AKATA WARRIOR

BOOKS BY

Nnedi Okorafor

Zahrah the Windseeker

The Shadow Speaker

Long Juju Man

Akata Witch

Akata Warrior

The Book of Phoenix

Lagoon

Kabu Kabu

Binti

Binti: Home

Binti: The Night Masquerade

Chicken in the Kitchen

The Girl with the Magic Hands

NNEDI OKORAFOR

AKATA WARRIOR

VIKING
An imprint of Penguin Random House LLC
375 Hudson Street
New York, New York 10014

First published in the United States of America by Viking,
an imprint of Penguin Random House LLC, 2017

LIBRARY OF CONGRESS CATALOGING-IN-PUBLICATION DATA
Names: Okorafor, Nnedi, author.
Title: Akata warrior / Nnedi Okorafor.
Description: New York : Viking, 2017. | Sequel to: Akata witch. | Summary:
Now stronger, feistier, and a bit older, Sunny Nwazue, along with her
friends from the Leopard Society, travel through worlds, both visible
and invisible, to the mysterious town of Osisi, where they fight in a
climactic battle to save humanity.
Identifiers: LCCN 2016055398 | ISBN 9780670785612 (hardback)
Subjects: | CYAC: Supernatural—Fiction. | Magic—Fiction. | Secret
societies—Fiction. | Albinos and albinism—Fiction. |
Blacks—Nigeria—Fiction. | Nigeria—Fiction.
Classification: LCC PZ7.O4157 Ah 2017 | DDC [Fic]—dc23 LC record available
at https://lccn.loc.gov/2016055398

Printed in the USA Design by Jim Hoover Set in LTC Kennerley

10 9 8 7 6 5 4 3 2 1

Dedicated to the stories that constantly breathe on my neck. I see you.

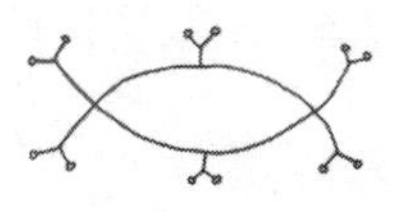

NSIBIDI FOR "LOVE"

AKATA WARRIOR

CONTENTS

ONYE NA-AGU EDEMEDE A MURU AKO:

Let the Reader Beware

Greetings from the Obi Library Collective of Leopard Knocks' Department of Responsibility. We are a busy organization with more important things to do. However, we've been ordered to write you this brief letter of information. It is necessary that you understand what you are getting into before you begin reading this book. If you already understand, then feel free to skip this warning and jump right into the continuation of Sunny's story at Chapter 1.

Okay, let's begin.

Let the reader beware that there is juju in this book.

"Juju" is what we West Africans like to loosely call magic, manipulatable mysticism, or alluring allures. It is wild, alive, and enigmatic, and it is interested in you. Juju always defies definition. It certainly includes all uncomprehended tricksy forces wrung from the deepest reservoirs of nature and spirit. There is control, but never absolute control. Do not take juju lightly, unless you are looking for unexpected death.

Juju cartwheels between these pages like dust in a sandstorm. We don't care if you are afraid. We don't care if you think this book will bring you good luck. We don't care if you are an outsider. We just care that you read this warning and are thus warned. This way, you have no one to blame but yourself if you enjoy this story.

Now, this girl Sunny Nwazue lives in southeastern Nigeria (which is considered Igboland) in a village not far from the thriving city of Aba. Sunny is about thirteen and a half now, of the Igbo ethnic group, and "Naijamerican" (which means "Nigerian American"—American-born to Nigerian parents, as if you couldn't consult the Internet for that information). Her two older brothers, Chukwu and Ugonna, were born in Nigeria. Sunny, on the other hand, was born in New York City. She and her family lived there until she was nine, when they moved back to Nigeria. This means she speaks Igbo with an American accent and says "soccer" instead of "football." It also means she has to sometimes deal with classmates calling her "*akata*" when trying to get on her nerves.

"*Akata*" is a word some of us Nigerians use to refer to and, more often, degrade black Americans or foreign-born blacks. Some say the word means "bush animal," others say it means "cotton picker," others say "wild animal" or "fox"—no one can agree. Whatever the meaning, it's not a kind word. Ask anyone who has ever been called an *akata* by Nigerians for the reasons Nigerians call people *akata* and you won't find one person who enjoys the experience.

Oh, and Sunny also happens to have albinism (an inherited genetic condition that reduces the amount of melanin pigment formed in the skin, hair, and/or eyes), but that is neither here nor there.

Let the reader be aware that a year and a half ago, Sunny Nwazue finally became conscious of her truest self and was officially brought into the local Leopard society. For clarity, let us quote the staple tome *Fast Facts for Free Agents* by Isong Abong Effiong Isong:

> *A Leopard Person goes by many names around the world. The term "Leopard Person" is a West African coinage, derived from the Efik term "ekpe," "leopard." All people of mystical true ability are Leopard People.*

We Leopard folk go by many other names in many other languages. A core characteristic of being a Leopard Person is that one of your greater natural "flaws" or your uniqueness is the key to your power. For Sunny, it was in her albinism. She's slowly learning what this means. Also, to be a Leopard Person is to have a spirit face; this is your truest face, the one that you will always have. And to expose your spirit face to people is like trotting around in public in the buff. Sunny is slowly getting used to the existence, privacy, and power of her spirit face (whose name is Anyanwu), as well.

Last year, Sunny learned that she was a free agent, one where the spirit of the Leopard had skipped a generation. Free agents don't have Leopard parents who have taught them who they are from birth. A free agent knows nothing of Leopard society—be it other Leopard People, knowledge of juju and the mystical world, or exposure to mystical places like Leopard Knocks. They have just become aware of their Leopardom and know what it is to have their world become chaos.

Sunny learned about her Leopardom when she was twelve. Her mysterious grandmother on her mother's side was the Leopard Person in Sunny's family, and if that grandmother hadn't been murdered by the student she was mentoring, she'd have brought Sunny in properly.

Be aware that Sunny's world is now occupied by mystical people and also beings only Leopard People can see, such as masquerades, *tungwas*, bush souls, ghost hoppers, and so on. This is especially true in the local Leopard society haven called Leopard Knocks, an isolated piece of land conjured by the ancestors and surrounded by a rushing river inhabited by a sneaky, vindictive water beast. The entrance to it is a bridge as narrow as an old telephone pole that runs over the river.

Understand that in order to appreciate this book, you must

comprehend what a masquerade is and is not. Masquerades are not men dressed in elaborate masks and costumes of raffia, cloth, beads, and such. Here is a quote about them from the book *Fast Facts for Free Agents* by Isong Abong Effiong Isong:

> *Ghosts, witches, demons, shape-shifters, and masquerades are all real. And masquerades are always dangerous. They can kill, steal your soul, take your mind, take your past, rewrite your future, bring the end of the world, even. As a free agent you will have nothing to do with the real thing, otherwise you face certain death. If you are smart, you will leave true masquerades up to those who know what to do with juju.*
>
> *Masquerades come in many sizes; they can be the size of a house or a bumblebee. They can even be invisible. They can be a dusty sheet draped over a heap of moths, look like a mound of dried grass, take the form of a spinning shadow, have many wooden heads. You really can never know until you know.*

Please note, however, that when the author of the book just quoted, Isong Abong Effiong Isong, was a teenager, she harassed a Mmuo Ifuru (flower masquerade) dwelling in her garden one too many times. That masquerade went on to make Isong's life a living hell for three years, and Isong's bias against them is reflected in her book. Not all masquerades are angry, mean, evil, or dangerous. Many are quite kind and beautiful; some are neither, wanting nothing to do with living beings, and so on.

Know that the more Sunny learns to read that Nsibidi book she bought last year, the more she will see. Nsibidi is a magical writing script from southwestern Nigeria. One must read deep Nsibidi with great care and skill; Nsibidi words carelessly read can lead to death. Be aware that as you read about Sunny, your own world may shift, expand, clarify, and grow more vibrant. No need to check beneath your bed every night, but you might want to make sure all the books in your bedroom are truly books.

Beware because this young lady Sunny has close friends who work juju as well. And when the four of them are together, they can save or destroy the world. Chichi is the girl who lives with her mother in the small hut sitting between the big modern houses, despite the fact that she is royalty from her mother's side and that her absent father is a famous highlife and afrobeat singer. Chichi could be older or younger than Sunny, who knows, who cares? Chichi may be short in stature, but her mouth and strong will rival the most successful market woman. Chichi's photographic memory and intense restlessness are the keys to her personal talent.

Orlu, who's almost fifteen, is the boy next door whom Sunny didn't talk to until destiny blossomed. Orlu is calm with an even temperament, qualities Sunny kind of likes in a boy. His dyslexia led him to his astounding ability to instinctively undo any juju he encounters. The best way to know if there is magical trouble is to watch Orlu's hands.

Sasha, who's fifteen, is from African America, the South Side of Chicago, to be exact. His parents sent him to Naija (slang for "Nigeria") because of his issues with authority, especially authority in the form of police. He's like Chichi: fast, hyper-intelligent, and he can remember like a computer. He's trouble in the Lamb (non-magical) world, but beautifully gifted in the Leopard world.

Understand that not long after entering the Leopard society, Sunny, Orlu, Chichi, and Sasha had to face a nasty ritual killer named Black Hat Otokoto, who was intent on bringing Ekwensu, the most powerful, ugliest, evilest masquerade, to the mundane world. Since they're all still alive, you can assume that things didn't go completely wrong with their encounter. Lastly, Sugar Cream, the head librarian at the Obi Library (the focal point of Leopard society), has, to Sunny's delight, finally agreed to be Sunny's mentor.

This book claims nothing, save that it strives to tell the story of the further comings and goings of this free agent girl named Sunny Nwazue.

Sincerely,

The Obi Library Collective of Leopard Knocks'
Department of Responsibility

1
TAINTED PEPPERS

It was stupid to come out here at night, especially considering the disturbing dreams Sunny had been having. The dreams Sunny suspected were not dreams at all. However, her mentor, Sugar Cream, had challenged her, and Sunny wanted to prove her wrong.

Sunny and Sugar Cream had gotten into one of their heated discussions; this one was about modern American girls and their general lack of skills in the kitchen. The old, twisted woman had looked condescendingly at Sunny, chuckled, and said, "You're so Americanized, you probably can't even make pepper soup."

"Yes, I can, ma," Sunny insisted, annoyed and insulted. Pepper soup wasn't hard to make at all.

"Oh, sure, but you're a Leopard Person, aren't you? So *your* soup should be made with *tainted* peppers, not those weak things the Lambs like to grind up and use."

Sunny had read a recipe for tainted pepper soup in her *Fast Facts for Free Agents* book but really, truthfully, honestly, she couldn't live up to Sugar Cream's challenge of making it. When making tainted pepper soup, if you made the tiniest mistake (like using table salt instead of sea salt), it resulted in some scary consequence like the soup becoming poisonous or exploding. This had discouraged Sunny from ever attempting to make it.

Nevertheless, she wasn't about to admit her inability to make the soup. Not to Sugar Cream, whom she'd had to prove herself to by defeating one of the most powerful criminals the Leopard community had seen in centuries. Sunny was a mere free agent, a Leopard Person raised among Lambs and therefore ignorant of so much. Still, her chi who showed itself as her spirit face was Anyanwu, someone great in the wilderness. But really, what did it matter if you had been a big badass in the spirit world? Now was now, and she was Sunny Nwazue. She still had to prove to the Head Librarian that she was worthy of having her as a mentor.

So instead, Sunny said she'd leave the Obi Library grounds, despite the fact that it was just after midnight, to go pick three tainted chili peppers from the patch that grew down the dirt road. Sugar Cream had only rolled her eyes and promised to have all the other ingredients for the soup on her office desk when Sunny returned. Including some freshly cut goat meat.

Sunny left her purse and glasses behind. She was especially glad to leave her glasses. They were made of green feather-light plastic, and she still wasn't used to them. Over the last year, though being a Leopard Person had lessened her sensitivity to light, it hadn't done a thing for her eyesight. She'd always had better eyes than most with albinism, but that didn't mean they were great.

After her eye exam last month, her doctor had finally said what Sunny knew he'd eventually say: "Let's get you some glasses." They were the type that grew shaded in the sunlight, and she hated them. She liked seeing true sunshine, though it hurt her eyes. Nevertheless, lately her eyes' inability to keep out sunlight had begun to make the world look so washed out that she could barely see any detail. She'd even tried wearing a baseball cap for a week, hoping the bill would shade her eyes. It didn't help at all, so glasses it was. But whenever she could, she took them off. And this was the best thing about the night.

"I hope the goat meat is hard for her to get at this hour," Sunny muttered to herself as she stomped out the Obi Library's entrance onto the narrow dirt road.

Not a minute later, she felt a mosquito bite her ankle. "Oh, come on," she muttered. She walked faster. The night was hot and cloying, a perfect companion to her foul mood. It was rainy season, and the clouds had dropped an hour's worth of rain the day before. The ground had expanded, and the trees and plants were breathing. Insects buzzed excitedly, and she heard small bats chirping as they fed on them. Back the other way, toward the entrance of Leopard Knocks, business was in full swing. It was the hour when both the quieter and noisier transactions were made. Even from where she was, she could hear a few of the noisier ones, including two Igbo men loudly discussing the limitations and the unreasonable cost of luck charms.

Sunny picked up her pace. The sooner she got to the field where the wild tainted peppers grew, the sooner she could get back to the Obi Library and show Sugar Cream that she indeed had no idea how to make tainted pepper soup, one of the most common dishes of Nigeria's Leopard People.

Sunny sighed. She'd come to this field several times with Chichi to pick tainted peppers. They grew wild here and were not as concentrated as the ones sold in the Leopard Knocks produce huts and shops, but Sunny liked having functioning taste buds, thank you very much. It was Chichi who always made the soup, and Chichi liked it mild, too. Plus, the tainted peppers here didn't cost a thing, and you could get them at any time, day or night.

It was the time of the year when the peppers grew fat, or so Orlu and Chichi said. Sunny had only learned of Leopard

Knocks' existence within the last year and a half. This was far from enough time to know the habits of the wild tainted peppers that grew near the fields of flowers used to make juju powder. Chichi and Orlu had been coming to Leopard Knocks all their lives. So Sunny was inclined to believe them. The peppers loved heat and sun, and despite the recent rains, there had been plenty of both.

When she reached the patch, she gathered two nice red ones and put them in her heat-resistant basket. The small patch of tainted peppers glowed like a little galaxy. The yellow-green flash of fireflies was like the occasional alien ship. Beyond the glowing peppers was a field of purple flowers with white centers, which would be picked, dried, and crushed to make many types of the common juju powders. Sunny admired the sight of the field in the late night.

She had been paying attention; she even noticed a *tungwa* lazily floating yards away just above some of the flowers. Round and large as a basketball, its thin brown skin grazed the tip of a flower. "Ridiculous thing," she muttered as it exploded with a soft pop, quietly showering tufts of black hair, bits of raw meat, white teeth, and bones on the pepper plants. She knelt down to look for the third pepper she wanted to pick. Two minutes later, she looked up again. All she could do was blink and stare.

"What . . . the . . . hell?" she whispered.

She clutched her basket of tainted peppers. She had a

sinking feeling that she needed all her senses right now. She was light-headed from the intensity of her confusion . . . and her fear.

"Am I dreaming?"

Where the field of purple flowers had been was a lake. Its waters were calm, reflecting the bright half moon like a mirror. Did the peppers exude some sort of fume that caused hallucinations? She wouldn't be surprised. When they were overly ripe, they softly smoked and sometimes even sizzled. But she was not only *seeing* a lake, she smelled it, too—jungly, with the tang of brine, wet. She could even hear frogs singing.

Sunny considered turning tail and running back to the Obi Library. *Best to pretend you don't see anything*, a little voice in her head warned. *Go back!* In Leopard Knocks, sometimes the smartest thing to do when you were a kid who stumbled across some unexplainable weirdness was to turn a blind eye and walk away.

Plus, she had her parents to consider. She was out late on a Saturday evening and she was in Leopard Knocks, a place non-Leopard folk including her parents weren't allowed to know about, let alone set foot on. Her parents couldn't know about anything Leopard related. All they knew was that Sunny was not home, and it was due to something similar to what Sunny's mother's mother used to do while she was alive.

Sunny's mother was probably worried sick but wouldn't ask a thing when Sunny returned home. And her father would angrily open the door and then wordlessly go back to his room where he, too, would finally be able to sleep. Regardless of the tension between her and her parents, Sunny quietly promised them in her mind that she would remain safe and sound.

But Sunny's dreams had been crazy lately. If she started having them while awake and on her feet, this would be a new type of problem. She had to make sure this wasn't that. She brought out her house key and clicked on the tiny flashlight she kept on the ring. Then she crept to the lip of the lake for a better look, pushing aside damp, thick green plants that were not tainted peppers or purple flowers. The ground stayed dry until she reached the edge of the water where it was spongy and waterlogged.

She picked up and threw a small stone. *Plunk*. The water looked deep. At least seven feet. She flashed her tiny weak beam across it just in time to see the tentacle shoot out and try to slap around her leg. It missed, grabbing and pulling up some of the tall plants instead. Sunny shrieked, stumbling away from the water. More of the squishy, large tentacles shot out.

She whirled around and took off, managing seven strides before tripping over a vine and then falling onto some flowers, yards from the lake. She looked back, relieved to be a safe distance from whatever was in the water. She shuddered and scrambled to her feet, horrified. She couldn't believe it. But not believing didn't make it any less true. The lake was now less than two feet from her, its waters creeping closer by the second. It moved fast like a rolling wave in the ocean, the land, flowers and all, quietly tumbling into it.

The tentacles slipped around her right ankle before she could move away. They yanked her off her feet, as two then three more tentacles slapped around her left ankle, torso, and thigh. Grass ground into her jeans and T-shirt and then bare skin on her back as it dragged her toward the water. Sunny had never been a great swimmer. When she was a young child, swimming was always something done in the sun, so she avoided it. It was nighttime, but she definitely wanted to avoid swimming now.

She thrashed and twisted, fighting terror; panic would get her nowhere. This was one of the first things Sugar Cream had taught her on the first day of her mentorship. Sugar Cream. She'd be wondering where Sunny was. She was almost to the water now.

Suddenly, one of the tentacles let go. Then another. And another. She was . . . free. She scrambled back from the water, feeling the mud and soggy leaves and flowers mash beneath her. She stared at the water, dizzy with adrenaline-fueled fright. For a moment, she bizarrely saw through two sets of eyes, those of her spirit face and her mortal one. Through them, she simultaneously saw water and somewhere else. The double vision made her stomach lurch. She held her belly, blinking several times. "But I'm okay, I'm okay," she whispered.

When she looked again, in the moonlight, bobbing at the surface of the lake was a black-skinned woman with what looked like bushy long, long dreadlocks. She laughed a guttural laugh and dove back into the deep. *She has a fin*, Sunny thought. She giggled. "Lake monsters are real and Mami Wata is real." Sunny leaned back on her elbows for a moment, shut her eyes, and took a deep breath. Orlu would know about the lake beast; he'd probably know every detail about it from its scientific name to its mating patterns. She giggled some more. Then she froze because there was loud splashing coming from behind her, and the land beneath her was growing wetter and wetter. Sunny dared a look back.

Roiling in the water was what looked like a ball of tentacles filling the lake. The beginnings of a bulbous wet head emerged. Octopus! A massive octopus. It tilted its head back, exposing a car-sized powerful beak. The monster loudly chomped down and opened it several times and then made a strong hacking sound that was more terrifying than if it had roared.

The woman bobbed between her and the monster, her back to Sunny. The beast paused, but Sunny could see it still eyeing her. Sunny jumped up, turned, and ran. She heard the flap of wings and looked up just in time to see a huge dark winged figure zip by overhead. "What?" she breathed. "Is that . . ." But she had to save her breath for running. She reached the dirt road and, without a look back or up, kept running.

The pepper soup smelled like the nectar of life. Strong. It was made with tainted peppers and goat meat. There was fish in it, too. Mackerel? The room was warm. She was alive. The pattering of rain came from outside through the window. The sound drew her to wakefulness. She opened her eyes to hundreds of ceremonial masks hanging on the wall—some smiling, some snarling, some staring. Big eyes, bulging eyes, narrow eyes. Gods and spirits of many colors, shapes, and attitudes. Sugar Cream had told her to shut up and sit down for ten minutes. When Sugar Cream left the office to "go get some things," Sunny must have dozed off.

Now the old woman knelt beside her, carrying a bowl of what Sunny assumed was pepper soup. She was hunched forward, her twisted spine making it difficult for her to kneel. "Since you had such a hard time getting the peppers, I went and bought them myself," she said. She slowly got up, looking pleased. "I met Miknikstic on the way to the all-night market."

"He . . . he was here?" *So that* was *him I saw fly by*, she thought.

"Sit up," Sugar Cream said.

She handed Sunny the bowl of soup. Sunny began to eat, and the soup warmed her body nicely. Sunny had been lying on a mat. She glanced around the floor for the tiny red spiders Sugar Cream always had lurking about in her office. She spotted one a few feet away and shivered. But she didn't get up. Sugar Cream said the spiders were poisonous, but if she didn't bother them, they would not bother her. They also didn't take well to rude treatment, so she wasn't allowed to move away from them immediately.

"There was a lake," Sunny said. "Where the tainted peppers and those purple flowers grow. I know it sounds crazy but . . ." She touched her hair and frowned. She was sporting a medium-length Afro these days, and something was in it. Her irrational mind told her it was a giant red spider, and her entire body seized up.

"You're fine," Sugar Cream said with a wave of a hand. "You met the lake beast, cousin of the river beast. I don't know why it tried to eat you, though."

Sunny felt dizzy as her attention split between trying to figure out what was on her head and processing the fact that the river beast had relatives. "The river beast has family?" Sunny asked.

"Doesn't everything?"

Sunny rubbed her face. The river beast dwelled beneath the narrow bridge that led to Leopard Knocks. The first time she'd crossed the bridge it had tried to trick her to her death. If Sasha hadn't grabbed her by her necklace, it would have succeeded. To think that that thing had family did not set her mind at ease.

"And then it was Ogbuide who saved you from it," Sugar Cream continued.

Sunny blinked, looking up. "You mean Mami Wata? The water spirit?" Sunny asked, her temples starting to throb. She reached up to touch her head, but then brought her hands down. "My mom always talks about her because she was terrified of being kidnapped by her as a child."

"Nonsense stories," Sugar Cream said. "Ogbuide doesn't kidnap anyone. When Lambs don't understand something or they forget the real story of things, they replace it with fear. Anyway, you're still fresh. Most Leopard People know to walk away when they see a lake that should not be where it is."

"Is there something on my head?" Sunny whispered, working hard not to drop her bowl. She wanted to ask if it was a spider, but she didn't want to irritate her mentor any more than she already had by nearly dying.

"It's a comb," Sugar Cream said.

Relieved, Sunny reached up and pulled it out. "Oooh," she quietly crooned. "Pretty." It looked like the inside of an oyster shell, shining iridescent blue and pink, but it was heavy and solid like metal. She looked at Sugar Cream for an explanation.

"She saved you," she said. "Then she gave you a gift."

Sunny had been attacked by an octopus monster that roamed around using a giant lake like a spider uses its web. Then she'd been saved by Ogbuide, the renowned deity of the water. *Then* she'd seen Miknikstic, a Zuma Wrestling Champion killed in a match and turned guardian angel, fly by. Sunny was speechless.

"Keep it well," Sugar Cream said. "And if I were you, I'd not cut my hair anytime soon, either. Ogbuide probably expects you to have hair that can hold that comb. Also, buy something nice and shiny and go to a real lake or pond or the beach and throw it in. She'll catch it."

Sunny finished her pepper soup. Then she endured another thirty minutes of Sugar Cream lecturing her about being a more cautious rational Leopard girl. As Sugar Cream walked Sunny out of the building into the rain, she handed Sunny a black umbrella very much like the one Sunny used to use a little more than a year ago. "Are you all right with crossing the bridge alone?"

Sunny bit her lip, paused, and then nodded. "I'll glide across." To glide was to drop her spirit into the wilderness (Leopard slang for the "spirit world") and shift her physical body into invisibility. She would make an agreement with the air and then zip through it as a swift-moving breeze.

She had first glided by instinct when crossing the Leopard Knocks Bridge for the third time, hoping to avoid the river beast. With Sugar Cream's subsequent instruction, Sunny had now perfected the skill so expertly that she didn't emit even the usual puff of warm air when she passed people by. With the help of juju powder, all Leopard People could glide, but Sunny's natural ability allowed her to glide powder-free. To do it this way was to dangerously step partially into the wilderness. However, Sunny did it so often and enjoyed it so much that she didn't fret over it.

"You have money for the funky train?"

"I do," Sunny said. "I'll be fine."

"I expect you to prepare a nice batch of tainted pepper soup for me by next week."

Sunny fought hard not to groan. She'd buy the tainted peppers this time. There was no way she was going back to the field down the road. Not for a while. Sunny held the umbrella over her head and stepped into the warm, rainy early morning. On the way home, she saw plenty of puddles and one rushing river, but thankfully no more lakes.

NSIBIDI FOR "NSIBIDI"

This book will never be a bestseller. The language in which it is written is much like that of the highest level of academia. It is selfishly exclusive by definition. It is self-indulgent. This is the nature of anything written in the mystic juju-rooted script known as Nsibidi.

You can hear me. You are special. You are in that exclusive group. You can do something most Leopard People cannot. So shut it down, turn it off, power down, log off. You feel the breeze; it is warm and fresh. It smells like palm and iroko leaves, damp red soil; they have not started drilling for oil here. There are few roads, so leaded fuel has not poisoned the air. There is a dove in the palm tree on your right, and it looks down at you with its soft, cautious black eyes. A mosquito tries to bite you and you slap your arm. Now you scratch your arm because you were too slow.

Walk with me . . .

—*from* Nsibidi: The Magical Language of the Spirits

2
YAAAAWN

"In social studies we learn about history, geography, and economics. We put it all together so that we can study how we live with one another," Mrs. Oluwatosin said as she sat in her chair at the front of the class. "But in many ways, social studies class is all about *you.* It should help you look at yourself and ask, 'Who am I? And who do I want to be when I am an adult?' So today, I want to ask you all: Who do you want to be? What do you want to do when you grow up?"

She paused, waiting. No one in the class raised a hand. Sunny yawned, pushing up her glasses for the millionth time. She was too busy navigating an intense magical world to figure out what she wanted to be when she grew up. She'd only managed two hours of sleep after she'd returned home. And those two hours were plagued by thoughts of the giant lake-dwelling octopus that had tried to grab her. *What the hell was its problem?* she wondered for the millionth time. She'd been too sluggish to bother with breakfast, and though she'd finished all her homework, she could barely remember what she'd done. Beside her, Precious Agu raised a hand. Mrs. Oluwatosin smiled with relief and nodded for her to speak.

"I want to be president," Precious said with a grand smile.

There was a pause, and then the entire class burst out laughing.

"You can't be president when you are not rich," Periwinkle said from the other side of the room.

"What will your husband think?" a boy beside him asked. They slapped hands.

Precious cut her eyes at them and turned away, hissing. "You people are still living in the Dark Ages," she muttered.

"Because we live on the Dark Continent," Periwinkle retorted, and the class laughed harder.

"Quiet!" Mrs. Oluwatosin snapped. "Precious, that is a fine idea. Nigeria could use its first female president. Hold on to your dream and study hard, and you may be the one to make it come true."

Precious seemed to swell with pride, despite the snickering of the boys. Sunny watched all this through her groggy haze. She liked Mrs. Oluwatosin. She had just joined the faculty at Sunny's exclusive secondary school, and she was a welcome addition; she was the type of teacher who truly believed in the potential of her students.

Periwinkle raised his hand. When Mrs. Oluwatosin called on him, he said, "I want to be chief of the police force."

"So that people can be dashing you money all over the place?" Jibaku asked.

More laughter.

Periwinkle nodded. "I plan to have many, many wives, so I'll need to make extra money to keep them all happy." He winked at Jibaku, and she sucked her teeth and rolled her eyes.

"You'll be lucky to even have one wife," she retorted. "With your fat head."

Sunny chuckled, resting her chin on her hands. Jibaku's meanness was certainly funnier when it wasn't aimed at her. She shut her eyes for a moment, feeling sleep try to take her. In the darkness behind her eyes she felt that thing again, like something was pulling her to the left and something else was pulling her to the right. It was unsettling, but for a moment she tried to analyze it. Doing so made her stomach lurch. She felt her body sway and was about to open her eyes when she heard snoring.

Oh no! I'm asleep, she thought, quickly opening her eyes, sure people would be staring at her. No one was, thank goodness. Apparently her snoring had been in her head.

"Orlu," Mrs. Oluwatosin said. "What do you want to be when you grow up?"

Sunny perked up. Orlu was at the front of the class so she

couldn't see his face. She'd barely had a chance to say hello to him this morning, but it seemed Orlu had gotten a fine night's sleep. She wondered what his mentor, Taiwo, had him doing last night and how he'd been able to return early enough to sleep well.

"A zoologist, I think," he said. "I love studying animals."

"Very nice," Mrs. Oluwatosin said. "That's an excellent career. And an exciting one, too."

Sunny agreed. Plus, Orlu was already like a walking encyclopedia when it came to creatures and beasts, magical or non-magical.

"Sunny? What about you?"

Sunny opened her mouth and then closed it. She didn't know what she wanted to be. *A professional soccer player?* she thought. *I'm good at that.*

For the past few months, she'd been playing soccer with her male classmates when they gathered in the field beside the school. Proving to them that she was worthy enough to play with them had been easy. All she had to do was take the soccer ball and do her thing; it came as naturally as breathing.

However, it was explaining how she could have albinism and yet play in the pounding Nigerian sun that was trickier; she certainly couldn't tell them that her ability to do this was linked to her being a Leopard Person. "My father had a drug delivered from America that makes me able to be in the sun," she told the boys who asked. She was such an excellent soccer player that they all accepted her answer and let her play.

When she was on the field, she was so so happy.

But being a soccer player wasn't a career. Not really. Not for a girl. And honestly, did she want to make such a spectacle of herself for a living? If she played, she'd play for Nigeria, and she'd stand out too much, having albinism. She frowned, her own thought stinging her. *I'm not really good at anything else*, she thought. "Um . . . I . . . I don't know, ma," she said. "I'm still figuring it out."

Mrs. Oluwatosin chuckled. "That's okay, you have plenty of time. But let yourself think about it. God has plans for you; you want to know what they are, right?"

"Yes, ma," Sunny said quietly. She was glad when Mrs. Oluwatosin moved on with the lesson. Considering the chaos of last year, Sunny wasn't quite sure if she wanted to know what "God had planned" for her. *I would be surprised if God took notice of me at all*, she thought tiredly.

"That lake beast and the river beast clearly have a thing for you," Sasha said that afternoon in Chichi's mother's hut. "What'd you do to them in your past life?" He laughed loudly. Chichi snickered, plopping down onto his lap and leaning back against his chest. She was carrying a large heavy book, and Sasha wheezed beneath her weight. "Jesus, Chichi, you trying to kill me?"

"Oh, you'll live," she said, kissing him on the cheek and nuzzling it with her nose. With effort, she brought the book up and began to flip through the pages. Sunny rolled her eyes but smiled. It was so nice to be around her friends after all that had happened in the last twenty-four hours.

"The lake beast is of the genus *Enteroctopus*," Orlu said. "They're born and raised in the full lands by large extended families. Most of them venture out into the world moving with their bodies of water. Why was it in Leopard Knocks?"

"What are 'full lands'?" Sunny asked.

"Places that mix evenly with the wilderness," he said. "A few places in Nigeria are known full lands: Osisi, Arochukwu, Ikare-Akoko, and sometimes Chibok gets a little full. Full places are a little bit of here and a little bit of there, layered over and meshed with each other."

"A beast attacked her in Leopard Knocks," Chichi said. "Who cares *why* it was there? Things come and go all the time for whatever reason. I'm more interested in who *saved* you! Hey, can I see the comb?!"

Sunny plucked it from the front of her hair and handed it to Chichi. As soon as it was out of her hair, she was very aware of it not being there. The comb was rather heavy, but it was a nice kind of heavy, comforting. The oysterlike coloring went well with Sunny's thick blonde Afro.

"What's this? Metal or shell?" Chichi asked.

Sunny shrugged as she got up. "I have to go home."

Chichi handed the comb back to her, and Sunny tucked it into her hair. She slapped hands with Sasha, and Chichi gave her a hug. "Are you all right?" Chichi asked.

"Yeah," she said. "It didn't get me; I'm alive."

"Don't know why that thing goes after you when it can more easily catch smaller weaker prey," Chichi said, pinching one of Sunny's strong arms.

Sunny smiled but looked away from Chichi. Sunny'd always been somewhat tall, but even she had to admit, she'd become quite strong. It was probably all the soccer she was playing with the boys, but there was something more to it, too. She wasn't bulking up like a body-builder, but there were . . . changes, like being able to squeeze someone's wrist into terrible pain, being able to kick the soccer ball so hard that it hurt if it hit anyone, and being able to lift things she hadn't been able to lift last year.

"You want me to work some juju on it to humiliate all of its ancestors and deform every single one of its offspring?" Sasha asked.

Sunny smiled, pausing to consider. "Nah," she said. "I'll let karma handle it."

"Juju works better and faster than karma," Chichi said.

Sunny walked out and Orlu followed her, gently taking her hand. When Sunny let go of his hand as she stepped onto the empty road, Orlu said, "See you tomorrow."

Sunny smiled at him, looking into his sweet eyes, and said, "Yeah."

You're not yet reading this correctly if this is your first time reading Nsibidi. Keep reading. It will come. But you can hear my voice and that's the first step. I am with you. I am your guide. Nsibidi is the script of the wilderness. It is not made for the use of humankind. However, just because it is not made for us does not mean we cannot use it. Some of us can. Nsibidi is to "play" and it is to truly see. If you lose this book, it will find you again but not without forcing you to suffer a punishment . . . if you deserve it. Don't lose this book . . .

—*from* Nsibidi: The Magical Language of the Spirits

3
HOME

Sunny's oldest brother, Chukwu, sat in his Jeep in front of the house staring at the screen of his cell phone as he furiously typed a text. Sunny watched him as she quietly crept closer. He was frowning deeply, his nostrils flared. He'd discovered his potential to easily bulk up last year, and his recently swollen biceps and pectorals twitched as he grasped the phone.

"What is wrong with this silly girl?" he muttered as Sunny leaned against the Jeep with her arm on the warm door. She didn't need to worry about dirt. As always, it was spotless. Sunny suspected he paid some of the younger boys in the neighborhood to wash it often. Chukwu had gotten the Jeep three weeks ago, and he would take it with him to the University of Port Harcourt in five days.

He didn't see her standing there. He never saw her. Since they were young, she could do this to him; to her other brother, Ugonna; to her father. She never crept up on her mother. Something in her, even when she was three years old, told her never to do that.

Sunny rolled her eyes. This was her oldest brother. Reeking of cologne. Wearing the finest clothes. His hair shaved close and perfect. Seventeen years, soon to be eighteen, and already adept at juggling four girlfriends he'd leave behind in less than a week. Going on five if he could convince the one he was texting to go out with him this weekend. Sunny read as his fingers flew over the touch screen.

`Just try me`, he typed. `U kno u interested, cuz u kno I show you a gud time.`

Sunny was glad that she'd never gotten that into texting. Look how it stupid it made you sound! Plus, she didn't need it. She only used her cell phone to call her parents to let them know where she was. When you knew juju, a lot of technology seemed primitive.

"Are you serious?" she finally said, when she couldn't stand watching him make an ass of himself any longer.

He screeched and jolted, dropping his cell phone on his lap. Then he glared at Sunny. "Shit! What is wrong with you?"

Sunny giggled.

"I hate when you do that!"

On his lap, his phone buzzed. He picked it up. "This is private. Go cook dinner or something. I'm hungry. Make yourself useful."

"Don't you have enough girlfriends?"

He flashed a toothy grin, quickly texting the girl back. "It's just so *easy*. I can't help myself."

"Stupid," Sunny muttered, walking toward the house.

"Where are you coming from all sweaty like that?" he asked her, looking up.

She'd been playing soccer with the boys. Chukwu's soccer group was older, so he had no idea she was playing now. If he did, Sunny didn't know how she'd explain. Really, she had more to worry about with Ugonna, who was sixteen. Sometimes her age mates played with the boys from his age group. Thankfully, he wasn't that interested in soccer. Thus, so far, so good.

"None of your business," she said over her shoulder, quickly going inside.

Her parents wouldn't be home for a few hours. Her mother was on call and had sent a text to all of them describing what they could eat. And their father always came home late on Thursdays. Ugonna was at the kitchen table nibbling on an orange. He had a pencil in his hand. He was drawing again. Sunny considered leaving the kitchen, but she was hungry.

Ugonna had always liked to draw; he'd sketch things like smiling faces and vague images of girls, trees, cars he liked, and gym shoes. But in the last year, after discovering an instruction website on the Internet, he'd gotten more serious with his skill. Instead of going out with his friends, he began to spend more and more time at the kitchen table, drawing. He was best at drawing faces and abstract images of forests.

Some of these abstract drawings reminded Sunny of the Nsibidi she was learning to read. Not that they looked the same, but they carried a similar energy. His drawings didn't literally move as the Nsibidi in her book did, but they *seemed* to move. The trees seemed to blow, the insects on the branches *seemed* to walk.

Then last month, he'd drawn what she'd been dreaming about since a week after facing Ekwensu. The city of smoke. It was a good drawing. Their mother had thought it was so beautiful she'd had it framed. Sunny had to look at that image on the family room wall every day now whenever she wanted to watch TV or exit the house. The dreams themselves were horrible enough.

They were worse than the vision of the world ending. The dreams were what happened *as* it ended. A city of smoke that rippled as it burned, that looked almost like another world entirely. It was like seeing through the eyes of a god. The first time she'd had the dream, she'd woken up, run to the bathroom in the dark, and vomited into the toilet. The second time, a week later, she'd fallen sick hours afterward and been unable to leave the house for two days while fighting a horrible case of malaria. The third time, she woke crying uncontrollably. She'd told no one about the dreams. Not even Sugar Cream. Yet her non-Leopard brother was drawing it, and her mother had framed and hung it on the family room wall.

"Hey," she grunted, walking quickly past Ugonna to the refrigerator.

"Good afternoon," he said, not taking his eyes from what he was drawing.

She opened the fridge, her belly growling horribly. She hadn't eaten breakfast, had forgotten her lunch, hadn't had enough money to buy a snack during lunch, didn't feel like asking Orlu yet again; essentially, she hadn't eaten since the pepper soup Sugar Cream had given her last night after the attack. She brought out three ripe plantain.

"Is Chukwu still in his Jeep?" Ugonna asked.

"Yeah."

"His head is so big," Ugonna said. "I don't know why Mummy and Daddy had to buy him that! He's staying in the government hostel, how's that even going to look?"

"Dad tried," Sunny said with a shrug. Chukwu was going to make a big splash at the university. Not only had he been one of the top students in his graduating class, he was the best soccer player in the area. Still, his father wanted his oldest son to really experience university life. Thus, instead of having Chukwu stay in one of the cushier private student hostels off campus, he'd insisted Chukwu stay at the more stripped-down government-owned hostels on campus. He'd have to stay in one large room with five other students. Chukwu had angrily protested, but he finally shut up when he learned that their mother had bought him the used Jeep.

Ugonna chuckled. Sunny did, too. She slit the black-yellow plantain skins and peeled them off. Then she sliced the plantain up into thin, round, slightly diagonal pieces and put them into a large bowl. She fired up a deep pan of hot oil and then dumped the plantain into it to fry. As she did all this, she resisted the urge to look at what her brother was drawing. Yet again she wondered how it was that he'd drawn that horrible burning city. He wasn't a Leopard Person. Was someone working some sort of juju on her? On her family?

She frowned, flipping the frying plantain over. She dished out the first batch and placed the hot slices on a plate covered with three paper towels. She picked one up and bit into it. Her mouth filled with saliva as it savored the tangy, sweet fried fruit that was so much like banana but not like banana at all. Perfect.

She focused on making the plantain and not on the talk she planned to have with Sugar Cream tomorrow night. Not on the fact that she had been keeping such deep secrets from her friends. From Orlu, in particular, it was the most difficult. Soon, she'd tell them. All three of them would hit the roof.

She put the plate of plantain in the middle of the table.

"You want some?" she asked, placing several on her plate.

Ugonna looked at the plantain, then got up to get a plate. "Thanks."

They both ate plantain and watched a Nollywood movie on the kitchen TV. Minutes later Chukwu joined them. As they laughed at the stupid woman who was so dumb that she'd left her baby in the taxi cab, Sunny glanced at Ugonna's drawing. It was of a tricked-out Viper with a sultry-looking woman draped on the hood.

She smiled and enjoyed her plantain and her brother.

That night, Sunny lay on her bed, gazing at the photo of her grandmother. Her grandmother, the only one of all her relatives who was a Leopard Person, the only person she could have talked to about all things Leopard. Where Sunny was albino, having pale skin, hair, and eyes, her grandmother was indigo black with closely cropped black hair. Sunny held the photo closer and looked at the juju knife her grandmother held to her chest.

It was particularly large, almost like a pointed machete, and looked made of a heavy raw iron. And both edges were notched with many sharp teeth and etched with deep designs. *Did they bury you with it?* Sunny wondered. *Did you even have a body to burn after Black Hat murdered you?* She shut her eyes. It was late and she was tired. This was not a place to go in her mind right before bed. She put the photo aside and unfolded the only other item that had been in the box with the letter from her grandma, the thin piece of paper with the Nsibidi symbols on it.

Sunny tried to read it yet again. When she felt the nausea setting in, she folded it back up. She shut her eyes, willing the nausea to pass. The first time, she hadn't heeded her body's warning; she kept trying and trying to read it. She wound up vomiting like crazy. It was so much that her father was overcome with wild worry no matter how much her mother, who was a medical doctor, assured him that Sunny was okay.

"What's wrong with taking her to the hospital, anyway?" he kept angrily asking, as he stood at her bedside with her mother. "*Kai!* This is a regular illness, isn't it? Then the cure is regular!" Eventually the nausea did pass, leaving Sunny with the nagging question of what the Nsibidi on the piece of paper said. She'd have to get better at reading Nsibidi in order to find out. She glanced at the piece of paper just for a brief second. Then she put all her grandmother's things away and grabbed her book *Nsibidi: The Magical Language of the Spirits* instead.

She wasn't ready to read her grandmother's complex Nsibidi page, but she *had* gotten a lot better at reading Nsibidi. Each day, she got better and better at "reading" Sugar Cream's book—particularly when she was rested, had eaten a good meal, and managed to go most of the day without talking to anyone. One did not simply read Nsibidi as one read a book or even music. Nsibidi was a magical writing script. It had to call you, and it only called those who could and wanted to change their shape.

Shape-shifters who saw Nsibidi would see the symbols moving and even hear it whispering. Sunny had experienced this the moment she picked up the book of Nsibidi at random in Bola's Store for Books last year. And though the book had cost some heavy *chittim* (Leopard currency that could only be earned by acquiring knowledge), it was worth it. It was her first lesson in mastering a Leopard art. Learning to read Nsibidi was initially intuitive, forcing the reader to reach deep within and understand that the symbols were alive and that they were shape-shifters, too. And when Nsibidi symbols changed shape for you, the whole world shifted.

The first time it happened had been two weeks ago, after Sunny thought she'd already learned to read Nsibidi. She'd managed to get through the first page, which was basically an introduction to the book, or at least, this was what she thought. Sugar Cream wrote that her book would never be a bestseller. So few could "hear" Nsibidi and even fewer wanted to listen. She said that Nsibidi was more a language of the spirits than one for the use of humankind. Then she began explaining how the book was split into sections. The book was quite thin, so the sections were very short. This was as far as Sunny had gotten.

For some reason, no matter how much she turned the wiggling symbols over in her head, unfocused her eyes, and strained to "hear" what the whispers were saying, she could get no further in her reading. She'd hit a wall.

Sweating and frustrated, she'd set the book down on her bed, the thick pages open. She leaned against the pillows on her bed.

"Come on," she tiredly whispered.

Understanding that first page had been deeply satisfying. With all that she'd experienced in the past year, here was something she felt made sense. Every part of her being loved and wanted to learn Nsibidi. And it seemed as if the understanding came to her *because* of this. It was exhausting, mentally taxing and frustrating, but she loved it. So it came. Then she hit this wall.

Now, as she looked at the thin book with thick cream-colored pages and maroon, almost jellylike symbols that wiggled and sometimes rotated, shrank, and stretched, she relaxed. She sighed.

"It will come," she whispered. She relaxed more. Her heartbeat slowed. She had other homework to do. Nsibidi was her friend, not a lion to tame or anything else to beat into submission. She was about to go get something to eat. Her stomach felt empty, though she had just eaten dinner.

"Sunny," she heard someone softly whisper.

When she looked at her book, she felt cool, soft hands press her cheeks to steady her head.

"Hold," the voice said.

Everything dropped. Away.

Nothing but the whispering symbols.

Oral and written words combined.

There was warmth on her face, like sunshine.

Sunshine now, not before her initiation into the *Ekpe* society. The Leopard society. The sunshine didn't burn.

She walked along a path, wild jungle to her left, wild jungle to her right. Drums beat but she could hear Sugar Cream's voice clearly; Sunny saw the symbols dancing before her when Sugar Cream called them, burrowing into the dirt when spoken, swirling into a tornadolike cycle when uttered.

"This book's titled *Nsibidi: The Magical Language of the Spirits*. But this book is tricky. Like me, it shape-shifts. It goes by another name, an inside name for those who can read it. *Trickster: My Life and My Lessons*, by Sugar Cream, is its inside name, its true name. This book is a part of me. It is wonderful that you are here and you are hearing. It is good."

Sugar Cream went on to tell/show Sunny that this jungle was where she grew up. She was introducing an old fluffy baboon from a clan that she called the Idiok when Sunny suddenly came back to herself. She had to blink several times to get her eyes and mind to focus. There was knocking at the door, and she glanced at her cell phone's time. Two hours had passed! She'd turned *one* page.

"Sunny?" her mother called again. Sunny tensed up. No one in her family knew a thing about a thing. They could not, by both juju and Leopard law. Among many other issues, this sometimes made reading the Nsibidi book difficult. Her mother knocked on the door. "What are you doing in there?"

Chink, chink, chink, chink! Ten heavy copper *chittim* fell onto the floor in front of Sunny's bed. The Leopard currency dropped whenever knowledge was earned, and these were the most prized kind. Shaped like curved rods, *chittim* came in many sizes and could be made of copper, bronze, silver, or gold—copper being the most valuable and gold being the least. No one knew who dropped them or why they never injured anyone when they fell.

Sunny jumped up and quickly grabbed the *chittim* and piled them in her purse. Yes, she'd learned something big, and she knew she could look into the book and "hear" Nsibidi in the same way again. "Wow," she whispered, putting her heavy purse beside her, the *chittim* inside clinking loudly. The pain in her belly hit her then, and she doubled over. Hunger, but a terrible aggressive hunger. She cleared her throat and tried to sound normal. "I'm just studying, Mom."

Her mother tried to open the door. "Why is the door locked, then?"

Sunny dragged herself to the edge of her bed. She placed her feet on the cool floor. "Sorry, Mom," she said, forcing herself to stand.

When she opened the door, her mother stared at her for

a long time. She searched Sunny's face, sniffing the room, listening for anything, anything at all. Sunny knew the routine. The unspoken between her and her mother increased every single day. But the love remained, too. So it was okay. "I'm . . . I'm okay, Mom," Sunny stammered. She smiled the most fake smile ever.

"Are you sure?" her mother whispered. Sunny wrapped her arms around her. At thirteen and a half, Sunny was as tall as her mother's five foot eight.

"Yes, Mom," she said. "Just studying . . . really hard."

"It's ten o'clock. You should get ready for bed." Her mother glanced over Sunny's shoulder at the book on her bed that was not a textbook.

"I will," Sunny said. "After I eat something."

"But you just ate dinner."

"I know. But I'm hungry again, I guess. A little."

"Okay, o," her mother sighed. "There's plenty of leftover plantain."

Sunny grinned. "Perfect." She could never eat enough fried, juicy, sweet, scrumptious yummies. When she finished, she brushed her teeth again and returned to her room. She shut off her light, fell back into bed, and was asleep within thirty seconds. Five minutes later, she was dreaming about the end of the world . . .

⌄⌄⌄⌄

The city was burning so furiously it looked like a city of smoke. She witnessed it from above the lush green forest. She was flying. But she was not a bird. What was she? Who am I? *she wondered.*

It was always like this here. She could smell it as she rushed toward the burning city. She did not smell smoke, however. The wind must have been tumbling away from her. She smelled flowers, instead. Sweetness, as if the trees below were seeding the air with pollen.

She tried to stop, but the force that she was riding wanted to go toward the city. She was a mind in a body that had other plans. There were spiraling edifices. Smaller structures on the ground, bulbous like giant smoky eggs. All of it undulated with smoke. This was the end. Was this Lagos? New York? Tokyo? Cairo?

Closer.

She felt like screaming. She didn't want to look anymore. But she had no body to look away with. It was like reading Nsibidi. Nsibidi? *she thought, panicky.* What is that?

She was too close to the burning city. Soon she'd be upon it. What were those flying out of it? Bits of incinerating building? They looked like bats. Demons.

She could feel her heart beating. Slamming in her chest; it wanted out. My heart? I have a heart? *She was shaking. She was falling now. The forest trees crashing toward her . . .*

Her body jerked as she hit the floor. Her eyes shot open as she thrashed in the darkness. The floor was hard. Familiar scents. She calmed. Her scent. She touched her mashed up Afro; she'd forgotten to take out the comb Mami Wata had given to her. Then she climbed back into bed and lay there until she slept a restless, yet thankfully dreamless sleep.

4

READING NSIBIDI IS RISKY

Saturday evening, Sunny went to see Sugar Cream in the Obi Library as usual. She was used to crossing the bridge to Leopard Knocks alone. The river beast made her nervous, but each and every time, she stared it down as she crossed. Even this time. It lurked just beneath the surface, a shadow the size of a house with eyes that glowed a dull yellow. Watching. Waiting. For what, Sunny didn't know. But when she brought forth her spirit face, and Anyanwu filled her up with confidence, poise, and courage, she didn't care. She dared the river beast to do its worst; then she'd have a reason to kick its backside once and for all.

When she arrived at Sugar Cream's office at around eight

P.M., her mentor was not there yet. One of the ancestral masks on the wall, the red one with inflated cheeks and wild eyes, opened its mouth and silently laughed at her. Another stuck its tongue out. The masks were so annoying. They were like having a chorus of children behind Sugar Cream's back who jeered and made fun of her as she was scolded or when she made mistakes.

"Oh, stop it," she said to the long-faced ebony mask that narrowed its eyes and sucked its teeth at her as she went to Sugar Cream's desk. There was a note on it. *Sit. We will practice gliding today. So clear your head. I will return shortly.*

Sunny groaned. "Sit" meant "Sit on the floor in front of her desk." She sighed, scanning the dark wooden floor. She spotted four of the large red spiders scrambling across the floor. There were always a few. Where they were going, Sunny didn't know, but they were *always* going somewhere. They were like scary ugly ants that were spiders.

She slowly sat on the floor. She shut her eyes and took a deep slow breath. She blocked out the spiders and took another deep slow breath. Unfortunately, as her mind cleared, it made room for the very thing she wanted to stop thinking about. Her dream. The smoking city. She frowned, trying harder to clear her mind. Sweat beaded on her forehead as the dream lost its sharp edges and began to grow fuzzy in her mind.

Her body began to relax. Her heartbeat slowed. Well-being. Nothing else. It would last about thirty seconds. So far, this was how long she could hold it. But this half minute was bliss. Ten seconds. A smile spread across her lips. Fifteen seconds. She began to hear that soft, slow hum again. It came from beneath her feet, beneath the floor—deep, deep, deep. It was beautiful. Eighteen seconds, she felt something scratchy.

Her eyes shot open, and she looked at her hand. One of the red spiders was crawling onto her pinky and ring finger.

"Eeeeeeeeee!" she screeched, flinging it off. It landed on the floor and ran toward Sugar Cream's desk. Sunny was on her feet, still in mid-screech when her eyes fell on the woman sitting behind the desk.

"Good evening," Sugar Cream said. Today, she wore a creamy yellow dress with a creamy yellow headwrap. The yellow bangles on her wrists clicked as she shifted her position.

"Spider! It was . . ." Sunny was so disoriented that she was out of breath and babbling. Anything *but* relaxed.

"You must have been deep in meditation," she said in Igbo. "I think it was going to check your pulse to make sure you were still alive." Behind her, the red mask laughed silently. "What would you like to discuss today?" Sugar Cream asked.

Sunny knew that whatever she answered was rarely taken into consideration, but she appreciated the question. She considered telling her about the dream. *But it was just a dream, really,* she thought. *I don't have any evidence.* When it came to the vision of the end of the world she'd seen while gazing into the flame of a candle two years ago, there were other elders who had also seen a similar vision. It wasn't just her. But then again, maybe others were having the dream, too. Maybe. A dream was a lot flimsier than an actual vision that one had while lucid and awake. She'd seen Black Hat slit his own throat, and then she'd faced Ekwensu very recently. Really, it was normal to have a few nightmares. She decided to go in another direction.

"How about teaching me more about reading Nsibidi," she said, slowly sitting back down. "I think . . . I think I've had a major breakthrough." She told Sugar Cream about her Nsibidi reading experience, and Sugar Cream was pleased.

"Finally," she said, smiling bigger than Sunny had ever seen her smile since starting her mentorship with the Head Librarian. Normally, Sugar Cream was so subdued and stoic. "Reading Nsibidi is not something I can teach you. Good, good, good. We can do more now."

"But why does it take so much from me?" Sunny asked. "I felt like I would die of hunger. I don't know how I was able to hide the pain from my mother."

"Trust me, your mother noticed." Sugar Cream chuckled. "But she's learning to accept what you are, even if she doesn't know exactly *what* you are, and that's good and safe for you both." She arched her back in her plush leather chair and shifted to the side. Sugar Cream's spine was curved in a dramatic S shape and thus, no chair was really made to suit her type of body. Sunny wondered why she didn't just have a special chair made for her. "Reading Nsibidi is give and take," she continued. "It gives you experience and knowledge, and in return the magic drinks your energy. This is fine if you replenish right afterward. Do what you've been doing. Read a tiny bit, then go eat well, sleep, relax. Don't go arguing with your brothers or watching something annoying on television, because next thing you know, you'll pass out and make a fool of yourself."

Sunny laughed.

"And expect a few nightmares now that you have unlocked the key to truly reading Nsibidi."

"Nightmares?" Sunny asked, her entire body prickling.

"Reading Nsibidi is similar to gliding through the wilderness in many ways," she said. "It, too, involves leaving your body. This will scare you, even if what you are reading is not scary. Your mind compensates by giving you nightmares."

"Oh," Sunny said.

Sugar Cream grew serious and held up a bony index finger, locking Sunny with her eyes. "Reading Nsibidi is risky. You're a free agent and for you to do this is not as rare as it is a bad combination. People have died from reading too much, Sunny," she said. "Beware of books written in excellent Nsibidi; you have to be truly strong to read them. Otherwise, you could get sucked into the story or the lessons or the information. When you return to yourself, it is only to wish this current life goodbye. Your body will have withered to bones; you'll have nothing left. It's not a good way to pass to your next life."

The sheet of Nsibidi her grandmother had left must have been that dangerous type of Nsibidi. She didn't know what it said, if it was fiction or nonfiction, but she knew how she felt when she tried to "read" it.

Sugar Cream stood up. "Now, then," she said. "Today, we're going for a walk."

"Where?"

"The tainted pepper patch," she said.

Sunny felt her entire body seize up.

"See the way you just reacted?" Sugar Cream asked. "It's not good to live a life dictated by fear. That is a lesson you especially must learn right here and now. Otherwise, you'll be miserable." She laughed. "Your spirit face is courageous and strong; do you want her to be ashamed of you?"

Sunny followed Sugar Cream out the door. Fine. *But I better not see even a small pond*, she thought.

5

AUNTIE UJU AND HER JUJU

By Monday, despite what Sugar Cream said and the fact that there was no lake beast near the tainted pepper patch, Sunny was back to fretting about her dream. Outside it was raining and the humidity made everything indoors damp. After school it was still raining, and Sunny had to meet Orlu at the school's front door. They walked off into the rain. Neither of them had an umbrella.

Sunny grumbled, grasping her juju knife in her pocket. She brought it with her everywhere, even to school, though she'd never use it for anything there. They reached the slick road, and Orlu started walking the other way, away from their homes. Sunny sighed. She could use a healthy dose of Orlu's quiet presence today. Chichi and Sasha might be around, but they might not be. Those two were always either at the market shopping for fresh juju powders or off in their "secret place" creating them. These days, aside from being boyfriend and girlfriend, Sasha and Chichi were like partnered mad scientists, always reeking of crushed flowers, having stained fingers and constant pleased and half-crazy grins on their faces. Sasha's hair had even grown twice its length, as if he were taking some kind of magical vitamins. The braids at the ends of his cornrows reached down his back now.

Sunny had hoped she and Orlu could go to her house and study together at the kitchen table while they listened to the rain. However, she'd forgotten, it was the day when Orlu went to visit his auntie in a nearby village.

"Can I go with?" she suddenly asked.

Orlu looked at her with raised eyebrows, rain dripping down his face. "Why?"

She shrugged. "If it's a problem, then . . ."

"No," he said. "It's fine. It's just . . . will your parents be okay with it?"

"I'll call," she said. "It should be fine."

"All right. But, let me warn you now, I love my auntie, but she's . . . she's very set in her ways."

Two minutes from the school, they managed to catch a *danfo*. The banged-up small bus was packed with sullen soaked people, and all the seats were taken. Sunny and Orlu squashed in with the people standing in the aisle. Orlu put an arm around Sunny when the jerky motion of the bus nearly threw her into the man sitting beside her.

The ride was only ten minutes. And despite having to stand, Sunny wished it were longer. As they drove, the rain began to come down harder. When they got off, it was like stepping into a waterfall. "Wish we could use an umbrella spell," Orlu muttered. But both of them knew this would only get them a trip to the Obi Library for punishment. All it would take was one Lamb seeing them walk down the street with not a drop touching their skin or clothes or backpacks.

His auntie's house was large and white with a green roof, surrounded by a thick white fence. Orlu knocked on the gate, and the gate man quickly opened it for them.

"Good afternoon," the gate man said. Then he ran back under the shelter of his gate man post. As they walked up to the house, Orlu suddenly stopped. "My auntie is a Lamb," he blurted.

"Okay," Sunny said. "So?"

Orlu shrugged.

"Orlu, I'm a free agent," she said. "You think I'm going to judge you for having Lamb relatives?"

He smiled sheepishly. "True," he said. "Come on, let's get out of this rain."

A young woman opened the door for them. "Good afternoon, Orlu," she said. She paused, looking Sunny over. Then her smile turned into a smirk. "You have got to be Sunny Nwazue."

"Kema, stop," Orlu said.

"Hi," Sunny said. Kema took her hand and shook it firmly.

"He talks a lot about you," Kema said. She touched the Mami Wata comb Sunny wore in her Afro. "Pretty comb."

"Thanks," Sunny said, nervous. If his auntie wasn't a Leopard, was Kema? What happened when Lambs touched gifts from Mami Wata?

"Where's Auntie?" Orlu asked.

Kema's smile lessened. "She's in the living room, watching a movie. She's not doing all that great today. Might be the rain."

Orlu took Sunny's hand. "Come on."

Sunny could smell Orlu's auntie before she saw her. A mix of cigarette smoke, expensive perfume, palm oil, and illness. She was sitting in front of a large flat-screen television, staring blankly. She wasn't much older than Sunny's mother and she was a healthy plump, with a face painted with bright makeup. Her eyelids were a deep purple, her eyebrows were shaven off and redrawn in the shape of thick black bars, her lips were a blood red, and her skin was flawless with light brown foundation. She clearly bleached it, for her light brown face was a great contrast to her dark brown neck and arms. She wore a white blouse and stylish black pants.

A Nollywood film was on, and a woman wearing a bad wig was shouting at another woman with an equally bad wig. When the second woman's eyes grew wide, and she slapped the other woman, Orlu's auntie didn't even react. The volume was way too high, and Orlu immediately turned it down. She did not react to this, either.

"Good afternoon, Auntie Uju," he softly said, kneeling in front of her and taking her hand.

Sunny's eyes began to water, and she suddenly felt like sneezing. Then she did. She nearly jumped as Auntie Uju suddenly looked at her. Sunny took several steps away from the woman; the look on her face was full of venom.

"Who is *this*?" Auntie Uju snapped.

"Auntie," Orlu said. "This is Sunny. She's my . . ."

"She is albeeno," she said, her face curling with disgust.

"Yes, Auntie," Orlu said. "That's obvious."

"Good afternoon," Sunny softly said, holding out a hand. The woman seemed ready to explode; best to tread lightly. Sunny's nose tickled again, and before she could take the woman's hand, she sneezed. Then she sneezed again and again.

"*Kai!*" his auntie exclaimed, staring at Sunny, who was holding her snotty nose.

"I'm sorry," Sunny said, embarrassed.

"Look at this evil girl!" his auntie shouted. "Look at her! Like ghost. She'll bring illness, poverty, bad luck into the house! Child witch full of witchcraft!"

"Auntie, come on," Orlu pleaded. He glanced at Sunny

apologetically. "Relax. This is my friend. My best friend. She . . ."

"*This* is your best friend?!" his auntie exclaimed, with bulging shocked eyes. She turned to Sunny with such a mean scary look, scrunching her painted face, that Sunny jumped back. "Go and die!" she shouted at Sunny.

Sunny whimpered. "What? I . . ."

"Our father, who art in heaven, ooooo," she suddenly started to wail. She held her hand in the air, jumped up, and stamped her foot as she shouted, "Fire! Fire! Fire! Be gone!"

"Auntie!" Orlu exclaimed, taking her shoulders and trying to get her to sit down.

But this only agitated his auntie more. "Fire! Fire! Fire! BE GONE!"

Sunny jerkily turned and walked out of the room. She moved down the hall, breathing heavily. She would not shed a tear in front of that crazy woman. She wasn't about to give her *that* satisfaction. She'd encountered this kind of thing many times. If Sunny cried, the woman would think her shouting and carrying on had caused Sunny to feel guilt for her "evil witchcraft."

Sunny stopped at the doorway and brought her shaky hands to her face. "But I am a witch," she whispered to herself. Though she was not a witch in the sense of what the woman and so many other delusional Nigerians believed. Leopard People had nothing to do with all of that. That stuff didn't even exist.

Why is it always about my being albino? she thought. *I never do anything to anyone, but yet they think I'm bad.* Her eyes stung as the tears came.

"Are you all right?" Kema asked, coming out of the bathroom.

"Fine," Sunny mumbled.

"Sunny," Orlu said, running up. "I'm sorry about that. Don't feel badly. Auntie Uju is not right in the head. She suffers a sort of dementia."

Sunny couldn't help the tears now. Nor could she help the sneezing. She looked at Orlu, wanting to ask the question that was on her mind. But Kema was there. Kema ran into the bathroom and brought Sunny a bunch of toilet paper.

"Thanks," Sunny said, blowing her nose. She sneezed again. "I think I should leave."

Orlu followed her out, and they stood at the front door as Sunny blew her nose again. Orlu handed her more of the toilet paper Kema had given him. "Sorry," he said.

Sunny only shook her head. "It's not the first time," she said. "People go crazy on albino people more often than you want to imagine."

"My auntie is involved in Mountain of Fire," Orlu said.

"So I noticed."

"I should have known this would happen, I guess. I'm just so used to you that I . . . I don't see your albinism as more than just part of what you are. I forget that other people . . . have issues."

"Like your auntie."

"Yeah," he said, sticking a foot in the rain.

"Orlu, you said she wasn't Leopard."

"She's not."

"Is Kema?"

"No. It's my uncle."

"Why does that room reek of juju powder?"

"That's why you're sneezing?" he asked.

"Yeah. Duh."

"My uncle thinks her dementia is . . . not natural. So he puts all these protective spells in the house. But as you can see, they don't work."

"Because maybe it *is* natural."

"Yes. It runs in her side of the family."

They were silent for a while. Orlu took her hand and squeezed it. "I'm sorry."

Sunny shook her head. "It's okay."

"Do you want me to ride back with you?"

"No, visit with your auntie. She needs you."

Kema came up the hall with an umbrella. "Here. Take," Kema said, handing it to Sunny. "Give it back to Orlu later." This was the second time someone had handed her a black umbrella in less than a week.

"Thanks," she said, taking it. She held it over her head and walked into the heavy rain. She stood waiting for a *danfo* for a half hour. The black umbrella was a godsend.

6
IDIOK'S DELIGHT

You are walking in virgin jungle. It has never been touched by shovel, brick, mortar, or tire. This place is full. Years back it was assumed to be an Evil Forest. Too evil a place for people to even dump the dead bodies of suicide victims, unwanted twins, murderers, and other people who were considered by Igbo and Ibibio traditional societies to be abominations. The Idiok baboons told me all of this when I was too young to really understand. But they have a way of teaching where the knowledge that is planted within you blossoms when you are ready to understand it. This is their own special way of teaching that human beings are still not able to master. I was taught in this way. Parts of this book are based on information they told me and experiences I had when I was under the age of three. It is clear to me as day.

This small patch of forest I show you was haunted. People believed that if you stepped even two feet inside, you would never be able to find your way out. Maybe this was true for Lambs. Superstitions are like stereotypes in a lot of ways. Not only are they based on fear and ignorance, they are also blended with fact. This place was the physical mundane world and the wilderness all in one. This was why these baboons loved it, for they were Leopard People, too. And for centuries, generation after generation, they made this place their home. Here they were safe and here they could speak with their ancestors, spirits, and other creatures of the wilderness.

You can smell the purity in the air, can't you? Stop and touch the leaves on this bush. Run your hand over them. They whisper, and if you look closely, you'll see that that brown cricket with the long antennae just walked through the leaf. You will not find it again. Spirits who do not like to be seen become unseen when they are accidently seen.

That is me, sitting with those four baboons. They told me that when I tell my story I should leave their names out of it. The baboons have names but not in the sense that we have names. Their names are not just their identities; they carry bloodline. Unlike with human beings, their names are the same as their spirit faces. So they don't share their names so freely. See the large one with the matted fur; he likes to swim in the ocean often, and the salt mats his hair and makes him smell like the sea. Many were sure he was close with Mami Wata. He taught me my first juju, which was how to open a coconut without losing the water. My first jujus were with Nsibidi, not powder or a knife.

The one with the patch of red fur near her eye hated me from the moment she saw me. She tried to tear me apart, but the others would not let her. She taught me how to climb trees by letting me fall. Then, impressed that I didn't die, she taught me how to climb the highest tree in the forest. It led to a place in the sky where you could walk because it was also the wilderness. Strange fruits grew there that only she and I enjoyed eating. The small one with the mangled leg was my best friend. We slept in the same nest until the day I was taken to live with humans.

And the fourth one with the white-gray fur is an elder. He is the oldest of the entire clan. No one knows how old he is, but his memory of Nsibidi is unmatched. Some say that his great skill with the language and storytelling is why he lives so far beyond everyone else. He moves slowly and only eats the softened fruits, but he could make the entire clan disappear if in danger. He is known throughout the wilderness. He speaks regularly with masquerades, and these powerful spirits love him because he can drop into the wilderness completely and return to the living world as if he were a ghost. As a matter of fact, that is his nickname, "Ghost." I know his true name and that used to make several of the others jealous, for only I and his companion, an old baboon elder who rarely left her nest, knew his true name.

I am about three years old. See me there beside the tree, sulking. The brown-skinned, naked little girl with a bracelet made from tiny shells, the one with the matted hair had found near the seaside. My arms are around my chest, my chin to my neck. Even having been raised by baboons, I still exhibit human traits. I know I am human. They made sure I understood that. The Idiok do not believe in lies. It is two weeks before the seventeen-year-old boy who would become my father would find me. I was happy the day before, but this day I am not.

I am so young, but Ghost has shown me the faces of my parents. I've seen humans before, from afar, as they drive past in their cars or hurry past our forest. I've listened to them speak and even picked up some of their words, to the Idiok's delight. But when Ghost made those signs before my face, something happened to me. I began to recall how I got there. I believe my parents were murdered. And this is why I am sulking. It is too much for someone as small as me.

However, stand here. Watch me. I will not stay

upset for long. I am a young child and the world is beautiful to me. But I will remember. That is one of the powers of Nsibidi. Memory. When you close this book, think of—

"Sunny!" her mother called.

Sunny came back to herself and leaned against her bed's pillow, her copy of Sugar Cream's *Nsibidi: The Magical Language of the Spirits* on her lap. She could smell the fresh leaves and pure dirt. It was warm and humid, and a breeze was blowing. She could hear the calls and chirps of strange birds. But the human mind often denies when it can't understand. *How can baboons teach a magical language?* she wondered. It was ridiculous. The entire book was all ridiculous, but cool, too. She'd ask Sugar Cream directly about this. And maybe she'd ask about Ghost and the Mami Wata baboon. And maybe she'd ask how one even *writes* a book in Nsibidi. She laughed. Sugar Cream had very strange origins, indeed. And "reading" about it was making Sunny feel equally strange. She yawned. Her body felt sluggish and thick.

"Sunny?!" her mother said, opening her door.

"Yes, Mom."

"Chukwu's leaving. Come say goodbye."

"Oh!" Sunny said. She'd been so wrapped up in her book that she'd lost track of time. Had two hours passed already?

She slowly got out of bed, closing her eyes for a moment and then opening them. She shook herself. "Wake up, Sunny," she said. She jumped up and down. It helped, but not much. She'd been "reading" her Nsibidi for two hours. Nothing could chase away the fatigue but a nap. She'd have to play it off.

Sunny's brother's Jeep was full of suitcases. "I can't wait," Chukwu declared. "First semester, I'll have chemistry and biology classes. I will show them what I am made of." His best friend, Adebayo Moses Oluwaseun, sat in the passenger seat. The two had been friends for years, but in the last year they'd become inseparable. Both were good soccer players, though Sunny's brother was easily better. And both had discovered weightlifting at the same time.

"I was going to say that you should watch for armed robbers on the road, but you two look too dangerous to bother." Their father laughed.

Adebayo flexed a muscular arm. "No bullet can penetrate my flesh," he said.

Chukwu laughed hard, and they both exchanged a look, sharing some sort of inside joke.

"Just drive carefully and quickly," Sunny's mother said. "Get to campus before dark."

"Mummy, campus is a half hour away," Chukwu said. "It's morning."

"Better to be safe," she said.

"Sunny," Chukwu said, smirking. "Stay out of my room."

"As if I have a reason to want to go in that smelly place," she said, leaning against the house. Her legs felt so weak. She sat down on the curb, gazing at her brother. He was really going off to university. "Wow," she said to herself.

"Ugonna, stay away from my side of the room," Chukwu said, waving a dismissive hand at Sunny.

"*Your* room?" Ugonna said. "You don't *have* a room anymore, and I have a big one."

"We'll see about that when I visit for Christmas," Chukwu said, starting the Jeep.

"Call when you get there," their mother added, opening the door and hugging him in the driver's seat.

"Study hard, my son," his father said, clapping him on the shoulder.

Sunny leaned to the side, her hand in the dirt, as they all watched him drive through the gate onto the road. Then he was gone. Sunny frowned, her mind jumping to what she'd just "read" in her Nsibidi book, that the Idiok who'd adopted Sugar Cream were Baboon Leopard People, and they all had the same name as their spirit faces. *That is just . . . bizarre,* she lazily thought. Then she laughed and slowly got up. *Good luck, Chukwu.*

7
THE NUT

Later that day, Sunny dribbled the soccer ball between her bare feet as she ran toward Ugonna. She moved it faster and faster the closer that she got to him. As she approached, Ugonna prepared to challenge her. As she did so, she watched his face shift from smiling to frowning.

"Shit," he exclaimed.

She kicked the ball to the left when she got to him, doing a quick whirl and catching it easily as she shot around him.

"Damn it!" he exclaimed, turning around to watch her.

She slowed down, working the ball with her feet. She flipped it onto the top of her foot and tapped it three times. Then she bopped it to her knee where she bounced it.

"Maybe you should try out for Arsenal."

Sunny's smile grew even broader. "They don't allow women." She popped the ball onto her head and then back to her feet. Then she kicked it to her brother.

"You can show them how to make an exception," he said, clumsily dribbling the ball between his feet.

"Maybe," she said, looking up at the shining evening sun. She'd gotten her Leopard teammates at the Zuma Cup in Abuja and then the group of boys from school to make exceptions, who said she couldn't do it a third time? "Maybe."

A car pulled up to the gate. It was Uncle Chibuzo, their father's oldest brother. He drove his shiny green BMW into the compound and parked it beside their father's black Honda.

"Ugonna, Sunny, how are you?" he asked, hopping out.

"Fine," they both said, each giving him a hug.

"How is school? Studying hard?"

"Yes, sir," Ugonna said.

"Always," Sunny said.

"I hear your brother went off to university today."

"Yes," Ugonna said. "He's probably meeting his hostel mates right now."

"You should be proud."

"We are," Sunny said. She gently kicked the soccer ball up, kneed it, and caught it in her hands.

"You are pretty good," Uncle Chibuzo said. "You want to be like your older brother?"

"No," Sunny said. "He's not as good as me."

Uncle Chibuzo laughed heartily. Too heartily. *Pff, he has no idea*, Sunny thought, annoyed. She wished he'd been there when she'd made five goals in a row last week playing with her classmates.

"This way," Ugonna said, taking the lead.

Their father had been expecting their uncle, and he was already waiting in the living room. As they greeted each other, slapping hands and laughing, Sunny and Ugonna tried to sneak away.

"Sunny," Uncle Chibuzo said, "bring kola."

Ugonna silently laughed, covering his mouth. And as Sunny turned away, she rolled her eyes. The ceremony of breaking the kola nut, more simply called "breaking kola," always relegated her to servant because she was always the youngest girl in the house. "Whatever," she muttered, going to the kitchen.

She placed a kola nut on the small wooden plate. Then she added a large dollop of peanut paste and a small pile of alligator pepper on the side. She brought it out to her uncle and father and tried her best not to look as irritated as she felt.

"Ah, kola has come," her uncle ceremoniously said, smiling wide with all his teeth.

"Very good," her father added.

Ugonna just stood there, clearly as impatient to have this over and done with as Sunny. She stood before her uncle because the kola was always presented to the oldest man in the room. She held the plate steady so that the balls of alligator pepper wouldn't roll off.

"Look at you presenting it like a miserable human being," her uncle snapped. "Wake up. This is not just something your elders do. It's an important ritual. You young people don't know anything."

Sunny wanted to heavily protest. She wanted to say that she knew more old ways than he *ever* would. She'd faced *real* masquerades and had her own juju knife, for goodness sake.

"Kola is important," her uncle said. "Not just to Igbo, to *all* Nigerians. The Yoruba grow it, the Hausa chew it, Igbos talk and talk about it. For us, Ndi Igbo people, the kola nut, the *oji*, symbolizes pure intention. It connects us to our ancestors. *Oji* is the channel of communication beyond the physical world and into the spirit world. Nothing starts without breaking kola."

He picked up the pinkish-yellow kola nut and broke it into four parts. "Four lobes," he said. "Very good."

He took a piece, scooped up some peanut paste with it, then some alligator pepper, and handed the plate back to Sunny as he ate it. Sunny next offered the plate to her father who did the same. When she served Ugonna, she refused to look at his smirking face. If he had been younger than her, she'd still have had to serve him, for maleness outdid age in Igbo culture. *Ridiculous*, Sunny thought as she always did when she got stuck serving the kola nut when her father had visitors.

She took her piece, dipped it into the peanut paste and then the pepper, and angrily crunched the combination. The bitter taste came from the fact that kola was full of caffeine. It used to be the ingredient in Coca-Cola that gave it its flavor and caffeine. The bitterness, the heat of the pepper, and the peanut flavor was always an explosion to her taste buds. She focused on that instead of her irritation.

Sunny studied well into the night, riding the caffeine wave of that one piece of kola nut. When she finished, she brought out the box from beneath her bed and opened it. Her kola nut buzz gave a kick to her curiosity. *I wonder*, she thought, bringing out the sheet of Nsibidi. She put it down, turned off by the idea of vomiting kola nut if she tried to read it. Then she picked it up again. She took a deep breath and then quickly unfolded it.

She looked at the symbols and nothing happened. She sighed, irritated. Nothing happening was even worse than feeling the nasty nausea. "Great," she muttered, still straining to "read" the Nsibidi. "Now I don't even—" The symbols started shifting. Her belly flipped with surprise; she grasped the sheet more tightly. "They're looking back at me," she whispered, feeling her lips go numb and her ears begin to plug up. She was being thrust high into the air or deep into the water. There was a strange smell, but it wasn't unpleasant. The smell was sweet and grassy—oily, too. Her belly rumbled and roiled.

Then Sunny heard the voice of her only Leopard relative, who'd been so powerful and loved and secretive and then brutally slain by her best student Black Hat Otokoto. Sunny's belly stopped rioting, the rising nausea disappearing. Her grandmother sounded almost exactly like Sunny's mother. The same high voice and rapid way of speaking. Then a strange place opened before Sunny—a city with beautiful stone buildings all etched with intricate designs. Mosaics, engravings, stone that contained mineral veins in natural, colorful, fractal patterns. Tall buildings that stretched high into the sky, but the buildings were rivaled by equally ambitious and strong trees, some palm, some more like fat baobab trees and hefty ebony trees. The roads were red packed dirt. And there was a small sunflower-yellow stone house with a stone roof . . .

The House is here. Yes, it smells like flowers, too. This surprises me. I love flowers. Everything here is stone, built to last. If it is wood, the trees will take offense and then take it apart. The winds can be strong in this place when it rains. A house must be solid and heavy, too. The front door is round and made from the wing of a giant Ntu Tu beetle. It's clearer than glass but won't break no matter what you do to it. That door is old, but it is not the oldest part of the house. Inside, you will find books, you will find heat, and flowers that have grown on the ceiling since the house was built.

Sunny, this is a place where if you seek, you will find. It took me years to find it. Maybe you will need to do the same at some point. If you are what I know you are, your life will not be easy, and there will be much that you have to answer to. But for now, you relax and see this place. See the street that leads to it. See the front door. And there is so much inside.

The floors are a mosaic that you can stare at for hours and think about the world. See the palm tree that grows through the center of the house? There is a clear roof that protects the opening from water when it rains. Come this way to the library. It smells of sandalwood all the time, and the walls are covered with amulets. The acoustics here bring any kind of music to life just as strongly as the words in these books bring ideas and stories to life. To learn is to live.

When the Nsibidi let her go, she was looking blankly at the bottom of the page. She could still smell sandalwood. *What a beautiful place that was*, she thought, lying back. "I want a place just like that when I grow up," she whispered. "Just like that." But what did it all mean? Why would her grandmother write a page of Nsibidi about this place? She hadn't even told Sunny where it was and whose place it was.

Maybe it's something she wants me to read when I'm under stress, Sunny thought. The fatigue that resulted from "reading" the powerful Nsibidi was tugging at her eyelids. She put the page away and closed the box. Then she lay in her bed. So relaxed. For several minutes, she thought about the house that sat in the strange city. *Maybe Grandma was a fiction writer*, Sunny thought with a chuckle. *Fiction written in Nsibidi, it would be better than a motion picture*. She chuckled some more. It was well past three A.M. As her eyes drifted shut, she hoped she'd dream about the beautiful house.

But she didn't.

Within minutes, she was dreaming . . .

She was in soft, warm water. Not choppy and rushing like when she was in the river during her initiation. No, this place was calm and blue, but she could feel its weight as she moved through it. And she could breathe here. She sped up. Her body seemed to know where it was going even if her mind did not. Faster and faster until the blue of the water became the blue of the sky.

She was flying. The rush of the cool air against her face took her breath away. She was high above a great forest, a rain forest. Mist moved through the trees like clouds that were too lazy to float. Then in the distance she saw it. A city of smoke. Burning so hot the buildings looked otherworldly. "Noooo!" she screamed, trying to stop herself. But she couldn't stop. She just kept hurtling toward it. She was going to burn, too . . .

She was falling. She was jarred awake by her body hitting the floor, again. "Oof!" She blinked in the dark, her eyes adjusting. She looked around her room and sat up. A bed, a dresser, a closet. There was a rolled-up newspaper on the floor. She felt a moment of panic. She couldn't remember her own name. "Who am I?" she whispered, frowning.

She could not remember. The room was nice, comfortable, and pleasing to her eye, but it was foreign. *Where am I? What is all this?* She got up, fighting panic. The bed had yellow-and-rose-colored sheets that she'd pulled half off when she'd fallen out. She looked down at her legs and frowned. Her skin was so pale. There was a flat-screen computer monitor on the desk and a small computer box on the floor beside it. Schoolbooks were also on the floor. Yes, those were schoolbooks.

As she looked around the room, unsure of who or where she was, she began to remember other things. The wilderness. Like an impossible wonderful jungle full of . . . everybody . . . but the living. Mostly green, but every other color and kind dwelled there, too. The wilderness made the physical world seem flat, dead, and quiet. "Ekwensu," she whispered. And when she spoke the name of the powerful terrifying masquerade who'd nearly killed her and her friends a year ago, she felt a deep anger rise in her. She hated no one; she didn't have the propensity for hatred. Nevertheless, the one who held that name was one she wanted to send to the darkest corner of the universe.

Her eye fell on the top of the wooden cabinet beside her window. She blinked. Then she burst out laughing. She sat down on her bed, her eyes still glued to the top of her dresser, and she laughed even harder. As she laughed, it was as if her spirit flew into her and filled her up; everything returned—her memories, her destiny, her self. She was Sunny Nwazue and she was Anyanwu. She was the daughter of Kingsley and Ugwu Nwazue and granddaughter of Ozoemena of the Nimm Warrior Clan. She was a Leopard society free agent, initiated over a year ago and witness to the suicide of the ritual killer Black Hat Otokoto and the banishment of the evil Ekwensu. And she was a most excellent soccer player.

Sunny was laughing because Della her wasp artist had created a brand-new sculpture out of some of the Oreo cookies in her backpack, a perfect replica of a stern-looking . . . Batman. As she watched and laughed some more, Della used a skinny leg to add one last flourish—a realistic sneer to Batman's lips probably made from the Oreo's cream.

Her belly cramped as she tried to stifle her giggles. She knew exactly where the large blue wasp had gotten its inspiration. She'd been reading her brother's copy of *Batman: Death by Design*, which their uncle had sent him from the

UK. There it was on the floor beside her schoolbooks.

"You are amazing, Della!" she said. "I love it!" She laughed again.

Della buzzed proudly and hovered beside it as Sunny snapped a picture with her cell phone. The wasp had grown to be about an inch and a half in length, its skills evolving beyond anything Sunny had ever imagined. Wasp artists that were happy were known to live as long as the human being they bonded to and develop skills that rivaled and even surpassed the greatest human workers of the arts. This Batman not only looked as if it would walk away at any time, but it resembled the dark, gritty Batman found in the recent films Ugonna had come to love so much.

Della buzzed happily and flew a gleeful loop the loop into the tiny mud nest it had built in the ceiling corner. Sunny sat on her bed. It was nearly dawn. She got dressed. Today was another day.

8
PEPPER BUGS

The next day was another day, too. A normal day. So was the next, and the next. For two months, things settled for Sunny. Well, it settled as much as it could for a free agent whose mentor was the Head Librarian of Leopard Knocks.

Sunny saw no more octopus-monster-propelled lakes, Mami Wata kept her distance, and reading Nsibidi was feeling more and more natural, though no less sublime. She didn't speak a word to anyone about her hardening body, and that made things easier, too. Better to just roll with it than try to explain it to anyone.

On the midnight of every Wednesday, she went with Chichi, Sasha, and Orlu for classes with Anatov. Half of these times were spent in his hut reviewing readings, learning and practicing new jujus, and being lectured on Leopard etiquette and history. Chichi and Sasha had recently passed to the *Mbawkwa* level, and Anatov taught them and had them practice higher-level jujus. Orlu and Sunny could only sit and listen. They weren't even allowed to ask questions during these portions of the lessons.

The other half of their Anatov nights were spent "learning by experience." Leopard education did not have any vacations or breaks aside from certain religious ones like Eid Al-Fitr, Eid Al-Adha, Christmas, and Easter. For Eid Al-Fitr, while Lamb school was on break, Anatov had all four of them volunteer at a local Muslim orphanage and then work later that night filling potholes along one of the smaller village roads. They'd used a dirt moving and packing juju that Anatov had taught them that very night. For days, Sunny was digging muck from beneath her nails and sweeping dirt from her bedroom.

For tonight's "learning by experience," Anatov was sending them into Night Runner Forest to capture four pepper bugs.

"What's a pepper bug?" Chichi asked, frowning.

Anatov smirked and pointed a long finger at her. "See, you and Sasha consume all the juju, Leopard history, and Leopard culture books, but yet you neglect the field guides. And, Sunny, you haven't had time to learn about the creatures of the Leopard world, except for those things you encounter personally, like ghost hoppers or the lake and river beasts. Knowledge gaps are no good."

"I know *tungwas* and bush souls, too," she added. "And wasp artists, and all those . . ."

Anatov waved a hand at her. "You know nothing of the millions of magical creatures of the world. And I have yet to assign you any field guides to read. For instance, you see *tungwas* all the time, but who can tell me what *tungwas* actually are?"

Sunny looked at the others, barely able to contain her delight. Even Orlu was silent, an annoyed frown on his face. Being new to the Leopard world, Sunny had been deeply disturbed by the basketball-sized skin covered balls that exploded into a shower of teeth, bones, giblets of meat, and tufts of hair. To calm her mind, she'd done a bit of research on them.

"Even in the Obi Library, there was no concrete information about them," Sunny announced, smugly looking at Orlu, Sasha, and Chichi. "One: no one really cares to know. Two: some things in the world are just beyond logic and the *tungwa* is one of them." She grinned and then added, "All this is according to Sugar Cream. I have to admit, I'm quite satisfied with both of these answers."

Everyone stared at Sunny, and she stared back at them, her grin fading.

"Well, *that* was surprising," Anatov said, after a moment.

"Anyway, for now, this exercise will do." He turned to Orlu. "I trust you know exactly what a pepper bug is."

Orlu nodded. "And I knew you'd ask us to go and find some."

"Why's that?" Anatov asked.

"For a few reasons," Orlu said. "The cost of tainted peppers just went up in the market. You like your food really hot. And the patch of peppers in your garden out back looks like something just came and ate it all."

Anatov grunted, irritably. "Yes, there is a small grasscutter that lives around my hut that has a taste for spicy food. Damn things are the woodchucks of Nigeria. They even look like them." He smiled at Orlu. "You are observant. Explain to them along the way."

Anatov gave Orlu a large metal pot, four spatulas, and oven mitts and then quickly ushered them out the IN door. "Good luck," he said. "And remember, the entrance to Night Runner Forest closes at dawn. Bring the bugs here before you go home."

Only Orlu was excited about the assignment. All of them remembered what Night Runner Forest was like as it had nearly killed them last year. But they'd all learned a lot since then. They knew how not to get killed or too badly hurt. Of course, that didn't make traipsing around in it at one A.M. any more tolerable.

"They shouldn't be that hard to find," Orlu said as Sasha

drew the tree symbol on the dirt not far from the Leopard Knocks bridge. Of all of them, Sasha was most used to entering Night Runner Forest because it was where his mentor Kehinde lived. "They are red and have long legs and square-shaped flat bodies that are kind of ridged, sort of like a leaf," Orlu said. "They look like tiny slabs of really lean beef or salmon."

"Disgusting," Chichi said.

Orlu ignored her. "They're about two inches in diameter, and they glow red in the dark."

"I'll bet they sting," Sunny said, as they stepped onto the path that opened up before them. "Things like that always sting."

"No, they don't," Orlu said. "They burn."

"Close enough," Sunny said.

According to Orlu, pepper bugs loved peppers. They would find a wild pepper plant and eat exactly one of the hottest peppers and then start to glow. This glow would nourish the plant and create a bond between the bug and plant. The bug would then inject the plant with a serum that would fortify the plant's health. So not only did the plant grow large, it grew healthier, too. Then the insect would defecate at the base of the plant and within one night another pepper plant would grow. Then another and another until there was an entire wildly growing pepper patch of at least ten plants. Then the pepper bug would do a glowing shaking dance that would attract a mate and this patch would become their home. Pepper bugs were happy to share peppers with human beings if the human watered the patch regularly and didn't pick too many peppers.

"Anatov wants to regrow his patch," Orlu said. "Then he'll taint the peppers himself so they will grow super hot just the way he likes it."

Note to self, Sunny thought. *Never eat Anatov's pepper soup.*

"Why can't he do this himself, then?" Sasha asked.

"He's our teacher, "Chichi snapped. "Students shop for their teachers all the time. Go to the market and everything. Don't you?"

"Not in America," Sasha said. "That's called ass-kissing."

They trudged through Night Runner Forest, trying hard not to disrupt, step on, bump into, or disturb anything. Of course, this was next to impossible. "I hate this place," Chichi hissed. She was blinking hard, her eye watering. An evil weevil, a long-snouted foul-tempered insect with the ability to hurl small objects, had thrown a small seed directly into Chichi's eye. Orlu grunted, scratching at a round orange-red patch on his arm where a Mars fly had bitten him.

"Yeah, there are days I want to just nuke this place," Sasha said, throwing yet another stick into the forest. He blew some powder and muttered some words, and the stick got up and stiffly began to smack at the patch of jungle to their left.

Something large ran off. "Too bad no one's written a juju that could do that."

"Time might take care of it," Sunny muttered.

They were all silent for a moment. A glint in the forest caught Sunny's eye. "Hey," she said, pointing. It was red, like a bunch of Christmas lights in the thick grass.

"Good eye, Sunny," Orlu said. They all ran up to the peppers. The stems reached past Sunny's waist, and the peppers on them were plump and plentiful. Up close they looked exactly like those chili pepper lights Sunny would see in Mexican restaurants back in the United States. The pepper bugs were easy to spot as they lumbered contently up and down the stems, batting and pressing on the peppers with their thick antennae.

"Damn, never seen these before," Sasha said.

"That's because you probably only take a path to Kehinde's," Orlu said. "Pepper bugs live off the beaten path."

Sasha rolled his eyes. "Ugh, whatever."

"So how do we get them?" Sunny asked. "If we were asked to do this, I assume it's not going to be easy."

"We have to get them in this pot," Orlu said. "They're hot, so they'd melt through a plastic jar."

"Are they fast?" Chichi asked, looking at them with disgust.

"No." He handed them each a metal spatula with a rubber handle. "Get them to walk onto it, put them in the pot, and put the lid on."

Sunny crept up to one and almost immediately started sneezing. Not from juju powder, but from the strong peppery fumes that suddenly emitted from the insect. "Ugh," she said, sneezing again.

"Jesus!" she heard Sasha exclaim a few feet away.

"Oh, sorry," Orlu said. "I forgot to add that when they feel threatened, they 'pepper up.' "

"Then how are we supposed to get them?" Chichi asked.

"Like this," Orlu said, creeping up to one. "Slowly. Move smoothly." He gently coaxed the glowing insect onto his spatula. It put a leg onto the flat metal and then took it off. Orlu nudged it a bit more and eventually the insect stepped on. Slowly, Orlu placed it in the pot, where it stepped off. He put the lid on. "There." The pot began to grow red with heat. "That's why Anatov gave me the oven mitts. When they realize they've been captured, they get really angry and heat up."

Once she stopped sneezing, Sunny was able to catch her bug pretty easily. With much cursing and sneezing, Sasha managed to get his, too. Chichi, however, kept getting hit with fumes. By this time, the entire colony of pepper bugs was on to them. When she was blasted with fumes a fourth time after taking five minutes to creep up on one bug, she shouted, "I HATE ALL OF YOU STUPID BEASTS! GO AND DIE!"

Orlu took her hand. "Sorry, o," he said, as she blew her

nose into the tissue Sunny had given her. "Let me try something."

He held up his hands and did that thing he naturally did that undid any negative juju. His hands bent, contorted, and twisted as he undid whatever juju the bugs had apparently worked. Then he said, "We mean no harm. We are just taking some of you to another place nearby to start a fresh pepper patch. I know you can fly. You can visit and cross-pollinate. If one of you wishes to be adventurous, come."

"Come on, dude, no insect is ever so reasonable." Sasha laughed.

But one of them was, for a pepper bug slowly walked up to Chichi. She looked at Orlu, who nodded. She bent down and let it walk voluntarily onto her spatula. When she put it in the pot, after about ten seconds, the pot's hot redness faded.

"It's cool," Orlu said when he touched the side of his pot tentatively. "That last bug must have told the others what I said." He picked up the pot using the oven mitts, regardless. "Most insects have a tricky side."

When they brought the bugs back to Anatov, they watched as he let them loose in his dying pepper patch. The four insects congregated in a square in the center of the dead and dying peppers and brought their legs and hands together, closing the square.

"You all did well," Anatov said, as they watched the insects perform their healing ceremony. "They'll be at this all night. By morning there will be fresh new shoots. You can go home now."

Sunny's lessons with Sugar Cream were even more challenging. Unlike Anatov, Sugar Cream didn't have Sunny go out and buy books. She was the Head Librarian; they had all the books they needed right there in the building. They always met in her office on the third floor of the Obi Library. Usually, they met Saturdays. But this weekend, they met on a Sunday evening because Sugar Cream had had an important meeting Saturday afternoon. Sunny couldn't help but suspect that Sugar Cream also wanted Sunny to journey to Leopard Knocks at night, forcing her to deal with the river beast and her fear of the lake beast. Thankfully, Sunny's journey to Leopard Knocks that evening had been uneventful and she'd arrived at Sugar Cream's office promptly at nine P.M.

Sugar Cream was leaning against the doorway when Sunny reached the top of the stairs. "There you are," Sugar Cream said, smirking. "Come in. Let's get started."

Sugar Cream's focus for the first two weeks had been on the rules and regulations of being a Leopard Person. She had Sunny not only read the thin and annoyingly prejudiced book *Fast Facts for Free Agents* two more times, but she also had Sunny write a research paper pointing out and deconstructing the book's bias. Sunny had never had to write such a difficult paper in her life. It forced her to not only look at the *way* she was given information but also at the background of the author Isong Abong Effiong Isong. It turned out that Isong was not only educated in the West but had fled from Nigeria after a terrible experience with armed robbers. For this reason, Isong had developed a fear and hatred of all things Nigerian. Though the research paper was tough to write, Sunny was glad she'd been forced to write it. Now she understood not only the rules the book taught but how to read those rules. Several small silver *chittim* had fallen during the writing of that paper.

Sugar Cream had also brought Sunny to several Library Council meetings where Sunny had to dress up and sit quietly behind Sugar Cream. Her mentor met with elders from all over the country and once with elders from all over the world. In this way, Sunny learned that the Leopard People were an organized group who kept many of the world's ills from being worse than they were. Who'd have thought that so much of Nigeria's corruption was stopped by the organized jujus of Leopard elders from a variety of Nigeria's states? Certainly not Sunny. The idea that things in Nigeria could have been a lot worse scared her deeply.

Sunny had also met some of Sugar Cream's important colleagues outside of meetings. Only two weeks ago, Sunny had entered Sugar Cream's office and nearly run into the chest of a tall Arab man. He'd worn white flowing garments and a white turban and smelled of sweet incense. Sunny had remembered him from a year ago during the meeting she and the others had with a group of Africa's greatest elders not long before they were sent to deal with Black Hat. From what she recalled, at least part of this man's name was Ali and he could shape-shift into a colorful toucan.

Sunny had stepped back. "I'm sorry, *Oga* Ali," she'd said in Igbo. Most library elders spoke many languages and at the meeting he'd expressed a serious dislike of Americans. Best to not speak her American-accented English.

He had surprised her with a smile. "Sunny Nwazue," he'd said. "You look well. Being mentored by Sugar Cream is good for you."

Sunny wasn't sure if this was a compliment or an insult. She'd smiled and said, "Thank you."

He had turned to her mentor, who had a frown on her face. "We will talk later, my dear."

Sugar Cream had nodded. "Go well."

"Inshallah," he'd said, closing the door behind him.

Sugar Cream fed Sunny books on African Leopard history and Leopard politics from around the world; she even gave Sunny a few novels by local Leopard authors. Sunny didn't think any of these were very good; Sugar Cream had laughed and agreed with her.

Nevertheless, it was the lessons in gliding that rocked

Sunny's world the most, and tonight, this was the focus. "Sit, Sunny. Sit," Sugar Cream told her. She set down her bunch of books on the floor, looked around for red spiders, and, when she saw none nearby, sat down. Sugar Cream settled at her desk, an agitated look on her face. She suddenly looked at Sunny. "I was going to test you on your Leopard history readings, but I have changed my mind. Watch closely."

As Sunny observed, she felt like screaming. Never had Sugar Cream changed before her. She'd only *spoken* of her natural talent. Sugar Cream could change into a snake, and then she could slip through time. Sunny had never been fond of snakes, so she wasn't eager to see her mentor do it. And now Sunny knew she'd been right to not ask.

Sugar Cream was a frail old woman of medium height. She had rich brown skin and a face that reminded Sunny of her grandmother on her father's side. She had no idea if her mentor was Igbo, Hausa, Yoruba, Efik, Ijaw, Fulani, or any other ethnicity. Sugar Cream didn't know either, really, since she'd been abandoned in the jungle when she was very young. If Sunny had to guess, she'd have said Yoruba. But all this began to melt. Her clothes billowed as they were emptied. The wrinkly skin on Sugar Cream's face began to shrink. Her entire body shriveled in on itself. Sunny felt nauseated and couldn't hide the look of complete disgust on her face. Her stomach lurched, and she hunched forward just as Sugar Cream's now lumpy flesh of a body collapsed forward on her desk with a soft thump. The same brown as her skin, it writhed and rolled.

Sunny gasped, shutting her eyes tightly. *Count to ten*, a papery and dry voice whispered within Sunny's head. *Then see me.*

Sunny slowly counted to ten. When she opened her eyes, she was looking into the green-yellow gaze of a large bright green snake. *To speak while in alternate form*, Sugar Cream said in her head, *must be learned. But to change, once you have mastered it, is not difficult.*

She did not move, her body still mostly in her clothes. When Sugar Cream changed back, Sunny understood why she'd stayed in place. She filled her clothes with the ease of an expert. "To see me change back does not have the nauseating effect," Sugar Cream said. "It's only the first time that throws one off. You will not experience that again when you see me change. Also, your gift is different from mine. When you change into mist and glide, you can bring your clothes."

They started first with breathing, for part of gliding between the wilderness and the physical world was understanding that you typically had to *stop* breathing to do it for any extended period of time. "You can glide across the bridge or through a keyhole. That is easy," Sugar Cream said. "But can you glide from here to your house?"

Gliding between the wilderness and the physical world was one thing, but Sunny knew what Sugar Cream was slowly working her toward. Dropping completely into the wilderness. To do so meant she'd have to die, really truly die. But she was born with this ability, so she would be able to always come back . . . if she did it correctly. She wasn't in any hurry to try, and Sugar Cream wasn't in a rush to have her try, either. "Not this year," Sugar Cream said. "But maybe next year or the year after that."

Sugar Cream worked her hard. After the gliding exercises, they worked on Night Frames, various states of being that you achieved only during the night. Night Frames required a combination of juju knife flourishes, humming deep in the throat, and a blue juju powder that left her skin oily. Night Frames were primary phases of slipping wholly into the wilderness.

"You don't want to enter the wilderness and not be able to come out," Sugar Cream firmly said. "That is death, of course. So you practice slipping in and then out, bit by bit. The night is when the barrier between the physical and spirit worlds is thinnest."

One had to die in order to go into the wilderness, so one had to birth her- or himself back. And one had to be strong to give birth. Though Sunny was born with the natural ability to do both, even she knew that talent and ability was best honed. Sunny had solemnly nodded and then the work began. They practiced two frames, which Sunny achieved easily enough but found she had to work to hold. Over and over, the humming, the blowing of the powder, the sneezing, then the colors that began to bleed into everything. By the time Sugar Cream sent her home, she felt as if her world was vibrating.

Sugar Cream's lessons; Anatov's teachings; Lamb school; hanging out with Chichi, Orlu, and Sasha; her strangely changing body—Sunny was overwhelmed, yet learning and absorbing so much. As she sat in her seat on the near-empty funky train home, she'd curled her body toward the window and shut her eyes. She took a deep breath, truly relaxing for the first time in hours, and this was when she felt that sensation of being pulled into two. Her eyes shot open and as she stared out the window, she began to quietly weep.

"Anyanwu?" she whispered. And then she heard herself respond in a deep voice, "Sleep, Sunny, I am here."

9

HOW FAR?

Sunny groaned as she opened the gate. The night sky hadn't begun to warm yet, but soon it would and the morning birds were already singing.

She'd slept the entire ride back on the funky train. Thankfully, the driver, a tall old woman named Magnificent, who saw her often at this late hour, knew Sunny's stop. Magnificent shouted, "Sunny! You're home! Go and sleep!" Sunny jumped to her feet and dragged herself from the juju-powered vehicle before she knew what was happening. The funky train silently glided off, leaving only a puff of rose-scented air and her in the dark standing before the gate to her house.

Her chin to her chest, she quietly unlocked and pushed

the gate open just enough to slip through. She trudged toward the front door. The house alarm wouldn't be on, nor would her father or mother be waiting up for her, though she suspected they were anxiously listening for her return. They didn't ask questions anymore. Good. That was one stress gone. Her skin still felt oily from the enhancement powder, and her sensitive nose was stuffed with snot. She'd need a good shower before going to bed and that would rob her of fifteen minutes out of the four hours of sleep she could snatch before she had to leave for school.

She stuck her key into the hole. She could pass through the keyhole, but there was always the chance that her brother or parents would be right there. Then she'd find herself sentenced to a caning by the Library Council for exposing the Leopard People's ways. Would they wipe or alter the memories of her family? Who knew what they did. Now that she didn't have to sneak around, it definitely wasn't worth the risk.

Creak!

She froze. Someone was opening the gate behind her. It was several yards away; she could throw the door open and lock it behind her. Or she could just risk it and pass through the keyhole. *Ekwensu*, she thought. *What if it's Ekwensu? But why would the physical world's greatest adversary have to push open a gate?* Armed robbers, then? But the gate was locked. Did they have a key? Was juju used to get in? Was the lock picked?

She whirled around, dropping her backpack and bringing out her juju knife. *What am I doing?* she thought, horrified.

The gate opened. Adrenaline flooded her system, causing a ringing in her ears and cold sweat to break from her skin. She crept closer. A shadow peeked around the gate. He looked right at her.

"Sunny?" he gasped.

"Chukwu?" She quickly put her knife into her pocket.

"What are you doing here?"

"Why aren't you at school?" Sunny blurted.

They stared at each other. Her brother was dark-skinned and standing in the shadows, so she couldn't quite see the expression on his face.

"I . . . I just got home," she said, stepping closer.

"From wherever it is you go?" he asked. He moved away from her, holding on to the gate.

"Where's your Jeep?" she asked.

"Parked it on the street," he said. "Don't . . ." He stepped away from her some more and, in doing so, moved into the dim moonlight.

Sunny clapped her hands over her mouth and gasped. "What happened?!"

Her brother had gotten quite muscular in the last year. He'd not only discovered weight-lifting, he'd discovered that he really, truly, madly loved it. Sunny knew that aside from kicking a soccer ball around, there was nothing he loved more than to be in the gym lifting until his muscles vibrated. Now Sunny could see that he'd gotten even bigger since leaving for school weeks ago. Still, at this moment, he looked like a pummeled, scared teenager. His left eye was swollen shut, and his mouth looked like it carried two golf balls. He held on to the gate with a big hand.

Sunny stepped up to him and touched his face. He looked away. "Chukwu, what . . ."

"Mummy and Daddy can't know that I'm here," he said.

"Why?"

"I need to get the money I have in my room. Then I'll leave." He looked into her eyes. "I don't want to put anyone here in danger." His face twitched and he frowned, one tear falling down his cheek.

Sunny felt her eyes sting, too. This was her brother Chukwu, whose name meant "Supreme Being," because he was "God's gift to women," or so he liked to brag. This was her oldest brother, who had tormented her since she was a baby, and protected her, too, in his own rough way.

"C-Come on," she said, her voice shaking. She wrapped her arm around his. "Lean on me. I'll get you inside."

They moved fast, heading straight to Sunny's room. Sunny banked on the fact that her parents would assume it was just her entering the house and not their oldest son who'd run away from the university they were paying so much for him to attend. She locked the door as he sat on her bed. In the light, she saw that he looked far worse than she'd thought. She took a deep breath and steadied herself; this was not a time to cry.

"Where is the money?" she asked. "I'll get it for you."

He frowned. "What? No, no, it's in a secret spot. It'll be . . ."

"In your room?"

"Yes," he said.

"What if Ugonna sees you?"

"He'll be sleeping."

"Not if you wake him up. And what if Mom or Dad comes out of their room? I know they heard us come in. Sometimes Mom checks on me. She'll come and listen at the door. She doesn't think I know, but I do."

"Shit," he hissed. "Well, what do you want me to do? I need that money."

"I'll get it."

He considered it for a moment. "What will you say if Ugonna wakes?"

"He won't. You know I'm better at sneaking than you ever will be."

Chukwu nodded. "True. Okay . . . There's a loose floorboard near the window. The front right leg of my bed is on top of it. The money is inside."

"Okay," she said. "I'll be right back." She paused. "Shut your eyes and close your ears."

"Why?"

"Just do it."

He frowned at her, but then did as she said. She ran to the door, made sure it was locked, glanced back quickly, and then passed through the keyhole before he opened his eyes and asked her why she was asking him to do something so weird. The feeling was one of compression and coolness. It wasn't the same as when she'd done it that first time, back when she thought she was working the first juju of her life but was really using her natural talent. Since then she'd done this many times and it was easier and easier. However, the feeling was sharper, too. More deliberate.

She came out on the other side of the door and then ran toward the room Chukwu and Ugonna used to share that was now just Ugonna's. She checked to make sure the door was locked. It was. She passed through the keyhole. Ugonna was sprawled out on his bed, sleeping noisily. He preferred to study on the floor, so this was where his schoolbooks and sheets of paper were scattered. His large-screen TV's screen saver flashed images of shiny sports cars into the darkness of his room. *Good*, she thought. She could see. Soft jazz music played. Even better, background noise, though she shouldn't need it. She ran to Chukwu's bed and waited.

She was still insubstantial, gravity affecting her but not as much as it would if she were all there. If Ugonna awoke and looked right at her, he'd see nothing, but he might sense her presence, even if he was a Lamb. Especially knowing how attuned he'd been lately. All the more reason to move faster.

She felt herself warm up and the smell of Ugonna's room slam into her. Sweat, cologne, and there might have been an orange rotting behind something somewhere in the room. She looked at Ugonna as he shifted positions. He was sensitive, all right. He was asleep but he *knew* she was there, that's how Anatov described this kind of thing. She didn't have much time.

Gently but firmly, she pushed the bed and touched the exposed floorboard. She felt around the edges and located the notch and lifted it up. There was the money. Rolls and rolls of American dollar bills and naira, held together tightly with rubber bands. She grabbed them and quickly began rubbing them on her arm. She rubbed and rubbed, watching her brother. He shifted in his bed again but then came to rest and didn't move.

She breathed on the wads of cash and then got up. He was now tossing and turning, trying to thrash himself awake. Unsure of what to do, she took the chance. If she failed and he saw her, she'd certainly be caned this time. Having Sugar Cream as a mentor, the very person who would decide on punishment, wouldn't ensure her of any sympathy. As a matter of fact, it would probably get her the harshest punishment. Sugar Cream was the best teacher she could have hoped for and one of Sunny's favorite people, but she was also a hard,

hard woman. There was a reason she was the Head Librarian.

Sunny ran toward the door, bringing forth her spirit face. She leaped over Ugonna's piles of books. Then she dove through the keyhole just as her brother sat up. Once on the other side, she ran off. She had seconds where she would not be heard. When she made it to her room, she waited quietly until she became substantial. Then she quickly grabbed the Mami Wata comb in her hair and used one of the teeth to pick the lock. She opened the door and went in.

"Did you get it?" Chukwu asked.

She looked down at her hands. Along with her comb, she was carrying the wads of cash. It had worked. She smiled, hearing a *chink* outside her door as a *chittim* fell in the hallway. She'd never carried anything with her before when she glided between the wilderness and the physical world like this.

She threw the money on Chukwu's lap. He grinned. "Thank you!"

She sat beside him on her bed. "You're not leaving until you tell me everything."

"No."

"Why?"

He looked at Sunny with eyes so ablaze that she nearly jumped off the bed and ran out of the room. "Why?" she asked again, grasping the rim of the bed to keep her steady. "What happened? Armed robbers? What . . ."

"Sunny. . . if I tell you, I'm putting you in danger. Even

seeing me here tonight isn't good," he said, looking away. "The less you know, the better it will be if they come looking for me here."

She touched his hard muscular shoulder and he winced. "Don't," he whispered.

"Is anything broken?" she quietly asked.

"I don't know," he said. "Maybe one or two of my ribs."

"Will you see a doctor?"

"Yes. When I can. I promise."

"Please, Chukwu, what happened?"

The pained look crossed his face again. And he thought for a long time. He glanced at the door. And then he started talking. And the very thing that Sunny suspected and had feared from the moment he left for school turned out to have happened.

10
BROTHERLY LOVE

Okay, Sunny. I'll tell you . . . but only you. You . . . you have a lot of secrets, but you know how to keep them, too.

I understand why Daddy wanted me to live in the government hostel, instead of the privately owned one. I'm not a fool. If you don't live life, you will be nothing. And to live life, you have to live with people. Real people. Yeah, I wanted to live with the high and mighty, the wealthy, the comfortable. Who wouldn't? Have you seen the satellite hostels, Sunny? They're self-contained. They've got laundry, a restaurant where they will make whatever you ask for, new furniture, you get your own room . . . or something like that. Of course, I wanted to live there. But it's expensive. It's a waste of money.

When Daddy said I had to live in the government hostel, I said fine. Whatever. It's all good. I knew he was trying to teach me a lesson. He thought I was soft after all those early years in America. I was just happy to get the hell out of the house and be on my own. My hostel room's hot and ugly. The beds are hard. You share the room with five guys, some are second and third year. They'll bring girls in there at night. I'm not even going to give you the details of that. You're too young.

Anyway, you know how I like to work out. There was a place in the basement of one of the off-campus hostels. They've got all sorts of free weights in there and a lot of the heavier weights where they'd use cement blocks and sand bags. Really serious stuff.

Adebayo and I started going there in the evenings after class, maybe three or four times a week. We both liked to pull heavyweight, so we had the same routine. You know Adebayo, right? We've been in the same class since we were little, and we played a lot of soccer together. Remember when I left for university? He was the one who went with me. Yes, him.

He and I, whenever there were parties we'd be the man show, you know, bodyguards, because we are so big and people are so afraid of us. And I was the head of the soccer team, so no one wanted to mess with me anyway. Adebayo and I, we were brothers from another mother. We thrived in that gym, like weeds. It was so hot in there, even though it was underground. It was just a bunch of guys, pulling weight like gorillas. Raw power. There were no women, so sometimes we'd be pulling in our underpants while these big fans would be blowing on us. It stank of sweat and the walls were real grimy. Sunny, you'd hate that place. But I loved it. My classes were tough; I'd go there to relax my head. Life was good . . . at first.

It all changed last week. Adebayo and I went there that early evening. It was Friday, so I was in a good mood. Later, we were going to meet up with some ladies; there was a party, too. We were working out. Pulling 10/10. We had just started at about 160 pounds. Then we'd load more, gradually. I remember, we were on our fifth round when Adebayo excused himself. He said he had to go to the bathroom. I just kept working out. I was at seven reps, pulling really hard, straining, screaming. I wanted to get that burn, you know? When you bench, it's no pain, no gain.

Not only had Adebayo left, but now I saw two guys come in. Not as swollen as me, but they were big enough and obviously a bit older. Taller. They started applauding me. I kept pushing up on the bar, putting on a show. I was the only one in the gym, but it was just two guys, Sunny. You don't know me; I can defend myself really good. I know boxing as well as I play soccer. You and Ugonna never knew about the places where the matches took place, but I used to win lots of money boxing. How do you think I got that money I put in the floor? You all just thought my bruises were from soccer. Who no know, no go know, right? So I wasn't afraid. But then another two guys came in. One of them was Adebayo, and he seemed to know the other three guys.

They all approached me. The three strangers were dressed for the street, so they must have come from outside. They were smiling and seemed nice enough.

"Well done," Adebayo said. But he didn't tell me the names of these guys.

"You are a strong man," the tallest one said, looking down at me as I struggled to put the bar and weights back on the bar rest. They didn't help me. "We are proud of you."

I smiled and sat up. I was wearing nothing but my boxer shorts and my muscles were bouncing. "Thank you," I said.

"We have something to tell you and it's very important." The other ones just stood behind him. "You need to know the rules and regulations of campus."

I immediately relaxed. This was all it was about, campus stuff. And I wanted to do well in school. These guys were here to help me. Great. Good. Since I'd gotten there, I hadn't had a mentor or any older student offer to show me how things were done and what was best. So this was a relief.

Right after that, we all went to a local cafeteria that we called the Cholera Joint. It was just down the road. The place is nothing special. They serve things like rice, beans, bread, and eba. Good, cheap food. You bring your plate to the stand and tell them what to put on it. Then you sit at one of the plastic tables and chairs and eat. It's mainly for us local students, but you get kabu kabu and okada drivers who come there often, too.

So there the five of us were. I saw all of them as my friends because Adebayo was my friend and they were his friends. I remember what everyone ordered. All of them chose rice, plantain, and beef. I chose my favorite, rice and beans. They make them nice at the Cholera Joint. I paid for all the food. It was a lot of money for me, but I had it. You know me, if I have it, then I spend it and when I don't have it, I don't miss it. Plus, I was in a good mood. These guys wanted to help me fold smoothly into university life. I don't know why I didn't put two and two together at the time. I do not know. Maybe I was blinded by hope.

Anyway, by the time we finished, it was almost eight o'clock and getting dark. We walked down the street about a half mile. The area was mainly occupied by the other two-story satellite hostels, the occasional tree. It is not a busy street. As a matter of fact, the street was so empty that we only met a few people along the way and there were no cars. It was a warm night, so because I'd recently worked out and then eaten, I was sweating. Eventually, they stopped under a low shaded mango tree. By this time it was completely dark and under that tree, no one could see us. Still, I wasn't scared. Adebayo was with me, and I just knew I could handle the other three if I needed to . . . if they turned out to not be so friendly.

One of them flicked on a torch and flashed it into the leaves above.

"Look, we've been watching you," the tall one said. "We have something important to tell you." At this point I glanced at Adebayo, and in the dim light that reflected from the flashlight, I saw him look away. "You're a strong guy, physically. Smart, get good grades, you were near the top of your high school class, the ladies like you . . ." He paused. "And we hear your little sister is albeeno, maybe even one of those child witches you hear about."

"What?" I exclaimed. "She's not . . ."

"No, no, relax. It's good. A child witch is power. We like what we see when we see you," he said, holding a hand up for me to stop talking. "We want only your success. And you will have all the advantages in school if you join us."

"Huh? How . . . Where? Be clear, I'm not understanding," I stammered. My mouth suddenly felt dry. Sunny, it was only at this time that I realized what was really going on, and it was something I heard was very common, but I never imagined would happen to me.

"We are the Great Red Sharks," he said.

Shit, shit, shit, I thought. You've probably even heard of them. "Fine . . . good," I said, still not sure what to say or think.

"Do you understand? The Red Sharks is one of the strongest confraternities in Nigeria."

He'd confirmed it. Now I was scared. Dad warned me about all this confraternity nonsense before I left. You and Ugonna have heard the stories of students going missing or getting killed *in fights. It's scarier and more common than all that Black Hat stuff from last year. Dad said they'd approach me and that I was to always say no. But it's not the same when you are right there looking into their eyes and they are looking into yours and they know who you are. My best friend, Adebayo, was in the Red Sharks. And that meant they knew everything about me already, because he did. How had he kept this kind of secret from me for so many weeks?! I didn't even notice any change in his behavior. I saw him often enough that I didn't know he snuck off anywhere else. But then again, it's a known fact that all confraternity meetings happen in the night.*

I almost ran. I considered it with every part of my being. I must have tensed up because Adebayo grabbed my arm and held it tightly. "Calm down," he said. "It's not what you think. You'll have a chance to get any grade you want. You'll get to be a lecturer! No one can harm you. You want money? Many of the Red Shark members are from filthy-rich families. They'll happily blow their wealth on you if you join."

I admit, I was a little dazzled. Especially by the idea of being a lecturer. I could already see the pride on Daddy's face when I told him about it. You know how he is. "I'll think about it," I said.

"You have three days," the tall one said.

For three days, I thought about it. I went out that night, met up with the girls, and partied. I studied hard the entire weekend. I worked out at the gym with Adebayo, and we acted like nothing was happening. Come Monday morning, they showed up at my room. Adebayo wasn't there. It was the tall one and one of the others.

"What is your response?" the tall one asked.

I asked them to explain exactly what they wanted again, and he didn't hesitate or get irritated. The tall one pulled me into the hallway and quietly told me that this was an invitation to join the Red Sharks. Then he and the other guy waited.

I laughed and nodded. "Okay."

They both smiled and we all shook hands, snapping fingers at the end. I began to relax again. Maybe Adebayo is right, I *thought.* Maybe it isn't so bad.

"We'll come back tonight," the tall one said.

At one thirty A.M.*, the tall one pounded on my door. The noise woke and angered my roommates; they got even angrier when they learned that it was for me. I quickly dressed and left with the tall guy. When I got outside, it was dark because the power had gone out. But there were three sets of eyes in the dark, and they belonged to three big guys. "You must agree to join the others," the tall guy said.*

I nodded. They blindfolded me with a red handkerchief and tied my hands. At this point, so much was going through my head. I was thinking I'd made a terrible mistake. Sunny, I kept seeing you, Mummy, Daddy, Ugonna, everyone. I kept wishing I were with you all and not where I was. I started wondering if I'd ever see any of you again!

We must have walked about three miles. It felt like it. It was a long way. When they took the blindfold off me, we were in the bush. One that I didn't recognize. They untied my hands. I looked around. Someone had a lamp, and I could see faces now. There were ten guys. Three of them were my professors, two of them were classmates, Adebayo was one of them, too.

They were all wearing red shirts, black trousers, black caps, and red armbands. One of them was singing some native song, and some were dancing and clapping to it. They were all older than me, except for Adebayo, but none was swollen like me and I was sure none of them knew how to box. If I had to fight, I would.

"What is your name?" a stocky guy of about nineteen asked me. He was light-skinned, probably Igbo, and had several keloids on his chin nestled in his slight beard.

"Chukwu," I said.

The man turned to the others. "His name is Chukwu."

They all stepped closer and grunted that they'd heard him. I tried to make eye contact with Adebayo, but he wouldn't look at my face. Neither would my professors and friends. It was like they were pretending not to know me.

"I am the leader, the Capo," the man with the keloids said.

"Okay," I said.

"Lie down," Capo said.

"Why?" I asked, surprised.

Before I knew it Adebayo, my best friend, stepped up to

me and slapped me hard across the face. I didn't even think; I hit him right back with a powerful uppercut blow. He fell to the ground. I know how to take a man out. Adebayo is my best friend, but I was terrified and angry as hell. No one slaps me!

They all jumped on me then. All ten of them, kicking, punching, stomping. I curled myself into a ball, trying to protect my body as much as I could. I remember being horrified but also very, very angry. I kept thinking, I'm going to get out of here. When I do, I'll beat them down one after the other. Just need to get out from under them. *But I couldn't, Sunny! When ten people attack you . . . you have no chance. The strikes, the weight, the pain, you CAN'T BREATHE!*

They beat you like that so that you will have no mercy in the future. What I later learned is that in the bush, if an initiate died from the beating, he was buried right then and there. That place was full of bones. It's haunted. How many dead students were watching me, wondering if I would join them in the spirit world that night? When you hear about students disappearing, this is one of the places where many of them go.

Those guys beat me until I was barely able to gasp for air. Everything was silver blue red, but somehow I didn't lose consciousness. I felt that if I did fall into the darkness that was calling me, I'd never return. I thought of you all. If I died, I'd be putting you in danger because Mummy and Daddy would come looking for me, asking questions. Who knows what the Red Sharks would do to them if they got too close to the truth?

So I stayed awake. I watched them start walking away, one after the other. Capo was the first to leave. "Let the devil that led you here guide you," he whispered into my ear. He firmly took Adebayo by the arm, dragging him away. Then the others left one by one. No one did a thing to help me.

I lay there, wheezing, painfully coughing, feeling the blood and sweat seep from me, mosquitoes coming in droves to bite me and drink my draining blood. I couldn't believe what had happened to me. It's one thing to take a few hits in a boxing match or a hard kick on the soccer field, it's another to be beaten down by ten big men. No mercy. No care for vital or sensitive organs. No rescue. I didn't know where I was and I was in the dark. In the bush. I was alone, Sunny. So alone.

I don't know how long I lay there. Maybe about a half hour. Sometimes things were very dim; other times, I was wide awake with terrible throbbing pain. Then I heard rustling and footsteps. Someone was beside me. That someone put his hands beneath my body and helped me stand up. I groaned and whimpered. I must have sounded like a dying old man. But at that time, I didn't care. I was barely conscious. The world was swimming, and I didn't know up from down. My chest was a knot of pain. My legs were numb. I felt wet all over. I could smell myself . . . I may have . . . there was more than the reek of sweat and blood on me. Slowly, we started walking.

"Never let anyone know I helped you," he said. I started weeping. He helped me get to my hostel. It was almost four A.M.

"That was the first phase of initiation," Adebayo said, looking at me gravely. "The next will be tomorrow night. It will go up to seven days."

"Oh my God," I whispered.

"Remember when I said I was robbed by those guys that first week we were here?"

When I realized, I gasped. "You were all bloody."

He nodded.

"And cut up. Your arms were . . . That was them?"

"If I can survive it," he said, "you can."

"No," I said. We stood outside my room whispering like devils in the night. Inside, my hostel mates were all asleep.

"There's nothing you can do to stop it now," he said. "You either make it through or you die. Now you know everyone's face. You can betray us." He gave me a first-aid kit and quickly left. That was the first initiation.

I cleaned myself up as best I could. I was aching all over, bleeding, cut. My hostel mates looked at me with fear, but none of them asked me a thing. I went to class that next day. No one was going to keep me down, I decided. I limped into class and stared my professor in the face as he lectured about mathematics. He acted like he was just my professor and I was just his student. He pretended that he was not one of the Red Shark members who'd tried to kill me the night before. Adebayo and I went to the Cholera Joint together for lunch. He, too, acted like nothing happened. He said nothing about my limping, but he did slow his walk for me.

Night fell. It had rained during the day, so it was cooler. My skin was itchy from mosquito bites and from scabbing skin. I felt inflamed all over. Again, I nearly ran. I wanted to jump in my Jeep and just drive. But . . . I don't know. I stayed. What could be worse than last night? *I thought. I wasn't going to run from anybody.*

They came at three A.M. *They didn't blindfold me or tie my hands. I knew where the place was, anyway. And I hadn't run, so to them I had resigned myself to my fate. I wasn't afraid. They brought me to the haunted bush where everyone was waiting for me. More than ten guys this time. Probably closer to thirty. All in red and black.*

They introduced me to "the family" from Capo *to me; my new name was* Yung C. *Then* Capo *asked me to step up.* When *I did,* Capo *grabbed my shoulders. I immediately tensed up, a thousand different flares of still-raw pain went through me. But I stayed calm. Some guys came up behind and beside me and held my arms.*

One of the members stepped up beside Capo *with something in his hand. Another member shined a flashlight on my other hand. Those guys holding me began to push me down. "Don't fight," one of them said, straining as I resisted. Another guy joined them, and they eventually wrestled me to the ground and . . . and* Capo *brought these clamps out of his pocket. They were holding me down, and two more guys came and held my head down. One of them squeezed my cheeks hard and said, "Open! Open your mouth!" After a while, the pain was so much that I did.*

Capo knelt over me with those clamps, and I understood exactly what was about to happen. I started bucking and trying to free myself. But there were so many guys, I was trapped.

"One of a Red Shark's teeth must be taken to signify he is one with the Sharks."

"You bite him and we kill you," the one squeezing my mouth open growled. The guy was serious. And he looked like he was hoping to have to do it.

"We take one of the ones near the back," Capo said. He was grinning, enjoying himself. How many times had he done this? I think he wanted me to give him a reason to bash my face with those clamps before pulling my tooth, anyway. I could see it in his eyes. So I stopped struggling. He took the one on the bottom right in the back. See the hole? I nearly blacked out. He pulled and pulled. Then I heard it rip. I whimpered with pain, saliva and blood filling my mouth.

"There it goes. Got it," he said. He didn't even wipe it off as he jiggled it about in his hand, laughing almost hysterically. Then he brought something out of his pocket and added it to my tooth in his hand. He shook them and together they made a clinking sound. Then he blew hard into his hand. When he shook it, there was no clinking sound. And when he opened his hand, my tooth was replaced with a larger, pointier yellow tooth—a shark tooth.

Several of the members gasped at his cheap magic trick. They all let go of me and I just lay there, feeling the mosquitoes biting me—my own bite one tooth less. I glared at Capo as he grinned down at me. That Capo. He is an evil man. Him, in particular.

I was exhausted, but there was more to come. They sat me up.

"You see this?" Capo said, kneeling before me, holding the shark tooth to my face. "This was your tooth. You have become a Red Shark like the rest of us now." The smile dropped from his face. "Hold out your hand."

The shark tooth looked sharp as hell. They had to grab me again and force my hand open. They cut me deeply on my hand. I didn't scream, but I stamped my foot really hard and fought not to struggle. If I did, the guys holding me would hold me tighter and I didn't want that. I breathed through my nostrils and tears bled from my eyes as a clay pot was held beneath my bleeding hand. My blood mixed with the blood of the other confraternity members who'd all done the same thing for their initiation.

"This is a symbol of our love for one another," Capo said. "Blood is blood."

The pact was sealed. Afterward, there was no beating. They sang traditional songs and gave speeches of welcome. I heard none of it. I only had one thing in my head at this point.

The Capo was always the first to leave. Then it was in order of rank. With Adebayo and I leaving together last. He told me that the next night, I'd be given three tasks to complete.

But, Sunny, there was no way in hell that I was going to stick around for any of it. I was sure one of those tasks was going to be that I hurt or kill someone! They are looking for me right now. Probably turning my entire hostel room upside down. I feel sorry for my roommates. I took all my things, though. I didn't tell Adebayo. How could I trust him? He's the one who told them about me. You see this? A medical student friend of mine gave me these stitches just before I left. I was lucky he helped me. Otherwise, my hand would probably be infected. I've been staying with lady friends, one night here, another night there, since Thursday.

So there it is, Sunny, I . . . I am a member of a secret society of the most dangerous kind and I've just gone AWOL, I've deserted, run off. They will *want to kill me. But if I stay . . .*

Sunny just gazed at her brother as he looked away, shaking his head. "If I stay, they'll turn me into a monster," he said.

She needed a moment to get her mind around it. Her oldest brother, Chukwu, was in a secret society . . . just as she was. He'd been through an initiation as she had been. But it wasn't the same. She loved her society; he was running from his. He could speak about it, but she could not. She blinked away tears as she felt something hard and hot in her chest. Rage. Her brother had been one of the banes of her existence for most of her childhood, though since she'd become a Leopard Person, their relationship had improved. Nonetheless, she could not ever, ever, ever bear anyone harming him. This realization surprised her as much as the intensity of her rage did.

"I have to go," he suddenly said.

"Where?" she asked, grabbing his arm.

Her brother frowned, looking at her hand gripping the flesh of his upper arm. "I have a lady friend in Aba who I can stay with for a few days. Then . . . I don't know."

Sunny's mind was so awash with anger and the pain of his story that she was finding it hard to focus. His face was so battered that he barely looked like her brother. Every motion he made was hindered by pain. On top of this, those idiots were robbing him of his future by scaring him away from school.

Her brother got up. Slowly.

"Wait," she said, running to her underwear drawer. She took out the plastic box where she kept the little naira she had and twenty American dollars from when they'd moved back from New York years ago. "Here," she said, shoving it in his hands. "Take this."

"I can't . . ."

"Yes, you can," she said. The wheels in her head had begun to turn. She wouldn't tell her parents. Not yet. "You have your phone?"

"Yes," he said.

"Okay . . . stay with your friend for now," she said. "But you're going to go back to school soon."

"Didn't you hear all I told you, Sunny? They'll kill me if I go back. They may even come here looking for me! I can't . . ."

"Have faith," Sunny said. "Have faith."

She gave him a gentle hug and then helped him quietly leave the house. She watched him slowly climb into his orange Jeep.

"Keep your phone close," she said. "Rest, eat, and . . . Chukwu, it's going to be okay."

He paused, looking into her eyes. "What makes you so sure?"

"Just trust me."

He smiled for the first time since he saw her. "Sunny, what's happened to you?"

She only smiled back.

"Whatever it is, it's good. It's good." He started the car.

"Keep your phone close," she repeated. Then she quickly added, "I'll call you in a day or so."

He nodded. "Not a word to Mummy, Daddy, or Ugonna."

She nodded.

Then he was gone. She went back inside and slept for three solid hours. She needed her rest. She had much more than school to handle come morning.

11
WAYS

As soon as Orlu climbed on the *okada* to go see his crazy auntie Uju, Sunny took off toward home. She leaped over the open gutter, leaving school grounds, and quickly jogged along the dirt path beside the road. She ran around students on their way home and avoided *okada* who drove dangerously close to the path as they sped and wove between cars and trucks.

She passed the usual shops and then the half-finished house that had been in construction for over five years. The run-down office building beside it looked even worse now that the house was almost complete. When she reached her neighborhood, she absentmindedly ran a hand over the smooth trunk of the palm tree growing on the corner of the street. She slowed down now, bringing out a handkerchief and dabbing her brow. She shut her eyes and took a deep breath. Getting through the school day had been hard. Not telling Orlu had been even harder. Sunny knew he'd disagree with what she planned to do. He'd push her to tell her parents.

Her eyes stung now. Then they grew moist. All day, she'd avoided thinking about her brother's story and his face, oh, his face, as best she could. But now that she was out of school and away from Orlu, she just wanted to sit in the road and cry her eyes out. She walked faster. Her parents wouldn't be home yet, but if Ugonna was home and she saw him, she'd break down and tell him everything.

When she arrived at Chichi's hut and saw her sitting on a chair outside, she knew she'd done the right thing. Her eyes filled with tears as she approached the one person she thought could help her. Chichi was reading a thick book and when she looked up at Sunny, she grinned. "You've gotta see this book! It's a novel set entirely in the *wilderness*! Of all people, you'll . . ." The smile dropped from her face. She closed the book and got to her feet. She placed the book on the chair. "Sunny! What's wrong?"

Sunny let her backpack drop to the dirt path that ran up to Chichi's hut, now unable to control her tears. "I . . . I . . . I . . ." she sobbed.

"What happened?" Chichi said, running up and taking

both of Sunny's hands. Chichi was already short and she hadn't grown any in the last year, whereas Sunny was pushing five foot nine and had gained several pounds of lean muscle. Still, Chichi managed to hold Sunny up and help her into the hut. Sunny sat down hard in one of the cushioned chairs inside the hut, tears still draining from her eyes. Chichi knelt before her and looked into her face.

"Sunny," she softly said. "Did someone . . ."

"It's my brother!" she managed to wail. "He's in *terrible* trouble! They'll kill him!"

Sunny told Chichi everything. Recounting Chukwu's story between tears, foot stamping, and cursing, something Sunny rarely ever did. Retelling the story to Chichi seemed to bring it alive that much more for Sunny. It was like stepping into Chukwu's shoes. There were three reasons Sunny went to Chichi. The first was that she knew Chichi had always liked Chukwu. Chichi thought he was pretty and liking him had always been a source of argument between her and Sasha. The second reason she went to Chichi was because Chichi could keep secrets, even from Orlu and Sasha. And the third was that Chichi would be willing to break the rules and risk punishment to help Chukwu because trouble-making and daring were in her blood.

"Did you know that these damn societies were originally formed to make sure there was always academic freedom and to cure society's problems?" Chichi shouted as she paced the floor. "People like Professor Wole Soyinka and Aig-Imokhuede started them!" She was as angry as Sunny. "Now these young people who know nothing are crippling the highest place of Lamb education?! The university is all the Lambs have! Without the university, they'd be intolerable. They have no other urge to learn. I didn't know it was full of . . . of social disease."

"It is," Sunny said. "You can't really be a top student there without having to join or at least deal with them."

They were quiet now. Chichi stood in the middle of the hut frowning. Sunny sat in the chair looking at her sandaled feet. There was no breeze outside and it was easily close to ninety degrees, yet inside the hut it was cool as a clam. The floor of the hut was dirt, the bed Chichi and her mother shared to the right and many stacks of books to the left. They had so little, yet Chichi and her mother combined were a force powerful enough to be of great importance to the Leopard Knocks elders.

"So what do you want to do?" Chichi quietly asked.

Sunny didn't look up. There was a storm rolling in her mind. She couldn't get the image of her brother's battered face out of her head. This was his life at stake and his future. "What happens if juju is performed against a Lamb?"

"You already know that," she said. "Remember what happened when you showed Jibaku your spirit face? You only got off easy because you were a new free agent."

"No, I don't mean minor stuff. Serious juju."

Chichi looked closely at Sunny, and Sunny didn't look away. "I don't know," Chichi said. She cocked her head. "Why?"

"I want to make them suffer," Sunny said, clenching her fists. It felt good to speak her thoughts to Chichi. "Not just his so-called friend Adebayo, or their Capo leader. I want to make *all* of them suffer."

They were quiet, staring into each other's eyes. Chichi looked away first.

"Even if you will suffer for making them suffer?" Chichi asked, looking at her feet.

"Yes," Sunny firmly said. "It will be worth the sacrifice. My brother will at least be able to go back to school. Just help me with what I have to do and then step back. I don't want you to . . ."

"Oh, I'm not going to let you take the fall alone," Chichi said, looking up.

"No . . . no, Chichi, if it's just me, maybe . . ."

"You came to me for a reason, right?" Chichi said. Now she was smiling that smile she only flashed when she was up to something. "You know I know . . . ways."

Sunny said nothing. She had never been a good liar.

"You waited until Orlu had to go see his auntie. You knew Sasha would be with Kehinde today. You wanted to speak to me alone," she said. "You're smart, Sunny. And when you need to use them, you have claws. Listen, I may know a way around the rules. We will get caught but not for the worst of it, if we do this right."

"Do what?"

"Well, they think his sister is a witch, right?"

"Yeah, but not a Leopard Person, just one of those child witches," Sunny said.

"Well, be what they say you are, then," she said. "The Red Sharks always meet at night. So, let's meet them in the night."

Sunny reported back to her mother to tell her where she was and that she'd be home in a half hour while Chichi made some tea. As soon as Sunny got off the phone, Chichi said, "Come sit down."

She's set up two mismatched and chipped porcelain cups and filled them with tea, making Sunny's just as she liked it, Lipton with just a hint of sugar. "Let's relax for a second before we do this," Chichi said, pulling up a stool and picking up a cup.

The tea was nice and Sunny allowed herself to settle down for the first time since before seeing her brother. Her tea was bitter and hot. It warmed her throat. She took a deep breath and slumped back into her seat, pushing away all the questions that tried to crowd her mind. All the while, Chichi leaned forward and watched her intensely as she, too, sipped her tea.

"You feel better now?" Chichi asked.

"Actually, yes, I do."

"Okay, let's call him," Chichi said.

"What? Now?"

"Yes, now. If we don't act soon, those crazies are going to show up at your house. We need to get fast and clear information."

"About what?"

"The Red Sharks," she said. "The members. Especially this Capo guy and Chukwu's friend Adebayo."

"Why? Why them?"

"You want to make them leave your brother alone, right?"

"Yeah."

"Then we need information."

Sunny frowned, squeezing her cup. She brought out her cell phone and brought up Chukwu's number and gave it to Chichi.

"What do I do?" she asked, looking at the screen.

"Just touch your finger to his picture," Sunny said.

"Right on it?"

"Yes."

Chichi fiddled with it and frowned. "Now there's a picture of some guy with dada hair kicking a football. What's Arsenal FC?"

"What'd you do? That's my background picture," Sunny said, taking the phone from her. She brought up her brother's number again. Not only did Chichi not have a cell phone, but she didn't even know how to use them. Sunny touched Chukwu's photo in her favorites list and handed it back to Chichi. "Just talk when he . . . Wait, give it to me."

Chichi gave it back, and Sunny listened to it ring. He picked up on the second ring. "Sunny?"

"Hello? Chukwu, how are you?"

"I'm . . . fine."

"You're at your friend's?"

"Yes. I'm at Ejike's apartment."

"Okay . . . um, hang on, Chichi wants to talk to you," she quickly said.

"What?" he said. "Didn't I . . ."

She quickly handed the phone to Chichi.

"Chuks," Chichi said. "How you body dey?"

Sunny got up and started pacing the room, bracing herself to hear Chichi say "Hello? Hello??" repeatedly because her brother had hung up the phone. But instead Chichi started laughing. Then she said, "Relax, *sha*. She didn't tell anyone else. But I know everything, yes." She paused. "About you and your cultist *wahala*. Look, we want to help you, but we need some information." She motioned to Sunny to relax as she slowly ambled out of the hut. "Names, descriptions, where they live, stuff like that . . ."

Sunny sat back and sipped her tea. But she couldn't relax.

When Chichi came back, she was smiling, the phone

pressed to her ear. "I don't have a cell phone, but you can always come to where I live and pick me up. Don't take me to any restaurant. I like roadside food only." She listened and then laughed hard. "That works. But give us three days. You will see. Nothing is more powerful than Mami Wata. Okay, o. Here is your sister." She handed the phone to Sunny. "We've got what we need."

"Hello?" Sunny said.

"What are you two going to do?" he asked.

"I don't really know yet. But . . . don't worry."

"Sunny," he said. "Can I ask you a question and will you answer it?"

"If I can." She glanced at Chichi, who was busy scribbling things down in a notebook.

"So you've joined Owumiri?"

"Huh?"

"Those Mami Wata women," he said. "Don't lie. Chichi told me so. I've heard a lot about them, and now I know why you've been sneaking around and acting funny."

Sunny frowned, utterly thrown off. She knew of Owumiri, too. They gathered at the river and the seaside and sang and danced and scared men. "I . . ."

"Look, I get it, Sunny," he said. "You need protection because . . . of your albino-ness."

"What?!" Sunny screeched.

"I understand," he said, ignoring her. "I haven't been the

best brother. Should have protected you more from all the bullshit."

"Chukwu . . . it's not . . ."

"Listen, Sunny, okay? Don't get close to these Red Shark guys. Work whatever it is you want to work from far away. The Red Sharks will kill you. They've killed before. You saw what they did to me, and that was just to become part of them! And don't expect me to go back to see if whatever you've done worked. Put it behind you."

"Just . . . sit tight," Sunny said.

"I plan to. And why'd you have to tell Chichi?! You want her to think I'm some sort of weakling? Look, call me in a few days, all right? By then I'll know more about my plans."

When he hung up, Sunny looked for Chichi and realized she was no longer in the hut. She went out the back door and found Chichi sitting on a mat reading outside. "I think I know what we should do." She laughed. "If we do it right, the worst punishment we'll get is a warning."

"What do you have in mind?"

"We'll set Murks on them," Chichi said. "Sasha and I have had to read up on these as second levelers. Anatov didn't spend much time on them, but it doesn't take much for Sasha and me." She grinned. Chichi's and Sasha's photographic memories were exactly what got them into so much trouble.

"What are Murks? Are they dangerous?"

"Of course they are. What do you think we *need* for

these guys? Fluffy pink talking bunnies? Murks look like tiny bats and dwell in pools of darkness—under a fallen tree in a lake, beneath houses, under beds, whatever. They are physical world–dwelling spirits so they can't be crushed and suffocated. Normally if you leave them alone, they will leave you alone, but what makes Leopard People interested in Murks is that they can be weaponized."

"What, you pack them in a gun or something?"

Chichi giggled. "No, no. You get them in the right mood, and they will do whatever mischief you ask them to do, especially when it comes to harming others. Murks have 'murky souls,' that's how they got their name. Give me a day or so to read up a bit more on them. Just follow my lead. I know exactly what to do."

12
MURKED

Sunny and Chichi lay on their bellies peeking through a bush beside a palm tree. They wore black pants and black sweatshirts with hoods they'd bought from Leopard Knocks.

It had taken one day to find them. Chichi had merely used Adebayo's full name in a dowsing charm she'd read about in a German book of juju. It took fifteen minutes for the funky train to get them to campus one night later, when the Red Sharks were set to meet and discuss what to do about Chukwu. Then Sunny and Chichi simply followed them into the bush. Once in, it had been easy enough to creep up on them, for they were singing and clapping. Sunny couldn't understand the words to the song, but Chichi could.

"What the hell?" Chichi whispered, looking disgusted.

"What?"

"They're calling to the devil in Yoruba," Chichi said.

Sunny shivered.

Two of the guys started building a fire, another two set down a cooler and one other set down a chair. A light-brown-skinned guy with keloids on his chin sat in the chair. This had to be Capo, the leader. The one who after having her brother beaten by ten guys had pulled out Chukwu's tooth, cut him with a shark tooth, enjoyed all of it, and then left him to live or die. In the firelight, Sunny memorized his silhouette. Looking straight at the firelight made it hard for Sunny to see his face. She wasn't wearing her glasses and in the night; they would not have helped anyway. But she could make him out well enough. Sunny felt her own fire, which had been burning in her chest since seeing her brother's battered face.

After a few minutes, they stopped singing and all the members sat on the ground before Capo. One big beefy guy, whose muscles looked ready to burst out of his red shirt, stood behind Capo with his meaty arms across his chest. Then Capo was speaking, but he spoke in a low tone, and neither Sunny nor Chichi could hear. Sunny and Chichi weren't concerned about what was being said; they were just waiting for the right time. It came about a half hour later, when it must have been well past three A.M. They'd opened the cooler and had been drinking and drinking. Then Capo grabbed a bottle of Guinness beer, drank it all at once, and started singing the devil song. Soon everyone joined him. As the minutes passed, their singing grew more drunken and frenzied.

"Okay," Chichi said. "I didn't plan for this, but it's *perfect.* We call the Murks on them, and they'll think it's the devil attacking them, not two Leopard girls hiding in the bushes. No council people can arrest us for that because we won't have broken the rules of exposure. I don't even think they'll have reason to give us a warning!"

Sunny grinned. "That's brilliant!" Her smile decreased a bit. "But what will the Murks do? Will it be enough? If we don't show ourselves, how will they know to leave us alone?"

"Just watch," Chichi said, bringing out her juju knife and a sack. "There's juju powder in here. Do *not* sneeze, no matter what."

The guys were singing crazily now. Sunny didn't think they'd notice if she sneezed her brains out.

"Bring your cell phone," Chichi whispered. "Remember, don't turn it on. The screen has to be dark."

Sunny brought it out and handed it to her. "I turned the contrast and brightness all the way down."

"Okay. And you set the timer, right?"

"Yes," she said. "It's ticking down now. Should have about thirty minutes before it stops."

"It won't ring or vibrate?"

"Right. It'll just stop timing."

"Okay. Here, touch the surface," Chichi said. "Run your fingertips over it."

After Sunny did this, Chichi took some powder between her fingertips. It looked like soot in the dim firelight. She blew it toward the men, and it traveled easily in a dark mist for several yards, mingling with and dimming the firelight. Chichi brought up her juju knife and spoke some rapid words in Efik, then she stabbed her knife into the soil and twisted it.

"Is that it?" Sunny asked, when nothing happened.

"Shhh," she said.

Sip! Something black flitted in front of them. Then it was gone. Then it came again and hovered before them. Even there in the dark, mere feet from the men who'd nearly killed her brother, Sunny found herself smiling. It was just so . . . *cute*! The small batlike creature was covered in downy black fur, its wings batting like those of a hummingbird. It hovered perfectly still so she could see its big black eyes, tiny snout, and pointy fox-like ears. It smelled strongly of perfumed oil.

"Who are you?" Chichi asked it.

It rapidly cheeped three times, and then said in a low voice that sounded like that of a very tall big man, "*Od'aro*."

Every hair went up on Sunny's body as she went from delighted to terrified.

"It calls itself 'goodnight' in Yoruba," Chichi said. "Typical." Then she spoke to it in either Yoruba or Efik. It did a quick turn and then zipped off. Sunny heard it cheep, and there were more responses from the treetops, which had started to shed leaves and shudder. The Red Shark members stopped singing, listening. One of them pointed at the fire, wobbling on his feet. But the fire was quickly dying, and soon they were all in darkness. Silence.

"Stupid boys think they are above reproach because they hurt and kill," Chichi whispered. "Let them learn."

"What are they going to do?"

"Watch."

The darkness that had fallen suddenly grew heavy and thick. The cheeping in the trees stopped, and the silence was as pure and weighted as the darkness. Sunny grabbed Chichi. She opened her mouth wide, to make sure there was still air and she could breathe it. She could. Then the screaming began.

"What is happening?" Sunny asked.

"Murks like to slap," Chichi said. "Their wings feel like hot steel."

Sunny and Chichi stood behind the bushes listening to the screams, yelps, and moans. *Let them hurt and remember my brother's face and his pain with every slap and scratch*, she thought. The sound of them running in all directions made Sunny freeze. For the amount of time Sunny had set the timer on her phone, the Murks would follow them to their homes, bringing their darkness and remaining quiet as air. And then when the members went to sleep, the Murks would bring the nightmares. Nightmares that would call up her brother's face and name and warn the members to leave him alone forever or suffer more consequences. Chichi's plan was flawless. But it wasn't enough. Not for Sunny.

The darkness was lifting as the Murks broke away from one another and chose which member to harass. The fire exploded with light and for a moment, Sunny had a clear view. She saw the backs of several members' red shirts as they fled into the bush, some toward the way they'd come, others in opposite or adjacent directions. One member ran right into a tree, falling onto his back, a Murk scratching and slapping at his head. And there was Capo on the ground. He'd fallen over his own chair and was too drunk to get up with any speed. Beside Sunny, Chichi was quietly laughing her head off.

Sunny jumped up.

Chichi hiccupped as she fought to speak. "What the hell are . . ."

Stop, Sunny thought. At the same time, she dug within and touched but did not bring forth her spirit face. She didn't touch her juju knife. This was hers. Natural. Her temples ached and her skin cooled, just as Sugar Cream had said it would be. She didn't hesitate. She held out her hands and pushed as one would push water. She'd stopped the rush of time. Silence. Complete and total silence. And stillness. She didn't look at Chichi. Nor the suspended Murk that was flying after one of the suspended members. There was Adebayo, looking over his shoulder, a Murk right above his head. Sunny didn't bother with him, either. She walked to where Adebayo was looking. Toward Capo.

As soon as she saw him up close, she didn't doubt what she'd done. The ground beneath him glowed a dull red, in the shape of curled and sprawled skeletons. She could see them all over, just beneath the ground. And Capo himself glowed with the same dull light, especially his hands and mouth. This guy was a Lamb version of Black Hat in the making. He'd killed with his hands and mouth. Cannibal. Ritual killer. Sunny felt her belly roll with nausea. How did her brother manage to fall in with these guys? This man? Chukwu was lucky to manage to fall out alive.

Capo was the only thing that was moving. He rolled onto his back, clasping his throat. He wheezed loudly, his watering eyes bulging. Sunny felt light-headed but otherwise perfectly fine. She looked down on him with disgust and pushed back her black hood. Capo's eyes grew wider.

"Do you know who I am?" she asked.

Still wheezing for air, slowly he nodded.

"You will die in less than a minute," she said. "You aren't albino, so you can't move outside of time." She paused, utterly enjoying the look of pure terror and approaching death on his face. And she enjoyed the fact that she was lying to him. This was far more than a mere medical condition; it was her being a Leopard Person born with a specific talent that she was practicing every day and . . . night. And it was her being *her*. "I'm Chukwu's child witch of a sister," she said. "You see me clearly. My name is Sunny Nwazue." His eyes were starting to close. "My brother will return to university. If any of you people lay a finger on him, I will bring a painful death to every one of your relatives and then you, especially you—I know what you've done. Do you understand?"

Capo nodded weakly as his eyes closed. Sunny quickly moved back to Chichi. Then she let go. Letting go was easier than getting ahold of time. She sank to her knees beside Chichi. She'd been standing on the other side of Chichi, and Chichi was still looking where she'd been. Now she turned to Sunny and did a double take. She looked where Sunny had been and then back to where Sunny now stood. "Sunny, what did you do?"

Sunny only shook her head, watching Capo yards away. All the others were gone. Capo wasn't moving.

"Did . . . did you kill him?" Chichi whispered. "Why didn't you just leave him?"

"You didn't see my brother," Sunny coldly said.

Capo twitched and suddenly jumped to his feet. He looked around drunkenly, and Sunny and Chichi ducked down. When he saw that he was alone, he started walking away. Then he turned back, dumped the water from the cooler on the fire, and then stumbled back the way they'd all come.

Chichi and Sunny stayed down for a while in the dark. When it was clear that everyone was gone, they stood up. "What did you do?" Chichi asked again.

"What needed to be done."

Chichi looked hard at Sunny. "You were beside me and then you weren't. And I didn't see you near Capo," she said. "But . . . I saw him slump after you disappeared." She frowned as she thought hard. "Did you hold? Hold time? Is that what you and Sugar Cream have been working on?"

"Some, but that was the first time I tried it."

"He saw your face?"

She nodded.

"Shit," Chichi said.

"It's okay."

"No, it's not."

They walked back to the main road. It took them a half hour in the darkness even with a torch. When they reached the main road it wasn't five minutes before the black council car drove up to them and demanded that Sunny get into it. Sunny did so without a word of protest.

"Let my mom know that I'm okay," she told Chichi.

"Okay," Chichi said. She paused. "Give me your phone. If you don't, they will take it from you."

Sunny handed Chichi her phone. They looked at each

other for a moment. Then Sunny said, "I'll . . . I'll be okay." *For now*, she thought. She didn't know about later. Still, as the car drove soundlessly down the dark empty road, past the satellite hostels where the university students who were not up to satanic mischief slept soundly, Sunny felt it was worth it.

13
DEBASEMENT

The ceremonial masks stared at Sunny. There were fifty-two of them. Over her months as Sugar Cream's student, she'd had plenty of time to count. The first time she was here, she'd thought there were only twenty, but then again, she'd been distracted by the fact that she was there at risk of being caned for showing her spirit face to Jibaku.

The masks didn't stay in the same spot, either. Every few days, some of them moved—sometimes across the wall, sometimes switching with the mask beside them. And some would change the expression on their faces. Sunny had learned early on not to touch them or mutter anything in anger near them. They would sometimes lick, smooch, try to bite or spit on her hand, and they'd tell Sugar Cream anything she said.

Now all the masks looked either angry or deeply interested. Sugar Cream was scowling at Sunny. Sunny gazed right back. It was five A.M. and she'd walked up the Obi Library stairs alone, since she knew the way to Sugar Cream's office and she knew the consequences would probably be greater if she fled. She found Sugar Cream in her office sitting at her desk wearing a cream-colored nightgown, a cup of warm milky coffee in her hand.

"What happened?" Sugar Cream icily asked.

Sunny told Sugar Cream everything. She'd stood with her back straight and chin up. She'd fought keep her eyes dry and won, though when she described her brother's ordeal, her voice cracked twice and she felt light-headed. When she told of holding time, only then did Sugar Cream's eyebrows rise. But only the tiniest bit. Otherwise, her face remained like stone. This early morning, Sunny's mentor looked ancient. This morning, Sunny knew that she'd be caned.

"Chichi was right," Sugar Cream said when Sunny finished talking. "Do you see her here?" She paused. "Huh?" she suddenly snapped, making Sunny jump. "DO YOU SEE CHICHI HERE TO BE PUNISHED?"

"No, ma'am," Sunny quickly said.

"No, you don't. And it's not only because she made sure you two remained hidden and that those foul young men thought it was the devil attacking them and not you two.

Those men rock the foundation of learning in this country. We Leopard People have been working for *years* to eliminate these confraternities at their root. You two were given a pass for what you did. But then *you* crossed the line. You let your rage get the best of you."

Sunny looked down, frowning. *I don't care*, she thought. She knew if she had it all to do again, she'd do the same thing. She had to protect her brother. Sugar Cream knew this, too.

"With great power comes great responsibility, Sunny," Sugar Cream said. "You're young. You're a free agent who knows very little, but who is bursting with potential and passion. You're not the best or smartest of your age mates, but you are . . . interesting. This is why I took you on. But you need to learn control." She took a sip of her coffee. "And you need to learn the consequences."

After explaining to Sunny what would happen to her, Sugar Cream called two older students in the building. They were not to speak to Sunny. They weren't even to look at her. All they were to do was walk in front of and behind her. They led Sunny down the hallway to a gray door, and one of the students opened it. It led to a stairway. Sunny followed him in, the other student following behind Sunny. The walls here were made of a gray stone that looked like it had been carved bit by bit with an ice pick.

The steps were also made of the same roughly chiseled stone. As they descended, Sunny couldn't help the tears that fell from her eyes. She counted thirty steps and still they kept going. It was like traveling into an underground cave. The air grew cooler and cooler until Sunny was shivering. She was glad that she still wore her jeans and the black hooded sweatshirt over her T-shirt.

Down, down, down they went. To the Obi Library's infamous basement. Sugar Cream had ordered Sunny to stay here for three days as punishment for pulling a Lamb outside of time, a severe violation of Leopard doctrine, even for someone of greater experience and age. Because Sunny was under twenty-five, her punishment was milder than if she were an adult. "If you were twenty-six," Sugar Cream had said, "you'd be caned and then sent down there for three months."

"Go in," one of the students now said. "And don't try to come up."

They left her. They didn't lock the door because there *was* no door, just an opening in the stone wall with the dimly lit stone stairway that led back up. Sunny turned around and took in her prison. The basement was large, smelled of dirt and mildew, and was filled with moldering bookshelves of moldering books. Books that had been replicated and brought down here to be disposed of in due time. The bookshelves had rotted, buckled, and fallen into decay. Obviously, some of the books had been forgotten. In the center of the basement was a dusty wooden platform with an old bronze statue of a squat toad with overly bulbous eyes. Sunny touched its large head with her hand and sat on it as she watched the students leave.

Each day, they would bring her a meal and a large pitcher of water. She was given a bucket as her toilet, which would also be taken and emptied daily. Other than that, she would be alone down there. No blanket, no bathing, no light other than the dim one high on the ceiling.

As the sound of their footsteps receded, the fear set in. She'd heard terrible things about the basement. She sunk to the floor, leaning her head against the toad's head. "I did the right thing," she whispered. "I don't care what anyone says."

There were red spiders all over the place, especially on the ceiling. As she stared up at it, she noticed a large patch of churning red in the far left corner over one of the few bookcases that still stood. Slowly, Sunny walked across the dusty floor, her sandals grinding on the white marble. It wasn't just covered with dust, there was sand, too. From where, who knew? She stopped feet from the ceiling corner above, her mouth curling with disgust. Hundreds, maybe thousands of nasty, mewling red spiders churned in the corner. She squinted and shuddered. They were all milling around one enormous red spider the size of a dinner plate.

"Oh . . . God," she whispered, stepping away slowly. She was sure the thing was watching her, watching closely with its many eyes. She stumbled back to the large bronze toad, the only thing in the room that felt . . . okay. She rested her back against it and wrapped her arms around her knees. The metal was comfortingly warm and immediately fatigue fell on her. It had to be nearing sunrise.

She'd snuck out of the house, journeyed to campus with Chichi, located and terrorized one of the most powerful confraternities in the area, and now here she was. This was the longest night of her life. Her eyes grew heavy. But there was no rest for the weary. The basement had no windows. She was deep beneath the ground; the place was like a tomb. And the one light bulb, which just *had* to be near the spiders, was greasy and dim, shining down on the older, used up, and discarded books. There were corners and crevices between fallen shelves, and the room was full of shadows and hiding places. All this made the scraping sound that much more terrifying.

The sound seemed to bear down on the marble floor. Then it dragged. Slow and steady. Then it stopped. Then it dragged and then stopped. It came from right behind one of the bookcases to Sunny's left. And she could see a bit of a shadow through two fallen shelves. But nothing more. Sunny had nothing with her. Nothing to throw. Nothing to clutch with fear.

"Oh," she whispered, trying to stay still. Willing herself to be invisible. She could become invisible. But not for very long. And to do so, she had to travel, to move. Would whatever it was come at her? *What* was it?

Scraaaaape. Pause. *Scraaaape.* Pause. It stopped just before it came into view. Sunny waited for what felt like fifteen minutes, but the thing didn't show itself. Instead, quiet as smoke, a flame burst from behind the books. A smokeless one. No smell. No burning. Just the light and shadow of a flame. Sunny, helpless and exhausted, leaned against the neck of the bronze toad, staring at that which she could not see. Soon her eyes went out of focus, and then slowly they shut.

Scraaaaape.

Sunny's eyes shot open and she jumped up. Her legs wobbled and buckled, and she fell against the toad, banging her hip. A rotten-egg smell of sulfur stung her nose. She winced, turning toward the sound and the stench. What she spotted beside the bookcase made every hair in her body stand up. Even from feet away, she could tell that they were human bones, and not only because the one piled at the top was a clearly human skull. One near the bottom was heavy and long. A femur. And there was a hand sticking out of the center. The pile looked about the size of one human being, the bones a dirty, rusty gray red.

Sunny didn't move. She couldn't move. Her eyes stared and stared. Then they started to water.

Tap, tap, tap. She gasped and looked toward the staircase. Someone was coming down. She looked back at the bones. They were gone.

It was Samya, one of Sugar Cream's closest assistants. She was one of the few third levelers under the age of thirty that Leopard Knocks had. To pass *Ndibu*, one had to attend a meeting of masquerades *and* get a masquerade's consent to be a third leveler. To attend such a meeting, one had to slip into the wilderness, which meant the person had to die and come back. Only third levelers and up knew how this was done when one was not born with the natural ability. To reach the third level of *Ndibu* was like earning a PhD, and it was rare for one to be under the age of thirty-five. Samya was twenty-four.

She was a bookish woman who wore red plastic glasses and a long red dress, and had reddish-brown skin like Chichi and Chichi's mother. She'd piled her long braids atop her head as she carried the small tray. "Oh, Sunny, are you all right?" she asked. The worried look on her face cracked Sunny's wall of strength like a sheet of thin ice.

Her body grew warm and tingly, and her eyes stung with tears. "No," she whispered as Samya quickly came to her. She put the tray of food on the floor beside Sunny and gathered her in her arms.

"Why did you do it?"

"I had to!" Sunny sobbed. "I *had* to! It was my brother! You didn't see what they . . ." She couldn't breathe.

"Shhh, shhh," Samya said, holding her back. "Relax. Get ahold of yourself."

But Sunny's entire body was shuddering. Images of her

brother's battered face, eyes swollen, mouth swollen. His pain. Capo's terrified face as he gasped for air. Lying in wait in the bushes. Darkness. Screams.

"Sunny," Samya said shaking her. "You need to *calm down*." She paused. "There is something down here that can't know you are weak."

Sunny felt her nerves zing. There *was* something down here. She felt faint as she pushed her body to calm down. "What is it?"

"I can't say, and I can't come back," Samya said. "When someone is sent to the basement, a different student must bring down food on each day. I think Sugar Cream sent me first because she knew you'd need me. Don't expect the others that come to be helpful. They will . . . follow the rules."

"What rules?"

"Never mind," she quickly said. "Some things are worth it. Now listen, Sunny, and listen closely if you want to come out of here sane and alive. These books are old. They are used. They have been replaced, then cast aside. They will be dealt with eventually, but for now they are down here. Every book has a soul, every book . . . carries and attracts. There are sterilization and soothing jujus all over this room, but this is the earth. Something will always come and live here. In this case it is a djinn. It guards and hides in the books."

"Does it make fire that doesn't burn?"

Samya nodded and frowned. "So you've already seen it."

"Yes . . . its bones. I fell asleep and I woke up and it was right over there." She pointed to mere feet away.

"Oh my God, so soon?" Samya said, circling her head and snapping her finger. Then she looked at Sunny and gave the most pathetic reassuring smile Sunny had ever seen. "Listen, Sunny. It will try you."

"Try what?"

"*You*. It knows . . . Sunny, you aren't learned yet. You are just a free agent, but you were . . . are someone who did something in the wilderness. It was a good thing, I think. Otherwise, why would Ekwensu fear you? The thing down here is a djinn, and it'll read your past life as you being powerful in your present one, some sort of chosen one. So it will try you. It will want to see what you've got." She frowned. "Damn, Sunny, why did you have to get yourself thrown down here?"

"What do I do?"

Samya got up. "I don't really know." She looked at the staircase as if someone were calling her. Then she looked at Sunny. "Don't let it take you." She paused. "And . . . don't believe the silly Lamb stereotypes about djinni. They don't grant wishes and what they show you can be an illusion, but more times than not, it is real. They *can* harm you. Okay . . . I have to go." She pointed to the tray. "Eat all of it," she said. She looked Sunny in the eye. "*All* of it. You need your strength."

"Wait, wait," Sunny said as Samya moved quickly to the

staircase. "My parents! My family. Will someone . . ."

"Good luck, Sunny," she said over her shoulder. "Stay strong. Stay alive." Then she rushed up the stairs.

Sunny watched her go, listening as her steps grew fainter and fainter and then were gone. She sat against the bronze toad and stared at her tray of food. A bowl of dry-looking jollof rice with one chunk of tough-looking goat meat in the middle of it, an orange, and a bottle of water. She ate it all quickly, her eyes darting around like a scared rabbit. She didn't taste a bite of it. The scraping sound had begun again.

There was water somewhere in the basement. But she couldn't see it. *Drip, drip, drip.* Then stop. Then *drip, drip, drip.* Then stop. As if there was some machine turning it off and on. Trying to drive her mad. That would make two things with the same intention. A machine and a djinn. Sunny giggled to herself. Quietly. She had to stay quiet. The thing that was clumping and scraping about the room didn't seem to really see her. As the hours passed, she began to believe it was because of the bronze toad. Maybe there was something in it that kept the djinn at bay. For since that first time, it had not shown its bones to her. *Maybe I didn't really see the bones at all,* she thought. She giggled again. *If I don't move, then I'll be safe.*

The scraping was on the other side of the large room, its

noise echoing about the high ceiling. From where she was, she had a clear view of the red spiders, too. The big one was still in its spot. That was good. Yes, that was good. Her head pounded. How long had it been since Samya left? Three hours? Nine? All she had was the hanging dim light near the spiders.

"Chukwu, you better thank me when I get out of here," she whispered to herself. It was good to hear her voice, even if she couldn't raise it. "*If* I get out of here." She hugged herself closer to the bronze toad's warm body, pressing her head to it. Her comb clicked against the metal. She took it out and examined it, glad to have something else to focus on. She held it to her nose and smelled it. It smelled briny like the sea, but there was also a hint of flowers. The smell was pleasant. It smelled of outside. She smiled and whispered "Thank you" to the lady of the sea who'd saved her and then given her a gift that she could admire during a dark time.

"Whooooo oh whoooooo is Sunny Nwazuuuue?" she heard an ancient male voice suddenly sing. *Scraaaaape.* "Whooooo oh whooooo is Sunny Nwazuuuue?" the voice said again. Then another *scraaaaape.*

It had seen her. It had known she was there all along. The bronze toad was just a bronze toad. A decoration. An ornament in a room that was more a giant trash container than anything else. Sunny knew this. She'd just needed something to grasp because they'd given her nothing. They'd thrown her down here, and they hadn't even given her a gun, a protective stone, a hard stick, nothing. She had her juju knife, but she didn't know any protective charms against djinni or ghosts.

She glanced up at the ceiling. The giant red spider was still there and even from where she was, she felt more positive than ever that it was watching her. But the other smaller ones had dissipated. Maybe they were all over the basement now . . . including on the floor. She looked down and wasn't surprised to see one scurrying across the sandy marble.

Suddenly, the entire room reeked so strongly of sulfur that it hurt to breathe. Sunny jumped up and took off toward the stairway that led out of the library basement, coughing. She hadn't moved much in hours and her muscles were stiff, but she ran up the stairway like a champion. Her sandals slapped the concrete. She didn't dare glance back. Thus, she couldn't have been more shocked when she found herself stumbling right back into the Obi Library basement. Her sense of direction and gravity reeled for several moments as she came to understand what had happened.

"What?!" she screeched.

"Whooo oh whooo is Sunny Nwazuuuue?" The voice vibrated, coming from every direction and within Sunny's head. She pressed her hands over her ears as she frantically looked for a place to hide. There! A small space between two fallen bookcases. Maybe she could hole up in that space for two days, a day and a half, whatever amount of time she had left here. About to run for it, she shivered and looked to her left. This time she did scream. Because she'd been about to run, her leg muscles were like a tightly wound spring. She tried to change directions by a few degrees and her legs tangled. As she went down, she didn't take her eyes off the pile of bones. The skull had its jaw broken. There was a foot at the top. A hand tumbled down and landed facing upward like a dead white spider.

Phoom! The dried old bones suddenly burst into quiet smokeless flames.

Sunny hit the ground, and her hip was an explosion of pain. Still, she managed to roll to her side and pull her juju knife from her pocket. She did a quick flourish and caught the cool invisible pouch in her hand as she lay on her side. Then she drew a square in the air while muttering into the pouch the words Chichi had taught her. The only difference was that she spoke them in her native tongue of English instead of Chichi's native tongue of Efik. "Bring a thick barrier. Hold strong, too. From the very air I breathe. It must hold true!"

When the tumbled hand rolled toward her and then perched on its fingertips so that it could tap on the barrier, Sunny shivered.

"Free agent weak frightened magic," the voice said. "Shatters like glass." With these words, there was the sound of glass breaking and falling to the marble floor. "What more do you have?"

Sunny had been practicing on her own and incorporating lessons Sugar Cream had taught her over the months. She calmed, forcing herself to look at the ancient pile of human bones that were engulfed in flames but not burning at all.

"Your entire body must relax, feel it drop. Then imagine your spirit dropping," Sugar Cream had said. "Think of Anyanwu. You are her and she is you. Remember your initiation? When you were pulled into the ground? Feel that. But feel it as if Anyanwu is pulling from your body." Before Sunny gave it a try, Sugar Cream had reminded her to make sure she was lying down.

Now Sunny was already on the floor. She rested her head back, keeping an eye on the bones. *Relax, relax, relax,* she thought. *Breathe.* She flared her nostrils, inhaling deeply through her nose. It took all she had, but she calmed herself. She would be okay. She might not have had too many real moments of terror in her thirteen years, but in her past life, she had. She couldn't remember them clearly, but she could feel those memories. Right on the tip of her mind. And she'd still gone on. Even if she died in this basement, she would go on in spirit. She relaxed more with the comfort of this remote knowledge. She relaxed. She dropped. She felt it physically, but it was much more than that.

"Oh, now it gets interesting," the voice said. "Welcome."

The marble floor was cool. It was a pure stone. An old, old stone. Maybe it had been in the earth longer than the Obi Library had existed. Maybe the basement was carved from what was already in the ground. It was so solid. Sunny got up. She flew, passing through the bookcases as if they were clouds. She was nothing but yellow mist. She knew there would be other things here, and she hoped she didn't run into them. But she couldn't afford to look around. She had to get away. And she couldn't stay partially in the wilderness for long. Not yet. Before she knew what she was doing or how quickly she'd traveled across the large room, she smashed into a wall.

They were made of the same marble. She could not pass through them, even if she dropped into the wilderness. How was this possible? *What kind of stone is this?* she wondered as she crumpled to the ground. *Scraaaape.* One by one, the bones dragged and tumbled toward her.

"Do you think this place is only *your* world?" the voice said. "It is physical and wilderness. It is a *full* place. You can't escape."

"What do you want?" she muttered. Not far from her on the floor were five red spiders. Two of them just stood there, seeming to watch her. The other three were running for cover.

"I want what you have," the voice said.

"Why?"

"They throw stupid Leopard People down here often. Timid, angry, weak-minded careless men and women who have nothing for me to take but a piece of their sanity, or some of a family member's future, meager gifts. But you . . . you have a soul that could release me from this place."

"Sunny?" someone called. "Sunny Nwazue?"

Sunny got to her feet, wobbly for a moment. Then steady. She'd hit the wall as something other than a physical body. She was shaken but okay.

"Sunny?" she heard the man call again. A human man. From near the staircase. Her second meal was here. She'd made it through the second day. But was it breakfast, lunch, or dinner?

"I'm here," she called, peeking around one of the bookshelves. He was a tall man of about her mother's age. He wore jeans and a black T-shirt and gym shoes. Not clothes she'd seen any of the Obi Library students wear during the day.

"Here is your dinner," he said, holding it out to her. If she had to guess, judging from his accent, this guy was from Lagos. He held the tray out to her. It was the same meal of jollof rice, goat meat, and water.

"Thank you," she said. "So, it's night, then? Do you know what time it is?"

The man didn't answer. He wouldn't even look her in the eye. He turned and started walking away.

"Sir? . . . *Oga?* Did you hear me?" Sunny asked, following

him as he walked toward the staircase. He moved quicker. Sunny put her tray on the ground, suddenly feeling panicky and invisible.

"Hey!" she shouted.

"I can't speak or look at you," he said stiffly, his back still to her. "The punishment is caning."

Sunny froze. Samya. She pressed her hand to her chest, shocked. "Oh," she breathed. "Oh no." She stepped away from the staircase, listening to the sound of the man's footsteps grow fainter and fainter. *Stay strong*, Sunny thought, tears in her eyes. *I have to survive this. Otherwise, Samya will have been caned in vain.*

She whirled around when she heard a crunch. Her plate of rice looked as if a stone as heavy as a car had fallen on it. A red spider had been crushed beside it, too. The bottled water rolled and came to rest beside a bookcase. She heard the djinn chuckle from the other side of the room.

"That's really funny," she said, trying to keep her voice steady. Her mother had once told her that if she ever found herself facing a wild animal, never ever show fear. The djinn wasn't an animal. Well, not one of the physical world at least, but it was certainly wild. Up to now, Sunny had worn her fear on her sleeve. She couldn't help it; she was *scared*. However, her mother also liked to say that it was never too late.

Her legs tingled and shuddered as she slowly walked toward her water bottle. She bent and picked it up, unscrewed the top, and took a deep, deep pull. The water washed into her parched body like rain on dry cracked earth. During the gliding lessons with Sugar Cream, she and Sunny never moved fully into the wilderness. Sunny was far from ready for that and to go in unready meant a quiet peaceful swift death to your physical body. However, Sugar Cream took Sunny "in and out," where she was in both the wilderness and the physical world, and instead of seeing one place, she saw two layered over each other. Sugar Cream described it as similar to looking at the world through an aquarium.

Learning how to go "in and out" or between was not so hard. Sunny had gone between naturally on her own when she'd first snuck out of the house through the keyhole thinking she'd worked her first juju. It was going into the wilderness completely that was extremely difficult. Whenever Sugar Cream had her do preparatory exercises for going into the wilderness, Sunny always found herself desperate for water afterward. "That's because water is life," Sugar Cream had said. "The body doesn't like for its soul to even *consider* entering the wilderness."

Sunny took another gulp and felt a little better. "You've forgotten what it's like to be human," she called out. "You should have crushed the water bottle. Humans need water more than food." Despite her fear, she smiled at her own words.

"I was never human," the djinn said.

As she drank, she looked around. More red spiders on the books feet away. The djinn's voice was still coming from the other side of the room but that didn't mean anything. Her eye went to one of the books in the fallen case in front of her. She pulled it from between two dusty hardcovers. Alex Haley's *Autobiography of Malcolm X*. A Lamb book. "What's that doing here?" she muttered. Beside it were several volumes on Leopard medicine and even more on Leopard world alliance law.

"Sunny!" She jumped. The voice was right behind her.

"Eep!"

She was yanked back. There was a bright flash in her mind and a metallic sting so intense that she couldn't tell where she felt it. Then she was plunging into cool water. There was a splash. It was like her initiation when she burst into the river and was pulled along, except this felt like she was being pulled down, down, down instead of horizontally. She felt her body struggling for breath. She couldn't breathe! The cool water pressed in on her as she descended into the deep blue. She could see the dull basement light above her, slowly pulling itself away as she sank.

She thrashed and clutched her neck. Her lungs burned. Water rushed into her mouth, down her throat, into her chest. Even then she fought, but she was growing weak. She was dying. The djinn was drowning her.

The water was cool. She was cooling.

She let go of her neck. She let go.

Then the sensation of falling without falling. She hit something hard. Colors zoomed around her. Mostly green. But she was vaguely aware of the library; she was in the library. Her chest felt heavy, full. She coughed sharply and grabbed for the bookcase. There was a red spider right beside her hand, but she didn't care. "No," the djinn said in her ear. "There is no escape. Come. Come completely." She could feel the bookcase melting in her hands, dissolving, as something yanked at her shoulders, pulling her back. She felt it in her chest, a warm sharp tearing sensation. Then she felt her spirit face rush forward.

"Oh," she heard the djinn say. Then it chuckled and drawled, "Who are you, Sunny Nwazue?"

She still felt the pain, but all over now, and she felt . . . dim, somehow muted. She'd held on to the case, trying to will herself out of the wilderness. But then she was holding on to nothing. Then the bookcase became a mass of bushes. But the spider on it didn't disappear; it sat there on the bush. She gasped. It was one of those creatures that existed in both worlds. It was still red but now the size of a basketball with fluorescent blue rings on its legs. The creature waved a leg at her and scurried away.

Sunny held on to the bush, realizing she wasn't breathing. She wore her spirit face. She was Anyanwu.

Her body. She was no body. She was yellow. The color of the sun. Light. In a sea of mostly green.

Green blobs undulated past. Pink and green insects with

green lines for wings. The wilderness looked like a jungle. There was sound, and it was thick and moist and fertile. Alive. She was afraid to speak.

"I see you," the djinn said. Its dusty voice was strong here. *It* was strong here.

All she could think of was death. How many seconds had passed? Would they find her body? Then the djinn was on her like a vampire. They went tumbling into some bushes as she fought to keep it from tearing off her mask. Was it a mask in the wilderness? Could it come *off*? She vaguely remembered what her father had said about masquerades: "Never unmask a masquerade. That is an abomination!" What happened if one's spirit face was torn off? Could the djinn then eat her soul like the meat of a cracked clam?

The djinn pinned her down in those bushes. It was stronger. It wasn't human. It wasn't dying. It knew this place. She was done for.

There was a large spider on its shoulder. It was red. With blue rings on it. Blue rings. Blue rings. Blue rings. The glimmer of sudden recognition was like a burning focal point of light in her brain, it was brilliant and it seared. She knew blue rings. She . . . *remembered.*

"I know you," she blurted, straining to hold the djinn off her.

"Yes, we've spent some time together," the djinn said, flashing a deeper red. "But don't worry. Soon, you won't know much else."

She wasn't talking to the djinn. As she desperately stared at the spider, she gasped, "I know you *all*."

The djinn's strength decreased as it tried to figure out what its prey was talking about and whom she was talking to. Then it noticed the spider on its shoulder. It released Anyanwu and scrambled back.

The spider leaped off the djinn and ran up to her and before she could say more, it turned its glowing backside to her and thrust its stinger into her yellow mist.

She was flying again. Backward, this time, across the marble floor. The sand beneath her bottom. Her skin was cool because she was soaking wet. She came to a stop just in front of the bronze toad. She opened her mouth and inhaled for what felt like forever. *Chink, chink, chink, chink!* Several tiny copper *chittim* fell beside her.

For several moments, her vision was distorted. She rubbed her eyes and tried to see. She was seeing too *much*! The green of the wilderness, the basement, through two sets of eyes, two minds, Sunny and Anyanwu. It was as if she was broken and her selves were sitting beside each other as opposed to being unified within. The sensation was horrifying. She heard her selves screaming. And just when she was sure she'd go mad, she came back together and her world snapped into focus.

She shivered and shuddered and then jumped up to find it. She ran to the bookshelf, looking at the ground. Where was it, where was it? There. She grabbed it and downed the rest of her water. She was soaking wet, yet she felt horribly dehydrated. She grabbed her shirt and began to suck the water from it, too.

"Gah!" she groaned, stumbling back. She'd been able to suck up quite a lot of water. She was that soaked. Her body began to calm, but her mind was popping and crackling, memories exploding like popcorn. "I . . . What is this? I . . . I remember them," she muttered, confused as her mind crowded. She whirled around. "I remember you all!" There, by the toad. Hundreds of them. She was lucky she hadn't crushed them. But then again, they could probably move much faster than she thought. They were not just spiders. Where was the big one?

The back of her neck prickled. She looked up. The thick-legged spider the size of a dinner plate was perched on the wall right above her head. Sunny addressed it in Igbo because she knew this was its preferred language. She knew so *much*. "Ogwu," she said. "Descendant of Udide the Great Spider of all Great Spiders, I remember you. I remember you and all of your children."

The spider's entire body scrunched up with surprise. *Good*, Sunny thought. Then it began to descend on a thick thread of webbing. Sunny knew she didn't have much time, so she spoke fast. "Do you remember me? My name is Anyanwu but here, my name is Sunny Nwazue. I am the granddaughter of Ozoemena Nimm. So . . ." She fought to remember what her grandmother had written in the letter she'd left for Sunny. She'd read it so many times, but she'd just died and come back to life. "So that makes me of the warrior folk of the Nimm clan, descendant . . . of Mgbafo of the warrior Efuru Nimm and Odili of the ghost people. I am thirteen years old, of Igbo ancestry and American birth, New York City. I am a free agent who only learned this fact a year and a half ago. So you have to know that I can't fight this djinn."

Its voice made her feel like a tuning fork was being held close to her flesh. The vibration made her want to stick her pinky in her ear. It was vaguely female. "I know you, Anyanwu," she said. She hung before Sunny's eyes. Even with her life being in danger, her fear of spiders made her tense up.

"I know what you all tried and failed at so long ago," Sunny said.

The spider clenched her legs to her body. Sunny suppressed a disgusted shudder.

"You were on the plane," Sunny said. "The *Enola Gay*. I know. You were on the bomb, and you tried to weave the storytelling juju your people are most known for. You wove a thick thread that was supposed to cause the bomb not to work when they dropped it on Hiroshima. But when you attached it, you misspoke one of the binding words, and it snapped when the bomb was released. You failed and no one has seen you since. So, this basement is where you came with all your descendants to hide from the world."

"No, this basement is where Udide cursed us to stay until I have completed my task," she said. "Which is impossible because I have already failed."

The lights flickered. And Sunny heard a scraping sound from across the room. The djinn had located its nerve. *Such things never give up so quickly*, she knew.

"Wait, please," Sunny said. "Help me."

"We will not," Ogwu said. "We can't help anyone. I am useless and my children are useless. The djinn takes from those sent down here for punishment, but we have only seen it kill one person punished down here. And that was forty years ago. A young man whose bones were so strong they could not break. Let it take from you, some blood, some years from your life, some of your life's good luck. Then leave this place and never do anything stupid enough to cause your return. Or . . . maybe yes, it will kill you, Anyanwu. I will see you in the wilderness." Ogwu started to ascend on her web, and Sunny began to panic. The djinn feared the spider. As soon as she was far enough from Sunny, it would have nothing to fear.

"Sunny Nwazuuuuue," the djinn sang. "I'm coming for youuuuu!"

"I know how you can break your curse," Sunny quickly said. Ogwu stopped. She waited.

"I need to do what you all tried to do but on a larger scale." She was making it up on the spot. Sunny had no clue why she'd been shown the vision in the candle and was having the strange dreams. But this wasn't a time to worry about flat-out lying. "I've seen the end. And this time it's not just a city in flames, it's the entire world. I've seen it in a candle. That's what caused me to discover I was a free agent Leopard Person. And I've been seeing it over and over in my dreams for the last few months! So maybe it's supposed to happen soon! Oh, saving the world will require more than just me, but I am *needed*. Please. Help me. If you do, you'll be doing what you should have done back in 1945! And this time, it'll be on a grander scale! You won't just be saving a city, you'll be saving the earth! Fear of failure leads to more failure! And you won't fail this time! You will be able to leave this place, trust me. Remember sunlight? You'll see it again, if you help!! I am . . . I am ignorant. I can't defeat a djinn!"

"You're Anyanwu; we knew each other well. You can crush this djinn like a pepper seed."

"I don't remember how!"

"Then you have no idea who you are!"

Sunny pressed her lips together but didn't argue.

Ogwu paused and then quickly ascended up her web. Sunny's stomach dropped. When she looked at the bronze toad, all of Ogwu's children were gone, too. Hiding wherever they liked to hide. Probably poised to watch the djinn take her life. Sunny would be like the guy from forty years ago. How could Sugar Cream throw her down here knowing *that* had happened? How could they send *anyone* down here knowing about it?! The Leopard People could be a callous people, especially when it came to adhering to certain rules. The damn rules.

Sunny brought out her juju knife. There were the bones. Right beside her. And the smell of sulfur. She ran through the handful of jujus she'd learned so far. How to bring music, how to keep mosquitoes away, healing minor injuries, staying dry in the rain, making a cup of polluted fresh water drinkable, testing if something was cursed or poisoned, how to push back a heavy aggressor, creating a barrier. She paused. The barrier, she was good at that one.

She held up her hand and opened her palm. Then she brought up her juju knife and made a circular flourish. She caught the pouch with the same hand while keeping the other one up. The invisible packet was cool and wet in her palm. "Stay back," she firmly said. Before she could speak the activating words the wilderness descended on her, layering her world. A black shadow flew from the pile of bones. Eyes wide, Sunny stood her ground. She opened her mouth to speak, but it was on her too quickly. Something sank into her arm like fifty needles. She screamed and her entire world, both physical and wilderness, flashed bright. She felt the djinn sucking as she tried to shake it off. But there was nothing to shake off. It had no body. Not even bones. There was nothing but a thick oily brown shade.

Suddenly, it froze. Then it let go. Sunny rolled away, avoiding her arm. She got to her feet and ran for the nearest bookcase. Only when she got around it did she chance a look back. It was disgusting. Hundreds of red spiders had pinned the djinn to the floor like a sheet of brown-red solid smoke. Sunny had to blink to fully understand what she was seeing. On one plane, the djinn was a pile of dry bones and the spiders were the size of American quarters, Ogwu the size of a dinner plate. On the other, the djinn was a large blob of brownish smoke and the spiders were large as basketballs, Ogwu the size of a small child. On both planes they were tearing the djinn apart.

She could hear the dry bones snapping, crunching, and crumbling. And she could hear the wet smacking as the large spiderlike creatures tore off tiny pieces of the djinn with their sharp legs and ate them. All the writhing legs and bodies made her stomach turn. The djinn didn't make a sound. It accepted its sudden defeat like an old man giving up on life.

As they ate, the hanging light bulb at the ceiling brightened, flooding the basement. It was like sunshine in its purity and warmth. Sunny shaded her eyes.

"Udide has seen us!" she heard Ogwu shout. "Udide has seen us!!"

The spiders left the mess that was the djinn and went

running to the wall, Ogwu leading the way. Up the wall they crept. Then they scrambled to the ceiling. Toward the hanging light. Ogwu stopped above it and pointed a leg at the light. "Go, my children, go! We're free! I will show you the world!"

Group by group they lowered themselves on their webs into the light, which flashed blue whenever a spider entered it.

"Anyanwu," Ogwu said. "Sunny Nwazue, good luck! We've saved you here, but all of our lives depend on what you and the others do. Stop Ekwensu."

"How do you know it's her?" Sunny asked. She hadn't mentioned Ekwensu. "You've been down here all . . ."

"I've been down here, but you know my children and I are not just of this place. We dwell in the wilderness also. We know the news there."

The basement flashed and flashed as if it contained its own lightning. Sunny looked back at the remains of the djinn. She was firmly in the physical world now and there was nothing but dust left of it. "Is it dead?" she asked Ogwu.

"It was never alive."

"Will it rise again?"

"Not for a while. Eventually. But we will not be here when it does."

Sunny smiled. She had one more night to spend here and she'd spend it alone. Thank goodness.

"Sunny Anyanwu, Anyanwu Sunny," Ogwu said. Her children were all gone, and she was finally lowering herself toward the light. "Thank you for giving me this chance to finally act, to play a role. The Great Spider Udide blesses you. If you ever meet her, send her my greetings and love." Then she was gone in a flash of blue light.

Silence. A good kind of silence. Sunny was safe. She held up her arm to look at where the djinn had bitten her and saw that her bicep was swollen and red. What did a bite from a djinn do? She had at least half a day left down here.

"The medical books!" she said, remembering. There were volumes of them in the case near the bronze toad. Her muscles felt sore and her head ached. But she felt good. She felt strong. The memory of Ogwu's failure and curse was vivid in her head. As Anyanwu, she had been part of the group that sent Ogwu to stop the atomic bomb from dropping. She'd been a part of a group trying to prevent one of the worst human-caused disasters of all time, back in 1945. *Wow.*

It didn't take Sunny long to find information in the medical books about the bite of a djinn. Apparently, they were common in the Sahara and all over the Middle East. They could kill you and take your soul if they held you in the wilderness long enough, which was probably what it had done to the man with the hard bones forty years ago and planned to do to Sunny. However, their bites only caused a low-grade fever and dryness in the mouth. Sunny would have to suffer until her final meal and release came.

Thankfully, the suffering was short-lived. Minutes after reading the djinni information, she sat beside the bronze toad and fell into a deep undisturbed exhausted sleep.

14
RELEASE

Pepper soup. Strong. With fish. She opened her eyes. Her stomach clenched with hunger. The light bulb was still shining brightly and Sugar Cream was glowing like Jesus Christ. The fact that she was wearing a long cream-colored dress and matching cream-colored veil added to the effect. Sunny's mouth and throat were so parched she couldn't speak. She was lying curled up on the sandy marble floor, her hoodie over her head, her sleeves pulled over her hands.

"Can you sit up?" Sugar Cream softly asked. She'd placed the tray of pepper soup and a large bottle of water beside Sunny.

She nodded, allowing Sugar Cream to help her sit up. She

scooted to Sugar Cream's desk, leaned against it, and gave her mentor a hard look. Her arm ached and itched, but she was alive. But she'd *almost* been killed.

"Oh, don't look at me like that," Sugar Cream snapped. "You suffer the consequences of *your* actions. Let that be your greatest lesson here. You make your bed, so you shall lie on it."

"It tried to kill me," Sunny whispered.

Sugar Cream stiffened for a moment, meeting Sunny's eyes. Then she picked up the bottle of water and handed it to Sunny. "Drink."

Cool, soothing, goodness. *Water is life; water is life; water is life*, she thought. She drank and drank, pulling in as much as she could. She finished more than half of the large bottle before bringing it down and sighing. "It bit me," she said.

"And what did you do about it?" Sugar Cream asked, handing her the bowl of soup. It was warm in her hands. A tainted pepper floated in the middle of the clear brown soup with large chunks of seasoned fish, tripe, and shrimp. It caused the soup to softly bubble. Sugar Cream handed Sunny a spoon, and she took it.

"I got the help of friends," she coldly said.

Sugar Cream grunted and smiled. "Ogwu and her children," she said. "Is that why the bulb burns as a portal?"

Sunny shrugged as she spooned the soup into her mouth. Her belly warmed and the rest of her body followed. For once it was good to eat hot, hot, hot tainted pepper soup. When she finished, Sugar Cream helped her up, inspected the bite on Sunny's arm, and then, after deeming it not serious, helped Sunny up the many flights of stairs. Sunny's punishment was complete.

The walk up and through the library was like a dream. She'd come to know the first three floors of this place well over the last year. But now, though she recognized everything, it felt slightly unfamiliar. There was a strange distancing effect, as if she hadn't been here in five years as opposed to three days. She'd changed down there. And she was exhausted.

By the time they reached ground level and stepped into the lobby, Sunny felt stronger. She no longer had to lean on Sugar Cream and her headache was gone. The bite was itchy, but she could at least move her arm. Sugar Cream said it was past midnight, yet there were several older students browsing the bookcases here as if all was normal. They glanced at Sunny and some of them smiled at her, patted her on the shoulder, and said "You look good" and "Handled like a soldier."

Samya slowly came up to her, and Sunny hugged her tightly. She felt Samya cringe, and she quickly let go. "I'm sorry," Sunny said, looking into Samya's brown eyes.

Samya smiled tiredly. "Don't be." She hugged Sunny

again and kissed her on the cheek. "I'm glad you are okay."

"They really caned you?" Sunny asked, her eyes tearing up.

"Don't cry. You walk out of here with dry eyes, okay? I'm fine. As you know, some punishments are worth it." Sunny nodded, working hard to fight her tears. Samya squeezed her hand. "Go," she said, gently pushing Sunny along.

"You've become a bit of a hero," Sugar Cream said drily, after they'd moved on toward the door.

If Sunny weren't so tired, she'd have been deeply confused. How did one come out of three days' punishment a hero? When she stepped out of the Obi Library, the air felt so sweet.

"Sunny!" Chichi screamed, running up and throwing her arms around her, nearly knocking her to the ground. Orlu and Sasha stood behind her. "They told us to wait out here. That you had to complete your punishment by walking unaided out of the Obi Library. Unaided!" She held Sunny back and looked her over. "You look terrible!"

"I feel worse," Sunny said, pressing her arm.

"Chichi . . ." Sasha paused, an angry look crossing his face, but then he looked at Sunny and smiled. "She told us everything. I'd have done the same thing, no matter the consequences. That's family, yo. Always gotta protect the fam."

Sunny only nodded. Not even Sasha would understand

the consequences. When he'd used juju to switch the minds of two police officers back in the United States, he'd been caned. She, on the other hand, had nearly lost her soul. But both he and Samya were right; it was worth it.

Her eyes met Orlu's and again she nearly melted into tears. It was as if he could see right through her, witness all that she'd been through. His hands were at his sides, clenching and unclenching. She stepped up to him and Orlu gathered her into a quiet hug. "It's all right," he said. "You're with us now."

Sugar Cream went back into the library as soon as Sunny was in the hands of her friends. She said that Sunny was to return for her lessons in a week. The four of them stopped at Mama Put's Putting Place on the way back when Sunny said that she was hungry.

"Don't worry," Orlu said, pulling out a white plastic chair for Sunny. "I'm paying. Order whatever you want."

Sunny's pockets were full of the gold *chittim* that had fallen in the basement, but she didn't argue with him. She'd been gone three days and all her friends could do was worry. They needed to feel as if they could do something. Especially Orlu.

"It's late," Sunny said. "My parents, my brother . . . maybe it's best if . . ."

"Don't worry about them," Chichi said. "I've been going over there. They know you are at least okay."

"What?! What have you been telling them?" she asked.

"Nothing," she said. "I can't. They already know you are part of . . . something. They're beginning to understand. So all I've said is that you're fine and will be back tonight. The first day, your father looked like he wanted to kill me." She laughed. "Honestly, Sunny, your father doesn't know if he is coming or going when it comes to you."

"Your mother came to see my mother yesterday, too," Orlu said. "My mother said she looked okay . . . just worried about the reason you were gone."

Sunny ordered a plate of stewed chicken. Mama Put said it came with jollof rice, but Sunny asked to replace it with more fried plantain. She didn't think she wanted to eat jollof rice for a while, or goat meat. She also ordered three bottles of water. When the food came, Sunny's entire body responded. As she ate and drank and ate and drank, Chichi told her some surprising things.

"I called your brother that next day," Chichi said. "Remember, you gave me your phone." She reached into her pocket and handed it to Sunny.

"Thanks," Sunny said. "What'd he say?"

"Nothing much," she said.

Sasha sucked his teeth loudly.

"Oh, stop," Chichi snapped.

Sasha muttered something under his breath, and Orlu's eyebrows went up.

"What did you say?" Chichi asked, frowning.

"My brother," Sunny interrupted. "My brother . . . is he okay?"

"He's back in school." Chichi grinned.

"What? Really?!"

"He didn't believe me at first when I said he could go back. But then later that day, he got a phone call. His friend Adebayo couldn't stop apologizing and telling him that it was safe to return. That the confraternity is disbanded. Chukwu didn't believe it until one of his other friends who was not in the confraternity and knew nothing about Chukwu's problem called his cell phone laughing and telling him that two of his professors had left their positions to join some born-again Christian group. When Chukwu returned, he found that the capo of the group had also become born-again, though he didn't drop out."

Her brother only missed a few days of school. Her parents never even knew he was gone. The next time he'd be home would be for Christmas, which was weeks away. He'd heal up nicely by then. Sunny looked at her phone. What was she going to tell him when she finally talked to him? She'd cross that bridge once she got to it.

When she returned home, she made it into the kitchen before anyone knew she was there. Her father stood in the doorway in his nightwear. "Sunny," he said in a low voice. "Where were you?"

Sunny's heart slammed in her chest and she felt her throat tighten. She couldn't tell him even if she wanted to. "Dad, I . . ."

He held up a hand. "Something has always been wrong with you," he muttered. "What kind of daughter has God given me?"

"I swear, Dad, I'm not . . ." She froze as it started to happen, her body filling with terror. But she couldn't help it, no matter how hard she willed. Her spirit face was coming forward! And as it began to happen, Sunny could feel Anyanwu's shock, too. She turned from her father.

"Don't swear," her father snapped. "Don't swear a *thing* to me. What are you . . . What is wrong with you?"

Sunny was afraid to speak. But as her spirit face retreated, she relaxed. She turned back to her father's angry face. Two years ago, he'd surely have beaten her when he was this angry . . . and this scared him. She could see it in his eyes. She was old enough now and had faced enough scary things herself to recognize it. "Are you all right?" he asked in a low voice.

She nodded.

"Did anyone hurt you?"

"I'm okay, Dad," she said. The djinni bite on her arm itched and ached. Was losing control of her spirit face a side effect?

He touched his forehead and closed his eyes, letting out a breath. He opened them. "Will this happen again, Sunny?"

She pressed her lips together, steadying herself. If her spirit face had slipped forward, would they have returned her right back to the basement? Or something even worse? Why did that even happen? And her father made her angry. She had always known he resented her for not being what he wanted. He was like so many other Igbo fathers. Sons, sons, sons, even when you had two. And if not a son, then a beautiful, polite, docile daughter. "No," she said, just wanting to escape to her room.

"I'll tell your mother that you're home," he said, making to leave. He turned back to Sunny. "We love you more than life itself." He paused, his own words seeming to take his breath away. Then his face became hard and angry as she'd known it most of her life when he looked at her, and he continued. "But you worry her like that again and I will disown you from this family and throw you out of this house."

Later on, her mother didn't come running to the kitchen or her room. But Sunny could hear her sobbing with relief in their bedroom. She heard Ugonna go to their room. Then he came to Sunny's room, peeked in, and without a word returned to his room. Sunny lay awake listening to her mother's sobbing and her father's soft consoling murmurs. She wished she could go to her parents' room as she used to when she was younger, before she became part of something that was entirely separate from her family.

She closed her eyes, tears streaming from the sides onto her pillow. Those days were over.

15
WAHALA DEY

A few nights later, Sunny walked into Anatov's hut with Chichi, Orlu, and Sasha. It was just past midnight. When they walked in through the OUT door and greeted their teacher, Anatov told them he had a special lesson for them tonight. Then he'd pulled Sunny aside.

"Come with me for a minute so we can talk," he said. "Excuse us," he told the others. He'd tied his bushy dreadlocks on top of his head tonight. Sunny noted this. When Anatov tied up his dreadlocks, it always meant the lessons that night would be tough.

They walked through the waist-high wooden front door labeled IN. It was painted with black and white squares that

Sunny had since learned were part of a protective juju that wove through the hut and the mile radius of forest around it.

As soon as they were outside, Anatov reached into his pocket. When he brought his hand up, he blew green juju powder in Sunny's face. She immediately began to sneeze and sneeze. She stumbled back. "What . . ." Then she was overcome by another sneezing fit.

Without a word, he brought out his juju knife and made several quick flourishes. He put his knife on the ground at his feet and then snapped both of his fingers in Sunny's direction. As soon as he did this, Sunny felt a force shove her backward. She stared at what remained in the place she'd just stood.

She sneezed another five times as she watched the green mist shaped like herself float there, slowly dissipating into the air like thick smoke. It looked around, as if shocked by its existence.

"What is that?!" Sunny said. Her stuffed nose made her sound nasally.

"You traveled fully into the wilderness. When people with your ability do that and then return, they always bring something back with them," he said, staring at the green Sunny-shaped mist. It was almost gone now, but it was still looking around in shock. It made no sound, but Sunny could smell something. She couldn't find the words to describe it. "It's like swimming in the ocean. You come out wet and when you dry, you're salty. You need to bathe."

"So I'm clean now?"

He chuckled. "Is being covered in sea salt dirty?"

"Well . . ."

"If I didn't do that to you, you'd become . . . strange," he said. "I've seen it happen. I didn't think I'd have to teach you how to perform bush medicine on yourself. Not so soon. But I guess when it comes to you all, things happen sooner rather than later. How do you feel?"

"I need a tissue."

He chuckled. "Aside from your juju powder allergy."

"I feel . . . lighter. Like I just took off a heavy coat."

Anatov looked pleased.

"And I . . . I can smell something," she said. "Even with my stuffed nose. What is that? Why's it so strong?"

Anatov nodded. "Can't describe it, right?"

Sunny shook her head.

"That's the wilderness," he said.

They paused, Anatov looking pensively at Sunny. Sunny sniffed loudly. Then Anatov smiled and shook his head. "What in Allah's name were you thinking when you did that to the society's capo, Sunny? I hope you've learned your lesson. You could have *died* in that basement. We'd all have been torn up, but the world would have moved on, eventually, and you'd have been gone. Don't you understand yet?"

"My bro—"

"I know it was your brother," he said stepping closer. "I

know you love him and that guy hurt him . . . badly. Nearly killed him. But *you* are in a secret society. A real *true* one that is older than time. And we have *rules*, strict, real, deeply upheld rules. While you were in the basement, Sugar Cream came to me angry as hell. She couldn't believe you'd do something so stupid. Do you know that? I have *never* seen her even break a sweat. But this night, she was shaking with fear and anger."

"I'm sorry," Sunny whispered.

"Tell that to your mentor and never ever cross that line again. We can't protect you if you do."

Sunny's nose ran and now her eyes were tearing up, too.

"You essentially died; that's what traveling fully into the wilderness requires," Anatov said bluntly. "When it pulled you in, if you weren't Sunny Nwazue, if you were Sasha or Orlu or Chichi or any other kid without your specific ability, you'd have *stayed* dead. Do you understand this?"

Sunny took a deep breath as his words sunk in. "I get it," she breathed.

"Good." He looked down his nose at her. "You set Ogwu and her young free."

"They were never really in prison," Sunny muttered. "She was just ashamed."

"Hmm," he said, putting a long arm around her shoulder. When she looked up at him, his nose ring glinted in the moonlight. Anatov the Defender of Frogs and All Things

Natural couldn't defend her from everything. "Come," he said. "I assume you brought your usual box of tissues?"

Sunny laughed and smiled, wiping her tears with her hand. "Yeah."

He grasped her shoulder warmly, pulling her into a hug. He smelled of his favorite scented oil—Egyptian musk—and his caftan was scratchy. "Good," he said. "Good, Sunny."

The four of them sat on the floor of Anatov's hut. Sunny had blown the heck out of her nose, but it still ran happily and freely. She pulled out another tissue, lifted her glasses a bit, and blew. By now her nose probably looked red as a cherry.

"You okay?" Orlu asked.

"Get her some water, man," Sasha said, chuckling. "With all that snot, she's going to get dehydrated."

"Tonight," Anatov loudly said. He spoke in Igbo. He did this often to help Sasha practice. "In celebration of Sunny's return, I've decided to throw out the planned lesson and replace it with something I think you all need: masking jujus. Jujus you use when you want to perform juju on or around Lambs but do not wish them to see or know it."

Sunny sat up straighter, deeply interested. There was juju for that? Leopards were allowed to perform juju on Lambs? She looked at Chichi, who looked equally surprised.

"One can perform juju on Lambs and around them," he

said. "We know this happens, sure. We can't live around these people and not be able to do this. However, you must take precautions. And those precautions are not so easy. And people are lazy." He switched to English, speaking with his African American accent. "They don't like to cover they asses. And if you mess up . . . well, y'all know the consequences."

He sat in his mahogany throne-like chair with its plush red seat. "Lord knows that Lambs can be damn annoying, with their silly materialism, hatred of education, and love of remaining stupid. They're obsessed with getting things fast, fast, fast, with the least amount of work, books, no instruction. It's universal." He chuckled. "Who can blame Leopards for wanting to throw some juju at them once in a while."

He went on to show them several jujus they could do. Empty Hands required a bit of common all-purpose juju powder and allowed one to punch someone without looking like one had done anything. Grace was a juju that you could do with only your juju knife; it allowed one to slip out of a situation unnoticed. *Ujo* only required a juju knife, too. This bit of juju filled a Lamb person with irrational crippling fear. It could be thrown from a distance of several feet, allowing the thrower to remain undetected.

Both Sasha and Chichi were especially good at performing this one. "I'm glad no Lambs are around," Anatov said, after watching both of them. "You'll both have to learn how to perform *Ujo* in strength grades . . . unless you want the

Lambs you work it on to run off screaming and vomiting with hysterical fear every single time you use it on them."

"Use *Ujo* sparingly," Anatov stressed to all of them. "Even a weak version of it can eventually cause brain damage when used on the same person more than once."

Of all the things Anatov showed them this day, Sunny's favorite was *Wahala Dey*. This was another juju knife spell that caused small things to randomly go wrong. One's pants would fall down, one would slip or trip, make a wrong turn, drop one's plate of food, one's computer would suddenly crash. It only worked on Lambs, and it was an excellent way to slip out of a bad situation or just ruin someone's day.

All four of them picked up on the jujus with only mild difficulty, and Anatov was pleased. "I hope this will keep all of you from any further trips to the Obi Library basement or, in your case, Sunny, worse." She felt her cheeks grow red. "And, Sasha, if you had known some of these, I doubt you'd have been sent here to Nigeria by your parents for being such a fool."

"Nah, I'd still have switched those two cops' minds," he said. "Police require something serious, *Oga*."

Chichi smiled at Sasha, and he looked ready to burst with pride. Orlu only rolled his eyes.

Anatov sucked his teeth with loathing, but in a fond kind of way. Their group wasn't his only group, but even Sunny knew they were his favorite. Chichi was his one mentee, and no elder took on a mentee unless he or she truly deeply loved and felt great, great confidence in that student. "Sasha, like me, you definitely have African America running through your veins—irrational rebelliousness straight out of Chicago. May the gods help you."

Sasha jumped up and did the Crip Walk.

"I said *Chicago*, not Compton," Anatov said.

"South Siiiide!" Sasha proclaimed, laughing.

Anatov's nostrils flared as he clearly stifled a laugh. "Anyway, so before you all return to the safety of your families, I'd like you to go to Leopard Knocks and pick up some of the all-purpose powder that we used for the jujus today."

"But we have plenty of that already," Chichi said.

"You have the yellow kind," he said. "Get the white kind. It's the purest and best and safest to use with Lambs. Just a tiny pound you can hide on your person or in your purse and keep it *only* for when you wish to deal with Lambs."

It was nearly one A.M. when they stepped up to the bridge to Leopard Knocks. Finding the white juju powder wouldn't be easy. Anatov said it wasn't a big seller, since it was juju powder that was exclusively for "use on Lambs." Sunny just hoped they could find it quickly so she could get a few hours of sleep before school tomorrow.

She was exhausted and could barely hear herself think as she looked at the tree bridge. The noise of the crashing river always seemed louder at night. She stepped up to the large smooth black stone and laid her hand on it. It was warm as she rubbed. The others were waiting behind her.

She was so, so tired, more tired than anyone understood. She yawned as she stepped up and faced the narrow slippery bridge. She relaxed herself and brought forth her spirit face. She was going to shift into mist and blow across the bridge, but she was just too tired. So instead, she felt her limber body stretch and she regally began to walk across the bridge.

Feeling tall and stately, she pointed her sandaled toes as she walked across. She was like a ballerina gracing the stage. Back straight, neck stiff, one foot in front of the other. She smiled softly as she looked down into the rushing water. The water gushed and coiled and thrashed as it tumbled downstream. What was it about this section of river that caused it to grow so turbulent? On each side, there were tangles of hanging trees, vines, and bushes both up- and downriver. How the trees grew at the river's edges was beyond her. The current should have carried them away.

"Hello," she whispered when she saw its great, round face just below the wild waters. The river beast. It was the size of a house and who knew what its full shape was. She'd never asked her friends, her teacher, or her mentor. She'd never wanted to show them that she was too curious about it. Their little game was between it and her, Anyanwu.

Every single time she crossed the bridge to Leopard

Knocks, even when she crossed as mist, it came up to watch her. Closely. Not casually. Not nicely. Initially, she had been afraid. The first time she'd crossed the bridge, it had nearly tricked her into falling into the river, and Sasha had saved her by grabbing her necklace. Lately, she was defiant, often stopping to look right back at the glaring monster who never broke the surface to show its certainly hideous face. Since her encounter with its cousin the lake beast, she was downright audacious when she crossed the bridge.

"Why do you wait?" Sunny said as Anyanwu. Her voice was deep and buttery, the voice of a sultry female radio DJ who played smooth jazz and midnight love songs. "I am right here. What is it you seek from me?"

It was hulking below her. She could see the girth of it now. She chuckled.

"Sunny?" Chichi called behind her. Her voice traveled through the mist as if from somewhere else. And technically it was, for the bridge linked the mundane world to the magical oasis that Leopard Knocks sat upon, which existed on no Lamb map.

"What is it you want?" Sunny asked, kneeling down to look the river beast in its submerged face. This beast's cousin had dragged her into its water. The djinn had dragged her into a sort of water that led to the wilderness. And now here was this damn thing, constantly threatening her with the same fate.

"Do you know who I am?" she said. She knocked her knuckles to her wooden spirit face. "I am Anyanwu." Sunny could only watch this other side of her taunt and heckle the river beast. Inside she shook and cowered. Normally, she felt right in line with her spirit self. Anyanwu was strong and old, and Sunny *loved* how she taunted the river beast. Anyanwu was Sunny. But, right now, Sunny was exhausted. She had no fight left in her. Not right now. And Anyanwu was picking another fight.

She rose up on her toes and then pointed her juju knife at the creature. The bridge shook, and Sunny felt like her heart would explode because not only was it shaking, something was cracking. Anyanwu gracefully crouched, her juju knife held firmly in her hand. There was something thick, green, and wet wrapped around the narrow bridge to her right. It looked like a mossy rope, a vine thicker than three fire hoses . . . no, a tentacle!

Oh come on, not again, Sunny thought. But Anyanwu laughed as the river beast finally surfaced. It was indeed the size of a house, as its shadow indicated. Craggy and pocked with calcium deposits and barnacle-like crustaceans, its horrible cranium was also covered with something like green-purple seaweed. The thing looked like a hideous sea garden. Its giant toothy maw was downturned and closed as it glared up at her with its dinner-plate-sized silvery eyes. She could smell it, too, like sea flowers if sea flowers had a scent. Sweet, briny, and oily.

It grunted and huffed and puffed out water at her, nearly blowing her from the bridge. The briny flower smell invaded her nostrils.

"Sunny!" she heard Orlu call. "Are you all right?"

"Yeah," she called back, still looking it in the eye.

None of them could come and get her. Only one person could be on the bridge at a time. Sunny was alone here. But she'd asked for this. Anyanwu had. A green seaweed-covered tentacle reached for her, and she danced back.

"You missed," she said. Then, without a thought, she leaped. This was Anyanwu's impulsiveness, but it felt great to Sunny. She wasn't a super-fast thinker like Sasha and Chichi, but there was a joy she experienced when she acted impulsively, and she felt it now. In mid-leap over the tentacle, she glanced down at the raging river below. She remembered how cold its waters had been when she'd moved through it during her initiation. With its wild, churning gray-white currents, no one would hear if she fell in and they would certainly spirit her away within seconds.

She landed gracefully on the side of the narrow bridge where she'd entered, the river beast's tentacle on the wood behind her; she was steps away from where Orlu, Chichi, and Sasha stood waiting to cross. She looked back and laughed, her voice Anyanwu's deep baritone that made her sound like an arrogant middle-aged chain-smoking woman. The river beast grunted wetly. Then it shivered with surprise and the crescent-shaped pupils of its silver eyes widened. Sunny stopped and nearly fell to her knees. The images that burst into her mind stung sharply like angry attacking bees behind her eyes. Then she could have sworn she heard the river beast laughing, or maybe it was shrieking because it, too, was experiencing the vision that moved through it to reach Sunny.

It flooded in like river water. There was haunted music. The flute and the talking drum filled Sunny's mind. Even the water below vibrated to the beat of the masquerade's tune. Then she was looking at Ekwensu, the terrifying spirit she'd faced here last year. She grabbed the sides of her head and shook it; she shut her eyes. "No, no, no, no." She was already so weak. The vision kept coming, though. Ekwensu looked the same; a house-sized mound of packed palm fronds standing in a place of green grass. The only difference was that she seemed to be constantly spilling out red beads from between her dry fronds, some tiny as ants, some big as horseflies. And she was rising from the grass now. Two of the red beads seemed to fly at Sunny, and she flinched, snapping from her vision.

One of the bigger beads hit Sunny square between the eyes, and for a moment there was a strange sensation of her drifting to the side when she wasn't. The bead bounced on the bridge's wood and rolled into the river. The second bead flew into the water, plunging in feet away from the river beast. This seemed to wake it and when it did, it fled back into the deep. Sunny stared at where the river beast had been, where the bead had flown, because the bead was real, a physical thing. Then she turned and ran off the bridge. Chichi screamed with relief as Sunny emerged from the bridge. "What happened?!" Chichi shouted. "We thought the river beast took you!"

"It tried," Sunny tiredly said.

Sasha and then Orlu came running. Sasha only touched Sunny's wet hair and hugged her head to his hip. Sunny leaned against him as Orlu knelt before her and took her hands. "What happened?" Orlu asked. His eyes were red and twitchy.

"Ekwensu," Sunny whispered. "She's back. She threw a bead and it was real and . . ."

Chichi used a drying juju on Sunny. She had to perform the spell twice because the first one left Sunny still damp and mildew-smelling. The second one left her dry, perfumed, and warm. "Thanks, Chichi," Sunny said. Chichi only looked at Sunny with stunned, puffy eyes. They hugged and didn't let go of each other for several minutes.

"Wait," Sunny finally said, pulling away from her friend. "I have to do something."

She stood up and brought out her juju knife and did the flourishes. When Anatov had shown her, she'd noticed that the shape he'd drawn in the air reminded her of Nsibidi. It was a skeleton of lines that was then dressed up with loops and swirls. When she finished, a strong force blew through her flesh, leaving a green mist in the shape of herself facing her. She stepped away from it, feeling her nose tingle.

"What is that?" Chichi asked.

"Residue from the wilderness," Sunny said. She blew and the green lost its shape and began to separate and mix into the air.

"You were in the wilderness?" Orlu asked.

"Partially, I think. Maybe that's how I saw Ekwensu. It was like she pulled me in."

"Like turning someone's head to look," Chichi said.

Sasha nodded. "She waited to catch Sunny when she was weak. It wasn't you she wanted to see; it was Anyanwu."

"I think the river beast was also a diversion," Chichi added. "So Sunny could be too weak and distracted to stop Ekwensu from tearing into the physical world."

The four of them were quiet for a moment.

Chichi turned to Orlu. "So what happens if you don't get rid of the residue?"

"She'll get sick," Orlu said. "Physically."

Sunny sneezed and rubbed between her eyes.

"Bless you," Orlu said.

"Let's cross and get you something to eat," Chichi said, helping Sunny up. "Then I want to hear all the details." She glanced at the river and then leaned closer to Sunny and whispered, "It's time to deal with the river beast."

Sunny nodded. "It's such a sellout, siding with Ekwensu like that."

"Do you think you can cross?" Chichi said. "I mean, you don't have to . . ."

"I'll cross," Sunny said. "This time I'll glide so it's fast." The soccer field and Leopard Knocks were the two places she felt she belonged. She was not about to let the river beast rob her of one of those. She rubbed the black stone and stepped up to the bridge. But she knew as soon as she raised her head and looked at the narrow bridge that even if she wanted to, her foot would not move. She felt pain at the tips of her sandaled feet, as if she'd knocked them against a wall. She stumbled back, her eyes wide.

"Wha—" She looked at her friends, tears filling her eyes.

"Sunny, what is it?" Chichi screeched, grabbing her hands. "Are you all right?"

"She's . . . she's not there," Sunny said. "I can't bring her forth. My spirit face . . . I can't . . . What's happening? Anyanwu, where are you?" Her toes ached and she felt the world swim around her; the spot between her eyes where the bead had hit her felt warm and itchy.

"Here," Orlu said, putting an arm around her waist. "Lean on me."

"You can't call your spirit face?" Sasha asked. "How can that be?" He looked at Chichi and blinked. "Oh, I can't even imagine that."

Chichi nodded but frowned for him to shut up, and this made Sunny panic even more. She couldn't cross the bridge without Anyanwu. Who was she without Anyanwu? Where had Anyanwu gone?

"She has to be with you somehow," Chichi said. "Your spirit face isn't just a face. It's *you*, your spirit memory, you spirit future, your chi. You'd be dead if she weren't there. You're probably just in shock. You need some jollof rice and stew and Fanta. Come on, we don't have to go to Leopard Knocks today. I know a nice Lamb restaurant where we can get some good food."

Uzoma's Chinese Restaurant was small and almost full to capacity. They managed to get a table near the back of the restaurant.

"Sasha and I come here all the time," Chichi said, trying to sound cheerful. "Though the food is terrible."

"I ordered the egg rolls here once, and they were just a boiled egg stuffed in a hard roll," Sasha said, putting an arm around Chichi.

Sunny attempted and failed a smile.

"You all right?" Orlu asked.

"No," she muttered. She felt dehydrated and ready to fall asleep right there at the table.

The four of them looked at one another with wide eyes and solemn faces. None of the people in the busy open-air restaurant could have imagined what they'd recently been through.

"I feel like an alien," Sunny said. "I don't belong

anywhere." She was dry, warm, and smelled good, thanks to Chichi. She was wearing her favorite jeans and a white T-shirt, and they were dry. Unlike those of all the other Africans in the restaurant, her thick, bushy Afro was blonde with a comb given to her by Mami Wata herself. Her skin was pale yellow pink, and her eyes were hazel. She'd just seen Ekwensu succeed in coming into the physical world, and she couldn't find Anyanwu.

"You belong with us," Orlu said. "You're a Leopard Person."

"Ekwensu is back," she whispered. "She will kill everything. But first she'll kill me. You sure you want me with you?"

"You don't know for sure what you saw," Orlu said. "You can do things with time, sometimes. You don't know if that was the future or . . . what."

They were all silent for a moment, the happy chatter of everyone else swelling around them. They ordered puff puffs, one of the only Nigerian dishes on the menu. In America, Nigerians explained to non-Nigerians that they were "Nigerian doughnuts," a description that Sunny always found annoying. It was verbal shorthand that sold puff puffs short. They were sweet, soft, perfectly round pastries that were simply what they were. Sunny also ordered a large bottle of water. When the waiter brought the puff puffs and water, she drank it all and ate five large puff puffs, feeling more like herself with each yummy bite. The others quietly watched her as she drank and ate.

Finally, Sunny took a deep breath and leaned forward. The others did so, too. "Do your spirit faces ever talk to you?" she asked. When they looked at her with perplexed eyes, she sat back and gazed at them for a long time. She bit her lip, frowned, and then just spilled it all; she told them how Anyanwu was her and she was Anyanwu, but Anyanwu spoke to her and she spoke back. Why not? Who else would she tell? Who else had her back? And now Anyanwu was gone. Sunny was glad for the noisy atmosphere; it covered up the cracking and wavering in her voice as she spoke. Then she told them about her dreams of the end of the world. When she finished, she wiped the tired confused tears from her eyes and ate the last puff puff.

"Who are you, Sunny Nwazue?" Chichi asked, imitating the djinn from the basement as she took Sunny's hand.

Orlu was staring at Sunny.

"I'm two people, and one of me is missing," Sunny said.

"Maybe you just need rest."

"Yeah. And you're a free agent, so your spirit face is new to you," Sasha said. "Maybe that's why it feels like a completely separate person. And yours is old, that's a lot of memory."

"And not just old, *busy*," Chichi added. "We're all old. Orlu and I have been to see the seer Bola, and we know things about our past lives. We just don't talk much about it. Sasha, too."

"Yeah, I saw a Gullah seer in North Carolina," he said. "She told me I'd done all sorts of crazy shit over the centuries. Slave rebellions of all kinds and some other *wahala* in the wilderness. On some level I'm aware of it. It's all good."

Sunny smiled, feeling a little better.

"I used to talk to my spirit face when I was little," Orlu said.

"Me too!" Chichi said.

"But Ekwensu," Orlu said. "What is it between you and one of the most powerful, scariest beings around?"

"Anyanwu is powerful, so she will have powerful enemies . . . and friends," Chichi said proudly, squeezing Sunny's hands.

"Word," Sasha said. "What you did to those confraternity guys, Sunny, that was you, not Anyanwu."

"I was just protecting my brother," Sunny quietly said.

"No, that Capo guy got so spooked that not only did he become born-again, but his hair has gone gray! I was at Chukwu's hostel yesterday," Chichi said. "He said—" She froze, then her eyes cut to Sasha.

Orlu dropped his face in his hands and shook his head. "Oh God."

"What?!" Sasha screeched, his voice cracking.

"Oh, come on," Chichi said, her voice shaking. "It was just . . ."

"Just *what*? Girl, tell another lie! All you *do* is lie! You're a pack of lies, and you think no one notices." Sasha glared at her with pure disgust and rage. "*Anuofia!*"

"*Kai!*" Orlu screeched. "Sasha!"

"We're sitting here asking Sunny who she is; we should be asking *you*, Chichi!" Sasha snapped, ignoring him. He stood up. Chichi stood up, too.

"Who do you think you are?" Chichi said, pointing in his face. "You don't own me!" She turned and thrust her backside rudely at Sasha.

Sasha's eyes grew wide, his nostrils flaring. He looked ready to explode.

"Come on," Orlu said, pushing the fuming Sasha along. "Let's take a walk." Sunny was beyond relieved when Sasha allowed himself to be shoved along. "I'll get him on an *okada* back home. Chichi, can you get Sunny home?"

"Yes, yes," Chichi snapped.

"Sunny, we go to Bola's on Saturday, okay?" he added. "I think it's time."

"I meet with Sugar Cream on Saturdays, and you meet with Taiwo."

"Yeah. We'll go in the morning," Orlu said. "It'll just be one long day."

Sunny slowly nodded. Chichi kept her back turned as she muttered, "Nonsense."

"You haven't seen nonsense yet," Sasha shouted over his shoulder.

"*Biko*, please, just stop, o!" Orlu said, pushing him along.

"What the hell did I do?" Sasha asked Orlu.

"Just be quiet until . . ."

Their voices lowered and faded as they left the restaurant. Only then could Sunny relax. She hated seeing Sasha and Chichi fighting, although it was more than inevitable. She'd seen Chichi getting into Chukwu's Jeep at least twice in the last two days. If her father had any idea his son was visiting home without stopping by to say hello to them, he'd be appalled. Chukwu was supposed to be immersed in his studies. He was, but he was also falling in love with Chichi.

At the same time, Chichi treated Sasha with the same affinity. And though just about every teenage Leopard girl younger and older in the area was infatuated with Sasha and his American bad boy ways, it was only Chichi whom Sasha gave his real time to.

"So, Chichi, what are *you* going to do?"

"About what?" Chichi asked as she applied some fresh lip gloss. Even from where she stood, Sunny could smell its fruity aroma.

"You know what." Sunny rolled her eyes and Chichi smirked.

"Maybe I'll let them fight it out Zuma wrestling style," she said. "To the death. I'll be like you and have my own guardian angel."

"You seem to keep forgetting that you are talking about my brother and my good friend," Sunny snapped. "These aren't just two random boys."

"I know, I know." She paused and then said, "I don't know."

"You don't know what you're going to do?"

"No," Chichi said, growing serious. "I like them *both.* Wish I had it easy like you. You and Orlu are made for each other."

"I don't know about that," Sunny said quietly.

Chichi smiled and shook her head.

"So you've been to see Mr. Mohammed's wife," Sunny said.

"Call him Alhaji Mohammed; he made his pilgrimage a few weeks ago," Chichi said.

"Oh," Sunny said. "*That's* why that other guy was managing the bookstore for so long."

"I happened to be there the Sunday he returned," Chichi said. "It was crazy. He was actually giving discounts on books . . . Well, for a few hours."

They both laughed. Alhaji Mohammed was a businessman to the bone, hajj or not.

"But yes, I've been to see Bola," Chichi said. "With my mother once, some years ago."

"What for?"

"We can talk about that some other time." She looked

at Sunny unsmilingly. Then Chichi's smile came back. "Bola Yusuf. They call her 'the woman with the breasts down to here.'" She gestured with her hands to mid-waist level. "She is an Owumiri initiate."

Sunny gasped and stopped. "A Mami Wata worshipper! Is she a Leopard Person, too?"

"Yeah."

This was the water worshipping group that Chichi had let Chukwu think Sunny was a part of. Sunny touched the comb she wore in her hair. "Should I take this out when I go?"

"Oh no!" Chichi said. "That'll get you much, much respect. She'll love you for that. And she'll love that the lake and river beasts can't seem to get enough of you, even if it's because they are Ekwensu's minions."

Sunny waited until right before bed to try it. She locked her bedroom door and, on shaky legs, walked to her window. She usually raised the screen just a crack so that her wasp artist could come and go as it pleased. Now she pushed the screen to the top of the windowsill and waited. It didn't take long. She watched the mosquitos slowly fly in, pushed by their own ambition and the night's breeze. When she counted five, she shut the screen and brought out her juju knife and worked a Carry Go, a juju that drove away insects with the intent to bite.

She felt the cool invisible juju sack drop into her upheld hand after she did the flourish with her knife, and she sighed with relief. She spoke the words as she watched two of the mosquitos land near the top of her white bedroom wall. She frowned as she watched one of the mosquitos migrate to her and then land on her arm. She smashed it with a hard slap.

Then she stepped to her bedroom mirror and looked at her face. She ignored her flushed cheeks and the tears rolling down them. She looked into her wet eyes and with her mind, she called Anyanwu. She dug deep within herself, and then she tried to bring her forth. Nothing. Sunny sat on her bed as the sobs wracked her body. Images of the river and the menacing Ekwensu flashed through her mind.

She crept under her covers and curled herself as tightly as she could. She still wore her sandals, and she didn't care. And when she got up in the morning and found an itchy mosquito bite on her arm and two on her left leg, she knew for sure Anyanwu was gone. Who was she now?

16

HEAD OF THE HOUSEHOLD

When she saw her father that evening, she went to him.

It had been a while since they had watched the local news together, but today Sunny needed his company. Anyanwu was still gone, and Sunny felt lost. She'd seen him settling down in his favorite chair to watch the news, a cold bottle of Guinness on the side table, a bowl of groundnuts on his lap. She sat down on the floor beside his chair, and he'd patted her on the shoulder, pointed at the TV, and said, "You heard about this oil spill in the Niger Delta?"

"No," she said. "I've been studying."

"These idiots are . . . Just watch, here it is. Turn it up," her father said. She grabbed the remote control and clicked up the volume on the large flat-screen TV.

A thin old man looked deep into the camera, a microphone held to his face. His voice was reedy, his expression perplexed. "I came here when there was no crude, no spillage, everything was so fine. People were enjoying back then," he said. "It's a strange thing to us. How could this occur? Are these oil companies stupid? *Ah-ah*, don't they know what true wealth is? How could they? These people aren't from here."

As he spoke, oil-drenched riverways, creeks, mangroves, and grassy vegetation were shown. The story cut to a journalist walking through the mucky forest in yellow hip boots as he spoke with a short young intense man, also in hip boots, named Murphy Bassey, head of the local watchdog group Friends of the Delta Organization. As they walked, they both pinched their noses.

"What's that smell?" the journalist asked in a nasally voice.

Murphy stepped over a fallen tree and stopped at a large black puddle in the soaked vegetation. "You see this here? It's not water." He brought a piece of yellow paper from his pocket, rolled it up, and stuck the end into the black liquid. Then he brought out a box of matches. When he used one to light the wet part of the paper, it burst into violent flames. "Whoo!" he exclaimed, dropping it on a dry patch of vegetation and quickly stamping it out. "See that?" he said as he stamped. "What is that? This place is already mutilated by oil pipelines; now the forest and waters are poisoned."

"So all it would probably take to set this whole forest and the towns near it on fire is dropping a match in the wrong place," the journalist said, looking very worried.

"Correct," Murphy said with a bitter chuckle. "We won't do that, though."

"I should hope not. I don't even think you should have lit that paper just now."

Murphy nodded, a bit out of breath. "I needed you to see, though. Give it a few days and the very *air* will be flammable. We have more than one oil spill every day here. In an area that's already polluted," Murphy said. "These oil companies are so sloppy in their mining of crude oil. They don't care. It's not *their* home. This new spill happened last night! It is not as big as the Exxon Valdez spill, but it is very, very bad. You see for yourself, do you see anyone here? No one is doing anything about it."

Sunny sighed as she watched, trying not to think of her own problems. As Anatov said, the world was bigger than her. In some parts, the world was literally dying. Her father held his bowl of groundnuts down for her and she took a few. As she shelled one of them, he offered his bottle of beer. "Need a sip?" he asked.

When she looked up and met his eyes, they both burst out laughing. He took a gulp and put the bottle back on the side table, and Sunny popped a groundnut into her mouth.

The only woman interviewed spoke in Pidgin English

and had a shell-shocked look about her. But her words made Sunny's skin prickle and her head feel light. "I come to see the water las' night. Wetin my eye see na one big thing wey be like animal as it dey descend into the water from air. Like some masquerade tin'. *Ah-ah*, mek these people stop wetin dem dey do, o . . . Because it don begin to attract evil, o!"

The woman's words hit Sunny hard. She opened her mouth and took a deep breath. A "masquerade thing" descending into the crude oil-soaked water? Was this Ekwensu? Did that Lamb woman just tell all of Nigeria that she'd seen Ekwensu? Sunny remembered when she'd encountered Ekwensu last year at the shrine beside the gas station, the oily, greasy smell, like car exhaust. Sunny could imagine Ekwensu tearing open a tanker and then bathing in the freshly spilled crude oil, a substance toxic to the flesh of the earth. If Ekwensu had just forced her way into the mundane world, such a "bath" would probably strengthen her.

Sunny moved closer to her father. He took another deep gulp of his beer and belched loudly. "This is not normal," he said. "Everything in that creek will be dead by tomorrow, the people are getting poisoned, the whole place could go up in flames. It's not even on international news."

Sunny slowly got up, her legs feeling like jelly. "I should finish studying," she said. Her father grunted, his eyes still on the TV where they were now talking about a murder in Lagos.

⌄⌄⌄⌄

The next morning, when she received her daily Leopard newspaper, she didn't find one mention of the oil spill in the entire paper. Her father was right; this wasn't normal at all.

17
BOLA YUSUF

"Thank goodness it's this way," Sunny said, rubbing a hand over her drying Afro. She absentmindedly took out the Mami Wata comb and used it to pick her hair out a bit. They were walking down a dirt path that ran through the forest that they usually took to get to Anatov's place.

Orlu sucked his teeth. "If it were back in Leopard Knocks, we'd find a way to get there."

"Tired of having to 'find a way,'" she muttered. "Just want to be normal, like everyone else."

"It's not far now," Orlu said.

They were walking side by side, shaded by the thickening trees. Sunny suddenly felt glad that it was the middle of the day. Who knew what was lurking in the bush. She giggled nervously to herself.

"What?" Orlu asked.

"I . . . I was just thinking, what could be worse than the river beast?"

"Sunny, there are crazy dangerous beasts like that in these forests, too."

Sunny quickly reached into her pocket for her juju knife. She fretfully babbled, "What . . . what kind of beasts? Are they big? Hidden like the lake beast? Do you think the lake beast would . . ."

"Put that away," Orlu said, chuckling. "The worst things around here and in Night Runner Forest come out at night, just after dusk. Relax."

When she still wouldn't put her knife away, he took her hand, and every hair on Sunny's arms and neck stood up. They walked in shy silence for the next five minutes, watching the trees or their feet. Then they came to a clearing in the trees. A large black solid steel gate stood here, with an image painted on each of the two doors. On the left was a painting of Mami Wata herself. She was more the Uhamiri version that Sunny didn't see very often. Instead of the long straight hair and Indian features of the more popular image of Mami Wata, the traditional Uhamiri version had skin black like a beetle's wings and long bushy dreadlocks that floated behind her like powerful-looking brown vines. She was grinning with white teeth and holding her long fin against her human torso.

On the other door of the gate was the contrasting image of a brown-skinned man with thick matted hair wearing chains around his ankles and wrists. Sunny frowned. The man had to be *onye ara*, a person suffering from madness.

"Bola's a Mami Wata priestess," Orlu said, seeming to read the question in Sunny's mind. "So she's a healer."

"Of what? Like malaria or . . ."

"No, stuff Lamb doctors can't address. You know, people suffering from being *ogbanjes* and women who can't have children no matter what the doctors do . . . and"—he pointed at the gate—"madness. A lot of Leopard People are struck with it. Maybe from some juju misfiring or someone being bitten by something in our forests, whatever. But Bola's also a really strong oracle. Her predictions and visions are never wrong, when she has them."

She can do all that and she married a bookstore owner? Sunny wondered. But then again, these were Leopard People. A bookstore owner was probably like marrying a brain surgeon.

Orlu knocked on the gate, and a minute later a tall woman wearing a long blue skirt and a white blouse peeked out. "Good afternoon," she said. She looked right at Sunny with such intense eyes that Sunny took a step back. Orlu nudged Sunny with his elbow.

"Good afternoon," Sunny said. "We're . . . I'm here to . . ."

"I know. She's expecting you," the woman said. "Remove your shoes and come in."

Sunny slipped off her sandals and, upon stepping past the gate, she felt it. First in the ground beneath her feet that went from warm to cool and almost damp. Then there was the rush of humidity; it was almost as if her skin's pores opened up and began to drink. She'd stepped onto sacred ground . . . or something. She opened her mouth and inhaled. When she looked at Orlu, he was frowning and picking his shirt from his skin.

In the center of the compound was a moderately sized white house. The ground around the house was neatly packed red dirt, tall wild bushes growing against the compound's wall. They were led around to the back where they entered a room with wooden benches. It must have been some sort of waiting area, for several women and men, some young, some old, sat on the wooden rickety benches in various states of anxiety and misery. One woman wearing a dirty orange-yellow wrapper and matching top was crying into the shoulder of another woman dressed in a yellow blouse and jeans. A man in a sweat suit jumped up and then sat down when they walked in. Another man dressed like a rapper was talking to himself, pulling at his skinny jeans and biting his nails.

One man even bore a striking resemblance to the madman in the painting on the entrance gate's door. He sat on the floor in the middle of the room, his long, unruly, matted hair flopped over his shoulder. He wore nothing but raggedy brown pants and a torn, dirty black T-shirt. He even had shackles on his wrists and bare feet.

"She will call you," the woman who'd led them in said. "Sit." Then she left.

Orlu and Sunny took a spot on the bench, squeezing between the crying woman and the mumbling man dressed like a rapper. After a few moments, Sunny realized he was actually speaking Arabic to himself.

"Glad I called and told my mom I'd be home late," Sunny said.

"Yeah, but we could be here all night," he said. "I've heard of . . ."

The door opened. "Anyanwu!" the little girl standing in the doorway called. "Who is Anyanwu?"

Sunny froze. She stood up and the little girl turned to her. The girl was about six years old, but she stood as if she belonged there and it was normal for her to order adults around. She even carried a clipboard. "Are you she?"

"Well, I'm Sunny, but my . . ."

"Yes or no?" the girl asked, holding up a pen.

"Y-yes."

"Come this way, then."

Sunny looked back at Orlu, who hadn't gotten up. "Come on," she whispered. "I'm *not* going by myself."

He got up and the little girl didn't stop him from following. She showed them down a narrow hallway with ocean-blue walls, and Sunny felt her eyes begin to water. She brought out the handkerchief in her pocket just in time to catch her sneeze.

"Sorry," the little girl said. "There's Catch 'Em in the walls. Eze Bola has had a few problems with imposters. People who are allergic always get sneezy here."

She wanted to ask the girl what constituted an "imposter" because maybe she was one now, but instead she asked, "What does Catch 'Em do to imposters?" She blew her nose.

The little girl giggled mischievously. "You don't want to know."

The girl led them to a large room with graceful high ceilings, white walls, wooden floors, and nothing in it but five white wooden chairs. They were arranged in a circle with blue cushions on the backs and seats. Bola Yusuf sat in one of the chairs, one leg crossed over the other.

Upon seeing her, Orlu stopped.

The little girl professionally grasped her clipboard. "Come on," she said, walking in. She motioned toward the chairs. "Have a seat, please."

Sunny followed her halfway across the room and then turned back to Orlu. "Come *on*," she whispered.

Orlu shook his head. He looked scared, sweat beading on his forehead.

Sunny bit her lip and frowned. "Geez, how old are you?! They're only boobs!"

It seemed to take all his effort to put one foot in front of the next. When he reached Sunny, she grabbed his hand and dragged him with her to Bola.

Bola was a thin middle-aged woman with long brown braids, three dark lines engraved on each cheek, and a large white oval painted across her forehead. She sat calmly in her chair wearing nothing but a flowing white skirt that reached her ankles. Her long skinny breasts did indeed hang well below her waist, touching her lap. She wore several blue and white bead necklaces that rested on her chest.

"You all look like students, and students can be stupid," she said in a hard voice. "So no photographs while you are in my compound. The last time someone did this, they angered Mami Wata and died in an accident upon leaving."

"We . . . we're students, but we're not here to study you," Sunny said.

"Good. Temitope, leave us now."

"Yes, ma," the little girl said, then she walked out.

"What is wrong with you?" Bola suddenly asked Orlu. He was sitting stiff as a piece of wood and looking at anything but Bola. "Haven't you ever seen a woman's breasts before? Weren't you ever a baby?" She lifted and swung them from side to side. Orlu looked as if he was going to pass out, and Bola laughed a loud raucous laugh. Before Sunny could control herself, she burst out laughing, too. She clapped her hands over her mouth and looked apologetically at Orlu. Then another giggle wracked her body, and her eyes began to water from the strain of holding it in.

"Look, boy, I am the servant of Mami Wata, goddess of the water, and as black Americans like to say, this is how we roll," she said. She looked at Sunny. "Did I say that right? You'd know better than me." She winked.

"Yeah," Sunny said.

"Relax, Orlu. Okay?"

Orlu only nodded, looking at the ground.

"I'm glad you brought him with." She paused, narrowing her eyes at Sunny. "My husband has spoken of you. Can you read the Nsibidi book he sold you yet?"

Sunny nodded.

"I like your hair comb," she said, grinning.

"Thanks."

"Now, you know I can't do a divination reading for you without you having something to give, right?"

"Oh," Sunny said. She reached into her pocket. "Of course. I don't have much but . . ."

"No, no, no, not *chittim*, not even your Lamb money," she said. "I want a story . . . one from Anyanwu."

"Huh?"

"I have heard of Anyanwu, that she may not be a good teller of stories, but she has good stories to tell."

"I . . ." Sunny looked at Orlu and then at Bola.

Bola gasped and said, "Oh. I see it now."

Sunny nodded. "Something happened to me." She felt her face flush hot, her eyes filling with tears. "I feel lost."

"You are," Bola said, growing very solemn. "How long have you been like . . . this?"

"Two days," Sunny said, her vision blurring from the tears. When she blinked, she saw that Bola was staring hard at her.

"But . . . it should have killed you," Bola said, her eyes wide.

"What are you talking about?" Orlu asked.

"My spirit face," Sunny said. "She's gone. I can't call her up! That's why I couldn't cross into Leopard Knocks on Thursday. That night, I tried working even a small juju and couldn't! And Anyanwu is gone and . . ."

The shock on Orlu's face was so much that Sunny stopped talking.

"All this time?" Orlu asked. "Since Thursday? You haven't had a spirit face?"

"Tell me what caused it," Bola said.

When Sunny told her all about the river beast, what she'd seen, and the bead hitting her in the face, Bola said, "This explains the oil spills in the delta."

Sunny nodded. "Ekwensu."

"We all sensed Mami Wata's fury yesterday morning,"

Bola said. "Yeeee, there is work to do, o." She sighed deeply and shook her head, looking troubled, and then looked up at Sunny. "Keep talking. Spit it all out." Sunny told her the details about her battle with the djinn in the basement and her previous encounter with the lake beast.

"*Kai!*" Bola exclaimed, clapping her hands to enunciate her outrage, when Sunny finished. She got up and paced back and forth. "This is something new. This is something new, o." She started speaking in rapid Yoruba to herself.

Sunny felt Orlu's gaze burning a hole into the side of her face, but she refused to meet his gaze. She wished she'd had him stay in the waiting room.

"Okay, okay, o," Bola said, sitting back before Sunny. "Focus," she whispered to herself. "There is so much." She took a deep breath as she gazed at Sunny. Then she exhaled, pointed at Sunny, and said, "Okay. You. Sunny Nwazue. I know of this problem you have. Never witnessed a victim of it who still carried life, but I know the condition. It's called doubling. It sounds like a misnomer because you have lost a part of yourself, but your spirit face is just not here. So in a sense, you've been doubled. Ekwensu did it to you.

"She threw one of her beads at you. The moment it hit you—" Bola snapped her fingers loudly enough to make Sunny jump. "Anyanwu was cut from you." Bola narrowed her eyes and tapped at her head. "Ekwensu is smart. It was the only way to distract Anyanwu enough so Ekwensu could push out of the wilderness without having to deal with Anyanwu while she was weak. But Ekwensu took a great risk, too. If you had caught that bead, you and Anyanwu could have destroyed Ekwensu right then and there. That bead was one of her *iyi-uwa*, her power.

"Anyway, it's done. She's in the world and you have been doubled, the connection between you and Anyanwu has been ripped apart . . . but somehow you both live. Your Anyanwu is out there. I don't know where she is."

Sunny felt ill. "Will she come back to me?" Sunny asked. Then she asked the question that had been nagging her since she realized Anyanwu was gone. "Even if the bond is broken, why would she leave me?" Tears welled up in her eyes again, and Orlu took her hand. "She's gone. I don't even feel her near. If this could kill me, why would she leave? Why . . ."

"Anyanwu is old," Bola said. "I know of her. All the elders, priestesses, priests, know her, Sunny. The ancient will travel; it is not for us to question. Especially with Ekwensu now probably able to occupy the mundane world *and* the wilderness, too."

"But . . ."

"Usually, I require payment for my services," she said. "My payment today is that you've shown me something I have never seen before: a living Leopard Person with no spirit face. I'd have said this was an abomination an hour ago, but you have taught me otherwise. Debt paid. Plus, I want to see what the cowries tell me about you."

She stood up and stretched her back. Then she brought out some cowries from her skirt pocket and moved to an open space in the room.

"So what is it that you especially want to know, Sunny? Aside from how to find your spirit face?"

Sunny paused for a moment, thinking. Since Anyanwu had disappeared, she hadn't thought about much else. What did anything else really matter? Then she remembered. "I've been having dreams of the . . . end," she said. "Before I discovered I was a free agent, I was shown the world's end in the flame of a candle. Sugar Cream says that some of my spirit friends or enemies from the wilderness showed all of that to me. I don't know why. But in a lot of ways, it led me to Leopard society. But these new dreams . . . they're different." *They leave me asking myself who I am*, she wanted to say. But she'd never admit something so pathetic in front of Orlu. "I just want to know . . . what the dreams mean. Do they mean that soon . . ."

"Yes, yes, yes," Bola said, dismissively waving her hand at Sunny. "Shut up now. I've got it."

Sunny was glad to shut up. Once she started talking, it was as if she had diarrhea of the mouth. *Words gushing forth like . . . water*, she thought, getting up. Orlu was already standing to Bola's left, his hands deep in his pockets, something he only did when he felt perfectly safe, which wasn't often at all. Bola's home must have really been protected.

"This can't be anything *but* interesting," Bola said as she knelt on the floor. "Let's see what the cowry catcher will show us today. Mouth open or mouth closed, only the cowry catcher knows." She blew on her handful of cowries. "I know some, but soon I'll know more."

"I hope it's good news," Orlu muttered.

"Whatever it is, at least I'll know what's going on," Sunny replied.

Bola brought the handful of shells to her lips and whispered something. Then she pointed and looked upward and said, "Inshallah. Chukwu is not concerned and only Allah can make it so." Then she threw the cowries. As they fell and tumbled to the hardwood floor, Sunny's right ear began to ring. She pressed her hand to it, and Bola looked at her and nodded. "That's the sound you hear when someone is talking about you. They are discussing your past, present, or future. I would tell you to whistle into your fist and say 'Let it be good,' but you cannot control those who inhabit the wilderness. Not when you are more than halfway there yourself."

Sunny pressed her ear harder as she watched the cowries settle. They took longer than was normal. Some of them tumbled in a circle over and over. Others hopped and bounced like popcorn kernels on a skillet. Some came to rest and then flipped back over. And several of them clicked together three times before going into a feverish dance on their sides. But finally, after nearly a minute, they all came to rest.

The room was silent as the three of them looked hard at the shells—Bola with the gaze of an excited, intrigued expert, and Sunny and Orlu with confusion. Ten minutes passed and Bola still hadn't moved. It almost looked as if she were in suspended animation.

"Is she breathing?" Sunny whispered.

But Orlu was looking around, his hands out of his pockets. "Did you hear something?"

Sunny frowned, suddenly on edge. "No."

"Shhh," Orlu said. "Someone's here."

Sunny scanned the entire room. No one. The sun shone through the large wall of windows and the room was pleasantly warm. But . . . she smelled something. She flared her nostrils. "What is that?" she whispered. It wasn't sour, pungent, sweet, oily, or foul. It wasn't stinky, delicious, stinging, perfumy, or dirty. She couldn't describe it. But it was strong and it was permeating the room. She and Orlu moved closer to one another.

Suddenly, Bola turned to Sunny. Her eyes were twitchy, her face blank of emotion. She stiffly stood up and came closer. Sunny grabbed Orlu's arm, but she stood her ground, facing Bola . . . or whoever it was possessing Bola's body.

"Sunny Nwazuuuue, who are youuuuuu?" she sang. She chuckled drily.

Sunny shuddered, pressing closer to Orlu.

"I see you."

Bola stopped, squinting her eyes at Sunny. "Yes, the free agent lucky enough to twin with Anyanwu and unlucky enough to be untwinned from her twin." She looked Sunny up and down. "So young and you've lost one so old." She stepped closer. "But you still live. I can speak to you. It is you who is having the dreams and asked what they are about."

"Yes," Sunny squeaked. "I want to know . . ."

"If the end of the world will come tomorrow. You wake up quietly afraid every morning that the sun will rise only to burn everything to ash and you'll have nowhere to hide but back on the other side where you were such a powerful guide. Warrior Sunny Nwazue of Nimm by way of Ozoemena of Nimm. But who are you really, anymore?"

Sunny felt her face growing hot, tears behind her eyes. The words of the one possessing Bola were like the slash of knives.

"Yes, words can cut deep," the one who was not Bola said. "They are clearer than images, more exact. Especially the magical kind, like the Nsibidi. Keep learning Nsibidi, you will need it; the answers are within it, and so much more. Your dreams, you have misinterpreted. Think, think hard. What you saw. It was not like what the wilderling forced upon you. This was something else and you know it. This was you using what you have. Shape-shifter, who can step into our wilderness when she learns that she can. Time folder, who can stop it when she hates someone enough." She crept closer to Sunny and cocked her head. "Smoking city or city of smoke?"

Orlu gasped. "Oh my God!"

"What?" Sunny asked.

"Ah, finally it dawns on you. See what happens when you only assume the negative?" Bola said, focusing for the first time on Orlu. "It's not always the worst."

"What? WHAT?!" Sunny asked him.

"Your man understands, that's what," she said. "The vision was just nudging toward where you must go to do what the world needs."

"But Osisi isn't . . . We can't *get* there," Orlu said.

"Yes, you can," Bola said. "Find Udide beneath the city of Lagos and have her weave you a flying grasscutter. Those can fly to Osisi easy. It will take you, if you can convince it."

"Lagos?" Sunny said. "How are we supposed to get to Lagos?! That's hours away! And what's Osisi?"

"Udide, she will be there? In Lagos?" Orlu asked.

"Yes."

"Through the market, as it says in the beast books?" he asked.

"Yes, for now."

"Flying grasscutters are obnoxious," he said, pinching his chin as he thought. "It'll get us all caned, or worse."

"Ekwensu has made it here. Time has run out and now

it'll be more difficult. A flying grasscutter is the fastest way to get to Osisi," Bola stressed. "If Ekwensu comes, a caning is the least of your worries."

Bola's face squeezed with pain and she stumbled back. She rubbed her eyes, opened her mouth, and hacked loudly. "Sunny," she gasped. "Both Leopards and Lambs in this world have jobs to do. It is not just you, but you have a job. You four, really. Ekwensu is getting her rest. She will strike soon. Gather yourselves. Sunny, you need Anyanwu. That old one is like an *ogbanje.* Tempt her back to you with love." She hacked again and sat down hard. Sunny then saw it, a periwinkle haze rising delicately from Bola's mouth and then dissipating into the air.

Slowly Bola stood up, straightening her skirt. She cleared her throat. "Temitope!" she gasped. She coughed and this time shouted, "Temitope!" The little girl came walking in with her professional walk.

"Yes, ma," she said in her tiny voice.

"We're done here," Bola said. "Send in the next client."

Once Sunny and Orlu were outside the gate, it was like stepping into another world. One that was not so full of water.

They walked in silence for several minutes. Then Orlu finally asked, "She's just . . . gone?"

Sunny nodded.

Silence for several more minutes.

"I'm sorry," Orlu finally said. "I can't even . . ."

"I'll get her back," Sunny said. Though she had no idea how. As she walked, she clenched and unclenched her fists. Doing so made her feel a little stronger. She kicked a large stone down the dirt road with her sandal and watched it sail far ahead. "I know her best."

"Yeah," Orlu said. But he sounded doubtful and . . . disturbed. As if Sunny had an unsightly gash in her cheek.

"What's Osisi?" Sunny immediately asked.

"You know how the living world and the wilderness are two places but they coexist?"

Sunny nodded. "Wait," she said, remembering. "I've read about full places. In Sugar Cream's Nsibidi book, she talks about how she and the baboons who raised her lived in a patch of forest that was full. Lambs were terrified of it because they saw it as a bit of forest they'd just never come out of."

Orlu nodded. "That can happen, yes. Osisi isn't just a patch of land, though. It's big. It's a town that is miles wide and long. It's somewhere between Igboland and Yorubaland and Hausaland . . . No one really knows exactly where but . . . wherever it is, you need to go there."

"Why?"

"Your dreams apparently are telling you to . . . probably yourself, somehow. Sunny, Osisi looks like a city made of smoke." He shook his head. "I don't know how Sasha, Chichi, and I didn't put two and two together. I guess we all just assumed . . ."

"The worst," Sunny said. So she wasn't dreaming of the world's end this time. She was seeing a world that was full.

"Yeah," Orlu said. "The only way to get there, for *us* to get there—you're not going alone—is by having a beast called a flying grasscutter take us. I've studied these before because they're fascinating. There was one living in Night Runner Forest some decades ago, and there's information about it in the book I have." He shook his head. "You'll have to just see it to understand it. Fact is, we have to get to Lagos somehow."

Sunny just held up a hand. Enough. Enough. Enough. "I'm going to Sugar Cream's. I'll see you later."

18
CLOUDY SKIES

The next morning was a Sunday and Sunny was glad. She hadn't slept at all. Every time she started to drift off, she remembered that her spirit face was missing and she'd wake up. "Sleep is the cousin of death," she'd once heard, and the saying came back to her now. She didn't want to meet death without Anyanwu.

So, all night, she stared at her ceiling. Thinking and thinking. Where could Anyanwu be? What if she met Ekwensu? Where did one's spirit face go? Did it actually "go" places like a thing with a physical body? Did it return to the wilderness, where it could lose itself in the ebb and flow of spirit? Or did it just wink out of existence like a puff of smoke? All of these possibilities made her feel ill with worry and self-pity.

She'd only been a Leopard Person for a little less than two years. Prior to that, she'd had no such relationship with the spiritual existence that was her spirit face. It shouldn't have been so devastating to return to the oneness of Lambdom. Nevertheless, if there was any evidence that she'd become a full-fledged Leopard girl, it was the fact that this was not the case. She felt the absence of Anyanwu so profoundly that she experienced moments of complete and total despair.

She lay in bed staring at the window watching the sun come up. She saw her wasp artist zoom out of its nest and out through the part of the screen she'd left open. She heard the morning activity of nearby neighbors. And she heard all this alone, as less than herself. While staring out the window, she had an idea. It made complete sense.

She rolled out of bed, glancing at the *Leopard Knocks Daily* newspaper on it. She considered reading through it for any possible news about Ekwensu or even more oil spills in the Niger Delta. Instead, she let it fall to the floor and went to her desktop computer. She put on her headphones and clicked on one of her favorite links, titled Six Hours of Mozart, and turned up the volume. The music washed over her and she closed her eyes, conjuring up an image in her mind of a ballerina she especially liked named Michaela DePrince.

She imagined her in a grassy field wearing jean shorts, a white T-shirt, and black pointe shoes. As the music danced, so did Michaela, leaping, stretching, and swaying. Sunny smiled as she sat back in her chair, feeling more relaxed than she'd felt since before the lake beast incident. She called Anyanwu to come and enjoy. She called and called. And then she opened her eyes, her joy gone. She slumped in her chair. She pulled off her headphones. She crawled back into her bed and got under the sheets. She didn't sleep.

She spent the day hanging around her mother, who was cooking her favorite red stew. She helped slice onions, ginger, and garlic, and blended tomatoes and bell peppers while her mother chopped and baked chicken and smoked turkey. As the stew boiled, she sat at the table and stared into space while her mother watched a Nollywood movie.

Sunny was glad her mother didn't ask why she wasn't out with Chichi, Orlu, and Sasha. She was glad her mother didn't ask her much of anything. It was nice. Just being around her, working with their hands, cooking. Then later on, it was nice just sitting at the dinner table with her father eating rice and stew. He read the newspaper and she read her current book, a graphic novel called *Aya: Love in Yop City*.

All this soothed her, but by the time night came, it all sat right back on her shoulders, weighty as bags of sand. It was an overcast night and thunder rumbled in the clouds above. She'd slept poorly, as she had for the last two nights. She hadn't spoken to Chichi, Orlu, or Sasha, she hadn't worked one small juju, no Leopard Knocks, which meant no Sugar

Cream. She'd have said that this was her life before realizing her Leopardom, but it wasn't. Before, she'd had a group of other friends, and she'd never known of that other side of her that was now gone, and Sunny knew she could never ever go back. It was like being left on an island. Her Saturday meetings with Sugar Cream and Wednesdays with Anatov and the others. Even Lamb school would be a problem. How would she face Orlu?

No going forward, no going backward. "It's like being dead," she whispered. The thunder rumbled some more and she suddenly jumped up and strode to her closet. She threw on some shorts and a T-shirt, sandals, grabbed her soccer ball, and was out the back door. Her parents might wonder where she'd gone, Ugonna, too. *Let them*, she thought, tears streaming down her face.

The field where they played soccer wasn't far. Especially when she walked with purpose. Her long, strong legs got her there in no time, and when she stepped onto the empty, slightly overgrown fields, she dropped the ball and kicked it hard. She jogged after the ball into the center of the field and stopped it with her foot. She looked up into the churning gray sky. There was a flash of lightning and then several seconds later, the rumble of thunder.

She knew the juju to prevent being struck by lightning, a variation of the rain-deflecting juju one used when caught in a downpour. Sunny chuckled bitterly to herself and kicked her soccer ball. "Let it strike," she muttered as she worked the ball with her fast feet. Back, to the side, tapping it in the air and catching it with the bottom of her foot behind her back, kick it lightly forward, behind, around. She smiled as she moved and dribbled the ball. She did a turn and kicked it back toward the other goal.

She ran across the field and shot it into the goal, the soft whisper of net against ball making her heart leap with a familiar joy. She grabbed the ball with her feet and worked it across the field to the other side and did it again. And then she did it again. All alone under the churning sunless sky, she enjoyed her own footwork, imagining that she was playing a one-on-one game against herself. The air rushed in and out of her lungs. She threw off her sandals so she could feel the hard, uneven ground with her tough feet.

She imagined she was trying to move the ball around her self, and this made her feet move faster. She did a bump and run, shoving herself out of the way and then taking off with the ball across the field. She laughed, because it had almost felt like she'd shoved someone. She'd shot the ball directly at the goal when she realized it. And her realization was immediately verified when the ball didn't go in. Instead, it was deflected by a seemingly invisible force.

Then the force became visible, and Sunny thought for a moment lightning had struck the field. She stood before the goal as the ball rolled to her feet. She rested a bare foot on it and wiped sweat from her brow. All the movement had cleared her mind, eased her muscles, and filled her with joy. Nevertheless, it was almost as if the clarity made it so that the anger could flow through her blood more easily. It flooded her system so hot and full that the world around her seemed to swell.

"Why'd you leave?" she shouted.

Then she blasted the soccer ball right toward the blurred but bright yellow figure standing in the goal. The ball sailed through it, and then the blur dissolved to nothing. Sunny stood there staring with wide eyes. Raindrops began to fall.

"I had to attend a meeting."

Sunny felt fury and surprise flip her belly as the rain came down harder. "A meeting?" she shouted. "You . . . you left me to go to a *meeting*?" Hot tears squeezed from her eyes and mixed with the cool rain.

"Rain Shelf yourself," Anyanwu said.

"I can't!" Sunny snapped. But maybe she could, now that Anyanwu was near. She decided to try, bringing out her juju knife. She blinked away tears as she worked the simple Rain Shelf juju and immediately the rain stopped falling on her, as if she held an umbrella.

"You're foolish," Anyanwu said. "And needy. And insecure."

Now the tears came harder for Sunny, and she plopped down on the grass. The squelchy wetness of the grass felt as awful as she felt. When she looked up, she found herself facing a figure of soft, glowing yellow light. They stared at each other for what felt like minutes. Around them, heavy rain splashed down, lightning flashed and thunder responded. They sat in the middle of the soccer field, and for the moment, to Sunny there was no one else on earth.

"Shut up," Sunny muttered. A flash of lightning nearby made her jump. She looked at Anyanwu. "You did that!"

"I didn't do anything," Anyanwu said.

Sunny didn't believe her. "You . . . you have always known who you are. You're old, you know everything." She had to stop to catch her breath, tears in her eyes again. "How am I supposed to believe in what I am when no one even knew this could happen? Even Orlu looked at me like I was an alien!"

"Yes. You are insecure."

Sunny grabbed a handful of wet grass and threw it at Anyanwu. She blinked when the clump hit the soft glow and fell to the ground. She threw more. Then Anyanwu grabbed an even bigger clump and flung it at Sunny, hitting her right in the face. Some of it got in her mouth, and she spit it out.

"Do you think I make you a Leopard Person?" Anyanwu asked.

"Yes!"

Anyanwu laughed. "I'm your spirit memory, I'm you outside of time, I'm your spirit face, I am *you*. You are me.

Our Leopardom is within all that makes us."

"Then why couldn't I go to Leopard Knocks that day?"

"Because, as I said, you're insecure."

Sunny pressed her lips together and frowned.

"Our bond's been broken," Anyanwu continued. "That trauma . . . few will ever know it. We've gone through it twice; it took two traumas to tear it completely. When that djinn pulled us in and when Ekwensu took advantage and finished the job."

Sunny nodded as they both felt a ghost of the sharp pains that had reverberated through their entire being. Twice.

"The second time, did you feel when we drifted?" Anyanwu asked.

"Yes."

"That was when we should have died. We'd have lost this connected duality and returned to the wilderness as one again. But we lived, because we are Sunny and Anyanwu." Sunny felt Anyanwu's confident pleasure at this fact. "Sunny, you can work whatever juju you please, whether I am there or not. That's why I say you're insecure. You couldn't get into Leopard Knocks because you didn't believe you were a Leopard Person without me."

"But . . ."

"Work a little harder and be more confident. Our bond is broken; some compensation is required. It's like loving and cherishing someone without needing the bonds of marriage to enforce it," Anyanwu said. "By sinister means, you and I are free."

Sunny sat with Anyanwu's words, staring into the pouring rain. The lightning and thunder were fading. But even if they didn't, she wasn't afraid of being struck anymore. Sunny took a deep breath and then asked, "What was the meeting?"

She could feel Anyanwu smile. "None of your business."

Sunny stared at Anyanwu for a moment and then burst out laughing. She got up and grabbed her soccer ball. It flew out of her hands as Anyanwu took off with it across the field. Sunny had to run fast to catch up with her. And the two played like that until the rain stopped.

On the way back, she came upon Sasha walking up the road, his hands shoved in the pockets of his jeans. By this time, the air had taken on so much humidity that breathing it was almost like drinking water.

"What are you doing in the rain?" Sunny asked, slapping and grasping hands with him.

"Looking for you."

"I was playing soccer," she said, tossing her wet ball up and catching it.

"With the lightning and thunder?"

"You could say that."

"You've been avoiding us all weekend."

Sunny shrugged. They began to walk.

"How come Orlu didn't come?"

Sasha shrugged again. "Said you probably needed some time to yourself. Me, I don't mess around. I came to see what's up. So, you good?"

"Yeah, I'm fine," she said.

"Even after . . . after what happened with . . ."

"Yeah. We can go to Leopard Knocks today, if you all want." She hesitated and then said, "The river beast won't stop me." She could feel Anyanwu within her as she said it. And she could feel that her presence was different. Not so locked. And this was verified when she realized she suddenly didn't feel Anyanwu within her. Anyanwu had gone off again, to wherever she went off to.

Sasha looked at her, narrowing his eyes. "You're different somehow."

"Yeah," she said. Then she laughed, tossing her soccer ball in the air and catching it with her feet. She passed it to Sasha, who caught it and then tapped it back to Sunny. She caught it, brought out her juju knife, and worked a quick juju that rubbed off the mud. It hadn't been difficult, but she noticed that she did have to concentrate a little harder on mentally aligning her words with her juju knife flourish.

"Jollof rice and goat meat at Mama Put's Putting Place?" Sasha asked.

Sunny smiled. "Definitely. My treat."

19
TRUST, *SHA*

"My clothes were ruined, but I knew that would happen," Orlu said, grinning wider than Sunny had ever seen him grin. "Nancy took me over the ocean!" His jeans were filthy with bright red palm oil and splashes of mud, as were his T-shirt and red Chuck Taylor gym shoes.

He'd been working closely with his mentor Taiwo's Miri Bird for the past two weeks, and he'd had a particularly interesting weekend. The bird, whose name was Nancy, regularly flew him up to Taiwo's palm tree hut, and the two had cultivated a friendship. Orlu had since taken it upon himself to study Nancy's species and ancestral bloodline. Flattered by his interest, the bird had agreed to take him for an extended ride to visit its mother forty miles east in the Cross River Forest.

"You're crazy to let that big chicken fly you that far, man," Sasha said.

Orlu only rolled his eyes. His general philosophy when it came to Sasha's smart mouth was, Do not engage. Sunny thought it worked every time.

Chichi, who sat in the doorway, loudly sucked her teeth and looked away. Sasha glared at her, and Sunny could practically feel the temperature rise a few degrees.

It was a rare Sunday where they'd all finished their chores, homework, and assignments, and none of them had any relatives or family friends to visit with their parents. It was Chichi's idea to meet in her hut. Her mother was at Leopard Knocks giving a lecture to some other third-level students. Thus, Chichi sat in the doorway, the cloth curtain piled on her back, a Banga brand herbal cigarette in her left hand. She took a puff and Sunny squeezed her face and looked away. Bangas were healthier than tobacco cigarettes and smelled nicer, but Sunny agreed with Orlu: a cigarette was a cigarette. And cigarettes were filthy.

"If you've got something to say, don't bother saying it," Sasha snapped. "Nothing comes from your mouth but lies."

"Come on, you guys," Sunny whined. "Can't you just . . ."

"Just what?!" Sasha screeched. "She's been cheating on me with your brother! She doesn't deny it!" He looked at Chichi. "Deny it."

Chichi slowly blew out smoke. "How old are we? We're not attached at the hip."

"Why am I even here?!" Sasha shouted. He started to walk away, but Orlu caught his shoulder.

"Because I asked you to come," he said. "Please. We're an *Oha* coven, remember? We can't . . ."

"Black Hat is dead," Sasha snapped. "Nigga killed himself. We all saw it. Our coven is *dissolved*."

"It's not over," Sunny said. "Ekwensu is here now! We . . ."

"If we are a coven, then there should be trust," Sasha insisted as he looked at Chichi.

"You think I don't know about Ronke? *Months*, you and her," Chichi spat. Sunny and Orlu looked at Sasha with raised eyebrows. Sasha's mouth hung open with shock.

"Trust, *sha*. It goes both ways," Chichi quietly said.

"Who is Ronke?" Sunny asked.

But Sasha's and Chichi's eyes were locked. They stayed like this for several moments. Chichi was the first to look away. She looked at Orlu. "There is a reason I asked you to have us meet here," she said. She momentarily looked at Sasha. "*All* of us. I have been thinking about it all. Black Hat, Ekwensu, Sunny, your dreams, that first vision you had in the candle. I've been thinking most about your . . . condition."

"You mean being doubled?" Sunny said. "Sheesh, it's not like Voldemort's name, you can say it aloud."

"Sorry," Chichi said, wrinkling her nose as if she smelled something bad. "It's just so . . . ugh."

"I know, right?" Sasha said. "I don't even know how you deal with it. It's like a guy waking up one day, looking down, and finding his . . ."

"Shut up, Sasha," Orlu groaned. "Chichi, what were you saying?"

"It's not your fault, Sunny," Chichi said. "Plus, I think you will change. Soon."

"What are you talking about?" Sunny asked, frowning. She'd told the three of them about being torn from Anyanwu, but not the full extent of it. Her relationship with Anyanwu who came and went as she pleased was as much her own business as the sight of her spirit face. But was there something else she needed to know about all this?

Sasha stepped closer. "It's obvious. Chichi has an idea," he said flatly. "What is it?"

Again, Chichi and Sasha looked at each other for a long time. Sunny looked from one to the other. She hated when they did this. Even when they were fighting, they shared some weird telepathy-like communication. It had something to do with their natural ability, that lightning-fast photographic thinking they both possessed. Orlu put his hands in his pockets, waiting. He was also used to it.

"Okay, so, Sunny, you . . . *we* have to get to Lagos to find Udide, according to Bola, right?" Chichi said. "You can't do this alone and it only makes sense for all of us to go."

"Well, yeah," Sunny said, biting her lip. "But how are we supposed to . . ."

"Your brother can take us," Chichi blurted.

Sasha cursed loudly and walked away.

"What?" Sunny said. "But Orlu and I are in school. It's not . . ."

Sasha had turned back and was looking at Chichi again, his face still angry. But not *as* angry. Chichi nodded at him. "This is messed up," he blurted.

Chichi shrugged. "But you know it's a good idea."

"Can you two please tell us your plan," Orlu said, sounding irritated, "since Sunny and I are too slow to follow your mind-reading?"

"I've asked Chukwu already," Chichi said. "Sunny, he knows he owes you. After making the greatest, most dangerous mistake of his life, he's back in school and alive because of *you*. He knows it was you, even if he doesn't know exactly *what* you did. He's got friends in Lagos and he's got his Jeep. We can go after Christmas, during your break."

"A road trip?" Sunny said. "We *drive?!*"

"Yes," Sasha said.

"But Aba Road is not friendly," Sunny darkly said. "It's . . ."

"I can't afford a plane ticket," Chichi said. "And I will never get on one of those filthy things, anyway. When I reach third level, I'll teach myself how to glide so I can travel distances in a more sophisticated *sanitary* way."

"Well, maybe my parents could . . ."

"Sunny, you know they'd ask too many questions," Chichi said.

"How about a funky train, then?" she asked. "There must be some that travel to Lagos."

"How will you explain going away for so many days, this time?" Chichi said. "You can convince your parents more easily if you go with Chukwu."

"What of Anatov and all our mentors?" Sunny asked. She hadn't told Sugar Cream about Bola's words or her doubling, nor Anatov. She wanted to, but she just didn't know *how*. Or maybe she wasn't ready.

"It's a road trip," Sasha said. "They'd all love for us to do that kind of thing."

"Well, it'll take forever, if we live," Sunny said. "I made that drive once with my father and brothers years ago. It was crazy."

"We can work some protection jujus," Orlu said. "It's doable."

"We're Leopard People and we've faced worse things," Chichi said.

Sunny couldn't argue with that.

Orlu turned to Sasha. "If we go, will you come?"

He paused. Then he said, "Yes. For Sunny. If Sunny goes."

Orlu smiled and so did Sunny.

"But my parents will never allow it," Sunny said. "That's, like, a ten-hour drive! And it's dangerous and . . ."

"Leave that to your brother," Chichi said. "He'll get them to say yes."

Chichi was right. Chukwu, God's Gift to Women, the Apple of Her Father's Eye, He Who Was Named After the Supreme Deity of Igbo Cosmology, could do no wrong. Ever since they were young children, her father had given Chukwu the freedom to do basically whatever he wanted. When Chukwu insisted on it, there wasn't a problem.

"And remember, he has friends in Lagos, too," Chichi added. "He can say he's going to see them and we're just going along for fun."

"Chichi," Sasha said.

"Fine," she said, getting up.

Neither Sunny nor Orlu said a word as Chichi and Sasha walked up the road, several feet between them, backs stiff, talking softly.

Orlu took Sunny's hand and Sunny smiled. He squeezed it.

"Do you really want to do this?"

"Do I have a choice?" Sunny asked. It wasn't a good time to do this, either. The doubling made working juju more difficult, and the effects of it still left her feeling . . . beside herself. And even if they made it to this full place, what effect would being there have on someone who'd been doubled?

"Yes," Orlu said.

Sunny chuckled. "If my parents allow it, I do. Will you come?"

"You need to ask me?"

"For this, I think I do."

He nodded. "I'll come."

"I'm not sure if I like the idea of being in a Jeep with Sasha and Chichi with Chukwu driving."

"Sasha will sit in the passenger seat," Orlu said. "That'll calm his ego. Chichi will sit behind him. You will sit in the middle and I will sit behind Chukwu. There will be less trouble that way and you'll be in the most protected position."

"You think I need to be . . ."

"Yes," he said. "Sunny, I don't think you fully understand your position in this."

"I do," she said.

"No, you don't."

They were quiet. Sunny thought of the last thing the possessed Bola had said just before the friendly wilderness spirit possessing her left her body: "Ekwensu is getting her rest. She will strike soon. Gather yourselves." Ekwensu would strike at her, Sunny, first.

"Maybe," Sunny said. "But Ekwensu hates me *and* I've seen what was in the candle, Orlu. I know better than anyone what's coming." She paused. "If I can help stop it, I'm ready to do what I need to do." She sighed. "Sometimes ignorance is bliss."

"Can't argue with you there."

20
ROAD TRIP

It was days before Christmas, and Chukwu had come home from university. Sunny was in the kitchen cooking rice and stew when she heard him drive into the compound blasting Nas. Sasha would have been impressed. Nas was Sasha's favorite rapper of all time.

Chukwu was with his best friend who'd nearly gotten him killed, Adebayo. Sunny eyed him as she added the last of the chicken wings to the stew and set it on low heat. She knew Adebayo but not that well. When he came by, he'd disappear into her brothers' room with Chukwu to play video games. As they grew older, they'd immediately be off to play soccer or join those boxing matches Chukwu had never told her about or whatever they did.

The Adebayo whom Sunny knew was from that fateful night with the Red Sharks. He hadn't seen her, but she'd seen him. All she could think now as she approached him and her brother, both of whom were bobbing their heads to the loud music, was that this idiot had slapped Chukwu across the face. How were they still friends? And from the swollen looks of the muscles bursting from their designer T-shirts, they'd continued working out in that dank sweaty basement of a gym.

"Welcome," Sunny said, smiling at Chukwu as she walked up to the car. "How na dey?"

"I dey kanpe," he said, giving her a hug. "I'm fine."

She looked at Adebayo and felt a cool satisfaction when even with his muscles he seemed to shrink in her presence. "Good afternoon," she said to him.

He grunted, "Hello."

Sunny waited for Chukwu to greet their parents with Adebayo, drop Adebayo off at his home, and come back. She cornered him in the kitchen when she knew Ugonna was in his room submerged in a video conversation on his computer and their parents were watching a Nollywood film in the living room. Chukwu was microwaving some jollof rice and two large pieces of goat meat.

"Is that supposed to be a snack?" she asked.

"Yes," he said, moving past her to sit at the table. He flexed his arms as he put the plate down. "Gotta feed these."

Sunny rolled her eyes and grabbed two plantain. "Want some?"

"Of course."

She brought out a knife and sliced the first one down the skin. She removed the thick peel and put the plantain on a plate and did the same with the next. "So how have things been?" she ventured. "At school." Her back was to him but she didn't have to look to see that he'd stiffened.

"Very well," he said.

"Good."

"Next semester, my biology professor wants me to be his assistant lecturer."

This time Sunny stiffened. To be a student lecturer was a highly respected position that students fought tooth and nail to get. It gave you valued teaching experience and broadcast to everyone that you were a top student. In addition, it showed that you had clout. It was one of the biggest reasons people joined confraternities.

"Really?" she said.

She turned around to find her brother looking straight at her. His face serious. "Yeah," he said. "Everyone is afraid of me." His face cracked into a smile. "They think I have strong juju, so they don't want to mess with me."

Sunny sat down across from him.

"What did you and Chichi do?" he asked.

"Can't tell you."

"So you did something?"

"Can't say."

He laughed. "That's what Chichi says. She gets all tricky and mysterious and tight-lipped. You want to know what Adebayo thinks?"

"What does he think?"

"He had terrible nightmares about me when I was gone," he said. "About me being sliced up and my parts given to some ritual killer. He said he woke up with his heart slamming in his chest. He thought he was having a heart attack. He thinks God sent witches to take his life. Capo, I have seen him, but he won't even look at me. He gets all shaky, starts muttering about Jesus, and practically runs in the opposite direction. All the teachers, I don't know what people are telling them. They smile a lot at me and ask me if I need any help with studying. My math professor offered to give me answers to the exam. I said no."

"Take no help," Sunny snapped with disgust. "What would be the point if it was all just . . ."

"I know," he said. "We both love soccer. What would be the point if we didn't have to play well to win, right? Same thing with school. I believe in *learning* . . . just like you."

Sunny nodded.

He smirked. "That's what I like about Chichi. Well, and because na dey beautiful, o."

Sunny rolled her eyes. *Does he even know about Sasha?!*

she wondered. She considered asking, then decided it wasn't her business.

"Chukwu," she said. "I've got a favor to ask you." She got up to finish slicing the plantain.

"What is it?"

She sliced for a bit before speaking. If he said no, she had no idea how they'd get to Lagos. Maybe they'd find a funky train that drove out there. But how would she get the time away . . . without their father disowning her? No, she had to do this very, very carefully.

"We need to go to Lagos for something," she blurted, turning to him. "Can you take us? It's important."

She quickly turned to her plantain, horrified with herself. She'd never been good at subtlety. That was Orlu's strength. This was her brother who used to punch her hard in the arm and call her Clorox as a way of showing sibling love. How could she be subtle or careful with *him*?

"What's so important there?" he asked.

"Don't tell Mom or Dad," she said. "I . . ."

"You aren't involved in some dangerous cult thing, right?" he asked.

"No," she said. "Nothing like that. I just need to . . . meet with someone. Please, I can't say more. You just have to trust me. Even if you won't take . . ."

"I'll take you," he said.

"Huh?"

"I'll take you."

"Really?"

"Yes. I owe you."

Sunny shook her head. "No, you don't."

"You did something that got me out of a bad situation."

"You'd do the same for me. You're my brother."

They stood looking at each other for a long time. Sunny's heart beat fast with emotion as she remembered how he'd looked that night. She couldn't keep the tears from welling up in her eyes.

"Okay," he said softly. "I don't owe you."

"So why help me?"

He shrugged. "I want to make sure you're safe."

"Okay," Sunny said, her throat tight. She turned back to her plantain, grabbing a pan and pouring vegetable oil into it. She added a bit of palm oil for flavor, just as her mother had taught her, and then turned on the heat.

"Plus, Adebayo will be there. He's spending the break at the house of his rich uncle and auntie. They're traveling to London, and they needed someone to watch their house." He laughed. "He'll have a huge mansion on Victoria Island all to himself. Living there like a king. Let me call him. When do you want to go?"

"Just after Christmas. We can spend New Year's there, maybe."

"So you and Chichi? And those other two, too?"

"Yes, me, Chichi, Orlu, and S-Sasha." Her face grew hot.

"Who is this Sasha? The American, right?" Chukwu asked.

Sunny bit her lip. "Yeah, he's . . ."

"Oh, I know about him," Chukwu said. He said no more and Sunny was relieved.

"You think Ugonna will want to come?" Sunny quickly asked.

"And not be here with his sweetheart to ring in the New Year? Doubtful."

Sunny scrunched her nose. "You mean Dolapo?" She'd met the girl once and was deeply annoyed by the way she looked Sunny up and down and then giggled. Since, Sunny hadn't spoken a word to her when Ugonna brought her around.

"The one and only."

"I'll ask anyway," Sunny said.

But Chukwu was right. Ugonna wasn't interested in Lagos, unless he could bring Dolapo. Plus, there wasn't enough room in the Jeep.

With Chukwu doing the asking, convincing their parents was even easier. "I guess you could use the break," her father said. He didn't say a thing about Sunny and her friends tagging along. He didn't even look at her. With the proud way he clapped Chukwu on the back, Sunny knew they'd be assured plenty of gas money and her father would entrust Chukwu with a nice amount of spending money, too. Good. She was going to Lagos to meet a giant spider.

21

BOOK OF SHADOWS

Today, it's raining in the forest. But by now you know that the water will not drench you. Not that badly. The Idiok have taken shelter, however. They don't like the mud, and the sound of the rain hitting the tree leaves is good for sleep. Those with young babies will be blessed with much-needed rest.

We are walking in my favorite part of the forest. I was attracted to this place, and that was how the Idiok knew to teach me Nsibidi. Look around you. Do you see that tree to your left with the smooth, narrow trunk and the tiny oval-shaped leaves? Yes, look all the way up and see that it stretches so high that it disappears into the rainclouds. It goes much higher than any normal tree. Imagine the things that crawl up and down that tree, into and out of the forest.

Do you see the vines that wind around it? Yes, you are seeing correctly. They have light green delicate leaves that look delicious enough to eat. I have eaten them; they taste fresh like lettuce. And see their white-pink flowers? See how they open and close, not slowly, not quickly? Like they are one great winding beast that is breathing? And see the ghost hopper perched on the tree trunk beside it? This part of my forest was full—a place that was both wilderness and physical world.

Lambs of the area avoided this place, deeming it long ago a forbidden forest. The patch of forest was small, no more than twenty square meters and easy to avoid, so for centuries, maybe even millennia, it had simply been left alone. For me, being a Leopard Person, it was seeing two layers of reality at once—the magical and the physical. I loved this place as the Idiok did.

By now, you may have come to understand. This book isn't about learning Nsibidi or my life or how to shape-shift. These are all things that I used to pull you off the ground. If you've gotten this far, you are strong in mind and body now. You know how to eat to live, you know how to plan, you know when you need rest, and you love Nsibidi. You are not my equal but you have my respect, for you are one of my kind. Good.

Right now, this book is about the city of smoke, a huge swath of land in this country that is full. Osisi. I pray that you will not have to see it, for it's not a place for any person who values his life, but if you have, if you have dreamed it, then you currently are the purpose of this book. There will be more than one of you, but only a handful. You . . .

Sunny had to fight her way out of the Nsibidi's grasp. This was one thing wholly unaffected by the doubling: her ability to read Nsibidi. She shook her head, flaring her nostrils and frowning, pressing Sugar Cream's book to her chest. As soon as she could see the light of her reading lamp and she could move her hands, she threw the book across the room. Tomorrow would be hard enough. Now this. All the threads of her life seemed to be winding into a tight bizarre rope that the universe expected her to walk across. Her brother, her questions, Sugar Cream's book . . . yes, *Trickster* was a damn good name for it. A perfect name for it. *Nsibidi: The Magical Language of the Spirits* literally shape-shifted, and not only in appearance (the symbols on the cover moved around like bugs) but in reasons for existing, in voice, in narrative. Was it even the same book for every reader?

And why did she have to get to this part on the morning they were leaving? "This is *wahala*," she whispered, lying back in her bed. She felt the usual reading fatigue that came with reading the book, and her head still ached from her fresh braids. Last night her mother had cornrowed her bushy yellow hair. The braids were long enough to touch her shoulders. Her hair was really growing. It was nearly the length it had been back when she'd burned it off while gazing into the candle. Two years ago. She'd pressed her Mami Wata comb into one of the side rows. It looked a little asymmetrically strange, but she'd come to see the comb as good luck. She wasn't about to stop wearing it when they were going where they were going to do what they were going to do.

Bzzz!

She smiled and got up to turn on her bedroom light. It was about five A.M. and still dark outside, and she'd been using her reading light. When she turned her light on, Della buzzed its wings louder. Sunny's eyebrows went up, and she slowly walked to her cabinet for a better look. Then she just stood there, her mouth open. Staring.

It was a head. She could not tell what Della had used to create it. Maybe the petals of some sort of yellow flower or maybe yellow paper or some kind of yellow paste that it had found in the market. There was gold, too. The face was ringed with pointy gold rays, like a sun. The nose was wide-nostriled and flat like her father's. The yellow lips were smiling. The eyes were hazel, as if "God had run out of the right color." They were her eyes. This was her. Della had sculpted a perfect blend of her human and spirit face, Sunny and Anyanwu. *How does one hug an insect?* she wondered. "Della," she whispered. "I . . ."

The insect quickly flew circles around her head and then hovered in front of her eyes. Sunny smiled. This was its way of saying, *No need for words.*

"Do you understand that I will be gone for a few days?"

The insect buzzed.

"You've been in here when Chichi and I were talking," she said. "So you know what is going on."

It buzzed again.

"Should I be afraid?"

It flew to its art, stood on top of it, and buzzed its wings.

Sunny chuckled. Her wasp artist seemed to know who she was more than she did. And it thought rather highly of her. Della flew up to her and touched her forehead with its long, limp legs and then zipped into its nest on the ceiling.

There was a knock on her door. It was Chukwu.

"Good morning," she said. "I'm going to get dressed in a little bit. I . . ."

"I need to know something," he quietly said, coming in.

Sunny shut the door behind him. "Okay," she said.

"You still can't talk about it, can you?"

She shook her head. If she spoke, her words would feel heavy and slow the way they always did when she skirted too close to speaking directly about being Leopard.

"Is . . . whatever you all are doing in Lagos dangerous?" he asked.

Sunny thought about it. "We can handle it," she said.

"It doesn't involve any of these ritual people? Because they're murderers and . . ."

"I've never ever been involved with those people," she firmly said.

"Lagos is a big crazy place for you," he added.

"No more than it is for you. Plus, Orlu and Chichi know it well," she said. "And Sasha has . . . international street smarts."

Chukwu scoffed. "Sasha? No comment."

"We'll be fine," she said. "And I'll have my cell phone." But if all went as planned, there would be a few days where he wouldn't be able to reach her. She'd cross that bridge when she got to it.

What Sunny was more worried about was Sasha and Chukwu being in the same space for so many hours. As far as Sunny knew, Chichi refused to make a choice between the two, and both refused to cut things off with Chichi, so the love triangle was very much intact. How was this even going to go?

There was another knock on the door.

"What are you talking about in here?" Ugonna said, coming in.

"Just the trip," Chukwu said. "Why are you up?"

"Are you planning something?" he asked, ignoring Chukwu's question. He was looking at Sunny.

"No . . ."

"Because I don't see why you and your friends are going," he continued.

"If you want to go," Sunny said, "you could squeeze in. We talked about this."

"I'm not going," he said. "I just want to know why *you*

are." He put his arms across his chest. "I got a weird feeling about it."

Sunny was about to say he was just imagining things. She was about to laugh and say he sounded like their superstitious aunt Udobi. But she couldn't do it. For months her brother had been sensing things about her, drawing and drawing pictures that she now realized were of Osisi. He was worried about her in a way that only a brother could worry about his sister. "It's something I have to do," Sunny said, taking his hands and looking right into his eyes.

He looked back into hers. He let go and said, "Okay."

Sunny breathed a sigh of relief. She couldn't have said more if she wanted to.

"Text me," Ugonna said. "Not Mom, not Dad, *me*. Both of you."

"We will," Sunny said.

There was an awkward pause among the three siblings. The air was so heavy with secrets that Sunny could practically feel them pressing down on her shoulders. But at the same time, never in her entire life had she felt so close to her brothers. And that's why she did something she'd never done: she reached out to both of them and pulled them to her in a tight hug. For a moment, they resisted, but then they gave in.

"Sunny, I will whoop the hell out of you myself if anything happens to you," Chukwu said into her neck.

"Okay," Sunny whispered.

When they let go, her brothers quickly left the room. "We leave in an hour and a half," Chukwu said as he closed the door behind him.

Sunny climbed back into bed. She was tired from reading her Nsibidi book. A good half hour would do. Plenty of time.

Orlu arrived within the hour, early as usual. Chichi and Sasha arrived together minutes later. Sunny stood in the kitchen watching as Sasha and Chukwu were introduced to each other by Chichi. She quickly took off her glasses, wiped the lenses, and put them back on. She wanted to see this clearly. Sasha and her brother were nearly the same height, Sasha being tall for his age and standing not far from Chukwu's six feet. But where Chukwu was made of bulky muscle, Sasha was lean, springy muscle. Chukwu seemed to flex his biceps more as he held out his hand to shake Sasha's. Sunny wished she could have been outside to hear them greet each other.

Sasha quickly used the excuse of packing his bag in the Jeep to walk away from Chukwu. Chichi came into the kitchen all grins.

"That is so wrong," Sunny said.

"What?"

Sunny just shook her head. "You brought *Udide's Book of Shadows*, right?"

"Right here," she said, putting her backpack down. She

brought forth the satchel slung over her right shoulder and took out a large brownish-black book. The pages were thick and yellowed with age and dirt. It carried the smell of burned paper that Sunny could smell from where she stood. The cover was etched with hundreds of slightly raised lines, like it was wrapped in the thin long legs of spiders. Sunny felt skittish just looking at it. She kept imagining the lines lifting from the cover, unfolding, and the book standing up. She shuddered.

"You want to see?" Chichi asked. "The writing is so neat, but really small. It's like a computer wrote it!"

Sunny held up her hands and shook her head. "No, that's okay."

Chichi giggled and put it back in the satchel. "Sasha finding it . . . He really has a good eye, *sha*. I hear that it can only be seen when it wants to be seen. It's got a mind of its own like that ring in Lord of the Rings. The book isn't all evil, but it's not all good, either. Sasha and I were studying it last night. Udide likes to speak in stories. The spell for how to find her is in there, but she tells it in third person as an adventure story about some stupid guy who doesn't know how to mind his own business. He was some teenage Yoruba guy from a long line of wealthy kings near Lagos who thought he was entitled to know everything."

Sunny chuckled. "I know a guy like that."

"We all do," Chichi said. "And he's not always a Yoruba guy."

"Yeah, but it's always a guy," Sunny said, grinning.

They both had a good laugh. "So anyway," Chichi continued. "Udide hears most things and she especially hears all things that involve her."

Sunny frowned at this. "So most likely, she knows we're coming."

Chichi nodded.

"I don't like that," Sunny said.

"Doesn't matter what you like. It is what it is. So this guy's nerve in trying to find Udide annoyed the hell out of Udide. Udide has always made it known that she has to allow people to find her. You cannot just decide to find her and find her."

"So we have to ask her?" Sunny interrupted. "Do we make some offering or . . ."

"Just listen," Chichi snapped. "Because of the guy's arrogance, Udide decided to give him what he wanted. She showed him the way in a dream. Of course, him being an arrogant *mumu*, he thought the dream was all him. He immediately jumped out of bed and ran to his little brother's room. He needed three blue marbles, and his little brother just happened to have plenty. Imagine that. He did as the dream instructed and sure enough, he found Udide in a cave beneath Lagos. But when he found her, the sheer *sight* of her . . ."

"He turned to stone?" Sunny screeched. "Oh my God, is

she like Medusa in Greek mythology?! We're doomed! How are we going . . . we need a mirror then. Or . . ."

"Sunny, shut UP!!" Chichi shouted. "Geez, did you drink coffee this morning, *sha*? Or some of your dad's *ogogoro*?"

"My dad doesn't drink that. He drinks Guinness."

"Just listen! When he saw her, she was such a horrifying sight to him that part of his hair turned white. Remember he was only about sixteen. So he looked very strange. He ran off and never looked for Udide again. She ended this story with this line, 'Without knowing a way through at daytime, never attempt to pass through at night.' Udide has a dark sense of humor."

"I guess," Sunny said. "But if she does, well, is it smart to use this same way to find her? And what if it's just a story?"

Chichi shook her head. "Udide's stories are *never* just stories. And I think it was more about the intent that got that guy messed up. We are looking for her for a *good* reason, Sunny. These dreams you're having about Osisi are serious. Something bad is going to happen, Ekwensu is on the loose and you are involved. There is something you need in Osisi and the only way to get there is by something only *she* can create. We're not seeking her out to prove how powerful we are."

Sunny hoped Chichi was right. Her hair was already yellow. She didn't need white streaks from terror to make it even lighter.

❤❤❤❤

The five of them stood in front of the Jeep as Sunny smoothed out the map on the car. Chukwu put his finger on the city of Aba. "Okay, so we're near here. We should take the Port Harcourt–Aba Expressway to . . ."

"I know the way," Chichi said. "I studied a local map I bought at the market." She tapped her forehead. "Got it all up here."

"Me too," Sasha said. "Plus, I checked out Google Earth and Mapquest. Nothing much there, unless you're looking at Lagos itself. But this map is more accurate than a GPS or anything online. Anyway, it's not the way that'll be difficult. It's not getting robbed or driving the car down a pothole that'll be the real test. I ain't from here, but I been here a minute now."

"We can stop in Benin City and stay with my uncle," Chichi added.

"Oh no, hon," Chukwu said with a chuckle. "If we leave soon, we'll get there by sundown, trust me. We'll be at my friend's aunt and uncle's house in no time."

Chichi paused. Then she smiled sweetly and said, "Okay, o."

Orlu laughed to himself.

Within fifteen minutes, they were all piled into the Jeep. Chukwu grasped the wheel, trying not to look at Sasha. Sasha plugged his phone into the Jeep's stereo system and was looking for just the right music so that he wouldn't have to talk to Chukwu. Chichi was behind Sasha, a Banga cigarette in hand that she planned to light as soon as they were past the sight of Sunny's parents. Orlu was behind Chukwu looking worried. And Sunny was in the middle waving at Ugonna.

"Call in a few hours," their father told Chukwu.

"And don't drive too fast," their mother said.

Sasha clicked PLAY and as soon as the song he'd chosen started, Chukwu's eyes lit up and he grinned. "Nas!"

Sasha looked surprised and then nodded appreciatively. And together they said, "*Illmatic.*"

They hit the road, the Jeep bouncing on a cloud of hip-hop beats.

Within a half hour, Sunny had a raging headache. Chukwu was speeding down a good stretch on the freeway. Sasha had the stereo bumping nearly as loud as it would go. At some point, Chukwu had installed a new, more powerful sound system, and this one was like the ones Sunny remembered from the streets of New York. She even suspected that Chukwu's system could do that thing where it set off car alarms if it was turned up to the highest volume.

As they sped, they bumped Nas's *Illmatic* so loudly that Sunny felt as if her head would explode. She could feel the bass vibrate through her entire body. The only time she'd ever felt anything remotely similar was when Ekwensu's drums were booming when she'd tried to break into the physical world last year. But this time, with each body-shaking beat, Sunny laughed and Sasha and Chukwu rapped "It Ain't Hard to Tell" along with Nas.

Sunny looked at Chichi; she looked annoyed. Sunny giggled. She couldn't have expected the two to bond over Nas. Orlu had fallen asleep, his head resting against the window. When he'd arrived, Sunny had noticed he looked tired.

"I'll be fine," he said when she asked him if he'd slept that night. "Stayed up late beading protective spells onto Chukwu's Jeep."

"Shit," Chukwu suddenly hissed. He slammed on the brakes.

"Whoa, whoa, whoa!" Sasha said.

Sunny, the only one who insisted on wearing a seat belt, was thrown against it, her glasses flying off. Sasha held on to his seat. Orlu quickly woke and threw a hand forward just in time to keep himself from mashing his head into the front seat. Chukwu managed to slow down and swerve, narrowly avoiding an enormous pothole.

"Didn't you see that coming?!" Orlu said.

"No!" Sasha said, shaking his head. He turned around. "Everyone okay?"

"Barely," Chichi said, picking up her book, which she'd dropped on the floor.

"Two words," Sunny said, putting her glasses on. "Seat belt."

Chukwu sucked his teeth and waved a dismissive hand at her.

"Weak American," Sasha said, grinning. "Don't you know we in Nigeria?"

Sunny shook her head, disgusted. Sasha had bragged from the moment he'd come to Nigeria about his hatred of "confining" seat belts and how he never wore them even when in the States and neither had his dad.

"The roads are going to get bad," Orlu said. "We should slow down from here on."

"I know how to drive," Chukwu snapped.

"And that's why we all just nearly died?" Orlu asked. "I'm not saying you're a bad driver, though. I'm just giving you sound advice."

Sunny smiled. Orlu was four years younger than Chukwu and far less beefy, but he'd always had a way of talking to Chukwu that Chukwu couldn't dominate. Even now Chukwu only looked at Orlu in the rearview mirror and said nothing. He slowed down, too.

Orlu glanced at Sunny and slipped an arm around her waist. Sunny felt tingles from her shoulders to her cheeks. For a moment, she even managed to pry her mind from Lagos and what they had to do there. She did not call Orlu her boyfriend and he didn't call her his girlfriend. The only kisses they'd exchanged were the one he'd given her on the cheek last year and the one she'd planted on his ear when he'd nearly killed himself bringing the two toddlers back from wherever Black Hat's cruel juju had taken them. Nevertheless, Chichi liked to joke that she and Orlu were "betrothed," and Sasha was always telling them to stop "beating around the bush." Chichi and Sasha were always so sure of and forward with everything. What Sunny knew was that she liked being near Orlu and they held hands often. Also, once in a while, he put his arm around her. He was her friend who was always on her mind.

Chukwu slowed the car down to nearly a full stop as they came upon a crater swallowing more than half the road. The sunken crust of asphalt quickly gave way to thick red dirt. There was a car stuck in the crater. Two young men stood on the raised asphalt staring at their car. They had their hands in their pockets and looked hopeless. An SUV crept around the stranded car by driving mostly in the dirt and plants on the roadside. When it was Chukwu's turn, he slowly drove past the car. Sasha opened the window.

"Do you . . . need help?" He added an Igbo accent to his speech to mask his Americanness. It was flawless. He switched to Pidgin English. "Wetin na want maka do fo' na? Na need any help?"

One of the men looked annoyed. "Anytin' wa u fit do to help, *sha*. Come lift am with bare hand." He sucked his teeth irritably and looked away and muttered, "Nonsense."

Sasha looked back at Orlu. Sunny looked from Orlu to

Sasha and back. Orlu looked at Chichi. Chichi was looking at Chukwu and then Sasha. Chukwu was looking at Orlu, Sunny, and Chichi in his rearview mirror and ignoring Sasha beside him.

"Chukwu," Sasha said. "Wait."

When Chukwu slowed down, Sasha got out. Chichi opened her door, too. "No, Chichi," Sasha firmly said. "Just Orlu." He paused. "We don't know these guys, *sha*." He was still speaking in his accent.

Sunny wanted to ask what was going on, but Chukwu was there. So she said nothing. Orlu got out on the other side of the Jeep and stepped into the tall grass. He walked up to Chukwu's window. "Drive all the way up," he said. "We'll meet you there."

"No," Chukwu said, putting the Jeep in park. "I'll help. I'm stronger than you both. And you don't know who these guys are, either. They won't mess with me."

"It'll be fine," Orlu said. "You need to stay in the car with Sunny and Chichi." He paused. "Don't worry."

Chukwu started to open the door. "Let me just . . ."

"No, none of us can drive," Orlu insisted. "What if another car comes and wants to get by?" He pushed Chukwu's door shut. "We'll be back in a second."

Sunny turned to look back as Chukwu reluctantly drove the Jeep a bit down the road. She could see Sasha talking to the guys, but Orlu was still watching them go.

"Keep going," Chichi said when Chukwu slowed to a stop about an eighth of a mile away. They rolled along a few more yards to where the road curved and they could no longer see Sasha, Orlu, and the guys.

"Okay," Chichi said. "That's good."

Chukwu frowned deeply as he put the Jeep in park. He didn't turn it off. "What are they doing?"

"Helping them, I guess," Chichi said vaguely.

"How the hell can they help those guys? That car needed a tow truck to pull it out. A powerful one."

Chichi shrugged.

"I should go and help," he said, turning the Jeep off and making to get out. "You two stay here."

"No!" both Chichi and Sunny said.

"Why? I'm the strongest and oldest. This makes no sense!"

Chichi quickly got out of the car and got into the passenger seat.

"They'll be back," she said. "No shaking." She smirked coyly and leaned closer to him. Chukwu's frown immediately began to melt.

Chichi was wearing one of her long, old-looking skirts and a T-shirt. She'd taken off her sandals and left them on the floor in the back. She was so small that she could easily and cutely curl herself into the passenger seat, pulling her long skirt demurely over her short legs.

"So how are you doing?" she asked, batting her eyes at Chukwu.

"Oh my God," Sunny muttered, looking at the trees outside the window.

Ten minutes later, Sunny heard a car zooming up the road. Chichi was sitting on Chukwu's lap telling him for the millionth time how amazing his muscles were and Sunny was outside the Jeep, leaning against her door. It was the car that had been stuck in the ditch, all right. But Sunny only recognized it from its color and shape. It zoomed past them at probably over ninety miles per hour. She barely caught a glimpse of the guys in the car, but she saw them, especially the driver. He looked terrified.

When she looked up the road she saw Orlu and Sasha coming, keeping to the side. She ran to them. A few cars passed, but otherwise the road was quiet. She was sweating by the time she met them. The day was growing humid.

"What'd you do?" she asked as they walked to the Jeep.

"A little bit of this and a little bit of that," Sasha said.

"Hardest part was getting them to turn away," Orlu said. "They started thinking we were armed robbers. But if we didn't get them to turn around and they saw what we were doing, we'd be in a Library Council car on our way to the Obi Library's basement like you."

"We had to use *Ujo* on them," Orlu muttered. "So they were too scared to look at what we were doing."

Sunny's eyebrows went up. That was the juju that Anatov had taught them that caused Lambs to feel a deep irrational crippling fear. So *that* was why they went speeding away.

Sasha suddenly picked up his pace, leaving Sunny and Orlu to walk together. "So you won't be taken to the council? I know you used juju on that car."

He shook his head. "Remember, part of being a good Leopard Person is doing your duty for your fellow human beings. When we saw those guys, if we could help, we would help."

"You've got to be kidding me," Sasha shouted. He was standing at the passenger window staring into the Jeep. "Oh, so this is how it is? This is what you are?"

"Oh no," Orlu said. They both ran to the Jeep.

Chichi climbed out from the driver's side. Then Chukwu came out, also from the driver's side.

"What the hell is wrong with you?!" Sasha shouted at Chichi.

"Lower your voice," Chukwu said, his voice booming.

"*You* don't speak to me," Sasha said, pointing a finger at Chukwu.

Chukwu laughed hard. "Or you'll what?"

Sasha's eyes grew very big, and he looked as if he was going to say something. Then he glanced at Sunny and seemed to change his mind. "I don't give a shit how big you are," Sasha said. He moved toward Chukwu.

"Come on, then," Chukwu growled.

"Okay," Orlu said, immediately putting himself between Sasha and Chukwu. "Okay, o. Okay, o."

"Keep your hands off her," Sasha said, pointing at Chukwu over Orlu's shoulder.

"Sure, but I can't help it if she can't keep her hands off *me*," Chukwu said, laughing.

Sasha turned to the side and spat. "We will see."

Sunny went and stood beside Chichi. "What were you thinking?" Sunny snapped.

"I wasn't exactly thinking," Chichi whispered, but Sunny caught the hint of the smile on her lips.

"Let's all just get back in the Jeep," Orlu said. "We have a long way ahead of us."

Sasha was looking at Chichi, who was looking right back at Sasha. Chukwu angrily got in the driver's seat, slamming his door. Sunny and Orlu got in. Then Chichi. Sasha was the last to get into the passenger seat. He glared at Chukwu, but Chukwu just started the Jeep, ignoring Sasha. Minutes later, Sasha put Nas back on, moving on to the next album, *It Was Written*. But the vibration of the beats wasn't nearly as delicious as before.

22

FRESH, FRESH, FINE *EWUJU*!

It was as if the roads were trying to kill them.

There were potholes and craters everywhere. In one place the road seemed to have sloughed off completely, and they'd had to bumble their way across the jagged remains. Somehow the tires did not flatten, but the poor roads made the going slow and dangerous. A few times they passed parts of the road that were so uneven from erosion that they nearly tipped over. Thankfully it was dry season; otherwise the roads would have been muddy impassable gullies.

Then there were the go-slows, traffic that robbed their trip of precious time. Two hours after suffering the pothole- and crater-riddled road, they'd sat on the expressway for a whole hour and a half without moving. On the sides of the road were occasional shanties and stretches of trees, and from both of these came an assortment of beggars and hawkers. One of the beggars was a young man in scruffy clothes with knotted hair and a mad look in his eyes. He reminded Sunny of the man they'd seen in Bola's waiting room. He leaned against Chichi's window staring at her. No matter how many times Sasha told him to go away, he wouldn't budge until Sasha had actually gotten out of the car and chased the man off.

The hawkers sold all sorts of things, from raw corn, pure water, and bread to skewers of beef *suya*, plantain chips, and roasted bush meat. One man had even held up a whole bush rat to Orlu's window. "Fresh, fresh, fine *ewuju*!" he proclaimed. He'd asked for six hundred naira and even offered to skin it while they waited. The bush rat looked as if it had been killed minutes ago, still dripping blood.

Orlu had simply waved him off.

When the go-slow finally let up, they began encountering the checkpoints where Chukwu was forced to "do Christmas" for the police in order to get by without being delayed. The blatant demand for bribes especially irritated Sasha, who held a particular hatred for police officers. Chichi had to grab his hand as Chukwu dealt with the road police so that Sasha would keep his mouth shut. When they were stopped by a third police checkpoint within two hours, Sasha was ready to jump from his seat and "slap the man across the face." This was when Orlu said they should stop and find a hotel.

They were in Benin City, only halfway there, and already the sun was going down. Thankfully, Chichi had planned ahead. "Chukwu, pull over. Sunny, give me your phone, let me call my uncle."

Chukwu pulled into the parking lot of a roadside market. Chichi dialed the number. "I told him we'd be coming," she said as she waited for him to pick up.

"You sure it'll be all right?" Sunny asked.

"Of course. They have a big house and they love me," Chichi said. "This is my aunt, my mother's sister . . ." She held up a hand. "Hello? Hello? Uncle Uyobong? Good evening." She grinned and laughed and then began to speak in rapid Efik.

"I'm not sure if I like the idea of being on the road New Year's Eve," Orlu said as Chichi talked to her uncle.

"I know," Sunny said. "But if we keep driving, trust me, we will be robbed . . . or have to fight robbers."

Chichi was laughing very hard as she cupped the phone to her ear.

"Do you know Chichi's uncle?" Sunny asked.

"I've heard of him but never met him."

"Good things?" Sunny asked.

"Yeah," Orlu said, smiling. "He likes flowers." He lowered his voice so Chukwu wouldn't hear. "They're both Leopard People, and her aunt's a third leveler like Chichi's mother."

"Okay, everyone," Chichi announced, handing Sunny her phone. "They have dinner waiting for us. Let's go."

"Which way?" Chukwu asked.

Ten minutes later, they pulled through the gates of a small but beautifully designed compound. The house was painted blue, and the compound was made pretty with tall palm trees and colorful flowers that seemed to glow even in the near darkness. The small parking lot in front of the house was black and smooth, as if it had been freshly tarred.

"Nice," Sasha said.

"I'm going to warn you all one more time, treat my uncle's flowers like little human beings," Chichi said. "And God help you if you step on one."

"What kind of man loves flowers that much?" Chukwu said with a laugh as he got out of the car. "What is he, some kind of wizard?"

They all froze, avoiding eye contact with one another.

"He's a botanist; he studied at the University of California in the States," Chichi said.

"Oh . . . okay," Chukwu said.

Sunny let out a breath.

A pathway led to the front door and along the sides were all sorts of plants: tiger lilies, sunflowers, a bush with red flowers, and there was even a tall cactus on the right side of the path's beginning. "Don't touch any of his flowers," Chichi stressed again.

"Ah!" Chukwu hissed. "Damn it!" He was ahead of Sunny, and Sunny had seen precisely what happened. The cactus had leaned forward and swiped at his arm with a thorn! Thankfully, Chukwu hadn't seen it do this. He'd only felt it. "I didn't touch it," he said. He looked at his arm with irritation. "It touched me or something. I wasn't even . . ."

"Who is that?" a deep voice said from inside. The door unlocked and a man peeked out, frowning. He had a smooth, bald head and a handlebar mustache and bushy beard that reminded Sunny of the man on the Internet years ago who was always complaining about the rent being "too damn high."

"Who is touching my plants?"

"Uncle Uyobong," Chichi sang. "It's us!"

He frowned and then his face broke into a smile when he saw Chichi. "*Ah-ah!* Chichi," he said, hugging her tightly. A woman with a bushy gray Afro and large gold earrings came to the doorway, and Chichi hugged her tightly, too. "Auntie," Chichi said.

"And this must be Sunny," her uncle said.

Sunny stepped forward. "Good evening."

She was quickly scooped into hugs from them both. "We've heard all about you," Chichi's auntie said. Sunny glanced at Chichi and she quickly shook her head. *She better not have told them*, Sunny thought. No one else needed to know of her doubling besides the four of them.

Sasha, Orlu, and Chukwu all received tight hugs, too.

"Chukwu," Chichi's uncle said, cocking his head. "You are at the University of Port Harcourt?"

"Yes."

Her aunt took his head in her hands and looked from one side to the other. "You heal up well," she said, hugging him.

Chukwu frowned at Chichi, who only shrugged. "Thank you, ma," Chukwu politely said.

"Come in," she said. "All of you. We've been waiting."

As soon as they stepped in, her uncle put his arm around Sasha's shoulder and said, "Come, you and I need to talk." Then they walked into another room.

Sunny was too busy taking in the spectacle that was the inside of their home to ask where Chichi's uncle and Sasha were going. The house . . . could she call this a house? A greenhouse maybe. It was nice and cool inside, yes, but there were plants . . . all over the place. They hung from the giant chandelier on the ceiling. Vines wrapped themselves around the banister of the stairs. There were potted trees flourishing against the walls.

"Wow," Chukwu said. "The house looks a lot bigger on the inside."

"It's the glass ceiling," Chichi's aunt said. They all looked up, and indeed in the large front room, the ceiling was made entirely of glass.

"This is my partner's home," Chichi's auntie said. "I own nothing."

"She and my uncle, they aren't married," Chichi said, moving closer to Sunny, so Chukwu wouldn't hear. "Remember, we are Nimm, and Nimm women can't marry."

"Oh," Sunny said. "Right." She'd been wondering this very thing. The house was lovely, but it looked extravagant. Chichi's mother lived in a hut and was proud of that. Still, even if she didn't own it, it seemed odd for a Nimm priestess to live so lavishly.

"My uncle built it for her but more for himself," Chichi said. "Did I tell you he loves flowers?"

"I don't think I've ever seen a place like this," Chukwu was saying to Chichi's auntie.

"Well, I'm glad to broaden your mind," she said. "Come, I'll show you where you'll be sleeping, and then you can eat dinner."

Sasha, Orlu, and Chukwu were to stay in a large room downstairs where every wall was taken up by a bookshelf. There was a large plush couch that curved into a horseshoe big enough for two of them to sleep on and a cot set up behind the horseshoe couch, which Chukwu quickly claimed.

"Why don't you boys get settled down?" Chichi's auntie said. "We'll be right back." She took Chichi and Sunny to a smaller bedroom upstairs. "You're fine sharing a bed, right?"

"Of course, Auntie," Chichi said.

Sunny nodded. "It's a lovely room."

And it was, with its large leafy plants winding up a pole

beside the curtains, creeping out through the cracked door over the balcony.

"Have you been good with your brother, Sunny?" her auntie asked.

"What do you mean?"

"You know what I mean, honey. Are things okay with his school? We don't need you dragged off to the library basement again."

Chichi snorted with laughter.

"I'm still here," Sunny said, embarrassed.

"Good," Chichi's auntie said, patting her on the back. "I know it's hard for free agents. You know the Lamb world better than us, and Leopard People can be assholes, so your kind can be short-tempered. For good reason. It's not easy living on the border of such different worlds."

A black cat smoothly skulked from beneath the bed and stood in front of Sunny and looked up at her. Waiting. Sunny ignored it as Chichi's auntie spoke.

"But you'll get used to it," she continued. "And you better do it fast, because I think something big is expected of you."

"I guess," Sunny said, glancing at the cat. It was still sitting there.

"Pick her up," her auntie said. "What do you think she's waiting for?"

Sunny bent down and slowly picked it up. She wasn't too familiar with cats, so she held it like a baby. It turned and twisted into a comfortable position in her arms. She petted it, and it began to purr.

"That's Paja," Chichi said, taking one of the cat's front paws in her hand. "See her paws? Cool, right?"

The cat had six digits on its paw.

"Is it . . . what if Chukwu sees it?"

"So?" Chichi said. "These aren't magical. Well, all cats are of the Leopard People, but Lambs have these cats, too. They're called polydactyl cats. It's a natural mutation. They're really smart, too."

The cat purred and rested its head against Sunny's chest, and Sunny nearly melted with delight. She sat on the bed with the cat in her arms and she stroked its soft black fur.

"I've contacted your mother," Chichi's auntie told Sunny. "She's glad you made it."

"Thank you," Sunny said. She'd also send Ugonna a text. He'd probably heard from her parents that they were okay, but she'd told him she'd keep in personal contact with him.

"Are you sure about this trip?" Chichi's auntie asked.

Sunny nodded.

"Okay," she said. "No more talk of it. Let's go have dinner."

Sunny brought the cat with her.

The dining room was in the back and also completely made of glass, various types of plants and potted trees stationed in the corners of the room. The table in the center was large and made of thick wood, as were the chairs. And the chairs were grooved with intricate designs, their edges smooth with age. Sunny found them extremely comfortable. The wood even felt warm.

Dinner was already set on the table in a large bowl and several smaller ones. The large white porcelain bowl was filled with *edikaikong* soup, and in each of the smaller bowls were fried plantain, puff puffs, and sliced mango. On a plate were fist-sized balls of gray *garri*. The soup was heavy with periwinkle snails, beef, and stockfish, and it was light in palm oil. The perfect balance. Sunny's mother didn't make this particular vegetable soup. *Edikaikong* soup was an Ibibio dish, not an Igbo one. However, since Chichi's mother was Efik, a subgroup of the Ibibios, Sunny had had it plenty of times at Chichi's house, so many times that she'd grown a taste for it. When she finished eating, she sat back, satisfied and exhausted. Her eyes were drooping when a sliver of the conversation happening around her floated into her ears.

"Sure, I'll go with you."

"Great," Sasha said, perking up. He'd eaten more than Sunny, but it seemed to have the opposite effect on him.

"I'm going with!" Chichi said. "You never take me out when *I* visit."

"Ah, but these three are men," Chichi's uncle said. "It's not the same."

"Go where?" Sunny asked.

"To taste the local nightlife," Sasha said. "It's almost New Year's Eve. Everyone's off work and partying already. We're in a new place, let's go see what it's like!"

Sunny looked at Chukwu, who wasn't saying anything. He clearly wanted to go, just not with Sasha. Orlu even looked interested. "Um, okay," Sunny reluctantly said. "I'll go if everyone else is going." And everyone else was. She groaned, but too quietly for anyone to hear. She'd rather climb into bed, read for a little bit, and then go to sleep. It had been a long, long day and tomorrow was probably going to be longer.

So this was how Sunny found herself at her first nightclub. Orlu had his arm tightly around her waist, and she was glad because the place was dark and packed with the undulating and wiggling bodies of people dancing, talking, and shouting. Not far away, she could see Sasha getting down on the dance floor, surrounded by five women who were close to twice his age. Chukwu was dancing with Chichi several feet away, but Chichi kept looking at Sasha. And who could forget Chichi's uncle and aunt who were out there dancing like maniacs, too? Chichi's uncle had a bottle of Guinness in his hand and was somehow not spilling it.

Sunny yawned, leaning on Orlu. Suddenly, he let go of her and started pushing his way farther in. "What are you doing?" Sunny asked.

Then the crowd surged forward, as people moved to get a better look. She was pushed along with it, and then she saw where Orlu was going. Two guys who looked to be in their twenties were swinging at Sasha. He ducked and one guy missed, but the other managed to punch him in the gut. Then there was Chukwu jumping on that guy, turning him around and socking him in the face. The guy stumbled back as two more of his friends joined him. They paused as they looked at Chukwu, who shouted over the music, "Come on, then!" He held up his fists. The guys weren't as dumb as they looked because none of them took Chukwu up on his invitation to fight. Orlu grabbed Sasha, and Chukwu pushed them both along.

Chichi's uncle joined them, shouting for the guys to stay back. Chichi's aunt was behind him looking angry and ready to fight, too. Sunny moved after them as they all exited the club. Once outside, Sunny was shocked to see that Sasha, Chukwu, and Chichi's uncle were all laughing. Even Orlu looked mildly amused.

"Damn," Sasha said, holding his aching belly. "Chukwu, I don't think I have *ever* seen four grown men afraid of one younger man. I don't even care, you get some dap for that. No doubt. Respect, respect." He grasped Chukwu's hand, slapping his other hand over it.

"I saw them coming at you," Chukwu said. "You had all their ladies, and you don't even look twenty."

"It's my American swag," Sasha said with a lopsided grin. He coughed and held his side.

"Are you all right?" Chichi's uncle asked.

"Yeah," Sasha said. "I managed to flex at the last minute. It's nothing a night's sleep won't cure."

They quickly got into the car in case the guys Sasha had angered came out for more. Sunny was just glad to leave that place earlier than they would have. Exactly an hour later, after the short drive back, showering in lukewarm water, brushing her teeth, and climbing into bed, Sunny closed her eyes. Chichi was already fast asleep, having taken an even shorter shower before Sunny. Ten minutes later, Sunny heard someone riffling through her and Chichi's bags not far from her head.

For a moment, Sunny just lay there in the darkness, reluctant to get up and switch on the light. She was exhausted and comfortable. *Maybe I'm just hearing things*, she thought. There was an air conditioner in the room that clanked and loudly dripped water. But the more she lay there, the clearer the sound came. *Crinkle, crinkle, rummage, rummage.*

Her juju knife was in the pocket of her night clothes and slowly, she reached for it. The light suddenly switched on. And what Sunny saw on her backpack shocked her, but only for a moment. It was a large black bat. And it was clutching her wallet, her glasses in their hard green case, and *Udide's Book of Shadows* in its strong sharp claws.

Without thinking, Sunny did the swift juju Sugar Cream had taught her for getting rid of those large wall spiders Sunny hated so much. She missed and the bat scrambled up the windowsill. "Oh no!" she breathed. She nearly dropped her juju knife but managed to grasp it and work the juju again. She caught the pouch in her hand and threw it at the bat as she said, "Stay there!" The bat dropped the book on the sill and her glasses and wallet fell to the floor. The bat was flattened right on the windowsill.

"Good thinking, Sunny!" Chichi said, looking impressed. She was standing at the light switch.

"You heard it?" Sunny asked, pressing her forehand. She'd had to focus her mind to a point to rework the juju correctly because of the doubling, and the effort was rewarding her with a throbbing headache.

"Yeah, after you woke me up by moving around. I was going to shred whatever it was to pieces. Your way is more humane."

They stepped up to the flattened bat. It was soft with black fur on its body and reddish fur on its head and had the delicately elegant face of a fox. It looked up at them with blank eyes.

"You think it was sent?" Sunny asked. *It was*, she heard Anyanwu whisper. Immediately, Sunny's headache went away.

"Of course."

"By who?"

"You *know* who."

"Udide?"

"No, *Ekwensu*," Chichi said.

Sunny gasped.

"It's a stupid thing to do," Chichi said, kneeling down to look at the bat. "She's toying with you. She just wants to scare you by letting you know that she knows. If she really wanted the book or your money, she'd have just made them disappear."

So Ekwensu knew she was going to Lagos in order to get to Osisi. Sunny shut her eyes. The thought of something powerful, terrible, and violent taking interest in her made her ill. Suddenly, she wanted to go home.

"What are we going to do with it?"

There was a soft meow at the door, and they looked at each other.

"No," Sunny said when Chichi went to open the door.

"Why not?" Chichi asked.

"What if it . . ."

Chichi opened the door and Paja skulked in. She trotted toward the immobile bat and looked at it. She meowed again. Then she arched her back and hissed, bringing her face right up to the bat, and the bat began to struggle against the charm Sunny had put on it. Then Paja appeared to gnaw at the air around the bat, and soon the bat flew out the window. Sunny shut it and smiled. "Paja," she said, picking up the black cat. "I'm glad you don't believe in capital punishment, either." The cat purred, rubbing its soft face against Sunny's.

Chichi rolled her eyes. "What kind of cat are you? You're *both* hopeless."

23
IBAFO

The next morning, after three hours of driving, they reached the town of Ibafo, about fifteen miles from Lagos. Almost there. The problem was that they were again caught in a go-slow, and not just any go-slow, a colossal go-slow. It was the wrong time to be there. Sunny could just barely see the source of their woes about a mile up the Lagos–Ibadan Expressway. There was a cluster of cream-colored buildings, and the parking lot around the largest of the buildings was packed. It was the Redemption Church Camp.

Being the early afternoon of New Year's Eve, people were just arriving. And those who could not find parking in the lot were parking right on the road. The go-slow was so thick that traffic wasn't moving at all. Some people even parked where they were stuck, left their car, and went on to the church.

"Are you kidding?" Sasha shouted out the window at some people in front of them who'd just left their car. They ignored him as they stepped into the grass and kept right on going, wearing their Sunday best, although it was Wednesday.

"Can you get around their car?" Orlu asked.

"I'll try," Chukwu said, driving onto the red dirt pathway near the center of the road. There was already a line of cars stuck there and Chukwu opened his window. "Excuse me, sir. Will you . . ."

The man in the passenger seat pinched his face and said, "Na no see way we dey hook here like person wey dey inside rat cage?"

The driver ducked down to see Chukwu. "You think I am fool?" he snapped. The man was old enough to be their father. "I let you in and the whole world will be squeezing."

"The people in the car in front of me have left it," Chukwu said. "Just let . . ."

The driver closed his window.

"What is wrong with the people here?" Orlu asked, disgusted.

"It's not them," Sunny said. "Chukwu, remember when we all came through here?"

Chukwu nodded.

"It wasn't this bad, but it was bad," Sunny told Orlu. "People know that, so they are mean. It's faster when you don't let anyone else in."

In front of them a large truck carrying about fifty people and a great pile of oranges belched out exhaust, and the people in the back coughed and waved at the polluted air. The exhaust soon reached them, and they coughed as Chukwu turned the Jeep on and closed the windows. When the air cleared, he opened them again. Best to save gas by not using the air conditioner.

"If this were a funky train, we wouldn't be here," Chichi whispered.

"Yeah, we wouldn't be here," Sunny said in a low voice so Chukwu wouldn't hear. "We'd still be at home because my parents wouldn't let me travel for so many days without Chukwu."

Chichi sucked her teeth and opened the door to stretch her legs. Sasha got out and leaned against the car with her.

It was hot and humid, and the shanties that housed a small market were booming with business, selling pure water, plantain chips, and cell phone car chargers. Sunny was looking at the cloudy sky, glad that a few of the puffier clouds were covering the sun, when the idea popped into her head. She had asked Sugar Cream about this very possibility, so she knew a little about it.

"Can Leopard People control the weather?" she'd questioned Sugar Cream one horribly hot day. The entire library had felt as if it would melt back into the earth from which it came. "Or even just temperature? I'd have thought there'd be some juju to at least cool it down in here."

Sugar Cream had laughed and said, "Can you imagine the world we would live in if we *could* do that? The entire Earth would be in chaos."

"Oh," Sunny'd said, leaning back on her elbows. As usual, she had been sitting on the floor of Sugar Cream's office. She'd tried her best to ignore the red spider scuttling across the floor a few feet away.

"The weather is the business of Chukwu," Sugar Cream had said.

For once, Sunny hadn't needed an explanation. Chukwu was her brother's name, but he was named after someone much greater. First and foremost, Chukwu was the name the Igbo people used for the Supreme Being. The great deity known as Chukwu was so inaccessible to human beings that one didn't even pray to it. If Chukwu gave you audience, you probably would have no idea why and you'd be in such awe, it wouldn't really matter.

"But," Sugar Cream had said, raising an index finger. "If the weather is already moving in a direction, we can sort of push it along. For example, if it's breezy, with some effort and consequence, a skilled Leopard Person can make it windy."

"What kind of consequence?"

Sugar Cream had laughed loudly. "Nothing worth discussing. There's a reason not many Leopard People play around with changing the weather."

Now, as Sunny looked up at the cloudy sky, she wondered. She climbed out of the Jeep and walked around to the other side where Sasha and Chichi stood smoking cigarettes.

"I don't want to hear it," Chichi said, rolling her eyes. "We're outside and there's a breeze."

Sasha blew out some smoke as he scrutinized Sunny. Then he said, "She's not here to whine. She's got an idea."

Sunny nodded. "I do," she said. "Well, it'll only work if one of you guys can do it. I know I can't." She glanced at Chukwu, who was fiddling with the stereo. Orlu was behind him reading the *Book of Shadows*, his brow furrowed with concentration.

Sunny nodded her head toward the sky. "It's supposed to rain later today. Can you make it rain now? Either of you?"

They were silent as they considered. It didn't take long. "If it rains, people will return to get their cars," Sasha said.

Sunny nodded.

"But only if it rains hard. A deluge that covers the roads," Chichi said.

"Exactly," Sunny said. "Can you . . ."

"Of course, we can," Sasha said. "But it's the consequences that bother me."

"What'll happen?" Sunny asked. "It can't kill you, right?"

"No, no," Chichi said. "Water no get enemy."

"Water is life," Sasha added. "*Aman iman*."

Chichi was quoting Fela, Sasha was quoting old proverbs and speaking in some Arabic type language; Sunny was completely lost.

"Sunny, get in the car," Sasha said, bringing out his juju knife. He lowered his voice. "Talk to your brother and Orlu for a while. We'll be right back."

Chichi poked her head in the Jeep window. "Chukwu, we're going into the market to find something real to eat. Do you want anything?"

Chukwu shook his head. "Just want to get the hell out of here."

"Orlu?"

"Nothing," he muttered, his eyes still on the book.

Sasha and Chichi quickly walked away, without a glance back. Sunny climbed into the car and sat beside Orlu. She wanted to explain to him what was going on, but Chukwu was right there. Orlu seemed too preoccupied with the book, anyway.

"Daddy warned me not to take this way today," Chukwu moaned. "I completely forgot. With all that craziness last night, I was distracted. We should have been there by now."

"Don't worry," Sunny said. "We'll get there."

"So close yet so far."

⌄⌄⌄⌄

A half hour had passed, and they'd only moved up about twenty feet thanks to two cars that were pushed off the road because they'd run out of gas. Drops of rain started falling just when Sasha and Chichi returned carrying bags of *chin chin*.

"That's all you got?" Chukwu asked as Chichi got in. "What took so long?"

"There wasn't much to eat," Chichi quickly said.

Sasha slowly climbed into the passenger seat. He looked ill, his face sweaty. Sunny frowned as he sat with his legs pressed together. He smiled weakly at her. Chukwu looked at him, frowned, and asked, "What is wrong with you?"

"Just gotta pee," he said.

"Then go do . . ."

The rain started hitting the car in large droplets. Then it began coming down like a waterfall.

Orlu looked up for the first time from the book. He looked at Sasha and then Sunny, and Sunny nodded.

"Turn the car on," Chichi shouted.

As soon as Chukwu did, she closed her window. They all followed suit as the car was pounded with rain. Sasha groaned and jumped out of the car. "Can't hold it!" he screeched. Sunny turned away as he stood in the rain right there beside the Jeep and relieved himself.

When he finished, he got back in the car, still looking strained. He pressed his legs together. Whatever he had done, it had only been him who did it. She couldn't imagine Chichi suffering the same problem. That would have been more complicated.

"What kind of rain is this?" Chukwu asked, leaning forward. Outside, they could see people running for shelter and to their cars. All around them, vehicles were starting and the paved double road ran with sludgy red mud. For several minutes, it was chaos. Women in their best church clothes took off their heels to hop into cars or beneath canopies. Men in church-appropriate suits and caftans jumped into driver's seats. The cloudburst above was like nothing Sunny had ever seen. And poor Sasha kept having to pee and pee. He was soaked from jumping outside to urinate and then getting back into the Jeep. Needless to say, Chukwu was perplexed and deeply annoyed by Sasha's problem.

"Did you eat some bad mango?" he asked, reaching beneath the seat and pulling out a blue battered towel. He threw it on Sasha's seat.

Thankfully, within minutes the go-slow began to move. Within a half hour, they'd outrun the strange weather and were cruising down the road. Sasha's peeing fit continued but decreased the farther they got from the Redemption Church Camp and soon, exhausted from the agony to his bladder, he fell into a deep sleep.

A half hour after that, they entered Africa's biggest megacity, Lagos.

24
THIS IS LAGOS

So many people. All in a rush.

In Lagos, people were perpetually on alert because anything could happen at any time. The roads were narrow, overcrowded, and littered with street traders and beggars of all kinds. There were so many rickety golden-yellow *danfo* packed with people. Even the air quality was different. At times it smelled like burning cedar wood, rotten medicine, garbage, exhaust. It was noxious. Was it even air? Sunny felt like she was breathing fumes, better yet, juju powder.

By the time they reached Victoria Island, her nose was running like crazy and she'd gone through half her box of Kleenex. Maybe Lagos really *was* dusted with juju powder. It was a crazy idea, but she had to wonder. She'd been to Lagos with her family many times before her initiation into Leopardom and never had this problem. She'd never had any type of allergy . . . other than being allergic to the sun.

When they entered the gated community where Adebayo's aunt and uncle lived, it was like driving into yet another world. A world of super wealthy people. Sunny had been to this part of Victoria Island before when the family had visited one of her father's friends. She'd felt displaced in the same way back then, and she didn't exactly come from poverty, either. Coming here after the crazy drive through Nigeria's many worlds of poverty, wealth, rural and city, trees to concrete jungle was even more unsettling. It was as if they'd left Nigeria and entered the cushiest part of the United States. The houses here were huge and gluttonous in the way that they were in the wealthiest suburbs of New York.

The streets were paved and pothole-free, clean and lined with flowers. A white woman walked a tiny white dog. A man in a jogging suit walked fast, sweating like crazy as he shouted into his cell phone in Yoruba.

"Okay, we're going left," Chukwu said into his phone. Adebayo was guiding him. "Oh . . . okay, I see it. White with the yellow Hummer in front." He laughed hard. "You can drive that? *Ah-ah*."

"Ugh," Chichi said, disgusted. "I'll bet half these people work for the government and oil companies."

"What's wrong with that?" Chukwu asked, holding the phone aside.

Sasha laughed hard and shook his head.

Chichi only looked salty.

"Okay," Chukwu said into his phone. He laughed loudly, playfully dropping into Pidgin English. "I dey road now, I dey come to your big, big house. I dey yahn you so that na go dey ready for me, o!" He listened for a moment and then laughed hard. "Okay, o!" Still chuckling, he ended the call. "Adebayo is ready for us."

Sunny didn't feel elated at arriving. The closer they got to the house, the closer they got to their destination. Tomorrow was New Year's Day. What did the New Year have in store for her?

Adebayo was waiting for them in front of the house as they drove onto the large curved driveway. He was wearing costly jeans and a brand-name T-shirt. Sunny rolled her eyes; he didn't normally dress so flashily. And the neighborhood must be incredibly safe. Sunny couldn't remember seeing this type of home that was *not* surrounded by a concrete gate.

Adebayo and Chukwu hugged and slapped hands. Then Chukwu introduced his friend to Sasha and Orlu. When he came to Chichi and Sunny, the smile on Adebayo's face wavered. His whole demeanor was false. How much did Adebayo understand about Sunny and Chichi's involvement in the destruction of his confraternity? Was that understanding conscious or subconscious? Judging by the way he quickly turned his back on them both, he recalled *something.* Sunny was glad. It would be a long time before she forgave him for introducing her brother to the Red Sharks and slapping him in the face that night, if she ever did.

"Welcome. Come in," Adebayo said, putting his arm around Chukwu's shoulder. "Let me show you everything."

The house was enormous. There were two kitchens, one for the mistress and master of the house and one for the house girls. Both had fully stocked and functioning refrigerators, cabinets, and cupboards, and both were used mainly by the house help, all of whom had traveled home to visit relatives until January second.

"And even then," Adebayo said as he gave them the full tour, "my aunt and uncle won't be back from London until the sixth."

The mansion had ten bedrooms, so they all had their pick of rooms. Sunny chose one on the third floor with a small balcony. It had a thick sliding glass door and a heavy-duty lock that she tested before choosing the room. It was a bit dusty and smelled as if it hadn't been occupied in some time, despite the gorgeous satin sheets, dreamlike bed with a canopy, and soft luxurious deep-blue rug. This wasn't surprising since only Adebayo's aunt and uncle lived here. Their children were at university overseas and the house help stayed in the small house out back.

"So wasteful, isn't it?" Chichi asked, coming in.

Sunny had put her things on the small plush lavender couch beside her bed and plopped onto the cool sheets. She sighed and grinned at Chichi, who rolled her eyes and sat on the floor. "I am so hungry."

"Me too," Chichi said. "I'll bet there's a whole market in all five of the refrigerators in the house."

"There are only two fridges."

"Same thing."

There was a knock on her door. "Come in," Sunny said.

Orlu had taken his shoes off and put on a fresh T-shirt. "I'm in the room across the hall," he said. "After your bat incident, it's probably best if I stay close."

"She can take care of herself," Chichi said. "And she's got me. I'm next door."

Orlu grunted, sitting on the couch.

Chichi smirked and pointed at the door. "Ten, nine, eight, seven, six, five, four, three, two . . ."

The door opened. "Sunny, you in here?" Sasha asked.

"Aren't you supposed to knock?" Chichi asked.

Sasha cut his eyes at her as he leaned against the wall, shutting the door behind him. He was carrying *Udide's Book of Shadows*. "I'm in the room downstairs near the front door," Sasha said. "Someone's got to stand guard, right? Especially with your . . . condition."

Sunny rolled her eyes.

"I put up a perimeter, too," Sasha added.

"Good idea," Orlu said. "Hopefully no one notices all the lizards that'll be on the outside walls."

"Yeah, it's not the most discreet juju, but it's powerful. Nothing will come in without me knowing. Like last night." Sasha looked at the door, locked it, and moved inside. He sat beside Chichi, and Orlu got up and sat beside Sunny on her bed. Sunny scooted up. They were all face-to-face, and for several moments, they didn't speak.

"We go tomorrow," Sunny said.

"Yeah," Orlu said.

"The market in J. City," Chichi said. "It's the biggest in Lagos. We can take a *kabu kabu*."

Sunny frowned. "But Ajegunle is . . ."

"Relax, I know how to deal with 'one chance' robbers and any other kind of stupidity," Chichi said, holding up a hand.

Ajegunle District, nicknamed "The Jungle" or "J. City," was the worst part of Lagos. Sunny's father described it as a slum, saying that it was full of garbage, poisonous water, filthy shantytowns built on muddy land and in some places islands of garbage. It was a place of rough, rough commerce.

"One chance" robbers were all over Lagos, but they thrived in Ajegunle and with vehicles that were heading to Ajegunle. "One chance" robbers were guys who drove *kabu kabu* or *danfo*. Their vehicles would be nearly full, so the drivers would advertise that they were giving people "one more chance" to get in at a reduced price. When the victim got in, he or she would be set upon by a bunch of thieves. Sunny had heard all kind of Lagos horror stories. And of course, there was the added danger of her being albino, and thus the target for ritual killers.

"Can't Adebayo just drop us off?" Sunny asked. Even as she spoke, she knew it was a stupid request.

"And bring all that attention to us with that hideous Hummer?" Chichi asked.

"And like your brother, Adebayo can't know where we are going, either," Orlu added.

"They can't," Sasha said, shaking his head. "Not even a little."

They were quiet again.

"It's New Year's Day, the markets will be empty," Sunny said, her throat tight. "It'll be easier for strangers to notice us, too."

"Some will," Chichi said. "But they aren't Chukwu and Adebayo."

"Fine," Sunny said. "We take a *kabu kabu* or *danfo*." She sat up straighter. "I have the marbles."

"Blue?" Sasha asked, looking pleased.

Sunny nodded. The juju required blue marbles to work.

"You've read it well," Sasha said. "I'm impressed."

"In the morning?" Orlu asked.

"People will be too tired from celebrating to notice us," Sunny said. "We leave at seven A.M." She paused, looking at all of them. "Sound right?"

They all agreed.

"Does anyone need to read more of this?" Sasha asked, holding up the book.

Orlu frowned. "That book is dangerous."

Sasha laughed. "I know. It's awesome."

Orlu sucked his teeth and shook his head in disgust.

"And if I'd never bought it, where would we be in all this?" Sasha said.

"You should give it to Sunny," Orlu said.

Sasha shrugged and handed it over. "I've read it three times, anyway. Plus, it feels like holding a million scratchy spiders." He tapped on the side of his head. "Got it all up here."

"Me too," Chichi added. They slapped and shook hands, snapping each other's fingers.

"I wouldn't keep it too close when you go to bed," Sasha said.

Sunny took the book and asked, "Why?" She shivered at its roughness and immediately glanced around her room, searching for spiders hiding in the corners. She'd seen a large wall spider in the room downstairs. She was reminded of one of the first lines in *Udide's Book of Shadows*: "Even in palaces, there are spiders."

"Just trust me," Sasha said.

"Oookay," Sunny said, putting the book on one of her cabinets. "So, what do we tell my brother?"

"I'll handle that," Chichi said.

Sasha groaned and got up. "On that note, I'm out of here. I'm going to explore around this edifice of excessive extravagance. If my boys from the States saw this place, their eyes would pop out. I had a friend ask me just before I came here if Africans have schools! He was a Lamb, sure, but he was a black dude, like me. Black folks be so *ignorant* sometimes."

"Overconsumption is a universal human trait," Orlu pointed out. "And so is ignorance."

"Yeah, but you've got to admit, black Americans, no, *blacks of the world* are into self-hate more than any other group of people. I know what I had to deal with when I was in the Chi. If it weren't for me being a Leopard, I'd have grown up as ignorant as anyone else. Leopard People read books by everybody and everything. We look outside *and* inside. But you have to be secure with yourself to do either . . ." He shook his head. "It's too hard to explain. Sunny, you know some of what I mean."

Sunny nodded. But her mind was not on the problems of the black African diaspora. She was thinking about what it was going to be like to meet with a giant sentient spider who was thousands, maybe millions, of years old while she was impaired by doubling.

Chukwu and Adebayo went out to the clubs to celebrate

the New Year. The four of them opted to stay in. Sunny and Chichi cooked up an elaborate meal of fried plantain, jollof rice, *egusi* soup and *garri*, fried chicken, and pepper soup heavy with fish (there were no tainted peppers, which was a shame). There was so much food in the house that what they'd cooked up would probably not even be missed. The business of cooking took Sunny's mind off what lay ahead, and she found herself laughing and joking with Chichi. When they finished, exhausted from cooking and wanting privacy, Chichi and Sunny sat down to eat before presenting the food to the others.

"Damn, this is good," Chichi said, savoring a spoonful of pepper soup.

Sunny took a bite out of a long slice of fried plantain. "Best dinner ever."

They ate for a while, Sunny's words lingering between them. Sunny knew they were both thinking the same thing, neither daring to speak those thoughts aloud: *Last supper.*

"I can't imagine this thing that's happened to you," Chichi suddenly said.

Sunny stopped eating. "You don't have to."

Chichi took a gulp from her glass of orange Fanta. "I mean, no, I don't mean it like that." She shook her head. "You're just full of surprises, Sunny."

"You're telling me," she muttered.

"You know you should be dead, right?"

Sunny slammed her fork down and looked at her friend. "What are . . ."

Chichi put both of her hands up, a grin on her face. "*Ah-ah, biko-nu*, don't kill me, o. I'm telling you, you are so *strong* and amazing, Sunny. And you don't even know it." She laughed, clapping Sunny on the back. "Eat your plantain and keep on surprising everyone."

Sunny bit into her plantain and as she did, she could feel Anyanwu's presence. Not like the stirring of herself, as Chichi would have felt her spirit face, but as the shifting of someone outside herself, yet who was herself. And for a moment, she saw through two sets of eyes. This had happened once before, about a week ago when she'd woken up after a good sleep. She'd lain in her bed staring at her room. And this had gotten her thinking about her cultural halves, American and Nigerian, how she'd always felt like two people in one. Then she'd wondered how Anyanwu felt about the American part of her. And then she knew for a moment because she was Anyanwu, but with the broken bond, it felt like Anyanwu was separate from her.

Now it wasn't so consuming because both she and Anyanwu were angry at Chichi for the same reason.

Chichi was watching her closely, and now Chichi laughed. "I see you! That's because of the doubling. Wow. I look in your eyes and see you *both*." She chuckled some more, picked a piece of fish from her soup, and ate it. "Full of surprises."

When the countdown began, Sunny was so stuffed with food that all she wanted to do was sleep.

But Chichi had found a bottle of wine and wine glasses, and before Sunny knew it, she was carrying her first glass of wine. They all screamed "Happy New Year" and clinked glasses when the time came. Chichi and Sasha shared a prolonged, nearly obscene, kiss.

"Happy New Year," Orlu said to Sunny, giving her a tight hug and planting a third kiss directly on her lips. It tasted like red wine.

"Happy New Year, Orlu," Sunny said, looking into his eyes. There was a hint of fear in them, and she wondered if, like Chichi, he saw Anyanwu in her eyes. However, she ignored this as she took another sip of wine. It tasted both awful and wonderful.

"Here's to saving the world," Sasha said. They all clinked their glasses again and sipped.

And surviving tomorrow, Sunny thought. She sipped again.

Sasha put on some rap music that Sunny wasn't familiar with. It was in the Ghanaian language of Twi. Both Sasha and Chichi started getting down, and even Orlu smiled and laughed, doing a few moves himself.

"*Ah-ah*, look at Orlu," Chichi shouted. "That's nice!" She imitated his steps and soon all three of them were doing Orlu's dance. Sunny felt a little dizzy from her wine, so she sat down, enjoying the moment with her closest friends. With her peripheral vision she saw a hint of a yellow figure sitting close beside her. "Happy New Year, Anyanwu," she whispered. The yellow intensified for a moment and then was gone. *But always there*, Sunny thought, taking another gulp of wine.

Later, after a brief phone call to her relieved parents and a ten-minute-long text message exchange with Ugonna, she stepped out onto her balcony. "Wow," she whispered, grasping the doorway. The railing was peopled with over thirty green and orange lizards. They looked at her, but not one ran away. She sat on the balcony floor and flipped through the *Book of Shadows* for a few minutes, but she was too tired to read.

When she went to bed, she placed the book on the other side of the room near her backpack. She must not have put the book far enough away because her dreams were full of scuttling and cartwheeling spiders. She stood, a glowing yellow figure, in a jungle that rippled and heaved with them—red ones, black ones, green ones, small ones, and an enormous one that waited for her in the deepest leafy darkness.

25
THE JUNGLE

When the rickety dented red *kabu kabu* stopped, the four of them piled in. Within seconds, five other guys tried to get in, too.

"Hey, no room!" Sasha said, kicking at a guy who tried to squeeze in. He shoved him out and slammed the door just in time. The car chugged off. "Damn, where are those guys going at this hour?"

"Home," the driver said, laughing.

"Oh," Sasha said. "Right."

"Where na wan' go?" the driver asked them.

"Ajegunle Market, please," Sunny said.

"Shey you know e close now," he said.

"It's okay," she said. "We're just meeting someone around there."

The drive took a half hour because of traffic. And by the time they got there, Sunny felt light-headed from the exhaust that wafted in through the car's floor. It was so old and rusted that you could even see the road through large holes.

"I'll pay," Orlu said when they arrived at the market. Judging from the grin and number of thank-yous the driver gave, Orlu had tipped him well.

"You didn't need to do that," Sasha said. "I've got plenty of cash."

"It's New Year's Day," Orlu said. "Plus, today is important. Don't worry about it."

The large market was a series of wooden dividers, shacks, benches, and stalls. All were vacant. It was like a ghost town. "Let's walk in a bit," Orlu said.

"*Na wao*," Chichi said, running a hand over a bench as they passed it. "I have never seen this place empty."

"I'll bet this is when the ghosts come to do business," Sasha said.

"I think the ghosts do business all the time," Chichi said. "They're not afraid of the living. Our world is nothing but a lesser version of this Osisi place we are trying to get to."

"True that," Sasha said. "Back in the States, I've got an uncle in Atlanta who says there's a place near a local farmers' market where once a year at midnight a spirit market opens and the only people who can go are old folks. If you're not old and you go, you come back all mentally messed up or mute or something."

"They have those here, too," Orlu said. "There's one in Ikare that my great-grandfather has been to twice."

"What does he buy there?" Sasha asked.

Sunny tuned out their chatter. She felt ill. The marbles were cool in her sweaty hand, but this didn't help. She didn't like spiders, for one thing. But that wasn't the worst of it. What if they succeeded in convincing Udide to weave them this flying grasscutter creature? What if the grasscutter took them to Osisi? What was waiting for her there?

Everyone agreed that it was a wilderling that had shown her the vision in the candle. But everyone also agreed that there was no way to tell if that wilderling was friend or foe. The wilderling's intentions in showing her the future were unclear. Was this the same with the dreams? What if this was all a trap?!

Her slick hands fumbled with the marbles. "What am I doing here?" she whispered. "Why am I doing this? I could just go home."

But she continued to lead the way, looking side to side as they walked through the empty market. She felt Anyanwu close and intimate, and this was comforting. They came to a large group of stalls covered by sheets of corrugated tin to make one big roof. It was cool in the shade. They stopped, quiet. The breeze blew and a small bird flew by cheeping. It flew through a ray of light, leaving a wake of dust. Sunny sneezed hard.

"There's . . ." Orlu stepped forward and held up his hands.

"Is there something to undo?" Chichi asked him.

"No," he said. "But . . . this part of the market . . . Leopard People sell here."

Sunny nodded, rubbing her nose. "Juju powder, I'll bet."

They walked on for another few minutes beneath the tin roof. "This place just goes on and on," Sunny said, her voice nasally from her stuffed nose. "It didn't look this big from the outside."

Sasha chuckled and shook his head. "Of course it didn't. This is a dark market. They can't be seen from the outside."

"Dark market?"

"Leopard market," he said. "They're common. The ones in the U.S. are actual buildings that move to a different place every month. They're nothing like the ones here. The prices are set and things are just . . . sterile."

"Dark markets are like the market in Leopard Knocks but nestled on Lamb grounds," Chichi added. "This one doesn't move around, but some other ones in Nigeria do. This one blends with the normal market, but you can only walk into it if you are Leopard."

"Well, once in a while a Lamb will walk in," Orlu said. "Usually sensitive Lambs. Those people are never the same afterward." He just shook his head. "Nothing is perfect or absolute."

"Yeah, except Library Council rules," Sunny said.

As they walked, she could feel the hairs on her arm stand up. Only the rays of light that crept between the roof's tin sheets lit their way. Nothing looked any different, not to her eyes. However, Sunny was sure there were . . . things around them. Small shadows in the corners kept moving right outside of her peripheral vision.

"Can we at least *get* somewhere?" Chichi impatiently said after another five minutes of walking.

Sunny looked back and indeed she could see the way they'd come in, just barely.

"Did you see the size of that ghost hopper?" Sasha asked.

"The one standing in that sun beam?" Orlu asked.

"Had to be over a foot long," Sasha said.

"Wonder what it sounds like when it sings," Orlu said.

"It probably sounds like a factory," Sasha said. "The bigger they are, the worse . . ."

"Oh, screw it." Sunny dropped to her knees. "I can't take it anymore. Let's just try it here." She rolled the marbles like small bowling balls, and they tumbled smoothly over the dirt ground. "Come on," Sunny said, jogging after them. They followed the marbles, which had begun to dimly—then strongly—glow light blue.

They ran and ran. Passing wooden booths, tables, medians, and stands. All empty. The marbles rolled straight ahead, maintaining their speed. Soon the corrugated roof ended, and they were in bright sunshine. They passed more empty tables, but there weren't as many. There was a lot more space with even trees growing between the tables. Then there were no tables and only a dirt path that ran through a back alley. Sunny could hear the hustle and bustle of the Lagos streets not far away.

When the dirt path began to slope downward, the marbles rolled slower. They decelerated to a fast walk. Then a slow walk. Then the marbles stopped completely. Sunny bent down and picked them up, and they continued to glow brightly in her hand.

They were about eight and a half feet below ground level, red dirt overrun with green creeping plants on each side. Above and to the left was the side of a tall office building and to the right was a busy expressway with people walking along the sides. Sunny could make out people in the office building. A man looked out the window but he didn't look down at them. And on the expressway, people walked on the narrow sidewalk without so much as a glance below.

This was yet another Leopard space hidden in plain sight. Sunny blew her nose and then inhaled through a somewhat unclogged nose. If direct juju was involved, it wasn't with the use of powder, at least not according to her nose.

"Oh God," she whispered.

The path descended at a steadier, sharper decline a few feet ahead. And this led right down into what could only be Udide's lair. The cave looked like the yawning cavernous mouth of a great beast of black jagged rock. And it fit so perfectly into the ground that Sunny could only accept the fact that the cave had probably been there before Udide made it one of her many homes. Maybe it had always been there. *Yet only a small part of the city's population can even see it*, Sunny thought. According to Sugar Cream, only .05 percent of humanity was Leopard People.

"Might as well keep going now," Chichi said. "She certainly knows we're coming."

She's known for a long time, Sunny heard Anyanwu say in her head. Sunny felt a shiver go up her spine as she remembered her dream. Of all things, why a spider? Why, why, why? She imagined Udide scrambling out of the cave lightning fast, right at them, her movements like thunder. Udide wasn't just a spider; she was one of the Great Ones. She was an ultimate storyteller. She was a weaver. And she was a really excellent writer. Sunny had read more of *Udide's Book of Shadows* than its numerous spells that Sasha and Chichi were obsessed with. Udide wrote short stories, too. Sunny had been most fond of those. There was one in particular about an alien invasion in Lagos that she especially enjoyed. It was set in the past, a few years back, and it was funny like a Nollywood comedy . . . with aliens.

Yes, Udide was not just some irrational arachnid that ate flies and looked horrifying. The thought that she was a creature that could be spoken to and possibly negotiated with set Sunny at ease a bit. At least she could beg for her life, if it came to that. She felt Anyanwu nearby bristle at the thought.

The closer they got to the cave the more strongly Sunny could smell it. Smoky, acrid, chemical. Sunny frowned. "Like burning houses," she whispered. She'd seen a house go up in flames once in New York not far from their townhouse. Sunny had only been five years old when she'd stood in the crowd a block away holding her mother's hand. However, she would never forget the smell. She shivered at the memory. "Why does it smell like burning houses?"

"What else is a giant spider going to smell like?" Sasha asked. He tried to smile, but it was clear that even he was afraid.

When they got to the opening of the cave, the smell was almost like inhaling smoke itself. The marbles in Sunny's hands lit everything up. The edges of the cave were covered with thick webbing and when Sunny looked closely she could see that the webbing was peopled with tiny black spiders and dead insects wrapped in more white webbing. This was going to be much worse than sitting on the floor of Sugar Cream's office.

"You think those are her children?" Chichi said, looking closely at the cave's wall.

"Either that or her minions," Sasha said.

"I wouldn't get too close to the walls if I were you," Orlu said as they entered the cave.

The ground was free of webbing but not of spiders. There were tiny and not so tiny spiders all over the place. For a while, Sunny looked down as she held up the marbles and tried not to step on them. But eventually she realized that these spiders weren't stupid and were not about to allow themselves to be crushed. With relief, she stopped looking down.

The cave was cool and damp, the burning house smell stronger than ever. The wide path led even deeper beneath the city. Then it opened wide and high as it came to an end. When Sunny laid her eyes on Udide the Ultimate Artist, the Great Hairy Spider, she screamed.

Udide not only smelled like burning houses, she was the size of a house. She was black with a gray sheen in the marble-light, and her many eyes glowed a rich brown, like truck-tire-sized jewels. She was covered with stiff hairs. Her abdomen was bulbous, the better to weave with, and tipped with a great black stinger. She was on her back, the spiked tips of her eight powerful legs pressed to the cave's ceiling. And Sunny saw her through both her and Anyanwu's point of view, which meant she saw Udide on both the spiritual and physical planes. Orlu clapped his hand over his mouth. Sasha started hyperventilating. Chichi just stood there staring, slack-jawed.

Sunny's eyes were watering as the great spider wriggled slowly, twisting and turning her body so that her legs were on the ground. Then she stood looking down at them. Sunny had watched this process through blurred twitching eyes. Her heart felt as if it was trying to beat itself to death against her rib cage. Of all the things she'd seen since entering Leopard society—ghost hoppers, bush souls, the river beast, the lake beast, the infamous Ekwensu—this creature was the one who threatened to break her grasp of reality.

Udide crouched down, bending her legs to get a closer look at them. Seeing the great spider move again filled Sunny with a strange warmth. The world around her began to swim.

"Do *not* faint," she heard Orlu say into her ear as he held her up. He spoke firmly and slowly. "Get a hold of yourself, or we're all dead."

His words touched her and she fought her fear with everything she had. Her body wanted to curl up and shut down into a defensive sleep. *No, no, no, no, no,* she thought. She reached for Anyanwu but couldn't grasp her. Where had she gone? Sunny wished she could go back in time, before any of this. When she was a different person in a different world. When she wore her hair longer because it looked nice and not because Mami Wata preferred it long. When she wasn't doubled and had no idea that she *could* be doubled.

Then she felt the sting on her leg, and she screamed again. There was a large spider on her pant leg working its fangs through the cloth deeper into her flesh. She shuddered and swiped at it, dropping the marbles. She felt Anyanwu start with surprise, and when she looked at the cave wall to her right, she saw a dim golden glow spread over the surface. She screeched again, stumbling into Orlu. Her leg felt like a rod of heat. Orlu began frantically looking at the ground, as he held her. "Are there more?" he babbled. "Sunny, you okay?"

"No!" Sunny screeched.

Udide used a leg to grip her webbing, and then Sunny saw her throw the web at Chichi. It hit Chichi in the chest and she screeched, too, pulling at the thick gray sticky rope in the dim marble light. Sasha grabbed Chichi from behind, but Udide yanked her right out of his grasp and then proceeded to wildly wrap Chichi around and around in webbing.

"Nimm princess," Udide said. Her deep booming female voice shook the cave so hard that dirt and pebbles tumbled from the ceiling and the walls. The spider's every hair vibrated at the sound, and all the spiders in the area ran in circles at the sound of her voice. "Trouble. *Wahala. Kata kata.* Tricky strong women and strong sneaky men. You have taken something from me."

"Taken what?" Sunny screamed as she strained with pain. "We just got here! We . . ."

"The beginning is never the beginning," Udide said. Chichi was wrapped now from feet to neck and struggling uselessly.

Sasha pulled out his juju knife and threw juju at Udide. Whatever it was, it didn't even move one of Udide's many hairs. He tried throwing another juju and received the same non-result. He picked up a rock and threw it. It bounced off Udide like a pebble.

"There is no juju that can kill a spider," Udide said. "We are sacred."

"Sasha, stop it!" Orlu said, his voice calm. But his eyes were watering with tears.

"She's going to kill her!" Sasha screamed, his voice cracking. He looked around and spotted a spider. He stamped on it.

Udide angrily puffed out a great stench of burning houses.

"You don't like that?!" Sasha screamed. He grabbed his backpack and brought out a can of Raid. "You think you're smart? I'm smarter!" Before he could fumble the cap off, Orlu let go of Sunny to grab Sasha. The can of Raid dropped to the ground. The two tussled, but Orlu was stronger. He held Sasha's wrists. "Stop!" Orlu said, straining, as Sasha looked around wildly.

"Please!" Chichi said. "I don't know what you're talking about!"

"But your name does, DNA does, your molecules do,"

Udide said. "I should kill you myself instead of letting my people feast on you."

Sunny had fallen to the ground, her heart beating dangerously faster than ever. She stared at the glow pressed to the wall feet away; she could hear Anyanwu in her mind, though she sounded so far away that Sunny couldn't understand what she was saying. When Sunny spoke to the great spider, she could barely catch her breath and her mouth felt slow and gummy. "Udide . . . Ma . . . *Oga* Udide, we came a long way . . . We need to . . ." She felt another sting, this time on her neck. She could feel the scratchy spider scramble to her cheek. She groaned.

"Nimm warrior," Udide said. "Something is wrong with you, and that is interesting to me. You are two, but you both are one. They will take you next. Thieves. All of you. I let you live out there only because you people make for good stories, and you have the nerve to come down here and face me."

She wrapped Chichi some more and more, thicker and thicker. Chichi wriggled and wriggled to no avail.

"*Oga* Udide," Orlu said, moving forward with Sasha. He pressed his hand to Sasha's mouth, and Sunny heard him whisper, "Not a word." He stood up straight and spoke loudly. "My friend Sasha here is from Chicago, in the United States. He grew up on the South Side, in a place called Hyde Park. His grandparents are from Mississippi and participated fully in the civil rights movement, though they were more on the

Malcolm X side than the Martin Luther King Jr. side. They passed that down to Sasha, too. He's a fighter, born and bred through the racist fire that still burns in the United States of America." He paused. "He . . . he was sent here to Nigeria to stay with my family and me because his parents wanted to keep him out of trouble. He's too smart and rebellious.

"He is the one who found your *Book of Shadows.* And Chichi, there, Chichi is the Nimm princess you are wrapping up and preparing to kill. But she is Sasha's girlfriend, and she, too, is obsessed with your words and ideas. Both of them used one of your jujus to call an Aku masquerade at a party almost a year ago. Your teachings are good and effective, though dangerous to the reckless.

"Me, I have read parts of your *Book of Shadows*, but it is not your spells and stories that I am interested in. It is *you*, Udide. I've read a book called *The Book of High Beasts.* In it, you are cited as the true creator of destiny. You are one of the few who answers only to Chukwu, the Supreme One. There is a Great Crab who lives deep in the Atlantic Ocean whom you love and see once every millennium. The hairs on your body can change the passage of time. You and Mami Wata have inspired human rebellions on every continent."

"You know much," Udide said.

Orlu nodded frantically. "And . . . and this girl here, Sunny Nwazue. That is her name. I love her very much." He glanced at Sunny. She could feel saliva running from the side of her mouth. "Sunny recently met and freed the spider named Ogwu and her children."

"She did *not* free Ogwu," Udide said. "Ogwu freed herself. Ogwu saved your Sunny from a djinn."

"Sorry, Ma Udide," Orlu said respectfully. "You are right. But Sunny helped Ogwu free herself, and Ogwu sends her greetings to you from a place of freedom." He paused, taking a breath. "Please, Chichi is like my sister. Please. We have come here for a good reason. I know your kind can sting venom *and* the antidote to the venom into a person. Please do this for the girl I love and my . . . my sister. Don't let them die. Please." He calmly nodded his head and again said, "Please."

There was a long, long pause. Then Udide hummed deep, sending out a vibration.

Sunny heard them first. More spiders. Then she saw them. These ones were tarantula-like with hairy abdomens and wiggling tails on those abdomens. They scuttled up to her. Then she also heard the sound of their fangs puncturing the skin on both her hands. She gritted her teeth against the pain. Immediately, even that pain began to fade and she started to feel better. Her muscles loosened and Orlu quickly helped her up. "Okay?" he asked.

"Weak . . ."

"Fake it," he whispered. "She doesn't respect weakness."

When she straightened in Orlu's arms and looked up, she

was positive that the great spider was looking directly at her. Into her. With her many, many eyes. *Fffffff!* The smell burst from the spider in a soft powerful warm blast. The whole cave could have been filled with a thousand burning houses. Sunny fought not to cough and fought even harder not to sneeze. Udide dumped Chichi on the ground, and Sasha ran to drag the wound-up Chichi away from the giant spider. When he got to Orlu and Sunny, he tore at the webbing. Chichi quickly wriggled out like a caterpillar. "Goddamn insane bug," Chichi muttered, rubbing her arm. "I think one of those spiders left a fang in me."

"Shut up," Orlu hissed.

"Sunny Nwazue," Udide said.

Sunny felt as if her head would explode from the sheer vibratory force of Udide's voice. She held her head and as she did, she felt Anyanwu come to her. Then she did the only thing that she could do, even with her friends there. She brought forth her spirit face.

"Greetings, *Oga* Udide," she said, her voice low and sultry. She stood up straighter. She could stand on her toes. Udide would see her as poised and graceful.

The great spider gave off her stench again, and Sunny stumbled back. "Anyanwu," Udide said.

"Yes."

Udide stared at her. "I know you."

"I know you, as well."

"In this life, you've been doubled and you live. You're strong in many ways."

"It's a strange life, this one."

"I want to speak to Sunny Nwazue. Because she wants to speak to me."

The others stood behind her as she let Anyanwu retreat into her.

"We're here, Sunny," Orlu whispered.

"Yes," Udide said. "But what difference does that make?"

"We're her friends," Chichi said, stepping up beside her. She leaned heavily on Orlu, trying to look tough. "We'll suffer whatever she suffers. She's not alone."

"And we don't suffer without making others suffer," Sasha added.

"Sasha from America," Udide said. "My *Book of Shadows* found you, and it will kill you. That will make a great story."

"Don't worry. I know how to use it," Sasha said with obviously false bravado.

"That's not how your story goes," Udide said. "You will die by that book."

"No, he won't," Chichi screeched. "We've both used it! We're . . ."

"I only have business with this incomplete, damaged one," Udide said. "Sunny Nwazue, why have you come?"

"I . . . I need something from you. A flying grasscutter."

"What will you give me in return?"

Sunny thought about it for a moment. Then she said what she'd planned to say, especially after Orlu had just saved all of them by doing the same thing. "A story," she said. Udide's hairs rippled with what Sunny could only guess was delight.

"You know me well," she said. "But you must remember, I am storyteller. I am old. I've dwelled for years at a time beneath this city over many decades. Since its birth. I lie on my back and I put my legs to the ceiling of this cave and I listen to the vibration of Lagos. I listen to its millions of stories. And I weave just as many. Lagos breathes stories. It is life and death; it is many worlds in one. And I have done the same in many cities of the world. New York, Cairo, Tokyo, Hong Kong, Dubai, Rio. Tell me a story I have not heard."

The spider got down low in front of Sunny. She came very close, within a foot. Sunny felt her bladder try to let go. She squeezed and stayed where she stood. Her friends were behind her, but as Udide stared deep into Sunny's eyes with her door-sized eyes, Sunny was alone. Alone with a giant storytelling, probably immortal, hyper-intelligent, merciless spider.

"No," Sunny said. She felt Anyanwu inside her, part of her. "I can't tell you a story you have not heard. But I can tell you my own particular story. It's mine. Only mine. There is only one me in this world. So in a way, maybe yes, this is the only story of its kind." She took a deep breath and then began to talk.

"I lived the first nine years of my life in New York City." Her legs were shaking, and something in her said she should sit down. Her experience with Sugar Cream's office told her that there would be spiders on the floor, but these spiders were smart and she doubted they'd climb on her. Even the ones in Sugar Cream's office knew not to do this . . . unless they meant to. So she sat before Udide in the dirt of the cave. She turned to her friends and nodded. They, too, sat. Then, miraculously, Udide also settled. She did not sit, because spiders do not sit. However, she rested her legs a bit and puffed out her fumes and made a contented hum that seemed to come from deep in her abdomen.

Sunny shut her eyes for a moment and calmed herself. *Anyanwu*, she said in her mind. *Give me strength. Help me tell this well.* Once Sunny started talking, she found that it wasn't as hard as she thought to tell a giant spider and her best friends about the most painful day of her childhood.

I went to a Catholic school in Manhattan. My classmates were all kinds. You had Africans; African Americans; American whites; all kinds of Caribbeans; some Asians, mostly from India and Pakistan; multiracial; Muslims, Jews, Christians, Hindus. I should have fit right in. Mostly, I did. I had a lot of friends. But though we were all mixed up there, the other kids really didn't mix, you know? Kids stayed with their own kinds, especially black and white. The African people kept to them-

selves in my school. The African Americans acted like they were kings. And queens.

I sort of moved from group to group. I didn't fit in anywhere. I was African, but not really African. I was born in America, but not really African American. Half the time, I didn't understand African American slang. I had a bit of a Nigerian accent that I'd picked up from my parents, which was strange since I was born in America. I loved the Caribbeans, but we all knew I wasn't one of them, either. I was light-skinned like the whites, but my puffy hair and the way I look, I could never fool anyone.

This one day when I was in third grade was bad. Those older African American girls, I don't know why they hated me so much. They truly truly hated me. I think if I had been hit by a car and was dying in the street, they'd point and laugh and watch my slow death. Anyway, this day, I went to the bathroom during my lunch, and they followed me in there. They must have followed me. You had to ask permission to go to the bathroom, and there were four of them. No teacher would have let them all go at the same time like that. They snuck out. To follow me. It wasn't a coincidence.

I knew they were in there with me while I was in my stall. So I waited and waited. But I could see their feet. They weren't going anywhere. They were waiting, too. For me to come out. Anytime a girl would come in, they'd bark at her to go use another bathroom. Eventually, I knew I had to come out. I couldn't stay in there all day and miss my classes. So I flushed the toilet and came out.

These were sixth graders. Big ones. The leader was this overweight, very angry girl named Faye Jackson. She was always getting into fights with other girls in her grade. She'd only spit cruel names at me; we'd never fought. I don't know why they came after me this day.

I moved quickly to the faucet to wash my hands. They stood at the sink near the door, blocking any quick exit I could make. So I was forced to go to the sink farthest away from them, near the foggy window on the far side of the bathroom, farthest from the door. Bad move. As soon as I did this, they closed in.

"Why you so ugly?" Faye asked as they stood over me.

"She so nasty," one of the other girls said. Her name was Shanika, and she was never mean to me except when she was with Faye. "Shouldn't you be at the retard school?"

"At least away from us," Yinka said. Yinka was Nigerian, but you wouldn't know it the way she tried to hide it. She was very dark-skinned, too, except for her face, which she was always slathering with skin-bleaching cream. And when she wasn't, her mother was. You'd see her mother do it to her every morning when she dropped her off at school. "Wouldn't want any disease that would eat all my color like that," Yinka added.

I could feel myself getting mad. I needed to get back to class, and I didn't know why they were trying to scare me. They were standing very close, towering over me. I was only eight, and I wasn't very tall for eight. I've grown a lot in the last three years. And in the last year, I've gotten really strong and muscular, but back then, I was small, and they were all tall and big.

"It's not contagious," I muttered, my hands wet as I turned off the faucet. And that's when Faye slapped me on the side of my head. I stumbled as the world got really bright and I saw stars. She'd hit me really hard. For no reason. Without me even speaking directly to her.

I was angry as hell now. I'd been harassed before and it upset me, but never had I grown angry like this. I was in there alone. I hadn't done a thing to them. They'd pressured me to move into the far part of the bathroom while one of them stood watch at the door. I was like prey to them. Because what? I don't know.

"Dirty African booty scratcher," Faye spat. "Filthy diseased Shaka Zulu bitch. Yo' mama probably got AIDS and yo' daddy got syphilis, that's why you came out looking like that."

Yinka cackled hysterically. I couldn't believe it. What was wrong with that girl? Who was diseased?! Even at eight years old I knew when something was completely twisted. Shanika looked a little worried, but she didn't do anything to shut her friend up. The one at the door, whose name I didn't know, was peeking back into the hallway. The bell rang. Lunch was over. I felt more rage boil in me.

Faye was about to hit me again when I looked her right in the face. I was sweating and shaking, and that's when I saw it.

Right there on Faye's white pants. A large circle of red. Blood. My mom had explained periods to me earlier that year. So I knew exactly what I was seeing and why Faye was probably so angry. I knew many things in that moment. So I went for the kill.

"I'm filthy?" I growled. "You, YOU'RE the one who is filthy! Look at your pants. You're bleeding all over them. Phew! Stinking! Filthy akata*! Who are you?"*

The word was something my mother sometimes called African Americans when she was talking to her friends. Some told me the word meant "cotton picker," others claimed it meant "bush animal." Whatever anyone thinks it means, it is a nasty word. At the time, the way those girls were behaving, I was glad to call them "akata." *I'd have loved to see the pain in their faces if they then learned what the word meant. But a word like that, you don't really need to know what it means. The meaning is all in the way it's said, the sound of it. It's ugly. It's an insult. It's like a dagger that is a word. She was bleeding, and I'd just drawn more blood.*

She looked down and saw the blood on her pants, and a look of horror passed over her face. She was so embarrassed. The other girls looked embarrassed, too, and a disgusted look passed over Yinka's face. Yinka was just a mean, foul person, turning on everyone in two seconds. In all the years I'd known her, she was always the same. Mean, and loyal to only herself. Faye's embarrassed face changed then to that look girls get when they are going to destroy something.

I tried to run, but there was nowhere to go. They descended upon me. Slapping me in the face, pulling my hair, shoving me against the wall. Then Faye dragged me to the coat hooks. She was so big that picking me up was easy. I struggled, but the other girls helped, too. They hung me there by my sweater. I couldn't get down, no matter how hard I tried. They laughed at me, and then they left me there.

I was bruised and achy. My face felt like it was on fire, and my nose was bleeding onto my white sweater. My cheeks were wet and itchy with tears. I was so mad, but I was also ashamed and scared . . . scared of myself. Even back then I knew what I'd said was evil. I was American, too. And their history was connected to mine, even if it was not exactly the same. Faye's ancestors had made America what it was, built it with their own blood, sweat, and tears, by force. They'd suffered and persevered. She was the product of survival. I knew this better than my mother, who wasn't born there. And I shouldn't have made fun of that girl's shame, either. I knew what it was like to be made fun of and hated because of the way I looked.

But they hurt me. Just because I was African and had a defect. They, too, called me dirty. Why do we people from Africa always call each other dirty? Even I did. And why did they hate me so much? Why? I know why I confuse people. When people are confused, sometimes they get mean and violent. I wonder if this has anything to do with what I saw in the candle. Confusion.

"That's my story," Sunny concluded. She let out a long breath, not wanting to look up at the spider or at her friends who now knew something about her that even her mother didn't know. "You may have heard it before, or not. But this version is mine."

When she heard nothing for several moments, she looked up. Udide seemed to be staring at her, her fuzzy black mandibles working in and out and her many hairs rippled. She felt a hand touch her shoulder and then squeeze, but she didn't look back to see whose it was.

When Udide finally spoke, her voice was deep and booming but less harsh. "Yours is part of a long story of humanity," she said. "Always a treat to my sensitive hairs." She blew out the burned house smell and stood up and turned around. "Home, one's house, dwellings doused. In flames, sad games, you'll all be ashamed. It'll be the greatest story ever told and only those like me will see it unfold."

Sunny ventured a look at Orlu, Chichi, and Sasha. It was Sasha's hand that was on her shoulder.

"Sorry," she said to him.

"For what?"

"That word."

He shrugged. "If I'd been in your shoes, I'd have said a lot worse."

"Step back," Udide said. She'd moved to the far side of the cave. "To weave one, I'll need space."

"The flying grasscutter?" Sunny asked.

"Step back," Udide repeated.

She held up a leg and pulled webbing to the tip of this leg with another leg. Then she moved both legs away, and the piece of webbing hovered softly in the air. She brought another thread of webbing to that one and then something stranger began to happen. All of the hairs on her body rippled in such a fluid motion that it looked as if she were encased in water. Sunny shuddered and again felt her bladder contract. She could even smell a hint of salt water over the smell of burning houses. Another smell accompanied these two conflicting smells of fire and water. She could not describe it but she knew its origin. The strange smell and the presence of water—Udide was calling on the wilderness.

"Three of you, move away, unless you want to abandon your bodies and cross over," Udide said. Her voice rumbled and vibrated; rocks fell from the cave's ceiling this time. "Sunny-Anyanwu, you may stay or move with your friends."

Sunny stayed. She wanted to see this. She could feel it rising around her now. It was like standing on the rising surf of a large beach. It was rising all around her, gradually. Sunny blinked as her perspective doubled with Anyanwu's, but her attention was on Udide and what she was weaving. Udide was still black and hairy, but she was also turning red and growing larger. And Sunny could see another version of Udide juxtaposed with the other two; this version of her looked as if she were made of shiny metal.

Udide worked fast, wrapping more webbing around the suspended strand. It took the shape of a white sticky-looking sphere about the size of a tennis ball. Then Udide raised a leg and started spinning. It whirled, slowly at first and then quickly. Then the great spider really began to work. She attached and wove and shaped so quickly now that Sunny's eye couldn't follow it. And as Udide worked, Sunny saw some of the spirits around her stop to watch. One looked like the shape of a man, only he was nothing but oily blue light. He stood beside Udide, a hand on a hip. Then he raised his other hand, brought it to his chin, and seemed to blow. His breath was blue, and it wafted right into the thing Udide was weaving.

Another wilderness creature came and did the same thing. And as they each added these ethereal ingredients, Udide's creature began to shift and take on different colors. It went from being spherical to a blob with many appendages on the sides, top, and bottom. It also began to grow. From tennis-ball sized to the size of a horse and then to the size of a van.

Sunny had since moved back to join her friends, who were all gawking.

One of what Sunny had begun to call colored-spirit people came and blew at the large still-growing mass Udide was weaving, and Udide seemed to get annoyed and shoved it away. For some reason, this made Sunny's belly cramp with hysterics.

"What is wrong with you?" Chichi whispered, frowning at her. "Are you all right?"

Sunny only shook her head. "Maybe the leftover spider poison is making me giddy, I don't know." Her body certainly still ached. But this didn't stop the laughs that kept bubbling up from within her. When she looked up, she saw Anyanwu's dimly luminescent form perched upside down on the cave's ceiling, surrounded by spiders as she watched Udide weave.

"What is so funny?" Sasha asked. When she looked at him, he was smirking.

"This . . . everything," she whispered.

And that got Sasha snickering, too. Orlu tried his best, but he, too, was clearly tired and overwhelmed and terrified. Soon, his eyes were watering from trying not to laugh. Only Chichi sulked, her arms across her chest.

Sunny was laughing so hard that when the large hovering mass that Udide was weaving plopped to the floor, she wasn't afraid. She took a deep breath and tried not to think about the fact that she was deep in a cave beneath the city of Lagos with a spider the size of a house who was weaving some mass of webbing that was starting to wriggle.

She turned away from everything and looked down the dark cave. That helped quell her giggles. The marbles she'd dropped lit the cavernous cave well enough, but their light didn't reach down the tunnel for even a few yards. It was as if the light bent toward Udide. Sunny inhaled and then exhaled and inhaled again. She could feel each place where the spiders had bitten her to inject venom and then the antidote. Those spots felt itchy and were probably red and swollen. But she was otherwise okay.

"What a life I have," she whispered.

To her left, she could see about thirty large spiders on the cave wall scrambling into the darkness. To where, she had no idea and didn't care one way or another.

All four of them bounced as Udide lifted the great web-wrapped mass and then let it fall to the ground again. They coughed and scrambled together, grabbing each other as the cloud of dust rushed over them. Everything was light blue as the blue marbles that sat on the ground between them, and Udide and her creation glowed brighter in the settling dust.

"Oh my God, it's exactly how I imagined," Orlu said. "*Thryonomys volante*, wow."

"You *imagined* this?" Sasha asked, pointing at it.

"Disgusting," Chichi said.

The mass was undulating. The blue marble light only lit part of it. There was something inside. *Unt*, *unt*, *unt*, the thing inside grunted. It sounded like a giant pig. Udide scurried around the mass three times, laying three of her legs on it after each rotation. Then she plucked a hair from her back and stuck it into the mass like a pin, using two of her legs.

The mass calmed, and Udide let out a great billow of her smoky stench, which made Sunny's eyes water. Then Udide stepped back and waited.

"One of us has to release it," Orlu said after several moments.

They all looked at Sunny. She shook her head. "I . . ."

"Because we'll all die if we get close to it," Chichi said. "We can't survive the wilderness."

"It is safe now," Udide said. "Just like Osisi is safe for you all; I have pulled down the veil of the wilderness. The creature is mortal and alive."

"Then you go," Sunny said to Orlu. "You're the one who likes animals so much."

"Yeah," Sasha agreed. "Which one of us knew its scientific name?"

"Okay," Orlu said.

"We can't all go?" Chichi asked.

"No, only one at first," Orlu said. He crept forward and slowly walked across the great cave. It took him nearly five minutes to get halfway across. He stopped, his hands clenching and unclenching. Then he started moving them quickly in the air.

"What is that?" Sunny shouted.

"It's . . ." He worked his hands some more. "Never mind. I'm okay."

"He's undoing jujus," Chichi said.

"It's protected itself," Orlu shouted. "And . . . well, I think it's joking with me. But not in a good way. If any of you had been in my shoes, you'd be on the floor itching and screaming right now from the stings of Seven Stinger Mosquitoes."

"Damn!" Sasha said. "I used that juju once in the Leopard Library of Chicago because this guy shoved me aside to get a book we both wanted. The man hollered like crazy."

"It's not even out of its cocoon, and it's already showing it's got a sick sense of humor," Orlu shouted. "This is why it's best for only one person to approach it." When he reached the cocoon, he paused and stared at Udide. "I know exactly what he's feeling," Sunny muttered. There was nothing like having Udide's undivided attention.

Orlu was too far for them to hear anything, but he was clearly speaking to Udide. Then he stepped up to the cocoon and brought out his juju knife. Sunny could hear the cutting from where she was, sort of an unzipping sound.

"Oh my God," Sunny whispered when she saw the shiny gray-brown head pop out of and then rip through the cut Orlu had made. Its big head was round, it had round fluffy-furred ears and large round blue eyes. It had some sort of black markings on its forehead, but she couldn't see them from where she was. It didn't look much like the grasscutters she was familiar with, large groundhoglike rodents related to porcupines. It sniffed around with its great nose. It sniffed Orlu, who stood very still. Then it looked at Udide, started, and retreated back into its cocoon.

Udide brought a leg up and kicked the back of the cocoon, and the flying grasscutter grunted loudly like a pig and shot out. It came running right at Sunny, Chichi, and Sasha; its huge blue eyes wide with fear and shock. They all turned to run. Then Sunny heard Orlu's voice right beside her ear. "Get down!" And because she was so used to trusting her friends, Sunny dropped to the ground, landing on top of Chichi. Sasha dropped right beside them.

Foooo! The flying grasscutter lived right up to its name as it took off low enough over their heads that they could feel and hear its wake. Sunny looked up just in time to see it whip and snap its long furry tail as it zoomed toward the cave ceiling and then disappeared.

"Just wait," Orlu's voice said. When she looked back, he was standing there, his juju knife to his neck. He was using voice-throwing juju and specifying it to just the three of them.

"There!" Sasha said, pointing at the entrance to the cave that led into darkness.

The flying grasscutter stood with its backside pressed to the wall as it looked into the cave.

"It wants to run, but it's too scared," Chichi said. She laughed.

From afar, the great creature looked forlorn and kind of cute as it grunted and pressed itself to the wall. It was basically a newborn. What a place to wake up to—a giant spider and a dark cave full of smaller spiders. "I'd be scared, too," Sunny muttered.

"Don't let it flee," Orlu's voice said. He was walking to them. "If it flies into the cave, it'll escape and we won't be able to catch it, trust me. They are intelligent. It's made by Udide, so it'll understand any language. Talk to it or . . . something . . . *softly*. But hurry."

They walked over to the grasscutter. It stared at them, its nostrils flaring widely. The marble light was dim here, but it reflected its eyes and in that moment, Sunny knew she could gaze into them for hours. They were like jewels and they were kind, too. But there was something else about the creature's face as a whole that made her want to slow down. It wasn't just cute, it was sneaky and sly. This was verified when she felt the ground pulled from beneath her feet. She fell awkwardly.

Chichi also tripped and fell as a tree root came up from the ground right in front of her foot. She cursed in Efik as she stumbled. Sasha looked at them, then he chuckled. "Just go," Chichi said. "If you haven't fallen, then maybe the damn animal likes you." She tried to get up, but the root wrapped more tightly around her foot. Sunny knew not to bother and just sat there.

"'Sup," Sasha said to it. "I think I've got wha'chu need, dude." He brought his backpack around. He looked back.

"Orlu," he said, as Orlu came up beside Chichi and Sunny. Sasha motioned him to come. "See if it lets you."

"Are you guys okay?" Orlu asked Chichi and Sunny.

"Yeah," Sunny said. "I think it just likes Sasha."

Orlu looked and then took a few steps forward. When nothing happened, he kept going and was soon standing beside Sasha. The flying grasscutter looked at them both with narrowed eyes. It took a tentative step back, but that was all. Sasha opened his backpack and Orlu looked inside. When Orlu laughed, the flying grasscutter didn't flee as Sunny had been sure it would. Instead, it moved forward to see what was in the backpack.

"Sasha, you're a genius." Orlu said.

"It dawned on me this morning," he said.

When he brought out the first handful of grass, the flying grasscutter lapped it from his hands with a giant blue tongue. It chewed and as it experienced its first taste of "foodular" pleasure, its entire body shivered with joy. Sasha fed it some more grass.

"Come," Orlu said to Sunny and Chichi. Slowly they got up and came toward the beast. It eyed them suspiciously but inflicted no more juju on them. Sasha handed the backpack to Sunny. "Give it some grass."

It didn't hesitate to take the handfuls she offered it. She watched as it ate, noticing that it wasn't just gray brown. When Anyanwu appeared beside her, so dim that Sunny suspected only she saw her, the grasscutter paused in its chewing. It sniffed at Anyanwu and then humphed and continued chewing. Its brown fur was tipped with white filaments that looked like thick spiderwebbing. Sunny frowned and took a chance and stepped closer. It watched her as she reached forth and touched its furry cheek. She'd been wondering what it felt like. Was it sticky like spiderwebbing? No. It was soft. So very soft.

When Chichi fed it, the creature left slobber all over her hand. Orlu shook his head at her, and she swallowed what was surely an exclamation of disgust. Sunny could have sworn she saw the grasscutter's eyes twinkle. Chichi quickly moved behind Orlu and Sasha, fighting the urge not to rub her wet hand on her clothes.

"My name is Orlu and I am a human being," he said. "This is Sasha. This is Sunny. And this is Chichi. We are on Earth, a planet. We will show you. Can you read?"

Sunny thought Orlu had lost his mind, but then the grasscutter grunted, shoving its tongue into the backpack and taking more than half the grass.

"Good," Orlu said, smiling. "What is your name?"

Sunny gasped as the image burst in her mind. A huge field of green, green grass under a lovely sun in the sky. *Chop! Chop! Chop!* an enormous pair of flat teeth cut at the grass like a lawnmower.

"Grasscutter?" Orlu said. "That's your name?"

It grunted. Another image burst into their heads. They saw *Udide's Book of Shadows* suspended in midair. The pages opened up and flipped this way and that way until they found one of Udide's many stories. An image of an old man and a grasscutter in deep discussion rose from the pages. The old Efik man had a strong accent. His yam farm was constantly raided by a grasscutter and he'd had to travel into one of its burrows to negotiate with it. In the story the grasscutter had liked how the man said its name.

Orlu pronounced it the way the old man did. "Grashcoatah? That's how you want us to say your name?"

It affirmed a happy assent by blowing air through its nose.

Sasha laughed. "Oh my God."

"Well, would you like another name?"

The grasscutter grunted an obvious no.

"Okay, Grashcoatah," Orlu said. "We understand."

"Ow!" Chichi screeched. "Who pinched me?!" She looked at Grashcoatah. "You did!"

Grashcoatah grunted gleefully and whipped and snapped its ten-foot-long narrow black tail.

"Well, most of us understand," Orlu said. "Will you come with us?"

It took more grass from the backpack.

"We can show you more than more of this grass," Sasha said. "We can show you a place where the grass is different colors!"

Grashcoatah purred deep in its belly, its eyes lidded with pleasure.

"Don't lie to it," Orlu said.

"I'm not," Sasha said. "I heard that there are all kinds of weird grasses in Osisi."

The ground vibrated as Udide approached them. "This is what you wanted?" she asked.

Grashcoatah suddenly disappeared down the cave behind them. But Sunny could hear its soft grunting. The creature was still there.

"Yes," Sunny said.

"You will treat it well?" she asked. Sunny could sense the threat behind Udide's question. Saying yes was only a small part of Udide's request. If anything happened to Grashcoatah, they would suffer.

"Yes," Sunny said.

"Then go," Udide said. "But there is one thing." She pointed a great leg at Chichi and then at Sunny. "The venom of my people is in both of you now. It will never leave you. It has decoded and bonded to your DNA. I can find you anywhere. I will know where you are at all times."

Sunny shivered. In all the excitement, the ache of the bites had retreated to the back of her mind. Now she felt their heated ache again.

Chichi gasped.

"Yes, you know what I am talking about, Chichi. You

know more than you let on. You are not ignorant. Not completely. You have heard rumor. You have heard myth. You have heard gossip. You know who to ask. When you finish this quest, bring me what is mine. Go to your people and bring it back. This one, Sunny, she is of the warrior clan of your people. She will be your 'woman show,' your bodyguard. If you don't bring it back, I know where to find you."

Chichi nodded, her eyes wide with terror.

"Smart child," Udide said. She walked back to where she'd been when they first arrived. She turned onto her back and pressed her thick hairy legs to the ceiling. "Leave me. It's a new year. Lagos is the tangled web I weave."

The marbles rolled back to Sunny, and she picked them up. As they left the cave, escorted by a parade of the nastiest spiders Sunny had ever seen, Orlu explained to Grashcoatah that it had the power to make itself invisible. Then Orlu explained *why* it had to keep itself invisible. Grashcoatah, who glided above them, only grunted that it understood. Whether it would cooperate or not was something they'd have to learn when they exited the cave.

26

FLYING GRASSCUTTER

When they emerged from Udide's cave into the harsh sun, Grashcoatah took its first look at the world outside. It grunted and then hummed deep in its belly. It did a slow turn in the sunshine, its large feet stomping on the dusty dirt ground. Then it shook out its furry brownish-white coat.

In the sunshine, Sunny could more clearly see its strange brown and white-tipped fur. The white parts were light and feathery and almost floated as if there was a breeze when there was none. She could also see that its eyes weren't quite blue but a soft periwinkle color, like that of an alien ocean. Its eyes were lovelier than she'd initially suspected.

When it turned those mysterious eyes to her, she sighed.

Its gaze was disarming. Yes, mysterious ocean was the perfect description; when Grashcoatah looked at her, she felt the flow of the ocean. The wilderness. Sunny wondered if the others felt the same watery sensation when it looked at them.

"Do you like the outside?" she asked.

It purred louder in affirmation.

Sunny smiled and said, "Well, you haven't seen anything yet. But . . ." She glanced at Orlu and he nodded. "But . . . so that we can show you things and so that no one will harm you, you need to stay hidden."

Grashcoatah suddenly disappeared right before her eyes. Sunny felt her entire body grow alarmed. This strange van-sized rodent with strange hair had been standing before her, and then, without one movement, it was gone. No matter how much magic she saw as a Leopard Person, she couldn't seem to stop having moments like this. Moments where she felt her brain would break; her entire foundation of what is right and what is wrong, what is normal and what is not, what is possible and what is not seemed constantly on the verge of a complete meltdown.

Grashcoatah reappeared and then began to snort as it watched her. It was laughing. It knew precisely the effect its disappearance had on her, and it found this very funny.

"That is just wrong," Chichi said, but she was smiling.

"Sunny, you should see the look on your face," Sasha said. When she frowned at him, he stepped back, holding his hands before him, as he grinned. "I'm just saying, your reactions are so extreme. I can see why it'd want to scare the hell out of you. It couldn't resist."

Before she said anything, the beast stopped laughing and looked her square in the eyes. It stepped forward, and then it bowed slowly. The gesture was so charming, especially coming from a giant rodent, that Sunny forgot her anger. Grashcoatah nodded and then disappeared.

"See, no shaking," Chichi said. "It's going to cooperate."

Mmmph, the invisible creature said. It was right beside Sunny, judging from the blast of warm beast breath Sunny felt on the side of her face, blowing between her cornrows. Its breath smelled like the sweet incense her auntie in America liked to burn when she was stressed out.

"Thank goodness," Sunny said. She turned toward where Grashcoatah probably was. "Thank you so much! We . . ."

"Not yet," Orlu quickly said.

"Oh," she said. "Oh . . . we, um, we really, really truly appreciate your understanding." She frowned at Orlu. Grashcoatah only thought it was going with them to Osisi. If they didn't ask it now about *carrying* them there, then when? When they needed to leave? No one, not even a smart beast, liked to be asked such things right before the favor had to be done. But for the moment, she was relieved. At least they would manage to get back to her brother's friend's place more easily. How long had they been gone? A few hours? He'd be really worried.

"One thing at a time," Orlu said.

She nodded. At least one phase of their journey was behind them now; they were done with Udide. And now Grashcoatah was going to stay invisible and thus avert the chaos and disaster of a bunch of Lambs seeing what they'd only deem a monster.

Getting the flying grasscutter back to Adebayo's aunt and uncle's house was a nightmare.

It was such a ridiculous disaster that Sunny couldn't stop laughing and saying, "There is a haunted basement with all of our names on it waiting for us at the bottom of the Obi Library!" Then she'd laughed harder as the driver of the *kabu kabu* carrying her, Chichi, Sasha, and Orlu whimpered and whined as he stared into the rearview mirror and pressed down on the accelerator. Grashcoatah had a sick sense of humor and he (Sunny had just seen Grashcoatah fly overhead and, yes, Grashcoatah was *definitely* a he) had zero intention of staying hidden to the world.

At first things were okay. Strange, but okay. When they'd arrived at the back entrance to the market, about a fifth of a mile from the entrance to Udide's cave, they found the market booming. It was packed with people as if it were the middle of any non-holiday week.

On top of this, as soon as they stepped past the first couple of booths, Sunny's cell phone began to buzz like crazy as it received text message after text message.

"Are you kidding?" Sunny whined as she shoved past a group of women waiting in front of a woman selling large tomatoes.

Orlu grabbed her hand when she got through, pulling her closer. She felt her phone buzz again, this time indicating that she had voicemails, too. "No, I'm not," he said. "What do your eyes tell you?"

Her eyes told her what she knew was the truth. At least a day had passed since they'd entered Udide's cave. The New Year was well on its way.

"Udide loves a good story," Orlu said. "So why not thicken our own plot by throwing us off a few days?"

Sunny felt ill. She knew exactly what all her messages were about. She just didn't know how severe. Were they from her brother or her parents?

"Hurry up," Chichi said over her shoulder. Sunny and Orlu hurried after them. Chichi was right. Grashcoatah had told them he would meet them on the outside of the market. It was best not to keep him waiting.

The chaos began long before they made it out of the market. It started with nervous whispering and people losing interest in buying. Sunny caught snippets of conversation.

"Need to get out of here . . ."

". . . . the other way."

"Something near the . . ."

". . . if they're armed robbers, I have my cutlass . . ."

The four of them kept moving, and soon they found themselves fighting against a tide of increasingly terrified people. Sunny and Orlu grabbed a wooden pole as the deluge of people increased, sweeping past them. Some were screaming, all were rapidly fleeing. When the tide of people slackened, Sunny saw that Sasha and Chichi were clinging to another pole. They silently looked at one another and then broke into a run. When they emerged from the market, the normally packed entrance was deserted. The last few people were fleeing in cars, *okada*, and on foot. There was a great cloud of dust rising in the open area in front of the market, and Sunny's stomach dropped.

"You didn't!" Sasha shouted at the settling dust.

"Don't!" Orlu said. "Don't acknowledge him."

Sasha immediately understood, closing his mouth. He stopped running and walked back between an abandoned cassava-and-melon stand and a booth selling bunches of bushy green *ugwu* and water leaves. Sunny stepped up behind him. "Why would he do that?"

Sasha laughed. "He thinks this is all funny."

"I'll bet he landed in the middle of everyone and appeared for a second and then disappeared," Chichi said. "Just long enough to make people think they saw something and not be sure of what they saw. There are Leopard rules for beasts like Grashcoatah, too. If he causes too much trouble, the Library Council would come and put him down."

Sasha nodded. "Yeah, appear for a millisecond and let Nigerians do the rest. Y'all already superstitious as hell. An owl landing in a tree will cause a riot. It doesn't take much."

"We have to get him out of here," Orlu said. "Before people come back, out of curiosity."

"I have an idea!" Sunny said. She felt giddy, pleased with herself. "Sasha, Chichi, throw out two *Ujo*. Strong ones. That way all Lambs will be too irrationally scared of this place to come near. And since both of you can produce strong *Ujo*, we'll have a large perimeter around the grasscutter." She pointed at the *ugwu* and water leaves beside them. "It's not grass, but maybe we can get his attention with it. He's certainly never tasted it before. Orlu, you're good with animals, you approach him. I'll stand behind you with more leaves."

They all paused, looking at Sunny. Then Sasha grinned. "Nice one."

Chichi brought out her juju knife and worked an *Ujo*. Sasha did the same, throwing his in the opposite direction. Orlu grabbed a bunch of leaves. Sunny reached into her pocket and brought out some naira and placed it in the money box beneath one of the largest bunches. Then she grabbed some *ugwu* leaves and followed Orlu.

As soon as they stepped out into the open, Sunny heard Grashcoatah *humph* deep in his throat. Then he made a wheezing laughing sound. "I hope you've had your fun," Orlu said firmly.

Grashcoatah laughed some more, appearing slowly before them. He eyed the leaves they carried, his nostrils flaring as he sniffed toward them. He took a step forward, and Orlu and Sunny stopped.

"Just as you know how to read," Orlu said, "you know what will happen to you if you show yourself again. Here, this is for you."

"Pff!" Grashcoatah said, defiant. He rushed forward, and Orlu and Sunny jumped back as Orlu told Grashcoatah, "No, no, no! Not like that."

Grashcoatah stopped, eyeing them with his large beautiful eyes.

"You want this? I know you can take it. But we know this world and you do not. You carry Udide's knowledge, but you don't have access to it all. I know. I've read about your kind. We'll explain our world to you, we can show you books to read, we can tell you about foods you'd love to eat." He held up his leaves. "These are *ugwu* leaves and we Igbo people use them in *ogbono* and *egusi* soup. They have a nice taste and . . ." He looked at Sunny. "Hold them up!"

Sunny held up her bunch of leaves. "Those," Orlu said, turning back to the listening creature, "are water leaves. They . . ." He turned to Sunny with a frown. "Do you know what they're used in? I'm not a cook. I barely know *ugwu*!"

Sunny shook her head.

"It's used in *edikaikong* soup. That's an Efik dish." Chichi said from behind Grashcoatah. As Grashcoatah turned to look at her, she pointed at her chest. "I'm half Efik and half Igbo."

"Sunny and I are Igbo people," Orlu added. "These are human . . . ethnic groups. Do you know the word 'ethnic'? Tribes?"

Grashcoatah grunted and stomped his foot. Then he looked at Sasha who was standing by his side.

"I'm . . . I'm American," he said. He grinned. "African American. I have no tribe. Not one that I know of at least." When the Grashcoatah just looked at him, waiting, Sasha quickly went on to tell Grashcoatah the story of the stolen Africans, the thieving Europeans who stole them, the Native American peoples who got wrapped up in it all, and how he was a descendant of "all that bullshit."

Grashcoatah listened with complete interest and attention. Clearly, he loved stories just like his mother, Udide the Spider. Then Grashcoatah ate the *ugwu* and water leaves ravenously; he liked the water leaves much more and went on to eat every leaf in the abandoned booth. The four of them had to pool several naira together to pay for the creature's meal.

Sunny was relieved when they finally got the grasscutter to consent to fly with them back to Adebayo's house on Victoria Island. Grashcoatah agreed to fly above them while they caught a *kabu kabu*. As soon as Grashcoatah disappeared, they got moving. Who knew how long it would be before the creature had another urge to scare the hell out of the citizens of Lagos.

They'd had to walk about a quarter of a mile before they found a *kabu kabu* who would stop. Chichi and Sasha's *Ujo* spell was indeed strong and far-reaching. Up to that point, if there was even a person nearby, he or she would have such a look of terror on his or her face that none of them even wanted to speak to the person. There were several *okada* that had been abandoned by their terrified drivers as well. Sunny was relieved that none of them had crashed. And people driving cars kept coming and then making a U-turn and screeching off.

"Make na come in!" the driver shouted at them. He was a young man with a shiny bald head, a neat goatee, and a wild nervous look in his eye. "Heard there was something happening around here and where things are happening, there are people who need rides. But the closer I get to the market, the more I feel like I SHOULDN'T BE HERE!"

They jumped in the car and Sunny was pulling the door shut as he sped into a wild U-turn and drove them off, shouting something frantic in Yoruba and then whooping with fear. The farther they got from the market, the more the man calmed, and soon he was back to being rational. As he drove, he apologized over and over. "I've had a long day," he said. "I get you where you need to go, no shaking, no shaking."

As they drove, Sunny looked into the air. Just as she did, she saw Grashcoatah do it again. Just for a split second, he showed himself. A man on an *okada* must have looked up in time to see him. So had a driver driving a loaded truck full of oranges. It all happened in slow motion, every moment drawn out.

"Oh no!" Sunny said, turning to Orlu. "He did it a—"

The truck full of oranges was in front of them, and it swerved across the dirt median of the road into oncoming traffic. Two cars and an SUV dodged the truck as the truck's driver panicked and tried to dodge the two cars and SUV and, in doing so, lost control. Tires burning rubber, it whipped sideways and capsized, spilling oranges all over the road.

As soon as the truck lost control, the *kabu kabu* driver took them right off the road and screeched to a stop. It was in this way that they also witnessed the *okada* and its driver fly into the ditch on their side of the road and tumble into the tall grass. He jumped up and looked at the sky with his mouth agape. Then he looked at them.

"Did you . . . I saw . . ." He looked toward the chaos in the street and forgot the rest of his words.

Sunny was sure she heard the grasscutter's sneaky laughter from nearby. She even thought she saw some of the spilled oranges disappear. "That is so wrong," she muttered.

"At least no one is dead," Chichi said.

They all got back into the *kabu kabu* and were quiet for the rest of the ten-minute drive, and as soon as they got out of the car, the driver sped off without even demanding his pay.

27
QUICK CHOICES

Sunny breathed a great sigh of relief. For one thing, no council car appeared. This meant that Grashcoatah's indiscretions hadn't been severe enough to warrant punishment. Secondly, Adebayo's car wasn't there. Her brother and Adebayo were out. They hadn't seen Chukwu and Adebayo since the two had left to party on New Year's Eve. But what of the house help? What day was it? The stress settled on her shoulders again. What would happen if Lambs saw the grasscutter? *Really* saw him? For more than a millisecond? Once inside Adebayo's compound they stood there. Waiting. Then the dust in the large parking lot puffed up as Grashcoatah softly landed.

"What'd you have to go and do all that for?" Sasha shouted at him. "People could have died!"

More grasscutter laughter.

"Please," Orlu softly said, stepping in front of Sunny. "Have some rest, Grashcoatah. You've just come into being. I know you're tired."

Sunny heard the grasscutter grunt.

"Take a nap," Orlu said. "No one will harm you here. You are safe and it's nice."

A soft wind picked up and the dust wafted up on the side of the compound close to the house. Grashcoatah purred softly. Sunny could see the weeds growing there flatten as the grasscutter settled down. When he made no more sound, the four of them congregated quietly in the doorway.

"Grasscutters turn invisible when they sleep," Orlu said. "It's a protective mechanism. They sleep for about five, six hours after birth, so at least we'll have until nightfall. I think we should get out of here by then. Otherwise someone's going to see him. He can't resist the temptation to scare humans. He's smart enough to keep it short. But sooner or later he'll slip and we'll all end up in the Obi Library basement and he'll be plant food."

Sunny knocked on the door. If days had passed, the house girl who lived in the servant house might be inside cleaning the house or cooking a meal. When no one answered, they all sat on the staircase in front of the house. Sunny brought out her phone. Without bothering to read all the messages, she called Chukwu. It rang once before he answered.

"Chukwu," Sunny said. "Hi! I . . ."

"Sunny? SUNNY?!"

She held the phone away from her ear, his shout was so loud. "Yes, it's me."

"WHERE ARE YOU? Are you all right? Where have you been?"

"I . . ."

"Are you all right?!"

"I'm fine," she said. "We are at the house."

"Oh, thank God! Thank God, o!! I thought ritual killers had taken you! I thought you were dead! I thought . . ."

"I told you, we have nothing to do with any of that."

"What the hell are you are involved in, then?" he snapped. "You disappeared for two days! Is this even you?"

"Yes!" Sunny shouted.

"I don't believe you, o," he said. But he sounded calmer. "Why should I?"

Sunny's eyebrows went up. Two days. That was bad but not too bad. She slapped her forehead. Why hadn't she thought to check her cell phone's date?! Days of being so close to Chichi, Orlu, and Sasha were rubbing off on her. She was losing her reliance on technology by the second. "Did you call Mom and Dad?"

He paused for several moments. "No," he finally said.

Sunny's legs wobbled with relief as she leaned against the door. "Thank goodness," she whispered.

"I wasn't sure," her brother said. "I should have but . . ."

"I'm glad you didn't! I'm fine. We . . . we did what we needed to do but, Chukwu, there's more. We have to stay here longer."

"What? How long? School starts in a few days. I have to go."

"Then . . . then go. I can . . ."

"No. I go home when you do. Where have you been?"

"I can't say."

"Then where are you going?"

"I can't say that, either."

There was a long pause.

"I'll be there in five minutes. I'm with Adebayo. Since you all disappeared, we've been searching for you all over." He was silent again for a moment. He was not telling her something. She didn't ask.

"Okay," she said. "See you soon." She clicked END and turned to the others. "He's on his way."

"As long as they don't try to park the car on that side of the compound," Orlu said, pointing to where Grashcoatah was sleeping, "we should be fine."

Adebayo wouldn't stop giving Sunny strange looks. Sunny's brother had hugged her tightly, and she even thought she saw tears in his eyes. "I'm okay," she told him. "Really."

Chukwu only grumbled something and pushed past her to scoop Chichi into his arms. Chichi giggled as he hugged her, and Sasha looked ready to burst.

"I gave the house girls a few more days off," Adebayo said, unlocking the door. "Your brother . . . he owes me. We've been eating trash for two days."

After taking long showers, Chichi and Sunny cooked up a meal of *edikaikong* soup and fried plantain. They all ate and then watched a Nollywood movie on the wide-screen TV. Then the sun was going down. Adebayo was engulfed in video games on the huge TV, and he'd put on bulky headphones to experience maximum sound. Chichi and Chukwu sat on the couch too close to each other, chatting quietly. At some point, Sasha had left the room. Orlu took Sunny aside.

"We need to leave tonight," he said.

Sunny rubbed her forehead and sighed. "This is all moving too fast; I can barely catch my breath."

Orlu nodded, patting her on the shoulder.

"Maybe we can convince the grasscutter to take us when it's dark," Sunny said.

Orlu nodded. "But what if he refuses?"

"And what if he makes too much noise? What if my brother comes out to see what is going on? What if . . . Orlu, I can't go in that basement again," she said. She shivered, suddenly feeling tears come to her eyes. She hardened herself, thinking of the damage that had happened there. "I won't."

"Don't worry," he said, taking her hand.

While Chichi kept Chukwu preoccupied with her batting eyes and idle conversation and Adebayo played his game, Sunny and Orlu went to the kitchen and packed some of the food into their backpacks. They filled plastic containers with frozen jollof rice and goat meat they found in the front of the fridge, and Sunny fried more plantain. They also found packets of biscuits and bottles of water in the cabinet. Her brother and Adebayo had cleared out most every other cooked item in the fridge.

"That should be enough for a day or two," Sunny said. "Hopefully, it won't take longer than that. Sugar Cream says time is different in Osisi. You know how days passed when we were in Udide's cave for an hour? It's the opposite in Osisi. If we can get there quickly, we won't have to worry about it so much. When the timeless wilderness mixes with our world, time dilutes, I guess."

"Can you hold that?" he asked as she tested out her full backpack on her back.

"It's heavy but . . ." She hoisted it up higher. "I think I'll be okay."

"Remember, if this goes right, you'll be hanging on to fur, hundreds of feet in the air, *and* holding that backpack."

"I can do it," Sunny insisted.

Orlu laughed and shrugged. "Okay."

They both looked at the window. It was dark outside. Time to go. In the living room, Sunny saw Sasha walk past Chichi and Chukwu on the couch. He gave them a dirty look and came straight to the kitchen. Chichi turned to watch him pass. The ends of Sasha's cornrowed braids were undone, his shirt was rumpled, and he weaved slightly as he walked. And the grin on his face was enormous and almost scary. He was carrying his MP3 player and ear buds in his shaking hands.

"Go outside!" Sasha mouthed to Sunny and Orlu. He didn't want Chukwu to hear. Sunny nodded and Orlu pretended to look somewhere else.

"There isn't much to eat," Orlu said, his voice, too loud.

"Just need a drink," Sasha said, grabbing one of the smaller bottles of water. He took a big gulp as Sunny and Orlu watched him.

"Are you okay?" Sunny quietly asked.

"Come with me outside," Sasha said in a low voice.

Grashcoatah was outside. What had he done? She hadn't heard any crashes or crunches. Had he eaten the trees? Was he visible? When Sasha left the kitchen, they both quickly followed.

"We'll be right back," Sunny said to Chichi, looking her full in the eye.

"Okay," she said, returning Sunny's look.

"Everything okay?" Chukwu asked.

"I don't think so," Sunny said over her shoulder.

Adebayo cursed loudly, and they all jumped and looked at him. But Adebayo didn't notice. He couldn't even hear them with his headphones. His eyes were locked on the military game he was playing with several people online. The guy was in another world. Sunny rolled her eyes and followed Sasha to the front door.

Outside, Grashcoatah stood in the spot where he'd slept. In full view. His head peeked over the concrete wall that surrounded the compound. His haunches were tense, his lovely eyes were wide, his strange brown-white fur was puffed up, and his nostrils were flared. If a giant rodent could smile, this one was smiling. Sasha walked right up to the grasscutter and put a hand on his fur. The grasscutter nudged him with his head and Sasha laughed.

"He just flew me high over Lagos!" Sasha said. "He . . ." Then he again laughed. "He and I have something *very* important in common." He fiddled with his MP3 player, and it began to play Nas's album *Hip Hop Is Dead* out loud. The grasscutter's eyes grew wider and his fur tensed, and then he started doing something that caused both Sunny's and Orlu's mouths to fall open. Grashcoatah was dancing, swaying side to side, rippling his fur and undulating his body in a sort of wavelike motion. All to the beat of the music.

"He's a hip-hop head!" Sasha proclaimed. "I came out here and put in my ear buds and was listening to my music and next thing you know, he's breathing over my shoulder. I put the ear buds to his ear, and he just came *alive*!" Sasha laughed again. "You should have seen it. It was like seeing a baby hearing music for the first time. I played jazz, blues, some metal, country; he liked them all but nothing got him moving like hip-hop."

Grashcoatah did a slow turn as he made his fur ripple like tiny waves on water. It was almost hypnotic.

"So I figured, he was digging my music and in a good mood and all, so I asked him what we needed to ask him."

Sunny held her breath.

"You . . . you asked if . . ."

"Yeah, I told him we needed to not only get there, but we needed a dang ride. He's cool with it. He took me up to show me how it would be. Better than any roller coaster! Whoo!! Was awesome."

Sunny needed to sit down, and she sat right there on the ground. Grashcoatah bobbed his head to the beat, resembling anyone enjoying the beats of Nas. "What am I seeing?" Sunny whispered. "This is . . . this is so weird."

"Eeeeeeeeeee!" The girlish-sounding screech came from the doorway right behind her.

"Don't!" she heard Chichi shout. "Just listen to me!"

When Sunny turned around she saw her brother's bulky form walking toward the open doorway, dragging Chichi along as she tried to pull him back inside.

"He wouldn't listen!" she shouted. "He wanted to see and he wouldn't listen!"

"What the hell is that?!" Chukwu screeched. "What is THAT?!"

The grasscutter roared with shock and disappeared. But Chukwu had gotten a nice five-second view of him.

"What was that?!" Chukwu screamed again. His eyes were red and wide, sweat beading on his face. "It's still here! I can smell it! It smells like incense! WHAT WAS THAT?!"

They all stood there in silence. Then Sasha said, "We have to leave!"

"Right now," Orlu added.

"WHAT WAS THAT?" Chukwu shouted again.

Soon curious neighbors would look out their windows or come out of their doors.

"Grashcoatah!" Sasha shouted. "Reappear!"

A few seconds passed and nothing happened. "Please," Sasha insisted. "He's seen you. It's too late. All we can do is go. But we can't go unless we can see you."

More seconds passed and then slowly, gradually, the grasscutter showed itself.

"Chineke!" Chukwu screamed. He grabbed Sunny and tried to shove her behind him. "WHAT IS THAT?!"

Sunny fought him, trying to get in front of him, but he was too strong. "It's not going to hurt you," she said, trying to move past him. He shoved her back.

"It's a monster! It's a spirit! *Mmuo!* This is witchcraft!"

Spit flew from his mouth as he spoke, and his red eyes were glistening with shock.

The bottle of water in her backpack and the containers of food sloshed and shifted as she tried to push past him.

"Get on," Sasha said. "The council will be here any minute now!"

He climbed onto the beast's back. Chichi hesitated for a moment. "Don't worry," Sasha said. "His fur is really, really strong. I don't even think it's completely fur. You can yank it and he doesn't feel it. Come on!"

Chichi grabbed the grasscutter's fur and climbed up. Orlu looked at Chukwu. "We . . . I'll keep her safe. We have to go or worse things will happen, trust me. You've seen what you shouldn't and we'll suffer the consequences. Not you."

"I'm not letting my little sister on that thing! Where are you even going?! WHAT IS THAT THING?!"

"It's a . . . grasscutter," Orlu said. He looked as if he were trying to say more but could not.

"Grasscutters are the size of cats! That's HUGE!" His eyes bulged and twitched as he held on to Sunny.

"I know," Orlu said.

"Shit!" Chukwu screeched. "Look at the head!! *Kai!*"

"Please, we have to go."

"I'm not . . . I'm coming with," he said, still grasping Sunny's arm and walking toward the grasscutter.

Orlu stepped in front of him. "You can't! You don't understand where we are going. I . . . I don't know if you'll survive."

"I'm not letting my sister go somewhere like that without me!"

"Of all people," Orlu said, "*she* will be fine."

Chukwu looked at Sunny, sweat pouring down his face. She pleaded to him with her eyes. He turned back to Orlu. "If . . . if you can tell me where you are going, then I will stay."

When Orlu could not, Chukwu let go of Sunny and pushed forward, about to grasp Grashcoatah's fur. Lightning fast, Sunny made a decision and she felt Anyanwu come, settling just below her flesh. Sunny felt strong and aligned. She grabbed her juju knife and worked as fast as she could. She caught the juju bag in her shaking hand. She could hear a vehicle pull up to the compound gate outside. The council had arrived. She threw the *Ujo* at Chukwu. She hated to do it, but it was better than seeing him harmed. A Lamb would surely go mad or die in Osisi . . . or worse.

The terror that bloomed on her brother's face made her want to weep. Hadn't he been through enough in the last few weeks? His wounds from his beating weren't even fully healed. The patch of healing skin from where they'd cut his face twitched as he backed away from Sunny.

"I'll be fine," she said, tears falling from her eyes. "Remember that. Tell Mom and Dad that I'm fine! And I'll be back."

But her brother wasn't seeing her. She didn't know what he was seeing. But whatever it was must have been horrifying for he opened his mouth and hollered loudly, turned, and ran wildly into the house. She just stood there. Then she felt someone grab the collar of her shirt. "Sunny, get on!" Chichi said, leaning almost upside down to grab Sunny.

But Sunny couldn't get her feet to move. All she could see was her brother's face. How it had broken into terror and how he'd run off like a madman. Had her *Ujo* been too strong? Had she just driven her own brother insane? Suddenly, her vision blossomed and she felt herself pulled physically backward. Then it was like she was a passenger in her own body watching herself climb onto Grashcoatah. As soon as she was on, Anyanwu mentally shoved her forward and Sunny gasped, looking wildly around.

Sasha was seated at Grashcoatah's neck, Chichi clasping Sasha's waist, and both staring at her with open mouths. She felt Orlu's arm grab her tightly as they took off. Instinctively, Sunny grasped handfuls of the creature's hair, her mind still trying to hold too many things at once. Grashcoatah's body was hard; it reminded her of the thick hide of a pig or an elephant. But its strong hairs were soft to the touch.

When the grasscutter flew into the air, Sunny felt no exhilaration. As they zoomed high over the house, away from the council car that was sitting at the gate as the council police pushed the gate open, Sunny cried and cried. All she could see in her mind was the look of terror on her brother's face. It was a look that said he was seeing a monster. *I am a monster*, she thought.

Yes, it was juju, but he was her older brother trying to protect her from danger. And make no mistake, she was heading to a very dangerous place. And she'd forced him to flee like a terrified child. If that wasn't something only a monster would do, she didn't know what it was.

28
THE YAM FARM

They were on the run. There was no getting out of this without being arrested. They could not return home without facing harsh punishment. No matter what they discovered in Osisi.

For the first half hour, Sunny could think of nothing but this fact and the look on her brother's face. Then, maybe it was the feel of the wind blowing in her face, or maybe it was the smooth motion of Grashcoatah's flight, or maybe it was the sound of Orlu's rare delighted laughter. Whatever it was, it caused the veil of sadness and doom to lift from her shoulders. And soon she, too, was in awe of the whole experience.

Grashcoatah flew high in the sky where it was cool and

silent. His body was remarkably warm, so none of them was uncomfortable. And he flew so smoothly. It was not like an airplane slicing through the air. It was as if his very presence caused the air to part and give way. There was no loud wind, though they flew fast. They were heading northeast.

Grashcoatah communicated in his own way that he instinctively knew the way to Osisi. According to Orlu, who was best at understanding the beast, Grashcoatah could smell the way. They were invisible to the world around them. When Grashcoatah made himself invisible, they also disappeared as long as they held on to his hairs. Sunny could even feel it, a warm sensation that traveled up from his body. At first, Sunny welcomed this visual nothingness. She was just wind passing through the air, similar to when she glided.

Once they were out of the city, they all agreed that it was okay for Grashcoatah to make himself visible. The night was dark and they were over mostly trees and small unlit villages. Sunny looked at her cell phone. It said NO SERVICE AVAILABLE. Grashcoatah was quiet as they flew. Sunny wondered if he was worried about what the council would do when they caught him. In Nigeria, intelligent beasts who broke protocol by showing themselves to Lambs would face execution.

"Even if we make it to Osisi without getting caught, I don't know what I'm looking for," Sunny said.

"Well, at least you'll arrive there in the same way that you arrived in your dream," Orlu said. "By air. Maybe you'll remember the rest of the dream when we get to that same point."

"*If* we do," Sunny said.

Hip-hop music began to play. Sasha was holding his MP3 player near Grashcoatah's ear. Grashcoatah purred, gleefully flying in a wavelike motion.

"Haha, yeah," Sasha said. "That's more like it. Cheer up!" He turned to Sunny and Orlu, Chichi holding on to his waist. "All of you, cheer up. We're going to a full place! How many of our peers will be able to say that? And we're doing it while on the run from the law. This is stuff that books are made of, man. Live in the moment. Don't know about y'all, but I'm going to make the most of this. I want to see this Osisi place."

"Me too," Chichi said. "The council won't be able to find us there anyway. Not even the best tracking juju can find anyone in a place that is blended with the wilderness. Worst they can do is catch us when we try to go home."

Sunny frowned. This didn't make her feel that much better.

"One thing at a time," Orlu grunted.

"Correct, my man," Sasha said. "One thing at a time." He turned his music all the way up.

They decided to stop at a small rural village after flying for hours. The sun was coming up and it was beautiful. Sunny couldn't help thinking about the last time she'd been out at dawn—when she'd been released from the Obi Library basement. She shivered, thinking yet again, *I can't go back there.*

She couldn't use the GPS on her phone; that rarely worked even during normal times. At the moment, the time on her cell wasn't even working. Maybe it was something about the grasscutter or maybe it was where they were. Whatever the case, she was left to guess their location. They'd been traveling northeast from Lagos. Maybe they were in Ondo State or even Kogi State. Grashcoatah was flying so fast, and without the sense of wind they could have traveled much farther than she thought. Whatever the case, the village below was quiet, cassava and yam farms stretching beyond the small cluster of houses.

They were invisible as they landed beside a large pond. "Shhh," Orlu said as they looked around. "Anyone see anyone?"

"There," Sasha whispered. "In that yam farm." They all looked. About a half mile from the pond, past lush blooming farmland, an old man with a machete was bending over and inspecting the vines and tubers of his farm. Aside from this man, the place was quiet. The pond looked clean and peaceful, several of the farm plants growing right at its edge to sip the water. It was the kind of place that women used to wash clothes or bathe. This village was lucky to have such a healthy pond.

"He probably won't even notice us," Sunny said.

"Maybe," Orlu said.

"*Ah-ah*, come on," Chichi said. She appeared as she let go of the grasscutter's fur and began to climb down. "I will die if I don't get off this thing for a bit." Once on the ground, she stretched her back and looked around.

The others followed suit, though Grashcoatah stayed invisible. When Sunny got to the ground, her thigh muscles cramped up. "Argh!" she said, stumbling.

"Riding a flying grasscutter is good exercise," Chichi laughed.

"I'm going to be sore for the rest of my life," Sunny said, gritting her teeth as she pounded on her thighs to loosen the lean muscles. "I feel like I've been playing ten hours of soccer. I need to eat two bananas, at *least*."

"Grashcoatah, there are plenty of plants," Orlu said. "I see wild grass, weeds, and things. Don't eat the man's crops, please!"

Grashcoatah grunted in a way that sounded sullen to Sunny.

They sat in a dry patch of dirt near the pond and ate a nice breakfast of plantain, bread, and groundnuts. It was communal eating, and they were all so hungry that no one cared about the dirt. The best they could do was wash their hands in the pond before eating.

When they finished, Sunny walked to the pond. She

dipped her hands in its clear water, marveling at the tiny brown fish darting away. One came back to eat the dollop of *egusi* soup that had washed off Sunny's hand. She strolled along the edge of the pond, in the opposite direction of the farmer, watching the tall grasses closely for snakes. She'd never imagined she'd ever be in a place like this, at this moment, for this reason.

She looked out at the still waters. The pond was so calm. And so . . . big. *We should get out of here*, she thought. Otherwise someone would see them. There were bound to be people using it this early morning. She brought out her phone. The battery was charged all the way up but still no service. She considered reading the text messages from her brother and parents that had been sent when she was in Udide's cave. She shook her head. *No, I'm keeping all that out of my mind until I finish this.*

She was putting the phone in her pocket when she noticed the red snake inches from her feet. *No!* she thought, her body filling with adrenaline. *That's* not *a snake!* As soon as this registered, the tentacle wrapped tightly around her ankle and pulled. She fell back, dropping her phone as she banged her elbow onto a rock. A second, bigger tentacle wrapped itself firmly around her waist and squeezed. Before she knew it, she was underwater.

Not a pond. A lake. One that wasn't normally there. The old

farmer hadn't looked beyond his precious yams. They must have been in Igboland. Only an Igbo farmer would be so focused on his yams that he didn't notice that an entire lake had arrived with the morning sun, sitting a half mile away.

All this spun around in Sunny's frantic mind as she fought with water, the tentacle, and for air. As she ran out of air, she felt her spirit face pulled from her. Just like that. As if they were being whipped about in a tornado and could no longer hold on to each other.

Anyanwu! she screamed in her mind. No response.

Pain burst in her chest as she was pulled deeper. Bubbles escaped her lips. The light retreated from the surface. Water entered her mouth, her eyes, her ears. Something yanked her by the neck. Pulling her backward. *Plash!* She landed in living grass, flopping onto her back like a fish out of water. She opened her mouth wide. She had a mouth, but she still felt herself fading. And then she felt Anyanwu jump into her. She breathed; death had not found her yet.

"Where?" She quickly sat up, her body aching. She touched her face; instead of flesh, she felt wood. Her spirit face. But her voice was not the low voice of Anyanwu. She heard a flute play a haunted tune, and she moaned.

Ekwensu spoke with the low voice of an earthquake, gravelly like tumbling stone. It made all the hairs on Sunny's arms stand up, for she'd somehow carried her body into the wilderness. "When crocodiles walk on waters, the ripples are obvious," Ekwensu rumbled. "I am deep in the water, so you cannot see my open mouth.

"Meet Death, my close friend and ally," Ekwensu said. "It is good that I've brought you fully here. He would like to acquaint himself with *all* of you."

He appeared behind Sunny. She could smell him, like decaying carrion. She could feel him, cool and damp. She could sense him, for his presence absorbed all the sound around him—it was as if a black hole stood behind her.

"Face me, child," he said in the voice of her father. "I've been waiting to meet you properly. The wilderness is not a place I normally come to, for there is no life here. But you are a special occasion. *Face me.*"

"Why?" she asked. She didn't dare turn around. "What do you want?"

"You make me feel powerless," he said with a chuckle. "You die and return, and your body is still alive. You come and go, come and go. You are unbound, but you still live. Why does your body not die *here* after so many seconds? Who are you?"

Have to get out of here, she thought. "I don't know," she said, gritting her teeth.

"Turn around," Death commanded.

Don't turn around, Anyanwu said in her mind. Sunny took several deep breaths. She hummed as she exhaled.

"It won't be painful," he said soothingly, sounding like

her father. She missed him so much. "Turn around. Both of you."

She shut her eyes, touching her wooden face and picturing the ocean, vast and full. Just beneath the water, schools of fish and larger beasts swam, the water protecting them from the sun's harsher rays. The waves rippled, never still, never at rest because water was life. Sunny would break the surface and Anyanwu would cause more waves, more ripples—because she was alive.

"Surface," she whispered. Death was at her back, but she had to focus her mind to a needle-sharp point, just as Sugar Cream had taught her. Never had she brought her physical body to the wilderness. Who would purposely *do* that? Even when she glided, Sugar Cream said that the essence that was her physical body became light and invisible and stayed in the physical world. Now, the lake beast had pulled her completely through, or maybe Ekwensu had used the creature to do it.

Nevertheless, the process of getting her body out had to be the same as coming here as spirit. She called her name in her mind, *Anyanwu Sunny Nwazue*. She grasped her shoulders, giving herself a hug, and she glowed a strong sunny yellow.

She took a deep breath, one last one, then slowly she turned to Death. Just before she faced Death, she shut her eyes. And just as she did, she kicked herself back as if she were in water.

She heard the angry growl of Death as her body shot

away. Her momentum slowed and she felt herself falling to the ground. *Oh no!* she thought. Then she plunged into water. She flailed, shocked by its wetness and weight. Her body was glowing like the sun, piercing the aqueous darkness. She turned and came face-to-face with the surprised eye of the lake beast. She looked right into it. Then she grinned. Her body was still glowing a yellow white, blinding the great water beast.

She kicked with both her legs, swam at the lake beast's eye, and buried her fist in it. She felt something burst, and the lake beast roared and began to thrash in pain. It spun, slapping around with its tentacles. Then it twisted, pulling all parts of its body into a huge tight ball, and then shot off into the depths.

Sunny flailed in the water. Still glowing, though the glow was fading. She felt pressure in her chest. She needed air. She swam to the surface until her head broke it. She threw her mouth open and inhaled deeply. Then she sputtered. The closest bank was at least forty meters away.

"Sunny!" she heard Orlu shout.

Sasha leaped wildly into the water. Sunny had always been a strong swimmer, but she was tired and overwhelmed. So she did what she always did when she got tired in the water; she floated on her back. She looked at the morning sky. So clear. So alive. She blinked and coughed a tired laugh. There was Grashcoatah, hovering in the treetops near the lake.

"Are you okay?" Sasha asked when he reached her.

"Yeah."

He was swimming with one of the large empty water bottles in his arms. Keeping the bottle between them, he linked his arms through hers from behind and began to swim with her backward toward the bank. "I took some lifeguard lessons two years ago," he said as they swam. "Just relax your body. I'm not tired at all, so I can carry you."

Sunny was glad to do so, and in no time, he had her out of the water. Orlu helped her to dry land. "What happened?" he asked.

Sunny was about to speak, but then she noticed the old farmer standing beside Chichi. She looked at Orlu.

"That lake beast knew you were coming," the farmer said in Igbo. "Seen it here before, but now I know what it was waiting for."

Sunny's mouth fell open.

"He helped us fight it on land," Orlu said. "*Oga* Udechukwu is a third leveler. We'd be dead if he weren't."

Only then did Sunny notice the tentacles lying in the cassava garden beside the water. There were three of them, thicker than fire hoses and frozen solid, white mist rising from them.

"It pulled me into the wilderness! It was trying to kill you guys at the same time? Was there more than one?"

"The lake beast has three brains," the farmer said. "I studied it, its cousin the river beast, and several of their other kin extensively when I was a youth. Fascinating beasts. But they have a habit of aligning themselves with negative or evil people or forces." He sucked his teeth, looking at the lake. "I knew that lake beast was up to something. *Kai!* I can't wait to tell my wife. She was sure that it was just passing through."

The old man took them to his small hut of a home and introduced them to his wife, who gave them each cups of hot tea, since they'd already eaten. She also took Sunny's clothes and dried them using a combination of the sun and a hot iron. "No use in using juju when nature has a better method," she said. She gave Sunny a long colorful caftan to wear in the meantime. The farmer and his wife were Leopard People who'd decided when they were young that after years as Obi Library students, they wanted to live like their forefathers and foremothers. "There is more knowledge to be gained from reading Earth's books than any book in the library," his wife said. She was a rail-thin old woman with strong arms and crinkly gray hair.

Chichi sniffed and shook her head. Sasha kicked her to shut up.

"We're on our way to Osisi," Orlu said. "Do you know of it?"

"Osisi?" he turned to his wife. "You see, Nwadike? Look at how they dress. They must be from Lagos. All the way out here hours from the border? Where else would they be going?"

His wife sucked her teeth. "Kids today are always trying to make their lives so complicated," she muttered, getting up and collecting their empty cups. "Cell phones, gadgets, silly juju, and always running to Osisi."

The farmer turned back to them. "Why?" he asked. "Why do you want to go to that dreadful place?"

"We have to find something there," Orlu said. "It's not for enjoyment or anything like that."

"We've never been," Sunny added. "We just . . ."

"You *shouldn't* go," the farmer said. "It's not a place for human beings; I don't care if it's full. Why can't you four just live a simple wholesome life? Study your books, then find husbands and wives, have children. Stay out of trouble. Be positive forces to the world."

"*Oga*," Sunny said. "This journey is important. Did you see our flying grasscutter? We even went to Udide to . . ."

"Grasscutter?" the farmer said, jumping up. "You brought a grasscutter here?!" He ran out of the hut, looking around, his skinny knees knocking together. "Where is it?! My farmland, my farmland! It'll be the end of me. I know what those things do. Some stupid kids flew one here ten years ago trying to get to Osisi the fast way. They couldn't control it and it ate *everything*!"

"We told it not to eat anything, sir," Sasha said.

"Oh, those things never listen," the old man said. "You all have to go. Now, now, now, *biko*!" He gently but firmly ushered them all out. When his wife found out about the grasscutter, she, too, went into a panic and brought Sunny's clothes all folded and fresh. "Take the caftan, it's yours. Just get your beast and go, please!"

"Grashcoatah!" Orlu called. Grashcoatah flew down, landing in the same place he'd landed before, beside the pond that became a lake.

They all climbed on. "Sorry," Sunny said. "But if it helps, you see that he did not destroy your garden."

The farmer nodded. "For the moment. Grasscutters are known liars and equally known for their trickiness. Trust me when I say that you can trust a flying grasscutter as far as you can throw it. Be careful!"

Grashcoatah humphed, offended.

"And please consider our advice about living a simple life," his wife added.

"We will," Sunny said. "Will you be okay with that?" she asked, pointing a thumb at the lake.

"Oh, sure," the farmer said. "It'll move on now that it's done what it came to do."

"And since you punched it in the face," his wife added. They all laughed.

They flew off, leaving the farmlands. As they climbed into the sky, Sunny looked back at the farm just in time to notice the sleek black BMW pulling up to the hut on the narrow dirt road. Even out in the middle of nowhere, the council had found them. They'd escaped completely by chance.

"We just have to make it to Osisi," Orlu said. "If that farmer was right, we won't have to make more stops."

The grasscutter grunted with relief, and Orlu patted him on his side. "Don't worry. We won't let them harm you."

"We forgot to ask them where we were," Sunny said, minutes later.

"Does it really matter?" Sasha asked. "As far as I'm concerned, that was very much the middle of nowhere."

For hours, they all were quiet as Grashcoatah flew on. Sunny didn't know what the others thought about as they stared into the clouds ahead, behind, or to the side, but she was glad for the silence. A chill had fallen over her flesh, a headache at her temples, and in her ears she heard a high-pitched screaming. And in the back of her mind, like the powerful afterimage left if one happened to see lightning strike, she saw the image of Death. She hadn't looked right at him, but she'd seen him with her peripheral vision as she pushed back.

And she was still seeing it—a blaring whiteness that could swallow anything if you faced it. She'd been so close. She shut her eyes, stifling a sob that came from deep within. Ekwensu had been there, Death had been there . . . and she was falling apart. *And if I had looked at Death, what makes me Sunny would have died. And I'd just be Anyanwu. Which means I wouldn't really be . . .* She felt Anyanwu hiss protest at her thought, and Sunny sat up straighter.

But it took hours for the image of Death to fade and even when it did, it didn't fade completely. Sunny didn't think it ever would.

29
FULL PLACE

Sunny didn't know exactly when they crossed the border into lands that were full. There was no obvious line. But within four hours things had shifted . . . drastically. Below them were miles and miles of the lushest green rain forest Sunny had ever seen. A massive, thick blanket of treetops. From above, it looked like the top of bunches of broccoli. She was sure they had to be somewhere near the Cross River Forest. What other part of the country could look like this? But that wouldn't have made sense with the northeast direction they were going. She'd tracked this by the location and movement of the sun.

Then, at first she thought Grashcoatah had decided to fly

lower. However, upon several minutes of closer inspection, she saw that it wasn't that they were lower; it was that the trees were higher, much higher, and bigger. Monstrously gargantuan trees of a type she'd never laid eyes on. They were over a thousand feet in the air, and Grashcoatah now had to weave around several of them.

Grashcoatah stopped making himself invisible. "What are you doing?" Orlu asked. "Someone will . . ."

"See him?" Sunny asked. They both laughed uncomfortably. There were far stranger things in the air and on the ground and in the trees. She'd seen some sort of insectile creature as big as Grashcoatah flying in the distance.

"Look!" Orlu said as they slowly passed the highest mahogany tree Sunny had ever seen. Its rough trunk was wide as a house, and within its top leaves were red furry creatures that looked like something right out of the Muppets. They had long swinging arms, and the fur on their bodies was so thick that they looked like giant red puff balls. They were picking and gathering the softball-shaped light green mahogany fruits and putting them into cloth sacks.

Sunny blinked and looked again. The sight was all types of abnormal. As they passed, mere yards away, Sunny saw that their eyes glowed orange yellow like setting suns. One of them raised its hand and let out an ear-splitting howl as the grasscutter flew by, and all the others waved with their big humanoid hands. They had no fur on their palms. Sunny,

Orlu, Chichi, and Sasha waved back. From that point on, it was strange creature after strange creature.

There was the flock of hummingbirds and praying mantises, all matching bright green, that flew with them for ten minutes. Some hitched a ride on Grashcoatah's tail, much to Grashcoatah's annoyance. They made cheeping sounds and seemed overly curious about Orlu's hands, flying around them and landing on them when he held them up. Then they let a draft of wind carry them off.

There was the shadowy thing that peeked up from a dead part of the jungle below, merely a set of staring huge eyes. This thing reminded Sunny of the river beast. She was willing to bet that it was another cousin of the river and lake beasts and that the farmer had probably studied this beast when he was a student. She was glad when the thing did not leap up and try to snatch them.

They saw what could only have been a small masquerade sitting at the center of a palm tree top. Then a patch of jungle that was all slowly undulating giant blades of grass. A pine tree with white ants the size of small children running up and down its trunk. And a hill-sized pile of what looked like dumped garbage and smelled like it, too. They passed over the first town that looked like smoke and, even without Grashcoatah's indifference, she knew this was not the place they were looking for.

"You're sure?" Orlu asked as they passed over the cluster

of modern-looking houses that wavered in the breeze. Smoky, wraithlike people walked on the very definite paved roads. There were no cars.

"Yeah," she said. "What I saw in my dream was much, much bigger. It was like New York."

Soon the trees gathered again, and they were back over dense jungle. Sasha and Chichi were near Grashcoatah's head quietly having an argument. Judging from the way they were snapping at each other, Sunny knew exactly what the argument was about. The state of their relationship was the last thing she was going to think about when they were so close to Osisi, so she ignored them.

Orlu sighed. "How come there are no *people*?"

Sunny hadn't thought of that. She shivered. What if Osisi was just full of spirits, even though it was technically a place where one was in both the physical world and the wilderness? "We're in the air," she said, hoping she sounded convincing. "People would mostly be on the ground, right?"

They saw Osisi an hour later. From afar, it seemed to be a burning city enveloped in smoke. Sunny had lost track of time but judging from the setting sun, evening was approaching. The effect of the orange sky and the orange city wreathed in black-gray smoke was overwhelming. It was just as it had looked in her dream, and she experienced a moment of vertigo as dream and real world, physical world and wilderness, meshed together.

She shut her eyes and when she opened them, they were right at the moment of her dream where she woke up. She gasped. Osisi *did* look like the apocalyptic place in her dreams. Her belly dropped. They were flying right to it.

"Grashcoatah," she screamed. "What are you doing?"

Sasha was cursing and shouting at Grashcoatah, and Chichi was looking everywhere for a way to get off the flying beast.

"Everyone, just get down," Orlu said. "Cover your heads!"

"But, but, but . . ." Sunny babbled. She was sitting straight up, unable to tear her eyes from the burning city. Orlu grabbed her and pulled her close to Grashcoatah's fur.

"He's not suicidal," Orlu said.

Grashcoatah grunted annoyed agreement.

Then they flew through the first of the flames. It felt like being slapped with a bucket of water, except it didn't leave them or Grashcoatah wet at all. "Oh," Sunny whispered as she peeked through Grashcoatah's warm fur. The flames dissolved the closer they got to the city, revealing a skyline more spectacular than New York's. Osisi was surrounded by a large ring of green. Sunny frowned. There were boats moving in it; was it bright green water?

"'When you walk through the fire, you shall not be burned; neither shall the flame scorch you.'" Sasha recited. "The book of Isaiah, chapter forty-three, verse two."

Grashcoatah flew low, playfully touching the surface with his forepaws. No, not green water, water covered with bright green algae. Once they'd passed the first wall of flames and smoke, the sky grew clear and blue. Osisi was a giant megacity of glittering glassy skyscrapers, large colorful stone buildings, and bulky wide leafy trees that looked older than time. It was simultaneously ancient and modern West African. And even from a third of a mile away, Sunny could see that it was full of spirits.

The first building they flew over was a large stone hut flanked by two skinny, impossibly tall palm trees. The hut sat so close to the water that it looked as if it would fall into it. At the very edge, Sunny could see the bottom of the building where the land was crumbling away to reveal roots . . . roots from the *building*, not the tree. There was also a large greasy shadow looming over the building's shingled roof that actually shrank away as Grashcoatah flew by.

Above the buildings, Sunny could see several large winged, floating, gliding, swooping creatures. Some were landing on buildings, others just passing through. A large batlike creature clambered its way up the side of a tall skyscraper, tearing at the building's façade with its claw-tipped wings as it climbed. They even passed another flying grasscutter, and this delighted Grashcoatah so much that he nearly flew into a building.

"Where should we land?" Orlu asked.

"Where the tallest buildings cluster," Chichi said. "That should be the downtown area where the action is."

"But we're not looking for action," Orlu said. "Not really." He turned and looked to Sunny. "Do you have any feeling about anything?"

She shook her head. "I know this is Osisi. It's the place where I was going in my dream. We were in the exact spot from my dream, somewhere back there. I don't know what to do next."

"Let's get on the ground," Sasha said. "This place is awesome. I'm dying to see more. Did you see that tree covered with spiders?"

Sunny hugged herself. "This place seems like a good place to get killed."

Chichi laughed. "Something tells me that dying here is not the same as dying back home."

"I mean, do people, like, work here? Do they pay rent and have mortgages?" Sasha asked. "What the hell? Did you see that building that disappeared and reappeared a block to the left? It created a new space!"

Sunny rubbed her forehead. "Let's just get on the ground."

Orlu leaned close to Grashcoatah's ear. "You all right?"

Grashcoatah grunted.

"Do you like this place?"

Grashcoatah grunted again and happily rippled his fur. Orlu smiled. "But it's not all great, right?"

An image flowered open in Sunny's mind. Judging by the looks on the faces of her friends, Grashcoatah was showing them all the same thing. There was a man standing beneath a tree. A coconut fell on his head and before he hit the ground, the tree had bent down, caught the man, opened a mouth full of sharp leaves, and chomped the man's head off. Blood spurted from the opening in his neck as the body fell and twitched.

Sunny shut her eyes, but the vision was in her mind. She felt her body seize up, ready to vomit what she'd eaten three hours ago. "Argh!" she shrieked. "Why'd you have to show us that?" Her eyes watered as she tried to hold back tears.

Sasha was shaking his head, as if trying to dislodge and discard the nasty image.

Orlu was frowning very, very deeply.

"I get it," Chichi solemnly said. "That's a warning."

Grashcoatah grunted.

"Best to know how dangerous the place is," Chichi continued. "It doesn't look so scary from up here."

"Speak for yourself," Sunny whispered.

"Take us down," Orlu said to Grashcoatah. "And . . . thanks for the warning."

An image of Udide flashed into their heads. Grashcoatah knew what he knew because of his mother.

Grashcoatah descended slowly between two large houses onto a wide quiet road. They climbed down and looked around. The building they'd landed in front of that looked so much like a house appeared to be a small library, a sign with a large open black book sitting in front of it, flanked by green bushes heavy with black berries. There was not a soul walking up or down the roads, nor was there anyone coming out of any of the buildings, at least as far as Sunny could see.

"So quiet," Chichi whispered.

"Shhh," Sasha said. "Looks can be deceiving. Can't you feel it? Someone's around."

Orlu's hands came up and he held them before his face. Sunny felt her heart flip. Orlu's natural gift was instinctively undoing harmful juju. His hands were like a radar, raising and preparing to dismantle before the bad juju attacked. Something was at work here.

Sunny looked at the road. It was packed red dirt. A strange contrast to the modern buildings that loomed all around her. She frowned as a memory tried to burrow its way up in her mind. She absentmindedly followed the others as they walked up the road. A warm breeze blasted as they passed a building made entirely of glass. Inside the building, what looked like human beings in traditional Hausa attire bustled about carrying papers and sitting in cubicles that housed computers and desks. The breeze materialized into one of these Hausa-looking people at the front door, but the man didn't open the door; he simply slipped into the wall.

The wackiness of Osisi made Leopard Knocks look mundanely normal. Osisi was the Lagos of Leopardom in Nigeria.

Sunny wanted to climb back on Grashcoatah and close her eyes, but she couldn't. She was on the verge of something. It was the road. "There are no paved roads here," she said to herself.

"Yes, I noticed that from above," Orlu said.

She pointed at an enormous stocky tree with a bouquet of leaves at the top, biting her lip as whatever she tried to remember moved right to the tip of her tongue. "And that's a baobab tree."

Orlu nodded, saying nothing. Grashcoatah was beside her, looking closely at her face. Chichi and Sasha were in front of them giggling about something. Sunny didn't want to speak. She didn't want to move. She didn't want to breathe. It was right there. Something. Something . . .

The wind suddenly blew, warm and damp. When it stopped, they were in the same place but a different place. At least to Sunny. She was seeing as both Sunny and Anyanwu again. They were standing in the empty dirt road where office buildings, houses, and a giant fat tree jostled for space, and people within the buildings looked and acted like . . . people. At the exact same time, Sunny was surrounded by a busy market that went for about a block.

Yards away, there was a woman who was not a woman selling fruits that were not fruits. When a man stepped up to her and picked up one of the applelike non-fruits, it disappeared. There were old women perched atop two of the booths, hungrily looking down at customers. One of them pointed at a young man, and they all grinned and nodded. A man walking by chatting on a cell phone stopped and then quietly slipped into a tear in reality. Sunny's mouth hung open. She inhaled loudly. "Can . . . can you all see this?" she asked. Again, she felt ill. This place felt heavy, packed, it felt . . . full.

"See what?" Orlu asked. A spirit of blue light passed right through him to step up to a booth run by a woman who looked barely there. She was selling small bags of popcorn.

"It feels a little cooler," Chichi said. "That's all."

Grashcoatah was looking around frantically, trying not to step on things from two different places. So he saw the wilderness, too.

"I see . . . There's . . ." Then she remembered. A red dirt road. Down one of these roads flanked by tall buildings and trees and bushes. Modern and old. A sunflower-yellow stone house. Her grandmother had shown her the place in the message she'd left Sunny. The sheet of Nsibidi. Her grandmother knew Osisi. And the house, Sunny knew what it looked like. And now that she was here, she knew where it was. When she looked up, it all snapped into place. She'd been here before. When she read her grandmother's Nsibidi note. *The house!* she thought.

"I know where to go," she said. She stared at Orlu as it all flooded her brain. "I . . . I know where to go!" She stumbled to Grashcoatah and grasped his fur. He bent his head toward her. "You see it, too?" she asked. Grashcoatah nodded, moving closer to her.

"Where?" Orlu asked.

"See what?" Sasha asked.

Chichi wrapped her arms around herself, shivering.

"There's a house," Sunny said, trying to stay focused. The wilderness market was all around her. If she and Grashcoatah stayed where they were, "people" willingly moved around them. "It's not far from here. Grashcoatah, we will climb on you, then fly straight up."

They all got back on, and Grashcoatah flew straight up as quickly as he could. Below, the empty road of the physical world and the busy market of the wilderness mingled in a profound act of coexisting. Staring at it made her eyes and temples throb harder than they had since entering Osisi, but she looked anyway. The market stretched along the road for about a half mile. So, though it was in the wilderness, it still acknowledged the road in the physical world, for the booths were set up along its edges. Yet the spirits walked right through people who could not see them, like Sasha, Orlu, and Chichi. And why did they make Chichi cold?

"Okay, hold on," Sunny said to Grashcoatah. He seemed relieved to hover in the air far above things for the moment. In the distance a large green glowing centipedelike creature spiraled between two skyscrapers. Sunny wondered if the others could see it.

"What was happening down there?" Orlu asked. "I didn't see anything. Just empty road and quiet buildings."

"Me neither," Sasha said.

"I dunno," Sunny said, rubbing her aching temples. She was tired in the same way that she was when she read Nsibidi. *Anyanwu*, she called in her mind. *What is happening?* Though she continued to see in the double vision, Anyanwu didn't respond. Where had she gone? Tears fell from Sunny's eyes, her nose ran, and her heart began to beat fast. She sniffled and shut her eyes tightly. She took a deep breath. Someone took her hands. "Inhale," Chichi said. Sunny inhaled. "Exhale." Sunny exhaled. "Do it again, Sunny. Breathe. We need you to be strong now," Chichi softly said.

Sunny inhaled and then exhaled, and each time she repeated this, Chichi squeezed her hands reassuringly. She opened her eyes and blinked away her tears.

"She's gone again," Sunny whispered.

"What?" Chichi asked.

I'm incomplete, she thought. *Can't you tell?* However, she didn't say this aloud. Sunny only shook her head. "Why are we even here? I had a vision I *thought* was the apocalypse, and then some crazy lady who refuses to wear a shirt told me to come here. What is that?"

"Anatov says the universe guides us all," Chichi said.

"It's up to us to listen. The universe is pushing you here. You know it. Stop being a coward. You're a Leopard girl, you should know better."

"The world is much bigger than me, right?" Sunny said.

"Right," Chichi said with a smile.

Oddly enough, the phrase she'd been told over and over by her Leopard teachers and mentors, the phrase that had always seemed so callous, made her feel better in that moment. The universe may have wanted to make use of her, but its purpose was not to specifically harm her.

Chichi brought out her juju knife and held it up. Sasha did the same, then Orlu. Sunny brought hers from her pocket. When they touched them together, as friends touch wine glasses together in a toast, there was a large periwinkle spark and a jolt. One felt through the tip of one's juju knife as if that tip was part of his or her body. However, when they touched their knives together, it was like feeling with four knives.

Also, for a moment, Sunny saw through four pairs of eyes at once. She saw herself, Orlu, Sasha, and Chichi in ways that she didn't normally see them. She saw herself as yellow-skinned and yellow-haired, but different. She was herself, but she was beautiful. Was this how Orlu saw her? She saw Sasha as lighter-skinned with sharper features and a warm red aura wafting from him; this was Sunny seeing through Chichi's eyes. She saw herself again, her yellow features glowing like the sun, her spirit face not visible but looking ready to burst forth at any moment. This was how Sasha saw her?

The periwinkle spark hovered in the air as they pulled their juju knives away. They watched it as it rose a few inches. Then it burst into white light, startling Grashcoatah. He roared with surprise and rose higher. Chichi exclaimed something in Efik as Sasha grabbed her arm so that she wouldn't tumble off.

"It's okay," Sunny said, patting Grashcoatah's side. "It's okay."

He slowed his ascent and grunted. Sasha climbed to his ear and put some music on. "Here, vibe to some Jill Scott, classic," he said, playing a song called "A Long Walk."

Grashcoatah's ears perked up and turned toward the soothing funky beat. Sasha leaned on the ear, a grin on his face as he held up his MP3 player.

"There's a house," Sunny pushed herself to say. She scanned the area. "Oh!" She pointed. "There! I see it! That yellow house! Grashcoatah, do you see it? Go there!" She paused. That was the one, all right. "That's the house my grandmother told me about."

As they flew, she told them about the piece of paper her grandmother had left her. It was hard to explain how one "read" Nsibidi. "It's something that you kind of have to *do* to understand it." But the fact that she could describe the smell of flowers that lingered around the yellow stone house and its thick clear front door that was round like a hobbit's door convinced them quickly to just go with it.

In front of the house was a lawn of tall thick overgrown blades of grass. In her grandmother's Nsibidi note, the lawn had been short and kept. This one was like a large wild field between two large stone librarylike buildings. No one had been here for a long, long while. Before they could climb off Grashcoatah, he went to work and started eating the grass like crazy. *Chop, chop, chop!* He was like the happiest lawnmower on earth. He didn't notice when they all tumbled off him and ran to the side.

"Jesus, look at him go," Orlu said as they watched the grasscutter do what his name said he would do . . . cut grass.

"Check out his flat teeth," Sasha said. "Reminds me of Barney."

Sunny laughed.

"Who the hell is Barney?" Chichi asked.

"Big annoying purple dinosaur for kids on TV," he said. "It's got this super fake, constant grin of flat white monoteeth on the top and bottom."

Grashcoatah grunted with pleasure as he went at the grass. But Sunny was more interested in the house. Even the overgrown lawn. She shaded her eyes in the sun.

"Why is . . ." Chichi tapered off.

"I don't know," Sunny said. "It didn't look this big in the Nsibidi." She called Anyanwu yet again. No response.

The overgrown area surrounding the house was like its own prairie, as opposed to a lawn. The yellow stone house itself was significantly bigger than the librarylike buildings beside it. From where she stood, she could see a palm tree with a very bushy top growing out of the center of the house. It, too, was wide and expansive. But in the Nsibidi the leaves had been green and alive. Now they were tan and dried up. Had the tree died since her grandmother had been here? They crossed the wild grass.

"So *that* door is made from some see-through beetle's wing?" Sasha asked as they walked up to it. "The beetle must have been as big as an SUV!"

The door stood over twenty feet high.

"Bigger than that," Orlu said, craning his neck to look up at it.

"*And* it's impossible to destroy," Sunny said. "Or so my grandmother said." *But why didn't she tell me that the house belonged to a giant?* Sunny wondered. *Hmm, so one can lie or omit facts in Nsibidi.* A tiny gold *chittim* fell to her feet. She wouldn't have noticed it if she hadn't been looking down at her feet thinking and trying to piece it all together. She bent down, picked it up, and placed it in her pocket.

"What was that for?" Chichi asked.

Sunny just shrugged. The simple two-story house took up the space of four houses. It was flanked by two normal-sized living palm trees and a large angry-looking bush growing in the back. Sunny stood there, looking up at the place. None of it made any sense. She'd thought that her grandmother had given her the Nsibidi because she found this house beautiful, a peaceful image to show Sunny. Or maybe it was a place that she wanted Sunny to eventually visit. But what could *live* here?

A group of four women carrying large jugs of water on their heads walked by on the dirt road that passed in front of the expansive patch of wild plants. They waved at the four of them as they passed and Sunny, Sasha, Orlu, and Chichi waved back. One of the women cupped her hands and shouted something in Yoruba.

Sasha and Chichi laughed. Grashcoatah grunted loudly and did a slow turn and then stretched a leg, rippling its fur. Sasha stepped forward, answering back. *When did Sasha learn to speak Yoruba?* Sunny wondered.

"What are they saying?" Sunny asked him.

"They're admiring Grashcoatah," he said. "And they are impressed that we met Udide in person."

Chichi ran over to the women and spoke with them for a bit. Sunny turned to the door and touched it. It was smooth and domed out toward them like a thick unpoppable bubble.

"Whose home is this?" Orlu asked.

"I don't know," she said. "I can't figure out why my grandmother took so much time to tell me all about it. I know what's inside, where everything is. But how come she didn't tell me that the house itself is gigantic?"

"Maybe she didn't want you to know," Orlu said.

Sunny frowned at him.

"There's no juju keeping it closed," he said, nodding toward the house.

"The door?"

"Yeah. I don't sense a thing. What if someone's in there?" Orlu asked. "We can't just . . ."

"No one is in there," Chichi said, coming up behind them. "Those women said this place is abandoned. They don't know who lives in it or owns the property, but most people stay away. They said some of the local elders will know."

"Did your grandmother say anything about how to get in?" Sasha asked.

"No," she said. "The door just opened or something. I dunno."

Chichi brought out her knife and blew on the tip, made a circular flourish, and tapped softly on the door. Her eyes grew wide. "Ouch!" she screeched, jumping back.

"Heh, I had a feeling a simple door-opening juju was not going to work," Sasha said.

"Felt like it *bit* me!" Chichi said, rubbing her right hand as she held her knife.

"I thought you said there's no juju protecting it," Sunny said to Orlu.

"It's not juju," Orlu said.

"Ancestral land, then," Sasha said.

"Exactly," Orlu said. "Whoever's ancestral land this is is not human."

"Let me see your hand, Chichi," Sasha said, taking it.

"See the red mark?" Chichi said, her voice softening as Sasha stepped closer to her.

"I see," he said. "Want me to kiss it?"

Sunny rolled her eyes and Orlu looked away, uncomfortable. "*Na wao*," Orlu muttered.

They stood there looking at the door for a moment. "Well, if your grandmother liked Nsibidi so much, maybe she used it to open the door," Chichi offered. "Do you know the Nsibidi for 'open'?"

Sunny was about to say that she only knew how to read Nsibidi. But then an image bubbled up in her mind. She saw the door opening when she'd read her grandmother's Nsibidi note. Slowly it swung open like a thick dome of glass. She was playing the image again in her head when she realized there was a flash of something. "Wait," she whispered. "Wait." She replayed the image in her mind; there it was again. She held up a hand, closing her eyes. "Wait. Nobody talk."

She replayed it again, this time slowing it way down. Again, but even slower. And that's when she saw the symbol. Clearly. It was more than "open." It was stronger. It was tricky demand and force. Her grandmother had broken into this house when she'd come here. A heavy bronze *chittim* fell. She heard it clink against the door and felt it land on her sandal. She opened her eyes, slowly bent down, and picked it up. She looked up and smiled at her friends. "Did you know that the images Nsibidi creates when read can be separated from the symbols?"

Always swift with understanding, Sasha and Chichi made her job so simple. "So . . . if you remember the image, you can call back the symbols?" Chichi asked.

Sunny nodded, putting the *chittim* in her backpack.

"Oh, I get it. You were remembering the image of the door opening," Sasha said, nodding. "And in that image is the Nsibidi symbol. Clever."

"Nsibidi, de tin' dey cool," Chichi said, impressed.

"I don't get it," Orlu said. "But if you can open the door, open it, *sha*."

Sunny put a hand on the door's cool surface. She brought out her juju knife. She paused. The blade of her knife was nearly identical to the substance of the door. Was her knife made from the wing of a beetle from some distant land? She'd consider this later. With her knife, she drew the symbol she'd seen in her grandmother's Nsibidi on the surface of the round door. She worked slowly, carefully, holding the image in her mind as she tried her best to duplicate it. Gradually, the surface of the door pulled her knife to it like a magnet pulled steel. *Pop!* The four of them jumped back. Then there was a deep hissing sound as the enormous door unsecured itself. A few budding plants and roots growing over and inside the door ripped and fell, and dust and dirt rained down. The strange clear door opened like a reluctant mouth.

Hands up, Orlu led the way in, then Sunny, Chichi, and Sasha. Once they were inside, the door softly shut behind them. However, only Sunny vaguely noticed. They were too busy looking ahead.

30
ABOMINATION

They slowly entered the high-ceilinged main room. It was like entering a palace. The sound of their footsteps echoed off the intricately mosaicked walls. A closer look at the walls revealed that the fractal patterns were made from the tiny wings of black, red, green, and blue beetles. As she walked toward the center of the tennis court–sized room, Sunny felt the temperature increase with each step. Orlu came up beside her, his hands raised and ready to undo the juju that came at them. He lowered them. "It stopped," he said.

"What did?" Sunny asked.

"Something was about to happen," Orlu said. "And then it didn't."

"I'll bet it's because of Sunny," Sasha said.

Sunny looked down at the floor. It was smooth and glossy, as if it had been polished an hour ago. And it was tiled with millions of flat circles that could have been glass, plastic, or something else. They were arranged in a fractal pattern that made Sunny woozy when she looked at it for too long. She couldn't say what color it was because it used every color she could imagine. It was like a constantly blooming flower. At the center of the room stood the trunk of the fat dead palm tree that reached through the wide circular hole in the ceiling. The top of the palm tree probably kept the rain out, if it did rain here.

Hung on the walls were large ceremonial masks, intricate and expressive. It reminded Sunny of Sugar Cream's office, if her office were magnified by ten and the masks were creepier. There was one that hung on the wall that looked made of solid gold. It was as tall as Sunny and as wide as the expanse of her arms. Its face was thick-lipped, wide-eyed, and bulbous-nosed. Its lips were pursed and puckered as if it was ready to spit a lot of something. Sunny moved out of its range.

She moved on to the one that appeared full of water, the wall visible through it. It had the expressive round face of a smirking woman with Yoruba tribal markings on her cheeks. Sunny couldn't resist; slowly she reached out to touch it. She hesitated. If this place were booby trapped with juju, maybe she shouldn't. But she'd always been this way with gelatin, bubbles, and any liquid substance that took a shape. She couldn't help just one poke. Her finger sank right into it. "It's water," she said to herself. Yet here it defied gravity and hung on the wall.

There were four others. One made of wood, but it sprouted roots that created a mane around the roaring face. It also hung from roots that burrowed into the wall. The next mask was made of bronze. It was the head of a wall-sized dragon creature. One was a small boulder of stone with rudimentary openings that made two eyes and a tiny hole for a mouth. And one was made out of pressed garbage, plastic bottles, tin cans, crumpled paper, dried orange and banana peels, cassette tapes, and more. This mask took up the entire wall on the far side of the room. It was grinning.

Sunny wondered if the masks could call out to Anyanwu. "Where are you?" Sunny whispered, trying to calm her nerves. Anyanwu had said they were always one, but why wasn't she answering? Where *was* she? Sunny did *not* like the feeling of being in this scary house with these scary powerful masks without her. There were doorways on the left, the right, and the center that led to other parts of the house. All of the doorways were enormous like the front door. Everything was huge. *Whose house is this?* Sunny wondered yet again.

They entered every single room in the house and indeed, all were rigged with some sort of juju. And each time Sunny walked into the room, the juju disarmed itself. Had her grandmother embedded something else in her Nsibidi note? Sunny wanted to stop and figure it out, but the longer they were in this place, the more nervous she felt. Whatever she needed to find here, she needed to find it soon. Even if there *was* something protecting her, the fact was this place was full of jujus that were meant to harm all of them.

For an hour they explored. Sasha and Chichi investigated a library upstairs where they had to work together to bring down and open even the smallest books. Sunny remembered this place from her grandmother's Nsibidi tour; she could even smell the sandalwood.

"Oh man, these books are soooo forbidden," Sasha excitedly said. "Not even fourth levelers are allowed to see these!" He and Chichi had dragged a book the size of a suitcase from the lower part of one of the bookcases and when they threw open the cover, it was like a universe slowly swirled within the pages—a billion blue, yellow, red, and white stars rotated in the giant swirl that occupied both pages. Sunny backed out of the room as they knelt down to further inspect the strange book.

"Is that safe?" Sunny asked from the doorway.

"Doubtful," Sasha said as he read some words that were appearing in the page's edges.

Chichi had brought out her notebook and pen and started writing things down. Sunny looked for Orlu and found that he'd managed to get the giant front door open again.

Apparently what had closed it was simple juju that he'd easily undone. He was outside with Grashcoatah showing him a book from the house.

"Come and help me get Sasha and Chichi out of that library," Sunny called out the door. "They're looking at some weird books in there!"

"They're not going to stop no matter what I say," he said, holding the book for Grashcoatah. Grashcoatah grunted and Orlu turned the page. He looked at Sunny. "We'll give them a few minutes."

Sunny nodded and decided to look around a bit more. Upstairs she found a spacious room with shiny marble floors. It was completely empty except for the trunk of the palm tree that grew through the center. There was a corner near a gigantic window where sunshine streamed in. She sat here and let her body grow quiet. She didn't like this house at all, despite its artistic walls, library, and masks. Since entering the place, she'd had a bad feeling. But then again, she suspected she'd have a bad feeling upon entering any house that looked like the house of the giant in Jack and the Beanstalk, especially without Anyanwu. All she could think was, *What about when the one who lives here comes back?*

But this *had* to be the place she was meant to find. All things pointed here. The Nsibidi note her grandmother had left, her tricky Nsibidi book, the lake and river beasts, Ekwensu's passive-aggressive attacks, Bola, her dreams. "So now what?" she muttered. She sighed and, despite it all, found herself relaxed by the warm sunshine and the quiet solitude of the grand room. She tilted her face toward the sun and shut her eyes. Everything glowed red behind her eyelids. She heard soft buzzing. When she opened her eyes, a red wasp was hovering right before her face. She stayed still as it lazily flew into the room, its limp legs hanging down.

Sunny slowly got up, as another wasp came through the open window. Then another. They didn't pay her any mind as they flew toward the palm tree. Where were they coming from? *Maybe there's a hive on the side of the house*, she thought. Something buzzed and landed on the edge of her ear, and her body tensed. She twitched and slapped the side of her head hard enough to cause her ear to ring. When she brought her hand away, she saw that she'd crushed a large flying ant or termite. "Ugh!" she said, wiping the crushed insect on the wall.

She made for the stairs, her heart pounding. Something wasn't right. "Chichi? Sasha?" she called as she jumped down the stairs. "We should get out of here! I . . ." They weren't in the library.

"We're down here," Sasha called. They were standing near the front door. The ceiling and walls were swarming with termites, and Sunny spotted more wasps and a few mosquitoes flying around, too. Chichi looked particularly horrified.

"What's going on?!" Sunny asked, running to them.

"Wait," Sasha said, frowning deeply as he held up a finger.

Suddenly, Chichi screeched, turned tail, and ran through the open door, out of the house.

"Chichi," Sunny called. "Where are you . . ."

Outside, Grashcoatah suddenly roared viciously. Sunny and Sasha looked at each other and ran to see what was happening. They stepped out just in time to see the great swarm of termites wrap around the screaming Chichi and whisk her into the air. The grass looked like an undulating black sea. It was writhing with black ants.

"Ow, shit!" Sasha said, slapping his arm.

Sunny felt a sting on her calf. Her leg involuntarily buckled from the pain, and she grabbed Sasha's arm. "Are you all right?" Sasha said, his face squeezed from the pain of his own sting.

"I . . ." she said. "Are you?" She looked down and saw a bee still wiggling its stinger into the leg of her pants. She brushed it off and nearly screamed from the pain.

"No," Sasha said, looking at his arm. "My arm's numb!"

Over the sea of ants, the swarm of stinging insects whirled into a chunky shape, swallowing Chichi's screaming form. There was a shimmery blue cloth that appeared at the base of the roiling form, and gradually the cloth ascended over the hovering mass of termite bodies. It looked like it was made of silk and was the deep blue of the ocean on a clear day.

"Okay, that's the Mmuo Aku Chichi called up last year,"

Sasha said. The one that had nearly killed them all at the social during the Zuma Festival. Oh yes, Sunny remembered it clearly. Death by stinging. Orlu had sent it back but before it left, it had whispered something to Chichi in Efik that even weeks later, Chichi refused to tell Sunny, insisting that what the Mmuo Aku said to her was "private business." Chichi liked being secretive, and this annoyed Sunny so she eventually just stopped asking. Now that very same Mmuo Aku had shown up in Osisi, found them, and swallowed Chichi, taking her to goodness knew where. Sunny made a key decision at the same time as Sasha.

"What are you doing?" they said to each other.

"Stay here," they both responded.

They stared at each other.

"Don't go near the Mmuo Aku! But get out of there!" Orlu shouted from the back of Grashcoatah, who hovered above.

THOOM! THOOM! THOOM! Sunny's ears itched and her teeth chattered from the sound. The deep beat continued as the crisp tune of a flute laced itself around it. The tune was like a sweet-throated bird serving as the harbinger of death and destruction. Ekwensu was here. Ekwensu was here. Ekwensu was here.

Sunny and Sasha looked at each other. Then Sasha ran one way and Sunny turned and ran in the other direction. Toward the trunk of the dead palm tree growing in the center of the house. The palm tree trunk whose roots now bulged upward as a termite mound pushed through the soil. Sunny clenched her fists and felt her knuckles crack. And still, Anyanwu did not come. The world around her sparkled with shades of a thousand colors. The masks on the walls were looking at her. They had been watching her since she'd entered this place, she realized. She just hadn't really taken notice.

She hadn't noticed a lot of things. Like how the leaves of the palm tree that grew through the house were dry. *Maybe they were never green*, she realized. *Maybe the greenness in Grandmother's Nsibidi was another lie.* Sunny felt faint as she understood. Maybe her grandmother knew Sunny wouldn't come here if she knew this was the home of Ekwensu. *Not just home*, Sunny thought. *Ancestral land.* She thought of the ancestral land her father owned and how he and his brothers (such land was only passed through the men) fought over it like dogs. To build on one's ancestral land was to keep one's family name alive. It was immortality. One was most powerful on one's ancestral land. *But also most vulnerable*, Sunny thought. *Right, Grandma?*

Termites wiggled out of the rising bulge and flew about the large space. Something also started happening to the tree's trunk; it had begun to swell, water droplets forming and then dribbling down the smooth bark. The wood snapped and split in several places, but still the trunk continued to swell. The space took on the acrid smell of oil and tar as it warmed.

She could hear commotion outside—Grashcoatah roaring, a squishy sound, buzzing, Sasha giving a warrior's cry. Something large hit the front of the house where she and Sasha had been standing moments before. A blast of frigid air flew in, conflicting with the warm air inside. But Sunny's focus was on the giant tree in the center of the house that wasn't really a tree, not anymore. It had expanded by ten feet in diameter, now twenty, thirty, bringing down the ceiling above and then the roofing. Then bark fell away to reveal tightly packed and layered dried palm leaves. There Ekwensu stood. Again.

And now, for the first time, Sunny could see her face. Faces. At the top of the great mound of tightly packed palm fronds was a cloth hood of wooden masks. Sunny could see three of the masks, one facing her and one on each side, and there was probably one more she couldn't see. Like the Aku masquerade Chichi had called last year, each mask had a different expression; the one facing her was smiling.

Water began trickling down through the open roof. It was raining. With the deep rhythmic drum that was beating, Sunny hadn't realized that a storm had come in, too. The rain hitting the dried palm leaves of Ekwensu made the sound of a large audience clapping.

Ekwensu began to dance. She rocked her huge body of packed dried fronds back and forth to the musical flute, bringing down more of the house. Chunks of stone fell; some landed right before Sunny. She was afraid, so afraid. But she didn't move. She stared at Ekwensu with dead eyes. Ekwensu began to spin.

Sunny heard the crash of lightning and Orlu screaming her name. Something meowed loudly like a giant cat. There were spirits lurking all around the room. She could see them clearly as she'd seen the market over the empty road. There were glowing blades of grass in the walkway that swayed to the rhythm of the flute music and large blobby white shapes pressing into the corners. Something green cartwheeled away from her on her left, leaping into the open mouth of the gold mask.

They feared Sunny. Even without Anyanwu. What did that mean? But they were not her concern. Sunny stretched her neck as she watched Ekwensu preparing to strike. That's how she'd always operated, Sunny remembered. Sunny flexed her legs and rolled her shoulders, the way she'd always seen Chukwu do just before running onto the soccer field for a game. She touched the juju knife in her pocket and focused on Ekwensu's spinning body, squinting as she tried to see individual leaves. If she waited any longer, Ekwensu would be spinning too fast. Sunny held her breath and ran forward. *If I die now, I die*, she briefly thought. And she meant it.

There!

She grabbed on to the first frond her eye caught. It

crumbled in her hand, and she quickly grabbed another, reaching as close to the root of the leaf as possible. The velocity took her, and soon she was spinning. For several moments, Ekwensu didn't notice and Sunny took advantage of this, using her strong, strong arms to pull in her body and then haul herself up as the great masquerade spun. She saw a red bead like the one that had hit her between the eyes tumble from between the fronds and drop to the floor. Then another. She gasped, looking frantically for more. Hadn't Sugar Cream said if Sunny caught one of those beads she could end Ekwensu?

She saw another bead, but it was too far to grab. "Damn it," Sunny hissed, out of breath. "Can't get it!" Ekwensu was spinning faster now, and the beads were flinging this way and that. Sunny decided to ignore them and keep climbing.

Ekwensu had always been arrogant, Sunny knew. She had expected and assumed Sunny, naked and so young without Anyanwu, would run *away* from her, not *to* her. Ekwensu's dried-up leaves were wet, making them easier to climb. And they were tightly packed, so as long as Sunny grabbed the right leaf, she found purchase and hauled herself higher. Sunny felt all her muscles flex. She was made for this. She was like an Idiok baboon in a forbidden forest. She focused on the wet leaves to avoid dizziness. She was almost there. She had to move faster!

Suddenly, Ekwensu stopped spinning, red beads clicking and clacking as they hit the walls and floor. Sunny held on with all her strength and managed not to go flying. When she looked up, one of Ekwensu's faces was looking right at her. The smiling one. Its angry smile widened as the blank wooden eyes glared at her.

Ekwensu roared and Sunny felt the powerful masquerade's warm body flex in a way that nothing made of dried leaves ever should flex. For a moment, Sunny nearly lost all her faculties. How could wet dried leaves not only be warm but *feel* like some kind of . . . flesh? The contradiction made her woozy, but she held on. A black substance began to ooze from between the leaves in millions of hairlike filaments. Wherever they touched Sunny's body, they stung.

Sunny couldn't hold on much longer. And she could feel it; Ekwensu was about to fly off. Sunny glanced below. If she let go and landed just right, maybe she would live to face Ekwensu another day? This thought gave her little comfort. And then a swarm of dragonflies was whipping around Sunny's head. No, not dragonflies. One of them slowed down right before her eyes and she gasped. Nsibidi. Loops, coils, swirls, lines of living yellow script. One of them stopped right before her eyes, and she grasped its meaning: *Remember, I never leave you. Read this*, it said.

"Anyanwu?" she whispered. "Is this from you?"

Ekwensu's body swayed and then slowly, she began to spin again. Sunny grunted and hung on tighter, as she fought to focus on the Nsibidi symbols floating before her. They moved with her, and the combination of trying to read them while Ekwensu rotated made her stomach violently lurch. She gagged as she read, then saw, heard, smelled . . .

Forest, silt, craggy waters, all drenched with greasy black ooze. Sunny knew this place. She'd seen it on the news. *The bitter smell of dead rotted trees, sulfurous like a thousand farts. The place is silent because everything is dead. Then I saw Ekwensu bubble up from a great pool of black-brown mud surrounded by a ring of dying trees. Mud bubbling and blurping as she rose. Then she began to spin and one of her faces spat out an orange-yellow spark. It arced into the pool of blackened mud and the whole place went up in flames. I pulled back far enough to see the forest burn, then the nearby town, and another town, all as Ekwensu danced in the burning forest.*

Sunny stopped reading the moment she understood. The Nsibidi disappeared. Setting the recently oil-soaked part of the Niger Delta on fire was only Ekwensu at play. It was only the first thing that would happen if Sunny didn't succeed right *now.* Once Ekwensu really got started, she would turn the world into the apocalyptic place Sunny had seen in the candle's flame. Her eyes were watering, not from tears but from Ekwensu's fumes and the pain of the stings as Ekwensu spun faster and faster. Sunny continued to climb. Everything depended on it.

The deep drumbeats grew rapid and the flute crescendoed into a shrill screech as the weakening Sunny climbed up the side of the masquerade, her body threatening to give out under the searing pain of the masquerade's stings. She was between the smiling and frowning face. Both of them twisted down and tried to bite her. She leaned out of reach. She knew what she was looking for and moments later, she saw it: a small space between the packed leaves and the faces, the bottom of the mask.

With all the brute strength she had left, she grabbed the edge of the masquerade's mask and yanked. It didn't give. It didn't budge. She'd gotten so close, yet now she would die. Sunny had fought Ekwensu once long ago in a past life, in the wilderness. She'd used her juju knife because it was a knife like the one she had now—one that could travel with her into both worlds. She'd been of both worlds back then, as she was now. And back then, she'd defeated Ekwensu and sent her away. Then, a year ago, Sunny had defeated Ekwensu with magical words she'd remembered from when she was only Anyanwu. She'd used juju again.

And now here they were, a third time. And this time, Sunny had turned things on their head and fought Ekwensu in a way that Ekwensu had not expected. Not with juju knives and magic, but with hand-to-hand combat, physical strength. And Sunny had almost won again. Almost. But Ekwensu's mask would not come off.

Sunny pulled and pulled. Deep and guttural, Ekwensu began to laugh an awful ugly sound that forced nauseous images of smoke, fire, death, and blood into Sunny's mind. She felt her gorge rise. Then she saw the very image that she'd seen in the candle two years ago. It wasn't a small sight in the flame of a candle this time. It bloomed before her with a certainty that spoke to her soul and the memories of her ancestors and the dreams of her future offspring. She shrieked and pulled again. And pulled. And puuuuuuuulllllllled!

It gave.

Like her last baby tooth that had hung by a thread for a week. The mask had been coming off all this time, it was just that neither she nor Ekwensu had realized it. Ekwensu's mask finally slipped off. And so did Sunny. As she fell, she could see her arms. They were dotted with red marks from being bitten all over. The lean muscles on her arms bulged. When had she grown so strong? Her veined hands were clutching the enormous mask that was bigger than her entire body.

She fell and fell. It felt as if she fell for days. Maybe time in a full place was not only different from time in the physical world but had a way of stopping and starting and slowing at certain moments. Maybe. Maybe this was the case now because Sunny saw everything around her clearly. Hundreds of red beads and several large bronze *chittim* fell with her. She could see Ekwensu's body, the black filaments breaking off now, stiffening like threads of pencil lead, the wet dried leaves beginning to fall apart and crumble on their own. She heard Ekwensu's spirit music falling out of rhythm one beat at a time, one note at a time.

"Eeeeeeeee!" The screams of Ekwensu made Sunny's eardrums vibrate, but even worse, the noise was physical. Like a thousand pins poking into her skin. And the mask that fell with Sunny was looking right at her. Only one of the faces faced her. The surprised face. Its eyes burrowed into hers. Its black O-shaped mouth was impossibly wide with shock. And the knob on its head glowed an angry red as it let out white smoke. Then Sunny hit the floor and her glasses flew off. She was pelted with red beads as the mask landed on top of her, and both air and sense were knocked from her body.

Sunny's father belonged to the local secret masquerade society. She'd never thought twice about this until now. At certain times of the year, her father would go meet with "his people" and come back late at night. And during celebrations like the New Yam Festival, he'd be gone, too. Usually, his disappearance coincided with when the masquerades would parade down the road. "None of your business," her father had snapped when she was five years old and had asked him about what it was like to dress up as a masquerade.

"Well, maybe next time I see one, I will snatch its mask off," she'd said defiantly.

Her father had looked at her with the most serious expression she'd ever seen him make and said, "Never unmask a masquerade. You hear me? That is an abomination!"

So Sunny had learned this long before she knew a thing about Leopard society. The fact that unmasking a masquerade was forbidden was common lore among Nigerians. So after all that she'd become and all the deep African juju she'd learned while spiritually crippled, she'd defeated Ekwensu with brute physical strength and local knowledge she'd possessed since she was a little girl. She smiled, a laugh on her lips.

There was no house, no mask, and no crumbling masquerade around her. She lay on her back in a field. A field of grass. "Grass." It was a fresh light green, and it wriggled playfully beneath her. The sky above was no longer broken open and dropping angry rain. Instead, the sun shone. She sat up, a hand pressed on the soft but firm squishy blades of "spirit grass." And in the bright light, she could see everything clearly despite the fact that she wasn't wearing her glasses.

When she looked down, she saw that she had hands and a body and her skin glowed a brilliant yellow. She was wearing a scratchy raffia dress that went to her knees. It was nearly identical to the one she'd found herself wearing when she was initiated. Was this some sort of second initiation? Or maybe she had died and this was the attire of the wilderness.

"Whatever," she grunted as she stood up, her bare feet pressing down on the worm-like grass. "It is what it is." She was relieved when the grass didn't bite her. She looked ahead, then to her left and right. Nothing but miles and miles of wriggling grass. She sighed and the sound of it carried as if she were in a large room. She exhaled and her breath was a soft yellow. She didn't want to speak; to speak would disturb the peace of this strange place. The back of her neck prickled, and the backs of her bare legs felt warm, as if she stood beside a space heater.

Slowly, she turned around. Then she pressed her hand to her chest and fought to stay on her feet. Now she *did* feel as if she was dying. She had seen masquerades before. She had just faced, climbed, and unmasked one of the most powerful ones. Now she felt this way because she understood that the being she was looking at was just projecting itself as a masquerade, because it was far more than one. She knew who it was but the very idea was impossible. It was impossible. So she let her eyes tell her what she saw. She was seeing one far more magnificent, infinitely more powerful and encompassing than Ekwensu could ever be.

The Unapproachable Supreme Creator of All Things. Chukwu!

And sitting beside it was a figure made of softly glowing yellow. Anyanwu.

The yellow aura wafting from Sunny's skin grew brighter. She was trembling, her throat was dry, and her voice cracked when she spoke. "I greet you, Great *Oga*."

Chukwu was the size of a large elephant. It looked like

a haystack made of layers of blue, yellow, red, and green soft cloth and it had multicolored mist bubbling from the top of its head which was a four-sided ebony mask. And on each side was a curious-looking face. It didn't look cruel or kind, and each face carried the same inquisitive expression as it scrutinized Sunny. Where it stood, dark green vines burst from the ground, stretched several feet, went limp, dried, and crumbled to dust. Yam vines swelled with large tubers that deflated, grew moldy, and finally melted back into the wriggling grass. Plants sprouted, bloomed with white flowers, dropped the flowers, fruited, and died. As Sunny stared up at the creature, her eyes dried and began to burn. She blinked and blinked, tears rolling down her cheeks. Terrified as she was, Sunny also felt fascination. She was drawn to the creature. No. Not creature. So much more.

"Sit," she heard it say. The voice was neither male nor female. Had it even spoken? She took her juju knife from her pocket and placed it on her lap as she sat beside Anyanwu. Before her, it seemed to sink ever so slightly into the wriggling ground, more plants blooming, fruiting, and dying around it. It was "sitting." She caught a whiff of its scent—soil, fruit, decay, and rain. It was a good smell.

Silence. Sunny stared at it and it stared at her. A white plate appeared between them. When the kola nut materialized on it, Sunny almost burst out laughing, and, beside her, Anyanwu actually did laugh. It wasn't enough that Chukwu had turned its eye toward her, but now it was going to break kola with her? She stifled her urge to giggle.

"Kola has come," Sunny and Anyanwu recited.

Chukwu's face did not change, but Sunny felt that it was pleased. The kola nut sat on its tip and then fell into seven lobes. From within the haystack of cloth came a long, thick arm of raffia and beads. When Chukwu touched the plate, two raffia stalks wrapped around a piece of kola. Several blue and red beads spilled onto the plate. Chukwu placed the piece of kola into the mouth of the face in front of Sunny. *Crunch, crunch, crunch, crunch.* The crunching was so loud that Sunny thought her head would pop. She was so mesmerized by the noise that she nearly forgot her role in the ritual.

Both she and her spirit self reached forward and took a piece of kola. Chukwu took another piece and for several minutes, Sunny, Anyanwu, and the Supreme Being watched one another and crunched away on kola nut. The kola had a nice flavor.

After what felt like an hour, Chukwu's head began to turn and each face took a look at Sunny and Anyanwu. First one face, then the next, then the next, and then the fourth. This one squinted at Sunny and then opened its eyes wide. Anyanwu slowly disappeared, and Sunny felt her settle comfortably within her, more comfortably than she'd felt since they'd been doubled. *Chukwu invited me here. All I could do was push you to fight; you had to fight Ekwensu alone,*

Anyanwu said. And Sunny understood. One did not decline an invitation to meet with the Supreme Being. Not ever.

"When did you learn to write in Nsibidi?" Sunny asked.

"I don't know," Anyanwu said. "But I suspect being close to God can cause . . . revelations."

Chukwu motioned at her with its strange arm. It seemed to be pointing at her head.

"What?" Sunny asked, touching her face. "Here?" When it kept motioning, she touched the comb on her head. She pulled it out, and the face on Chukwu smiled. "This was a gift," Sunny said. "From Mami Wata." She held it out and Chukwu took it. In Chukwu's hands the comb broke, and the iridescent part of it fell to the grass as three large iridescent shells. Then the shells started moving, ghostlike snails with long, bulbous antennae pushing out and dragging the shells.

"Oh," Sunny said, watching the snails munch their way through the grass. Chukwu reached forward. As the arm came toward her face, there were two things she could do, flee or stay still. One didn't run from God. She held very still. When Chukwu's arm was inches from her face, she saw that it was tipped with what looked like a sharp needle. Sunny shut her eyes and gave in to her fate. Chukwu touched her forehead and the world exploded.

When the world came back together again, Sunny was in a coconut grove. She was standing, wearing the raffia dress, her juju knife in hand. The air here was light and when she inhaled, she felt it fill her chest and then leave through her nose. She was breathing. She was back in Osisi. She touched her face and found that she was wearing her glasses. And she was glad because in *this* sunshine, it was hard to see clearly.

She touched her forehead. There was a slightly sore spot in the center, but otherwise she felt fine. She frowned. When she tried to remember that part of her that was from over a lifetime ago, she couldn't grasp anything—not even the depth of her hatred and fury with Ekwensu. All she could recall was that they'd once fought in the wilderness and she'd used her juju knife.

The coconut grove was a few blocks wide and long. Like all the coconut trees she'd seen in Osisi, these ones were heavy with coconuts. Behind her was a tall skyscraper that looked as if it was made of blue marble. There was no sign on the building, nor did any of the windows have glass. Inside, the building looked empty, except for the occasional shadow that passed by. To her right were more trees. And to her left, past the coconut grove, was a librarylike stone building that she recognized. *Oh thank goodness*, she thought. *The house is just on the other side.* She felt blood rush down from her head and leaned against one of the slim trunks. There was a great crashing sound and a cloud of dust or smoke rose from the other side of the building.

Sunny froze as things grew quiet again. A coconut fell

from one of the trees beside her. Then another from another. Then another. She looked up just in time to see another coconut fall. Her body was so sore and slow that she couldn't react quickly enough. Just before the coconut smashed into her head, a large brown hand appeared and caught it.

Over ten feet tall, the being was humanoid with skin fibrous and rough like the husk of a coconut. Its long head's face was a mere imprint with no definition, as if its face were covered with a layer of coconut skin. It had long arms and long legs, and its shape seemed vaguely male. Gracefully, it handed the coconut to Sunny.

"Thank you," Sunny said, putting her juju knife in the large pocket at the front of her dress and taking the coconut in both hands. She'd been offered kola by Chukwu and now was offered a coconut by a coconut masquerade. What next? The masquerade stepped into a coconut tree's trunk and was gone. She put her coconut down and then did the cleansing flourish with her knife. The green wilderness residue that she left when she stepped to the side was so thick that it was like standing beside a solid green shadow of herself. She stared at it as it turned to her and seemed to stare back. Then it began to dissipate in the gentle breeze. When it was gone, she picked up her coconut and walked past the trees onto the street toward Ekwensu's land.

As she walked, others joined her, heading toward the noise. There were people who looked as if they'd come from her town, some who were dressed more fashionably like they were from Lagos, some who didn't seem quite human, and some who looked as if they were in the wilderness. Sunny was part of a crowd by the time she arrived at the house . . . or at least where the house used to be. It had crumbled into dust, leaving nothing but a tall lonely palm tree. The dust glowed like embers in a fire and was slowly disappearing back into the wilderness.

"Orlu!" Sunny shouted, pushing past the various people in the crowd. She decided to glide through them, feeling her body cool and separate in that strange way she was still getting used to. She flew through misty blobs and felt them question where she was going. *They're my friends*, she thought to them as she passed.

When she reappeared in front of Orlu, a silver *chittim* dropped and she caught it in her hand absentmindedly as she stared into Orlu's wet eyes. He was covered in the strange dust, and it glowed orange yellow on his skin like jewels. He twitched as his eyes met Sunny's, then his eyes grew wide. "Sunny?" he whispered.

Sunny grinned.

Orlu removed her glasses, placed both hands on her cheeks, and pulled her face to his. His lips were warm and the glowing dust on them made Sunny's lips tingle. Then he pulled her into a tight hug. "You were dead. We were sure you were dead," he said into her ear.

Over his shoulder, Sunny saw Grashcoatah standing to the far side of where the house had been. Sasha and Chichi were using their juju knives to cut long, long hairs that hung from his back and sides. At Grashcoatah's feet was a big pile of bronze *chittim*. He was nudging some of them with an inquisitive foot. Sunny frowned and let go of Orlu.

"I . . . No, I didn't die. But . . ." What was she going to say? That she'd broken kola with Chukwu the Supreme Being? What would that *sound* like? Would Orlu even believe her? She touched her forehead and for a moment, the world brightened and deepened. She took her hand quickly away from the spot. "I pulled off Ekwensu's mask."

Orlu held her away from him, put her glasses back on her face, and really looked at her. He touched her arm, rubbing a finger over the red marks from Ekwensu's stings. He brought up his hand and was about to touch the center of her forehead. She caught his hand. "What happened? Did something hit you there?" he asked.

Sunny shook her head.

"Then what is . . ."

"Sunny!" Chichi screamed, running over. Orlu stepped back, his eyes still on Sunny's forehead. When Chichi got closer, Sunny noticed that there was blood on her shirt and that her arms were covered with raised welts. Then Chichi was hugging her. She smelled of sweat and something sour.

"That Aku masquerade wanted to settle a score," Chichi

said. "It thought that it had a better chance of getting me when Ekwensu attacked you. But it hadn't counted on dealing with Sasha, the world's best bug killer." She laughed and slapped hands with Sasha. Sasha flashed a look at Sunny, his smile faltering the slightest bit. She glanced at Orlu and he looked away.

"Are you all right?" Sunny asked Chichi. "Where . . . The blood, where'd it come from?"

Chichi pressed her lips together in a smile and then shook her head. "I'm fine. Alive."

The various people who'd gathered began rummaging through what was left of Ekwensu's home. Some were actively eating the disappearing sparkling dust, others were scooping it into their pockets, bags, and even shirts. They cautiously kept a distance from Sunny and her friends, though some boys were standing around Grashcoatah. They were helping him gather the *chittim* he didn't seem to want and offering him handfuls of grass. Grashcoatah happily accepted the grass.

Orlu related the story of what had happened as they watched the people of Osisi collect the dust. The Aku masquerade had tried to pull Chichi into the wilderness so that Chichi could die while it watched. The masquerade saw Chichi's conjuring it at the Zuma Festival as an attempt to enslave it, and it hadn't forgotten the insult of such an attempt. It had probably been tracking Chichi from the moment they entered Osisi. Waiting for the right time to strike.

Only Sasha's quick desperate thinking saved Chichi as the masquerade swallowed her and prepared to cross over with her. Sasha had enhanced the common mosquito-repelling juju, wrapped himself with it, and dove into the swarm. Insects burst around him as he swam deep, deep, deep into the swarm of stinging biting ants, termites, bees, and wasps that were the physical body of the masquerade until he found Chichi. Horrified and defeated, the masquerade vomited them out and fled, but not before inflicting a painful wound on Chichi's chest. Chichi only felt it after Sasha had dragged her away.

"Turn around," Chichi said to Orlu and Sasha.

"Why should I?" Sasha said, looking annoyed. "I saved your life. And it's not like it's anything I haven't seen already . . ." He grinned. "More than once."

"Stop it," Chichi said, growing serious. "Just turn around."

Sasha and Orlu both turned away. Chichi stepped closer to Sunny as she looked around to make sure people were still more occupied with collecting the strange dust than watching her. Then she undid a few buttons on her shirt and opened the top. Sunny leaned forward to look. She gasped and stepped back.

"Sasha used some of the ants from the Mmuo Aku to close it up," Chichi said.

"Is that what those stitches are?" Sunny asked, through her hands covering her mouth. Her eyes watered.

"Yeah, they have big and strong biting pincers," she said. "You get them to bite down, then clip the body off with your nail."

"That's nasty," Sunny said, disgusted.

Chichi only shrugged. "Better than dying. I remembered Orlu talking a few years ago about ants used for sutures."

Chichi's swift photographic memory had saved her yet again. As she lay there with the large wound on her chest bleeding and bleeding, she'd remembered what Orlu had told her. Then she told Sasha to find the ants. He'd turned around and found a large group of them at his feet, almost waiting for him. "They *were* waiting," Chichi said. "I made them come and wait as soon as I could see them clearly in my head." Sasha and Chichi's natural gifts were always unclear to Sunny. But every so often, like now, she was in awe of their power.

When Sasha had rescued Chichi, swimming up through an avalanche of exploding insects, the opening to the wilderness just behind him, one of the Aku masquerade's insects had struck. Chichi said that she felt it crawl into her shirt and that it was large. But she was so focused on getting out that she couldn't do anything about it. It was big and it tried to cut out her heart. If Chichi hadn't fallen on her chest just as they emerged and crushed it, she would have been dead. It turned out to be a giant brown sticklike insect with razor-sharp front legs. It had cut a gash beside Chichi's heart that was two inches long. It wasn't too deep, so it didn't get to her sternum; the nasty bug was just getting started.

"And there was more," Orlu said. Ekwensu had planned to deal with Sunny without any interference. Thus, when Orlu and Grashcoatah tried to get into the house, several of Ekwensu's minions had attacked. They were shadowy and brilliantly colored spirits that could somehow affect the physical world, and they started with knocking Orlu off Grashcoatah's back. Then they tried to push Grashcoatah to the ground as well. Orlu had hit the ground hard and lost consciousness for at least thirty seconds. When he came to, there was insanity happening right above him.

"Grashcoatah was like Spider-Man," Orlu said. "He was hovering over me to protect me, and there were spiderwebs shooting from his fur! They'd wrap and wind around the spirits, and the spirits would fall wriggling to the ground and then dissolve, I guess, back into the wilderness." He shook his head. "Sunny, you might have been able to see where they went because you can see both places. Grashcoatah was amazing."

When the fight was over, Grashcoatah had many ropes of webbing hanging from his fur, but there was no time to pull or cut it off. There was a great flash from within Ekwensu's house, and everything went dead silent. "I'll bet people all over Osisi felt it!" Chichi said. Then Ekwensu's house began to crumble. With Sunny seemingly inside it, it crumbled to dust. To nothing. Nothing but a palm tree.

Sunny told her friends everything . . . Everything except the part about meeting Chukwu. That was hers. None of them asked where her Mami Wata comb was, and she was thankful. Let them assume that it had been knocked off when she fell from Ekwensu. Or something like that. It was better this way.

"So are you still . . . doubled?" Chichi asked.

Sunny nodded. "But I'm . . . we're okay with it."

The three of them looked at her skeptically.

As they flew out of Osisi minutes later, glad to leave the place behind, Sunny used her knife to crack open the coconut the masquerade had handed to her. She gave it to Chichi. "Drink," Sunny said. Chichi happily obliged and said it was delicious. Moments later, the wound on her chest grew warm and itchy. When it began to flake off along with the ant stiches, revealing new skin underneath, Chichi wept. "It hurt a lot more than I said it did," she whispered, wiping her tears. "I wasn't sure if I could take the pain much longer." Sunny broke the coconut fully open, and they shared the sweet, buttery meat. Even Grashcoatah ate a piece, though he preferred to eat the crunchy shell.

31

AND SO IT WAS DECIDED

As soon as Lagos came into sight, Sunny checked her phone. It was evening and in the darkness the screen of her phone glowed like a star. It had one bar of energy left. When she saw the date and the time, she laughed. She leaned back, her hand pressed to her chest. She shut her eyes. Only a few hours had passed since they'd flown away from her irrationally terrified brother.

Her relief only lasted a few seconds. She sat up. "If no one else is going to ask, I will," she said. "What are we going to do?"

"Let them whoop our asses and throw us in one of the other library basements where you haven't killed whatever is lurking in there," Sasha said.

Sunny gasped, whispering, "Oh God, we're all going to die."

Sasha shrugged. "What else can we do? Go on the run? I ain't. I've got an education to obtain. I'd rather just face the music . . . whatever it is."

"But what about Grashcoatah?" Sunny said. "Maybe he should have stayed in Osisi. There are more of his kind there, anyway."

"I thought about that," Orlu said. "But he'd never really be safe. They'll still eventually find him." He patted Grashcoatah's back, and Grashcoatah grunted. "We've already talked it over."

"You and Grashcoatah?" Chichi asked.

"Yes," Orlu said. "I wanted him to stay in Osisi, but he convinced me that it was better if he took the chance and tried to clear his name. He doesn't believe he did anything wrong; it was an accident. Really, there are moments of breach between the Lamb and Leopard worlds all the time. Someone sees, hears, or walks into something. And usually Lambs don't believe or understand what they see. No one gets punished for those because they're *accidents*. Well, this was an accident, too."

"True," Sasha said.

"It's still risky, though," Chichi said. "The council's rigid as hell."

"We have to state our case well," Orlu said. "Really well. Grashcoatah could lose his life."

"So could we, if they put us with something like that djinn," Sunny said. But she understood the difference. For Grashcoatah, death could be guaranteed.

"Sunny just defeated Ekwensu," Orlu said. "She sent her back into the wilderness, and now she can't cause the *apocalypse*. I think the council will take well to the idea that Grashcoatah helped make that happen. We need to explain things. Sunny's brother *had* to be with us, or Sunny wouldn't have been allowed to come to Lagos to meet Udide who wove Grashcoatah who took us to Osisi. You see?"

They all did. And so it was decided.

Invisible, Grashcoatah softly landed in the compound. They all climbed off, making sure to hang on to his fur. Adebayo's Hummer and Chukwu's Jeep were parked and the house was quiet except for the sound of the TV in a room on the second floor. It was close to midnight.

"Okay," Orlu whispered. "One, two, three!"

They all let go of Grashcoatah's fur at the same time. The warm breeze met Sunny's face. They were visible now. She could hear Grashcoatah quietly move to the side of the house. "Goodnight," she whispered. Part of one of the bushes disappeared and she could hear Grashcoatah chewing.

They rang the doorbell, Sunny standing in the front. She took a deep breath, holding on to the doorway to steady herself. Was her brother even *here*? Maybe they had taken him. Maybe he'd run off into the street and been killed by oncoming traffic. The door opened. He took one look at her. His eyes grew wide and his nostrils flared. Then he grabbed her into a hug. "Thank God," he said.

When he let her go, he looked at the others and they looked at him. He clearly wanted to say something. Then his mouth pressed shut. "Have . . . have you had dinner yet?" he finally asked.

They all said no.

"You and Chichi can go make it, then," he said with a laugh. "Adebayo and I haven't eaten, either."

They all went inside. Before following them in, Chukwu looked outside at the parked cars and the rest of the compound. Sunny stayed back and caught his shoulder. "Are you all right?" she asked.

He opened his mouth to say something. Then instead paused for a very long time, an uncomfortable look on his face, again. "I . . . I am now, Sunny," he said. "You should call Mummy and Daddy."

She nodded, bringing out her cell phone. She watched Chukwu join the others in the kitchen. From his behavior, it was clear. The council had performed a trust knot on him, yet they hadn't altered his memory. How much did he know? And why was he *allowed* to know? She called her parents.

32
REALIGNED

The drive back to Aba was different from the drive to Lagos. Chukwu gritted his teeth as he looked ahead at the road and mashed down on the accelerator. They were speeding down the expressway at eighty miles per hour.

"You might want to slow down," Sunny said. She was sitting in the passenger seat this time, and her seat belt felt like a flimsy piece of toilet paper over her chest. Chukwu's favorite album of all time was playing yet again, but in this moment, it was *not* helping matters at all. Track four of *Who Is Jill Scott?*, "Gettin' in the Way," belted out of the speakers. It added another layer of attitude to the foul one that Chukwu was cultivating.

"I know how to drive," he muttered, looking straight ahead.

Behind him, Chichi sat snuggled close to Sasha, his arm over her shoulder. They were looking at one of Sasha's books, whispering to each other, oblivious to Chukwu's growing rage. They'd been this way since Sasha had saved Chichi from the Aku masquerade. Chichi hinted to Sunny that there was something amazing Sasha had done while in the maelstrom of biting insects that had cleared her mind and reminded her of why Sasha was her "truest love." Of course Chichi didn't bother to explain even the most mundane aspects of this to Chukwu. That wasn't Chichi's style.

Sunny looked back at her, giving her a dirty look. "Stop it!" she mouthed when Chichi glanced up at her.

"What?" Chichi asked.

Sasha smirked, pulling Chichi closer as he looked Chukwu in the eye through the rearview mirror.

Sunny turned back to the front as Chukwu pushed the car to drive faster.

"You're not going to be able to get away from them by doing that," Sunny muttered.

"Yeah, but we'll get home faster," he said.

Behind Sunny, Orlu was fast asleep. He hadn't told her all that he'd been through with Grashcoatah, but it must have been something. He and the grasscutter had spent most of last night in quiet conversation, Orlu taking a mat and sitting beside the invisible creature, quietly speaking to him, and Grashcoatah grunting and sharing mental images with Orlu. Sunny had left them alone and gone to bed. Come morning, when she looked out the window, she saw Orlu lying on the mat, assumedly beside the still-invisible grasscutter.

To cover for his behavior, Chichi rather convincingly explained to Chukwu and Adebayo that Orlu was from some remote Christian sect where they liked to pray for hours outside and then sleep where they prayed. Nigeria was full of so many different types of Christians that neither Sunny's brother nor Adebayo thought anything of it. Sunny wondered what Orlu and Grashcoatah had spoken about as she watched Orlu sleep so deeply that he didn't notice the shenanigans among Sasha and Chichi and Chukwu.

Grashcoatah flew above the Jeep, invisible to the world. Sunny would have rather been up in the sky with Grashcoatah, even if it was drizzling. Anyanwu was up there, sitting on Grashcoatah's back, feeling free as a bird.

33
GRASSCUTTER STEW

An hour later, about halfway through the drive back, they stopped at a raggedy-looking shack on the side of the road. It looked as if the next rainy season would wash it away. The walls were made of worn-out wood, the roof made of tin. Behind and beside it were tangles of trees, bushes, and plants. There were no buildings to its left or right. The shack had no sign. Yet there were cars parked all along the roadside.

"What are we doing here?" Chichi snapped.

"Lunch," Chukwu said, putting the car in park.

"They serve food in *there*?" Chichi asked. "And you want to go in and eat it? *Kai!* Do you want to die of dysentery?"

Sasha snickered.

"Why not just wait until we see a better place?" Sunny asked.

"Don't let the look of the place fool you," Chukwu said. "I'm not just stopping here randomly. Adebayo told me about this place. He said it serves some of the best grasscutter stew he's ever tasted. He said the meat is so sweet you'd think they fed the thing chocolate for a year before they slaughtered it."

"Let's do it!" Sasha said, getting out of the Jeep. "My father had grasscutter meat the first time he came to Nigeria and hasn't stopped talking about it since. I want to try it."

Chichi got out, too. "I know good grasscutter stew. Let's see if Adebayo knows what he is talking about."

Orlu was still in the car, frowning. Sunny got out and opened his door. He didn't have to say anything; she knew what he was thinking and why he was frowning. She took his hand. "Come on. They are not going to be serving the meat of *flying* grasscutters. Just the regular kind. And you can eat something else. If it makes you feel better, I will, too. I've never liked eating grasscutter, even before we made friends with a giant flying one."

Orlu sighed and got out of the Jeep. They both heard a soft grunt directly above them. An image of lush bush bloomed in Sunny's mind. Grashcoatah was going into the bush behind the building to see what he could find to eat.

"Okay," Orlu said.

"How will he know when we leave?" Sunny quietly asked

Orlu, as they followed Chukwu, Sasha, and Chichi.

Orlu smiled mysteriously. "I'll tell him."

The grasscutter stew was indeed the best on Earth, at least according to Chichi. Sasha ate three bowls, Chukwu four. By the time they were all done, he and Chukwu were in such high spirits that they were talking and laughing at each other's jokes.

"It's like they are drunk on stew," Sunny told Chichi, as they walked out the front door. The owner of the restaurant had told them the restrooms were in the back. Sunny wasn't too confident about what she thought they'd find. If worse came to worst, she was content with going in the bushes.

"Well, it *was* good stew," Chichi said, picking at her teeth with a pinky finger.

"They make good *ogbono* soup, too," Sunny said. "With chicken."

"They just need to do some remodeling," Chichi said. "At *least* a sign for the place. Word of mouth can only go so far."

The sun was setting, but the heat of the day seemed intent on staying. The pepper soup Sunny had eaten was extra spicy. Not tainted-pepper spicy that left her tongue and mouth tingly while enhancing the flavor of everything else she ate, just a normal type of spicy that warmed every part of her and cleared out her sinuses. This warmth mixed with the heat of outside made her feel a little dizzy.

As soon as they walked to the side of the shack, the chatter from the filled dining room receded. The grass here was tall and unkempt, a narrow path through it roughly hacked. When they got to the back, the grass was shorter. Sunny expected to see Grashcoatah at work here making the grass even shorter, but he was nowhere in sight.

On the back of the shack was a large door with garbage bags on both sides of it. The door was ajar, and Sunny heard the clink and splash of cutlery, cups, and dishes being washed. There was a small clearing of dirt directly behind the shack where a large thick wooden table sat. Behind the table were three red outhouses with tin roofs. And behind the outhouses, more trees and bushes grew.

"Disgusting," Chichi said, stepping up to the large table. It was slick with congealing and dried blood, bits of meat (there was even a chopped-off paw), and milling flies. "I hope this isn't where they cut the meat they use in the restaurant."

"It probably is," Sunny said, the food in her belly rolling.

Chichi picked up the grasscutter paw and held it up.

"Ugh!" Sunny said "How can you touch th—"

Click. Click, clack, click.

Chichi looked past Sunny and her eyes grew wide. "Oh my God."

Sunny stared at the source of the clicking. Then she quickly slapped the grasscutter paw out of Chichi's hand. But really it was a useless gesture. If the oily-looking black vultures with wingspans wider than her height standing on top of the outhouses had wanted the paw, they'd have taken it long ago. There were five in all. The click-clacking sound was their talons on the tin roofs of the outhouses as they moved around.

"They're probably here for the meat when they are chopping it up," Sunny said. "Disgusting, lazy birds. I'll bet they live here, scavenging off of whatever the restaurant people throw away." She shook her head and started to step away. "I'm going to go pee in the bushes. I'm not going near those vultures, let alone those nasty outhouses. I can smell them from . . ."

"Sunny," Chichi said. And that's when Sunny noticed that Chichi wasn't even looking at the vultures. She was looking toward the trees. As Sunny turned her eyes in that direction, she felt every hair on her body stand up. There was a ringing in her ears and pressure on her face. Sunny's nostrils flared. She smelled smoke. A very specific type of smoke.

"Shhh," Chichi said, still staring toward the trees. "Don't speak."

Sunny had to resist the urge to scream. If she screamed, someone from the kitchen might hear and come to investigate. Then he or she would see the glorious giant bristly spider with legs powerful enough to part trees standing in the shadows. Would seeing Udide be a breach of the Leopard rules? Udide was more than a magical beast. Udide was one of Chukwu's deputies . . . a deity.

Udide blasted a thick puff of breath at them. Burned houses, that was the specific smoky smell. Sunny and Chichi clutched each other, the soon-to-set sun beating against their backs.

"Didn't I tell you that I can find you anywhere?" Udide asked, her voice vibrating in Sunny's head like a passing train. By the look on Chichi's face, the same was happening to her, too. "The venom of my people is bound to your very DNA."

"I know what you want," Chichi said, straining. A line of red tumbled from her nose to her lip. Sunny touched her nose and found that hers was bleeding, as well. "Please!"

"You have heard rumor," Udide said. "You have heard myth. You have heard gossip. You know what I ask."

Sunny shook her head. "We don't . . ."

"We can't go in there," Chichi said. She paused. Sunny was shocked to see that Chichi looked absolutely horrid, tears streaming down her face. "The last time my mother was there, they nearly killed her!" She took a deep breath. "Because of *me*. They . . . they nearly killed her."

"It is a story," the spider said. "My story. Written as a ghazal on a tablet-shaped Möbius band made of the same material as your juju knife, albino girl of Nimm, so you will recognize it. It will call to you. It cannot be broken. It is mine. One of my greatest masterpieces. It belongs to me. Go there, get it, and bring it back to me. My venom is in your blood. The doubled albino girl is a Nimm warrior; this story has made that clear. She will be your woman show."

Sunny frowned, rolling the idea in her mind. Woman show? Her brother had worked as a "man show" during wrestling matches when he wasn't wrestling. A bodyguard. She would be Chichi's bodyguard.

"You are a Nimm warrior, Sunny. Like your grandmother," Udide said, retreating into the trees. Her voice was fading now. "My venom is adhered to your DNA." Then she was gone. Chichi stood there, silent, tears flowing from her eyes.

"Let's go," Sunny said, putting an arm around Chichi. Never had she felt so much taller than her best friend. So much bigger. Physically so much stronger. Chichi looked up at her with trembling eyes and pressed lips.

"What is it?" Sunny asked. "Why are you looking like that?"

Chichi only shook her head and tiredly looked away.

"Let's just get home," Sunny said. "We'll deal with all this later."

34

JUDGMENT DAY

The council came three hours before daybreak.

Chukwu was able to drop off Chichi at her hut. Then he dropped Orlu and Sasha at Orlu's house, Grashcoatah following Orlu and landing in his compound safely hidden behind the house's surrounding wall. At home, Sunny had time to greet her parents, peek into Ugonna's room where he just grunted a hello and went back to sleep, take a shower, and unpack her things. It was just as she lay down to get a few hours of sleep that she felt her toes tingle. Then she felt the tingle travel up her body all the way to the top of her head. And it was in the center of her head that she felt the tug.

"Oh no," she whispered as she was pulled through her

bedsheets and window. Then there she was, standing barefoot in her nightgown in front of the council car.

"Get in," the driver said in American-accented Igbo. She was a small woman with long straight black hair, lots of makeup, and large earrings that clinked when she turned her head. Sunny got in.

On the front lawn of the library, Grashcoatah was chained, shackled, and muzzled. He lay there, looking forlornly at Sunny as she passed. He would flicker into invisibility and then reappear, groaning in despair and biting at his chains.

"Hang in there," Sunny said as she was ushered inside. "We'll get you free!" She hoped. She hoped.

"Move," Sunny's escort said, shoving her along. "Worry about yourself."

Sunny would never forget the black classroom in the Obi Library. Even the leather seats and table were black. Sitting in the plush chairs were Library Council members or officials or executioners, Sunny didn't know or care. They all looked like they could be her angry mean aunt or unforgiving uncle. The only one Sunny recognized was Sugar Cream. Sunny went and stood with the others before the table of adults, feeling irrational with fatigue and anger. She fought back tears of rage.

"Pull yourself together," Orlu whispered to her. "Grashcoatah's life depends on it."

Anyanwu, she said in her mind.

I'm here, Anyanwu responded.

She felt her muscles flex as she stood up straight and faced the stern, mostly unfamiliar council members. Some were her mother's age; most of them were much older. But Sunny didn't care. She was in a sort of zone.

"Again, here you are, Sunny Nwazue," an old woman said to her in Igbo. She wore her hair in thin white-gray braids and she looked more ancient than Sugar Cream. "Your third offense. You'd think nearly dying at the hands of a djinn would teach you to follow the rules. Yet here you are, and you've dragged your *Oha* coven and a grasscutter into the trouble with you."

Orlu stepped forward. Sunny put her hand on his shoulder. "I've got this," she told him. She was shaking, but it wasn't from fear; she felt she would burst if she didn't say what she desperately wanted to say. She told them everything, from the beginning to the current moment. She spoke about her brother being in the secret society, how she ended up thrown into the Obi Library basement, the djinn, the dreams, being doubled, meeting with Bola, Lagos, Udide, almost facing Death, and then Osisi and their great battle with Ekwensu, the Aku masquerade, and Ekwensu's minions. But again, she kept her encounter with Chukwu to herself.

When she finished talking, the council officials just stared at the four of them. For several minutes, it was like this. They did not discuss among themselves. They did not write things down. They did not ask questions. They didn't even move. They just stared.

"To be doubled is very sad," Sugar Cream finally said. "Death is always close by, but for you, he will always stand behind you."

Recalling the image of Death in her peripheral vision, Sunny felt the shiver run up her spine and an uncontrollable urge to burst into tears. Almost. She remained stoic, mostly due to Anyanwu holding her steady.

"Your brother," a tiny dark-skinned man about her mother's age said. "We didn't alter his memory. We gave him the choice of forgetting or entering a trust knot. We told him that to enter the trust knot was the hazardous choice. He was still under the *Ujo*, screaming with terror every few moments. And even then, he chose not to forget. Instead he chose to remember and suffer because he can never share the memory. We don't normally allow this with Lambs, because with the wrong people this can cause madness. But for your brother, due to the circumstances and his passion to protect you, we allowed it. What will you do with him now?"

"Protect him," Sunny said, before she'd fully thought her answer through.

Again the silence.

Not long after that, the four of them were told that they could go. Outside, Grashcoatah was released. And quickly, calmly, steadily, they all walked away from the Obi Library. It didn't matter that it was nearly morning and they weren't sure how they'd get home. Best to leave before the shock the council members were in wore off. Best to not run in order to maintain the look of innocence. Once they reached the Leopard Knocks shops, they climbed on Grashcoatah and off they flew.

35
HOME, AGAIN

Sunny arrived back at home around eleven A.M.

It was Saturday and her parents weren't home. Ugonna was at his girlfriend's house. But Chukwu was there sitting on the doorstep as if he'd known she was coming. He had his cell phone in his hands and it buzzed as Sunny walked up to him.

"You all right?" he asked, glancing at the text message he'd just received. He put the phone in his pocket and looked up at Sunny. He was wearing sweatpants, Adidas slippers, and a T-shirt. All clothes their aunt had sent from America, clothes that Chukwu only wore when he was trying to passive-aggressively impress.

"Yeah," she said.

There was a long pause. Neither of them could speak their thoughts to the other and the cause for this was juju, not reluctance.

"Why are you home?" Sunny asked.

"Came to see Akunna. She's coming over," he said. "Of all the girls, she's the coolest. Otherwise, I'd just ask her to come to the university to see *me*."

Sunny smiled, sitting beside him. "Such a gentleman."

They sat like that for a while. Shoulder to shoulder. Full of questions. But relieved. Relieved to be alive and well and home. When Akunna arrived, Sunny waved at her and got up and went inside.

In her room, Sunny threw her purse on the floor, shut and locked the door, and lay on her bed. She savored the quiet. The stillness. Her brothers were visiting with girlfriends. Her parents were at work or food shopping. They were okay. Everything was okay. But she couldn't quite smile. She looked at her barely used computer, her dresser and cabinets, her pile of books, the early edition of the Leopard Knocks newspaper on her bed, and the window. Then she hugged herself. She looked around her room again. The effect remained. Her room didn't feel the same. This place felt cramped, useless. It felt like it belonged to someone else.

She frowned, trying to hold the tears in. She'd gone out to find herself and in the process lost her home . . . and in a way, herself. How had that happened? At the same time, she and Chukwu were closer than ever, she and Ugonna, too. And though her parents felt more distant, a sort of understanding had developed between her and them. They had not stayed home and waited for her to return. But maybe they'd gone out because they couldn't stand the waiting. So much had changed in the last two years.

Something buzzed beside her ear. "Oh," she said, sitting up. "Della!!" In all the adventure and trouble, she'd forgotten about her wasp artist! Her entire body tensed up. Wasp artists were known to be overly emotional, especially when neglected. Their response to neglect was stinging their owner/audience with a paralysis-inducing compound. The paralyzed victim was then forced to watch the wasp artist dramatically commit suicide. Sunny had been gone for over a week and when she'd returned last night, she hadn't had time to check on Della. She frantically looked around the room.

There was a loud buzzing coming from her closet. She crept up to it and paused before sliding it open. If Della was in there, maybe it was better to keep it trapped. But it clearly could get out, since it had just been right beside her ear. She threw open the closet door. For a moment, Sunny wasn't sure what she was looking at. Then she wondered if she was seeing correctly. Could wasp artists create things like this? Della had indeed been improving in its artistic skill but . . . "Is this . . ." She knelt down and picked it up. "For me?" she whispered. "Is it mine?"

Della buzzed loudly, now hovering above her head, watching Sunny's reaction closely.

"I was gone for so long," she said, holding the hair comb. "You knew I was coming back?"

It buzzed again. How did it know that she no longer had the hair comb Mami Wata had given her? *Only Chukwu knows*, she thought, as she pressed the comb into the side of one of her cornrows. She went to admire herself in the mirror. The comb looked like it was made of tiny shiny multicolored glass beads, even the teeth. Yet it had a way of sparkling yellow orange when she turned her head just so. She took it out and held it to her eyes. When she looked closely, she saw only shiny sparkling pin-sized dots of light. "What is this made of?" she asked.

Della flew circles around her head until she let her question go and laughed. "Yes," she said. "I love it. I love it so much. It's the most beautiful thing I've ever seen!"

More loop-the-loops, and then Della zoomed into its mud hive on her ceiling and was quiet. "Wow," Sunny said, admiring the piece of wasp art. She lay back on her bed, smiling as she tucked it into her hair. There was a flash of red on her dresser. A ghost hopper was walking down the side. As it walked, it slowly disappeared.

Now her room felt more like her room.

36

THE ZUMA ROCK FESTIVAL

The Zuma Rock Festival came a month later. All of them went, except Orlu. He and Grashcoatah had gone instead with Taiwo and Nancy the Miri Bird to witness the mass spawning of some sort of butterfly in the Cross River Forest. Sunny missed him, but Orlu's excitement about going delighted her more than his absence depressed her.

Despite all that she'd been through, she was still able to experience the festival with fresh eyes. The three of them went to the art fair, and Sunny bought a new wrapper and matching top. Chichi bought a bookmark made of shed Eji Onu masquerade raffia. When placed between the pages of a book while reading the book, it made the images one imagined that much more alive. Sasha didn't buy anything because he was saving all his money for the book fair near the end of the festival.

A jewelry maker was awed by the hair comb Della had made for Sunny. He offered to pay her an insane amount of *chittim* AND naira for it. He said that it was made of zyzzyx glass, a serum that wasp artists secrete when they reach their first artistic peak. Few wasp artists willingly gave away their zyzzyx glass artwork; it was too beautiful to merely be worn as a "bauble by some young girl." Insulted and intrigued, needless to say, Sunny refused to sell her zyzzyx glass hair comb.

They moved on to the book fair. It was enormous. They hadn't been to this last year, and Sunny was kind of glad. The festival had been so overwhelming back then that she'd nearly gone catatonic. If she'd been to the book fair, she would have screamed to go home and never had her amazing experience of playing soccer in the Zuma Cup.

The book fair consisted of row after row of books packed on the field that would later be used for the Zuma Cup soccer match. Here, people argued and sometimes fought over books, and some of the books argued with and fought people. Sasha got into a disturbing altercation with a dark-skinned man wearing a Tuareg-style indigo face veil. All Sasha had done to spark it was reach for a thick, brand-new-looking book with *The Great Book* burned into the spine in Arabic. To Sunny's shock, the man had slapped Sasha's hands and then slapped him hard across the face as he shouted something in Arabic.

Sasha had shouted right back at the man in Arabic. The man simply ignored him, turning his attention to the book as he grabbed and opened it. Sasha was too angry to notice and Chichi was too busy trying to pull him away. However, Sunny saw the inside of this book. It wasn't really a book at all. Its inside looked more like the touch screen of a tablet.

Then she was helping Chichi shove Sasha away from the man. After looking at other books, Sasha settled on a book that was the size of his hand. It was sticky with old honey and had print so small that even a child with 20/20 vision would need a magnifying glass to read it. It also had several pages torn out of it. "But it's a book of practical joke jujus written by an Abatwa!" Sasha said. He purchased it for a whole bronze *chittim*, managing to haggle a discount due to the missing pages. He refused to talk about *The Great Book*.

They skipped the wrestling match and from what they heard it was again a bloody match, though neither of the champions was killed like last year. Nevertheless, Sunny found herself watching the sky and the constant milling festival crowd around her, looking for the fallen champion turned guardian angel Miknikstic. She even snuck to the spot where she'd first met him last year in front of the soccer field. Sasha and Chichi were at the table where they'd all just eaten lunch. They were debating the recent election of the governor of some state, and their discussion was so heated that they hadn't even noticed her slip away.

Now she stood in the very spot looking at the field. It was here where Sunny had felt so out of place, so overwhelmed . . . by everything. Not this time. The festival now felt almost underwhelming, even with the intriguing and fascinating parts like the book and art fairs, even the wrestling match.

She turned around and looked at the Leopard People going about their business. They laughed, talked, explored, did their juju. They were so comfortable. Like her parents and all the Lambs she knew. When did she wind up on the outside again? She'd met Miknikstic here, as well, a man who less than an hour later would transform into so much more. She crossed her arms over her chest, squeezing the muscles of her strong ropy biceps with her hands. With her right foot she sketched a series of loops and swirls into the dirt—the Nsibidi symbol for "I am here." She paused for a moment, looking for any sign of movement in the symbols. As if she were good enough at it yet. She chuckled and returned to her friends.

An hour later, she stood center on the field holding the soccer ball. The field had been cleared of the stacks and cases and shelves of books. Now there was nothing but uneven grass and the white lines of the field, bold and perfect. She felt good in her white uniform, and this time she wore brand-new soccer cleats that she'd bought with some of her *chittim* in Leopard Knocks, months ago. Sasha was behind her to her left.

She looked at Godwin, the green team's leader. He was playing goalie. He gave a nod of confidence.

"I'm going to wipe the field with you, ghost girl," Ibou said. Sunny grinned at him, setting the ball down. "No," she said. "You're not." Ibou had grown about three inches and his shoulders were even broader. But Sunny had grown taller and become more muscular, too. The ref blew his whistle, and Sunny took the ball with her dancing feet. She felt Anyanwu reveling in the art of motion and grace. She kicked the ball to Ibou's left as he came at her. She did a turn, moved behind him, and caught the ball with her feet. She laughed, spotting her teammate Agaja to her right. He was open. As she passed the ball to him, she could already see Agaja blasting it into the goal.

Goooooooooal!

ACKNOWLEDGMENTS

First and foremost, a gracious thanks to the Universe for bringing this novel together on its own time.

I'd like to thank my former Penguin editor Sharyn November for helping me strengthen the continuation of Sunny's story. Thanks to my current editor Regina Hayes for jumping in and making this novel really shine. Thanks to my Nigerian editor Bibi Bakare-Yusuf for helping me smooth away so many of the Americanisms I couldn't help putting in the novel. Thanks to producer Mark Ceryak and filmmaker Barry Jenkins for those days years ago working on that film treatment that ended up helping me generate some of the ideas in this novel. Thanks so so much to Success T for letting me weave the nonfiction of his own experiences with confraternities into this novel; that chapter was practically word for word. Thanks to illustrator Greg Ruth for the two stunning renderings of Sunny Nwazue that are the covers of *Akata Witch* and *Akata Warrior.* Thanks to Jim Hoover, who designed this book's beautiful jacket, for his meticulous eye for detail and zing. And thank you to my mother, my father, my daughter Anyaugo, Ifeoma, Ngozi, Emezie, Dika, Obioma, Chinedu, and the rest of my family in Nigeria and scattered about the Diaspora, because family na family, o.

The masquerades dance and the ancestors smile,
And these in themselves make it all worthwhile.

NNEDI OKORAFOR is a novelist of African-based science fiction, fantasy, and magical realism for both children and adults. Born in the United States to Nigerian immigrant parents, Nnedi is known for weaving African culture into creative evocative settings and memorable characters. In a profile of Nnedi's work, *The New York Times* called Nnedi's imagination "stunning." Nnedi has received the World Fantasy Award, the Hugo Award, and the Nebula Award, among others, for her novels. Her fans include Neil Gaiman, Rick Riordan, John Green, Laurie Halse Anderson, and Ursula K. Le Guin among others.

Nnedi Okorafor holds a PhD in English and is a professor at SUNY Buffalo. She divides her time between Buffalo and the suburbs of Chicago, where she lives with her daughter. Learn more at nnedi.com or follow her on Twitter @nnedi.